IN THE
SHADOW
OF THE
WATER TOWER

A NOVEL BY ALAN KIRBY

MILL CITY PRESS

MINNEAPOLIS, MN

MILL CITY PRESS, INC.

322 FIRST AVENUE N, 5TH FLOOR

MINNEAPOLIS, MN 55401

612.455.2293

WWW.MILLCITYPUBLISHING.COM

THIS BOOK IS A WORK OF FICTION. NAMES AND PLACES ARE THE PRODUCT OF THE AUTHOR'S IMAGINATION.

ISBN-13: 978-1-63413-004-2

LCCN: 2014948059

COVER DESIGN BY ALAN PRANKE

TYPESET BY JENNI WHEELER

PRINTED IN THE UNITED STATES OF AMERICA

For Mike

Contents

CHAPTER 1

THE PHONE CALL

A year ago my life changed with a simple phone call. My brother's life also fundamentally changed with that call. And the town of Glenville, Indiana, would forever be altered as a result of that call and what transpired over the subsequent thirty days.

"Please hold for Mr. Borland."

The call came from a lawyer's office in Glenville and I was asked to "hold" while a conference call was connected to include my brother, Joe, the lawyer, and myself. I'm old enough to still believe that conference calls are something that someone with a unique skill set establishes for you when there is a need to conduct business with multiple people. If you were in management, then you clearly lacked the skill to orchestrate one yourself and needed help setting it up. Therefore, I still think of a conference call as something that involves some degree of competence and, therefore it commands a level of significance.

I realize that conference calls now might just involve three college sophomores on separate cell phones figuring out what to wear to a party that night. My daughter Jenny, and her friends Trisha, and Jackie really don't need any help figuring out how to make the call. But in my little protected world, there is still a certain gravitas attached to the event. Something important was to be discussed. Plus, a lawyer was on the other end of this call and that can never be good.

"Mr. Kelly?"

Stereo response: "Yes?" My brother and I were already keenly on the same wavelength even though he was talking from the East Coast and I was in California.

"Splendid. I guess we should use first names so I can tell you apart. Would that be acceptable to both of you?" Borland asked. Never trust a guy who uses the word "splendid." A normal person would never say that. "Splendid" is only used in old BBC Agatha Christie movies. I don't trust people who watch those and then mimic the dialogue.

My brother, Joe, gets to the point, "I'm fine with first names. What's yours?"

Borland hesitated a beat. That seemed odd. He then replied, "I'm Thomas Borland. Please feel free to call me Tom." I had a feeling that he was the kind of guy who would have been more comfortable remaining "Mr. Borland." He already seemed a little uptight by Indiana standards. My brother and I then clarified who was on the line (Joseph, "Joe," and Darren Kelly) so the conversation could get started.

"Gentlemen, I am aware that this phone call is a surprise to you and that you are anxious to get to the point; therefore, I won't waste your time. I presume both of you are familiar with the name Clarence Hazelton, often referred to as Shorty Hazelton." There was a long silence on the line before I finally said, "Sure, we knew Shorty."

This was getting interesting. Shorty Hazelton was all of five foot four inches tall. I always thought it was just a little cruel that he was tagged with that nickname, but with Clarence as your alternative, Shorty probably sounded pretty good to him. A black cloud of potential litigation just disappeared. Nothing in my imagination suggested that Shorty Hazelton was suing us. The fact that he had been dead for several years gave me some comfort in that regard. The additional consideration that he had been a neighbor and life-long friend of the Kelly family also led me to believe that no harm would ever come to us from Shorty.

Borland continued, "As you are aware, Mr. Hazelton passed away three years ago. I was his personal lawyer for approximately the last two years of his life. I handled all matters related to his investments and taxes, his Declaration of Trust, and the creation of his Last Will and Testament."

The Shorty Hazelton that we knew could not possibly require the services of a lawyer for anything but the bare minimum to get him buried. We're talking about "Uncle" Shorty. He had always been Uncle Shorty to us. I don't know why. We weren't related, but he had been a part of the Kelly family as long as I can remember. This was a guy who lived in a tiny, one-story house in little Glenville, Indiana. The house might have been a thousand square feet, at most.

He lived there the entire time we knew him. When his wife, Meta, passed away, he continued to live there until his death. Only an empty field separated his house from ours for many years. Joe and I spent hours and hours eating Aunt Meta's cookies, watching TV, and sitting on a sofa in a living room that never seemed to be updated.

He drove an old blue Plymouth, as I recall, and never looked as if he bought new clothes. He always looked the same year after year—only a little shorter as time marched on. A wisp of gray hair covered his head. That, too, never seemed to change as long as we knew him. He seemed prematurely old when we met him and still older when we last saw him. He was funny, kind, encouraging, and always interested in what we were doing. We loved him like a real uncle and chose to spend time with him when we could have been off doing something else. That's a pretty big statement when you think about what a couple of teenage boys might have been doing otherwise.

"Mr. Hazelton directed me to keep the contents of his will private for three years after his death before revealing its contents and directing the disbursement of funds according to his wishes. He confided in me that he had no living relatives or close confidantes, but wanted to make certain that no one would suddenly appear after his death claiming a right to access his estate. Since the money was held in a charitable trust and managed according to his directions, we avoided probate activity. No inquiries have been made and I am now ready to proceed with his directions." Borland then asked, "Do either of you have any questions at this time?"

"Yeah, I have a question," I said. "Are you sure you have the right Shorty Hazelton and the right Kelly brothers? The Uncle Shorty we knew wasn't exactly throwing money around and clearly didn't need a lawyer to settle his 'estate.' Joe, does this make any sense to you?"

"No. It makes no sense at all. Maybe his old Plymouth is a classic now and worth some serious money. Maybe he left that to us."

"Gentlemen," interrupted Borland, "perhaps we can get on with the task at hand so you won't have to speculate about Mr. Hazelton's intentions." This guy was beginning to annoy me. "We have now completed the first step in Mr. Hazelton's directives. I have contacted you both and you are hereby notified that you have been mentioned in Mr. Hazelton's will. The second step in the process requires your immediate attention and must be conducted in a private meeting with me, here in Glenville. I realize this will cause an inconvenience for you both, but we need to proceed in this fashion according to Mr. Hazelton's wishes."

"Mr. Borland," I offered, "this is all just a little strange and it's real hard to believe that we need to travel from both coasts to Glenville just to hear that Shorty left us his favorite set of checkers. Do you remember that checkerboard, Joe?"

"Sure, I remember it," Joe replied. "Fine looking checkerboard, but not worth traveling halfway across the country to retrieve. Plus, how do we split it?"

An exasperated Borland blurted out, "Gentlemen, this is not about a checkerboard or some old car. I cannot reveal the contents of the will over the phone, but I can tell you this. The value of what we will discuss is significant—very, very significant. I can promise you that by attending this meeting and hearing Mr. Hazelton's wishes, both of your lives could be changed forever. I suggest that you arrange to get here as soon as possible."

CHAPTER 2

BACK HOME, AGAIN, IN INDIANA

As my plane begins its descent into Indianapolis International Airport (formerly Weir-Cook Municipal when I grew up), the words to Indiana's unofficial state song, "Back Home Again In Indiana," creep their way into my thoughts. That is always the case when I go home. Lyric images of sycamore trees, new-mowed hay, and the moonlight on the Wabash River surface from the deeper recesses of my brain. Every Hoosier knows this song primarily from its prominence in the opening ceremonies of the Indianapolis 500—"The Greatest Spectacle in Racing."

It is performed each Memorial Day before a crowd of roughly four hundred thousand racing/drinking fans. Backed by the Purdue All-American Marching Band, the song naturally takes its rightful place in the loyalty hierarchy right after "The Star Spangled Banner" and just before the invocation. Of course, what makes this rendition so special is that it has been sung in most years since 1972 by the one and only Jim Nabors. That's right. Jim Nabors—Gomer Pyle from *The Andy Griffith Show*. Also known as *Gomer Pyle, U.S.M.C.*, the dim-witted character with the baritone voice and slack-jaw expression. Of all the people in the state of Indiana who could probably do a decent job of singing this song while truly representing the spirit and dignity of Indiana, we chose Gomer Pyle! And, to make it worse, he isn't even from Indiana. He's from Alabama. We had to go to Alabama to find someone to sing our state song? John Mellencamp could have handled it. He's a real Hoosier and he was even a founding member for the Farm Aid concerts. What says Hoosier better than supporting farms and singing about life in a small town? Gomer Pyle, my ass. I still like the song, though. Brings a tear to my eye every Memorial Day.

I was flying in from California and my brother, Joe, was driving to Indiana from his home in Maryland. We figured whatever business we had with the lawyer wouldn't take long and we could spend a couple of days in town and take in a few sites in Indianapolis. It had been so long since either of us had been home that we were anxious to see how the place had changed. Indianapolis had obviously grown from a sleepy small city to a supercharged sports town with all the accompanying restaurants, hotels, and bars to drive the local economy.

Glenville was less that thirty minutes down the road from Indy and I knew it had changed as well. I was aware that most of the local businesses had moved from the small downtown area to be closer to the interstate out at the far edge of town. That area used to be nothing but farmland, but over the past few years its fertile soil produced a Home Depot, Steak 'n Shake, Bob Evans restaurant, Applebee's, and several small hotels where weary strangers could rest within eyeball distance from the interstate.

Those travelers had to be on their way to somewhere else since Glenville wasn't exactly a tourist destination.

With the addition of a Walmart, my beloved small town had nearly completed the all too familiar transformation to being just another nondescript spot along the interstate. It would always hold a place in my heart and I never fail to declare myself a Hoosier even though I've spent nearly my entire adulthood in California. However, the few Glenville friends that I stayed in touch with let me know that the town just wasn't the same. It was losing its identity. Now doubled in size from when we grew up there, it is still a fairly small town of roughly 20,000 people. I guess at least this trip will give me the chance to judge for myself whether Glenville still feels like home.

Both Joe and I had previously come back for exactly one high school class reunion each. We both waited roughly twenty years before returning even though there seemed to be reunions every five or ten years. Joe and I were three years apart in school and that worked greatly to my advantage. He was a senior when I was a freshman. The anxiety of raising the first son gave way to the routine of dealing with the youngest as various rules and restrictions fell by the wayside. The subtlety of this social transformation was a thing of beauty to watch from my perspective and a source of great irritation to my brother.

After we had returned from our respective reunions, we compared notes and agreed that they were fun and worth attending. However, we were glad that we had waited a number

of years before going back to our home town. It made it more
challenging to recognize people. Several times I had to take a
second look to peel back the layers and find that eighteen-year-
old kid's face in the person who just greeted me. I'm not saying
my old classmates were unattractive. They just didn't look like
the same people I remembered.

Let's face it. Life looks a little different when you're approaching forty and your memories are still frozen in time from
your senior year in high school. We had all started to become
our parents in different ways and that was more than a little
scary. Folks spent the evening sharing a few of life's highlights
and minimizing the lows. After all, what was the point in con-
fessing to someone you wouldn't see again that your life was
pretty much in the toilet?

A group of guys surrounded me at the reunion. With the
help of nametags, I quickly identified each one and shook hands.
Most of them were much thicker than they had been in high
school. Thicker necks and thicker stomachs prevailed. However,
one guy actually looked exactly as he had in high school. That
just seemed unnatural to me. I took an immediate disliking to
him. They started telling stories and I was reminded of the way
that Indiana men tend to preface any story they're going to tell
you. They have to first get your attention:

"I'll tell you what now, Kelly . . ."

"Now, Kelly, listen here . . ."

"Let me tell you one thing . . ."

It's as if every story will have a profound impact on my life. "Now, Kelly, let me tell you something—those ribs you'll get down there at Smokin' Hog are the finest you will ever have in your life. I guarantee it." The guy could have been talking about the weather. "I'll tell you what now—you can bet on rain tomorrow." Profound. I love that way of talking. Get their attention. Make your point. Nod your head in satisfaction for a comment well made.

I enjoyed catching up with a number of women who had been friends of mine in high school. Most had successful careers in a variety of occupations, including banking, teaching, real estate, and engineering (a Purdue University graduate of course). A couple of old friends had predictably stayed at home to raise fairly large families just as their mothers had done. I suspected they were very good at it since they had both been the eldest siblings who often nurtured the younger ones in their families when we were in school. I learned later that one of these mothers, Kathy Nelson, also volunteered in town and was on the board of nearly every important organization, including the School Board.

Two women approached me later in the evening. One was short and tending toward round, but still attractive in a short, round sort of way. The other was tall, thin, and very attractive in a gorgeous, slutty sort of way. Karen Bowers beamed up at me from her disadvantaged position and threw her arms out for a hug. To compound the problem, I initially had no clue about her identity. I saw a little familiarity in the face, but the woman in her late thirties with light shades of gray in her hair did not resemble any cute, young eighteen-year-old that I could remember lusting after in high school. She was attractive enough; she just wasn't eighteen anymore, and that's where my mind was stuck.

She caught my dumb look and shrieked, "It's Karen! Karen Bowers. Don't you remember me?"

I stumbled and bumbled and offered an apology for my momentary lapse. Nice recovery.

It should have been abundantly clear to those standing nearby that I was much smoother than I used to be in high school.

Actually, Karen, I had no clue about your identity because I was staring at the gorgeous, tall, bleached blonde goddess next to you. In a timid voice that sounded exactly like that of a teenager, I quietly managed a forced greeting, "Hello, Donna. . . . You're still looking terrific." I was pathetic. She smiled, surreptitiously checked my nametag, and gave me a hug that was considerably less enthusiastic than the one clamped on me by Karen. Let's simply say that my chest never touched her chest. Just like in high school. In a nanosecond she had put me right back in my rightful place on the male sex-appeal continuum.

After twenty years, I was barely worthy of an acknowledgement by the gorgeous bad girl of Glenview High School. Some things don't change. Every guy in high school chased after Donna Taylor, but only the guys who had spent a few nights in juvenile hall would get a chance at her. At thirty-eight, she must be dating guys from Vegas adorned with gold chains.

Putting the disheartening effects of aging aside, my memories of that high school reunion are still very positive. Glenville had been a great place to grow up, with good people who seemed to have a handle on what was really important in life. By West Coast standards it clearly wasn't the most sophisticated spot in America, but I've generally found that Californians overrate the concept of sophistication. There was a great deal about small-town Indiana that I really missed. However, once I left Indiana after college, I saw little need to go back and reminisce. One class reunion was probably enough, but here I was going home again and looking forward to seeing some of my old friends who remained in the area.

* * *

Joe pulled into a curbside spot at the Indianapolis airport just as I came out of the baggage claim area. He had made the ten-hour drive over from his home near the Chesapeake Bay in Maryland. It always amazes me how many states you can cross in the East Coast and Midwest compared to driving in California. I could make a ten-hour drive from southern California to northern California and never leave the state. He cut through Maryland, Pennsylvania, West Virginia, Ohio, and half of Indiana to meet me, and showed up right on time.

Joe jumped out of the car and greeted me with the traditional Kelly handshake. That is to say there were no hugs. No full frontal hug, no one arm on the shoulder, no man-hug with a half-handshake and half-hug. Not even a Bill Clinton hand-over-hand handshake where you shake hands and then place your free hand over the top just to indicate that "you are really special to me . . . I'm demonstrating that with my extra hand."

The Kelly men simply look you in the eye, smile (if warranted), and shake your hand. Joe and I shake hands in the same manner that we always did with our father. We're not a hugging family. Never were. I cannot remember ever being hugged by my father. He loved me. He was very good to me. He just didn't hug me. I don't feel any worse for it and neither does Joe. Others might suggest it explains a few things about us. Good luck with that analysis.

CHAPTER 3

ON THE ROAD TO GLENVILLE

We cruised out of the airport in Joe's Chrysler 300 sedan. This is currently the car of choice for gangbangers in L.A. They all have the black version with wire rims and tinted windows. Joe, naturally, has the all-white version, which just doesn't carry the same cachet as the black one. However, it's a great car, fully loaded, and plenty of trunk space for drugs, guns, or dead bodies. Joe generally just carries groceries and gardening supplies.

We head out on Interstate 465 to circle Indianapolis and then head east on I-70 to Glenville. This interstate didn't even exist when we grew up in Glenville. Highway 40 was the main east/west route to and from Indianapolis and it seemed like a sufficiently major thoroughfare at the time. Now it was a secondary route dotted with retail stores, stoplights, and small communities along the way. It was basically just farmland when we drove it in the past. The farms are still there, but they are now pushed off into the distance, farther away from the highway.

Joe and I caught up on life in California and Maryland. Though we don't get together very often, we talk all the time. We seem to have been frozen in time somewhere back in Indiana when we were sharing a bedroom. Once when we were twenty years removed from Glenville and laughing about something stupid, I asked Joe, "Do you think we're ever going to grow out of our adolescent relationship? Here we are both respectable professionals and I still feel like whenever we're together I'm viewing the world through the eyes of a smartass kid—only with a better perspective. I don't normally feel that way, but you seem to bring out the worst in me."

"Darren, little brother, just be thankful that we haven't grown up yet. And let's hope we never do."

That was twenty years ago and nothing has changed. We just dial each other up on FaceTime and chat away. It's like we're in the same room together, catching up on the latest sports and news, playing guitar back and forth as Joe tries to help me along through my beginner stages, and generally just being brothers who share a similar sense of humor and perspective on life. No one makes me laugh easier than my brother. His powers of observation are unique and often result in a sarcastic remark whispered quietly to a confidant. At other times a droll comment will be uttered out loud that generally flies right over the head of his intended target.

Mind you, he likes people a great deal and people like him. He really is a very nice guy. It's just that those who think too highly of themselves, have quirky physical attributes, or have obvious shortcomings (like stupidity or moronic behavior) will without question draw his attention. Most of those people won't know he's already formed a skeptical opinion of them and they will remain firm in their belief that he is a wonderfully sweet guy.

To give you an idea of how Joe's mind works, he called me one day from Maryland and explained a scheme he cooked up to impress my young son and daughter. I arranged for an evening when both kids would be home and I could casually direct their attention to *Wheel of Fortune* on the television. With the three-hour time difference between coasts, Joe had already watched the show and phoned me the solution to every puzzle.

I started slowly and waited until I had a few vowels to solve "Home Improvement." The kids weren't that impressed. Solving "All You Need Is Love" with just one *a* and an *o* got their attention. They excitedly called their mother in to witness my genius when I solved "Little Big Man" with just an *a*. Prematurely solving the last puzzle with only a *u* apparently pushed the envelope of credibility when I blurted out Thoreau's warning to the masses, "Beware Of All Enterprises That Require New Clothes!"

For a brief moment, I was the smartest father on the face of the planet thanks to Joe. But one questioning glance at their mother when I pushed it too far and it became clear that I was just another adult fake. My wife, Beth, just smiled and slowly shook her head. I pleaded for one more try as both kids stomped out of the room. Beth looked at me and simply asked, "Joe?" I indignantly answered, "No, I'm just really good at this stuff."

Joe and I are both young men. And by "young" I mean younger than most card-carrying AARP members. I just turned sixty and Joe is sixty-three. That might sound old if you're thirty. It sounds downright youthful if you're seventy-five.

Aside from a few aches, pains, and replacement parts, we are both relatively fit and healthy and in full possession of the most important attribute shallow and narcissistic men can retain— our hair. In the very dim light of a bar near closing time when visual acuity and sobriety are greatly impaired, we might be able to pass for fifty-five. That's an important and interesting bench- mark that any guy can relate to, but also completely useless in our case since we are both happily married and have never been approached by any woman in a bar at closing time since our mid-twenties.

Joe and I were fortunately blessed with a high rate of me- tabolism that allowed us to eat just about anything we wanted without getting heavy. Being skinny as a kid was challenging, but eating junk food, as an adult, was very gratifying when I didn't put on any weight. As a single guy in my late twenties I regu- larly frequented the McDonald's located next to my apartment complex to enjoy a "triple play"—breakfast, lunch, and dinner. Those days have now been ruined for me with the proliferation of educational propaganda about fast food.

However, it is impossible to ignore the care and concern our wives demonstrate at home as they place salads and lean protein products in front of us. The Kelly boys are still not heavy at all, but we have both accepted the reality that exercise and better eating habits are now a part of our routine for reasons other than weight. What a drag. The good news is that all rules about eating can be—no, must be—ignored whenever one is on vacation. Though it might be a stretch of the definition, this trip to Glenville has officially been declared a vacation.

So, to be honest, we're just average guys albeit slightly on the tall side at six feet two inches. Not short, not fat, not bald . . . no limp, no lisp, no Amish beard—nothing that would draw attention to either of us. Joe generally spends his free time cruising the Chesapeake on his sailboat with his wife and friends. He worked hard for his money and now gets to enjoy spending some of it.

Conversely, I spend much of my time cruising golf courses. I like land-based activities that pose little threat to my health and generally involve competition, small wagers, and a beer or two. Though I live in the beautiful Ojai Valley only twenty minutes from the Pacific Ocean, the sea holds little fascination for me other than the occasional impressive sunset out over the water.

Yes, my brother and I have long ago gone our separate ways to the opposite coasts of our country. He retired fairly early from a successful career as a director of visual communications with a large pharmaceutical firm and later worked as an independent consultant to the industry. I followed an academic path purely because I never wanted to leave college. It was yet another example of not growing up. A few degrees later, including a Ph.D. in counseling psychology, and I was set for life in a quirky but relatively stress-free environment where I could be marginally helpful to others as a counselor and professor. Recently retired, I was just beginning to fully realize the joys of retiring at an age still young enough to pursue all sorts of other interests. Despite our divergent paths, our bond is a close one and we are about to be tested in a manner that neither of us ever experienced before. As we drove together toward Glenville, we reminisced some more about growing up in Indiana and wondered what Uncle Shorty had left us. Tomorrow we meet the lawyer, Thomas Borland.

CHAPTER 4
UNCLE SHORTY'S WILL

We woke the next morning to a beautiful Indiana spring day. It doesn't get any better than spring and fall in Indiana. Despite my fond memories of summers in Glenville, the reality is that it's incredibly hot and humid and only fun for children who don't know better. Winters are simply what make people move to Florida—as my parents did a few years after Joe and I finished college.

This April day was bright and sunny with a slight breeze in the air. Any Midwesterner could tell you that coming out of winter into the warm months of April and May brings a sense of hope and optimism that borders on euphoria. It happens every year. As a male teenager in Indiana, I suspect this sudden contentment had something to do with the proliferation of bikinis that seem to appear overnight. Girls in Indiana didn't need a beach to turn their white skin to a beautiful golden brown. They simply gathered in small groups out on their front lawns. With a towel and some sunscreen, they were prepared to cause accidents as teenage boys drove by slowly to catch a glimpse of the most important seasonal change of the year. The practice nearly caused riots in college as girls found their spots on the lawn beneath the dorm windows. Guys above ran from room to room colliding with one another in search of the best vantage point.

Unfortunately, the morning breeze could often turn to a windy afternoon that might then evolve into a thunderstorm that rumbles through the area. That could ultimately turn into a tornado that selectively trashes a local trailer park. That can be a bummer. But it really doesn't happen that often. Generally, hope and optimism—and bikinis—abound. All in all, spring is still an excellent time of year. Perhaps not as good as fall now that I think about it carefully, but very good nonetheless.

Joe and I left the Residence Inn and headed across the street to do what we do best. Eat. We narrowed our choice between Bob's Big Boy and Cracker Barrel. We chose the latter since we thought it might be healthier. We figured Bob was a big fat guy with a fat son and that just didn't sit right with us.

Without question, breakfast is the greatest meal of the day. First . . . it's first. Second, it's cheap. And, third, you can combine all sorts of edibles together in any fashion and just keep changing them around for a new taste experience every time you visit the same restaurant. Joe and I settled into our window table with a lovely view of the parking lot at Cracker Barrel and proceeded to order sufficient quantities of eggs, sausage, and potatoes. The meal was, of course, topped off with side orders of biscuits and gravy. After we polished off our plates, we both sheepishly admitted that we could have handled a second helping of biscuits and gravy. However, we showed some restraint and decided that we had a big day ahead of us with the lawyer and we didn't want to feel uncomfortable. Plus, we previously saw a Steak 'n Shake that might be a good place for lunch. We didn't want to get too full.

Perhaps you're thinking that this obsession with food might not be healthy for two young guys in their sixties, but I am happy to report that we both enjoy cholesterol levels that are barely within the acceptable range (pharmaceutically induced, of course). That's good enough for us. And, remember, we're on vacation. It's okay.

* * *

We left Cracker Barrel and headed into downtown Glenville to meet with Lawyer Borland. That exhaustive drive took approximately five minutes. Borland's office was right on Main Street in one of the original red brick buildings that used to dominate the downtown area that we knew as kids.

The new combined city government center and police headquarters was also located right downtown. On the same side of the street were a few little shops, insurance agents, and several storefronts for lawyers who presumably needed to be located nearby the hub of legal activity for the thriving criminal population of Glenville. That's where we found Thomas Borland, upstairs in an office overlooking Main Street. No doubt it was a great spot for viewing the annual Fourth of July parade.

The door to Mr. Borland's office was open, so we knocked gently on the glass inset and stepped into an entryway. There was no receptionist to greet us. This was a one-man shop, but the place was impressive nonetheless. The entire office was probably a thousand square feet and gave the impression that the owner knew exactly where every document was located, every pen and pencil stored, and when a picture tilted on the wall more than an inch.

A huge and very impressive mahogany desk with two high-back side chairs stood out for their elegance in a room that already could be deemed elegant. Everything about this man on the phone suggested neat and tidy, and clearly that is what we found. The walls were adorned with personal photographs and a couple of East Coast landmark prints, which looked particularly out of place in an Indiana office. Of particular note, though not placed in a prominent location, was a framed diploma from the Yale Law School. Impressive.

Interestingly, the wall of photos did not contain the usual vanity shots of Lawyer Borland shaking hands with a variety of dark suits enveloping homogenous-looking men who presumably shared some small degree of fame or fortune. That was a deviation from the standard law office mold. Borland's photos showed a young man progressing in age while posing with what appeared to be members of an attractive family. As my eye moved across the wall, I watched three boys and an attractive woman gradually age along with a proud and happy father.

The older version of the man in those pictures quickly rose from behind his desk. He must have stopped taking pictures a few years ago since the traces of gray in this man's hair were not visible in the photos. He looked like what I might expect of an East Coast lawyer—a little stiff compared to the typical Midwesterner. Maybe I had been too heavily influenced by his clipped speech, with a slight accent that I couldn't place, over the phone. The Yale diploma and East Coast images on his wall probably further influenced my preconception of him.

He was several inches short of six feet tall with mostly dark, thick hair combed straight back, and he wore thin wire-rim glasses. He wore an expensive-looking suit, a crisp light blue shirt, a smartly knotted tie, and dark wingtip shoes that were polished to a high shine. Thomas Borland appeared to be in his early fifties and seemed impressively fit and energetic. My guess is this was not a guy who loosened up easily. I didn't see him going home and throwing on a Hawaiian shirt, shorts, white socks, and black sandals while he popped the top on his first Pabst Blue Ribbon.

"Gentlemen, you must be the Kelly brothers. Right on time! Splendid!"

Oh, God, here we go again. Splendid. Now that I've seen the man, my bet is that his speech mannerisms have been cultivated at private schools before being further drilled into him at Yale.

He quickly offered, "I'm Tom Borland. Which of you would be Joe and which of you would be Darren?"

Joe was quick on the draw and shrugged before responding. "I'll be Joe," he offered as if he had a choice of which name to pick. That response puzzled Borland, but he shook hands with Joe anyway and then greeted me in the same manner. His handshake was firm and he looked me right in the eyes as if he was taking my measure.

"Gentlemen," Borland gestured toward the chairs, "please be seated. Can I get you anything before we get started? Water, coffee, tea?"

We both declined since we just wanted to get this over with to begin our nostalgic visit around town. Borland began, "Well, then, let's get started, shall we?"

"We shall," Joe and I responded together with a sideways glance that has often been repeated over the years.

"As you know from our phone conversation," said Borland, "I represented Mr. Hazelton for several years before his death. He was a very private man who never wanted anyone to know that he had accrued a substantial amount of wealth over the years. I realize from our phone call that you had no idea he was wealthy."

"Tom," I said, "that would be putting it mildly. Uncle Shorty had no signs of wealth and there was no indication that he spent money on anything. The only exception was that his garage was set up with a bunch of woodworking equipment and he liked to make stuff and give it away."

In fact, Uncle Shorty saved Christmas one year when he produced a wooden platform with an intricate train track attached. Our folks must have bought us the train set and then conspired with Uncle Shorty to make it the greatest Christmas present of all time by having it mounted. Other kids had to lay their track out each time they wanted to use it and then break it down and put it away. In the meantime, every time the train came around a curve for them it would knock the tracks out of alignment and the cars would fly off and presumably cause an imaginary chemical spill and evacuation of the area. Our set had bridges and cool railroad crossings where near misses could occur with strategic precision. It even had a train station.

My Christmas miracle came on the heels of our next-door neighbor, Luke Jackson, informing me that there was no Santa Claus and that I wasn't going to get my beloved train set. I knew my parents didn't have much money for presents, but I figured Santa had a bottomless toy bag and I had been good enough to warrant a decent reward.

Joe was already dialed in on the Santa deception and had accepted the fact that we likely weren't getting a train set. He didn't have the heart to tell me about Santa, but Luke figured it was time I grew up and faced the facts. He told me he was doing it for my own good—and because I was too old to be talking about Santa *and* because other kids were making fun of me. It had become embarrassing for Joe and Luke.

As my mind wandered through images of that train set in our garage, I was brought back to reality when Joe asked, "How much money?" He generally liked to cut to the chase. But Borland was clearly not the kind of guy who jumped ahead. His presentation was carefully planned.

"First," Borland cautioned, "Mr. Hazelton wanted you two gentlemen to understand why he chose to share his estate information with you. He remained a very private person until he died and only seemed to have a few friends from church. He had no family and remained in his little house in Westside Village until the end. He often told me that his best years were spent in that house with his wife, Meta, enjoying the friendship of neighbors such as your family. He spoke very fondly of your father, Michael, and looked up to him as an outstanding individual."

I remembered that Uncle Shorty really did admire my father. I'm not exactly certain why. Clearly, Joe was having the same thoughts as he glanced at me and raised an eyebrow at the description of our father as an outstanding individual. Dad was older than Uncle Shorty (and taller). He was certainly a good person who seldom spoke badly about others. He was a good provider and I have no doubt that he would never stray in his fidelity to our mother. Not that she wouldn't test any man to look elsewhere from time to time, but Dad just never would exert that much energy. Plus, he feared her wrath.

Our father cruised through life accepting his role and making the most of it. He earned a decent living, wore a suit every day, didn't have to work on weekends, got home by 5:30 every evening in time to have one cold beer while Mom got the food ready for our 6:00 p.m. supper. In Indiana in the 1960s we had supper—not dinner. He seldom raised his voice in anger, but also showed only a marginal interest in the youthful exploits of his two sons. He was a calming influence in the Kelly household that could sometimes become volatile when our mother set her mind to something new.

Born and raised in Dublin, Ireland, our father came to this country in his early twenties. His intelligence and soft Irish accent seemed to open doors for him and no doubt cast a sort of romantic notion about who he was. Our mother, more than once, observed that Michael Kelly's accent likely lured her into marriage more than anything else about him. Uncle Shorty wasn't wrong in thinking our father was a good person. Joe and I loved him and even admired him in many ways. However, Uncle Shorty may have given him a little more credit than he deserved. I guess that didn't hurt anyone.

Borland continued, "Mr. Hazelton also spoke highly of Michael Kelly's two sons. He told stories of how you two would visit for hours and always treated his wife and him with respect. He said you weren't like other kids who didn't have time for older people. You laughed at his stories and always were happy to just hang around. He felt that you were part of the family."

It is true that we enjoyed crossing the field and hanging out at Uncle Shorty's place. Of course, that generally meant we could get a second meal over there. After polishing off lunch at our house on a Saturday, we could just stroll over there and know that the first question would be, "Are you boys hungry?" Of course, the answer was always "yes." We figured it wasn't incumbent on us to disclose that we had just eaten. They didn't specifically ask, "Did you eat lunch yet?" Thus, there was no need to lie. We should have been lawyers.

"Mr. Hazelton was most impressed that you both wrote to him long after you moved away from Glenville," said the lawyer. "He was quite moved by your efforts and looked forward to every note, however brief it might have been." Here is where Joe and I have our mother to thank. Does anyone really think that two young guys would voluntarily write letters to a neighbor after moving away from home? Just to touch base and keep him updated on our changing lives and locales? We were brainwashed.

Our mother brainwashed us in many ways and this was one. She drilled into us that a handwritten letter was worth more than gold. Thank-you notes were written no later than 5:00 p.m. the day after receiving a gift. After visiting someone's house for supper, a thank-you note followed the next day. If someone did you a favor, you thanked him or her in person and you confirmed it in writing. This was the law according to Violet Kelly. And the Kelly boys did not break the law.

Like Pavlov's dog, the Kelly boys were verbally rewarded sufficiently to create a pattern of behavior that no longer relied on prompting, threats of punishment, or even rewards. We had developed a life-long habit that extended far beyond just thanking people for birthday presents. When we moved away, we both continued to send home update notes to our parents and to our only other local "extended family," the Hazelton's. Our mother brilliantly engaged in periodic reinforcement by letting us know how much Uncle Shorty and Aunt Meta enjoyed our notes. That set our behavior in stone.

So, it is true that from an outsider's perspective, we might have been uncommonly kind to Uncle Shorty over the years just because we took an interest in him. It just seemed to be the natural thing to do (following our early behavioral therapy sessions). After Aunt Meta passed away, we both made sure to keep in touch with cards and notes. Though neither of us returned to Glenville with the exception of our class reunions, we continued our correspondence until Uncle Shorty's death.

* * *

I missed much of what Borland said next as I reminisced about the Hazelton's. He caught my attention when he asked, "Would you like to know how he made his money?"

"Absolutely," we answered together with a bit too much enthusiasm.

"I have two words for you," Borland dramatically proclaimed.

"Berkshire Hathaway."

Joe and I looked at each other and exchanged quizzical looks. Neither of us was particularly knowledgeable about the stock market, but even we had heard of Berkshire Hathaway. Joe blurted out with feigned enthusiasm, "Warren Buffett? You mean the Oracle of Omaha? Also known as the Omaha Sage? Also known as the Sultan of Swat? The Great Bambino?" Joe paused. "No . . . wait . . . those last two were Babe Ruth."

Borland just stared at him as if he were a child—albeit an unusual sixty-three-year-old child. Joe got the message and started to squirm. He was right back in Mrs. Gephardt's third-grade class trying to disappear under his desk. Lawyer Borland then proceeded to very calmly educate Joe and me about the history of Uncle Shorty's investments.

"You see," started Borland, "Mr. Hazelton was a very, very early investor in the stock market. As a young man he received a modest settlement from an insurance company for a car accident that damaged his leg (it's true that Uncle Shorty walked with a very slight limp). The money sat in a savings account until sometime later when a good friend of Mr. Hazelton, a local banker at the Glenville Banking Company, gave him some advice. That friend advised Mr. Hazelton that he should invest the money with a small brokerage firm that was led by a former classmate of his at the University of Nebraska. They had graduated together in 1950 and then the classmate went on to earn a masters degree in economics at Columbia University.

"This classmate so impressed the banker that he told Mr. Hazelton that his friend was the smartest person he had ever met and could be trusted completely to invest Mr. Hazelton's money wisely. His name? Warren Buffet. Mr. Hazelton took his friend's advice and in the mid-1950s invested with a firm led by Mr. Buffet that would eventually evolve to what became known as Berkshire Hathaway."

Borland continued. "The genius of Mr. Hazelton's approach was that he never wavered from his investment strategy. He started with a small lump sum. He then lived as frugally as possible, committing most of his pay increases to his investment fund just as if it was a simple savings account. He never panicked and withdrew funds and he simply reinvested everything that he earned. The beauty of the stock market is that it inevitably keeps moving forward in spite of dramatic dips in value that might send investors reeling in a panic to sell.

"Mr. Hazelton never bought other individual stocks; he didn't chase the latest great idea or dump it in a panic when the stock faltered. He simply stayed the course with Berkshire Hathaway and trusted Warren Buffet to make the right decisions. In fact, Mr. Hazelton didn't even pay attention to the fund for many years and only realized later in life that he had accumulated far more than he had imagined.

"Buffet's decisions were legendary. During a ten-year stretch early in Buffet's career, his partnership's assets were up by over 1,000 percent compared to the Dow's 123 percent. Every month Mr. Hazelton would contribute to his funds and never take anything out. If others had just followed this simple philosophy with any balanced portfolio, they could have made enormous sums of money over time.

"For most of us, life gets in the way. We need money for education, a car, a mortgage, or an unforgettable vacation that eventually becomes forgettable. Or, we just panic when the market goes south. We pull our money out when the market is low and reinvest again when it shows signs of recovery. By then it is too late to reap the real rewards of the upswing. Mr. Hazelton never made that mistake."

By this time Joe and I are mesmerized. I was wondering just how much money Uncle Shorty might have accumulated over sixty years of investing, but I was also remembering how many times I had made bad investment choices and missed out on a chance for serious accumulated wealth. Someone needed to give me this little Financial Investment 101 lecture long, long ago. It also seemed clear that Borland was not a novice when it came to the topic of accumulating wealth. He might be a bit annoying with his stiff demeanor, but he was no slouch.

So once again, Joe asked the question, "How much are we talking about here?"

And, once again, Tom Borland chose not to answer directly. He said, "First I must tell you both something that you probably won't care to hear. Mr. Hazelton's last will and testament stipulates that none of his estate will pass to either one of you personally. You will receive no money."

Joe and I look at each other searching for a clue. We flew across the country and learned that Uncle Shorty cared for us a great deal and, incidentally, was worth a great sum of money as well. His lawyer called us in to read his will and one might presume that there was something in it for us. How about a checkerboard? Nothing? Well, that was mildly disappointing.

"You must be joking," I lamely commented.

"I never joke about the reading of a will." Borland's right eye twitched a bit and he shook his head as if he'd been insulted. He then looked over his reading glasses and down his nose at me—a practiced effect no doubt used countless times before.

"Then why are we here?" asked Joe. Those were my sentiments as well. We never expected or looked for any sort of inheritance from Uncle Shorty. And even though he may have left an estate that was certainly more than expected, we still had no reason to believe that we deserved any of it. So, why were we there?

Borland let out a huge sigh. "You are here because Mr. Hazelton has a plan for the citizens of Glenville that involves his estate and your willingness to be involved in the disbursement of those funds. I tried to advise him that there were much better and more well-established approaches to this type of philanthropy, but he would not listen. He was determined that his money would not go toward exorbitant overhead costs, excessive administrator salaries, or government waste.

"He rarely had a kind word for bureaucrats of any type whether they were in government, the school system, or even churches. He admired some of our local volunteer organizations and even received some assistance from them in his last years.

Yet, he also was critical of how disorganized he thought some of those organizations were since their leadership was fairly transient by nature."

"So, what did Uncle Shorty hope to accomplish? How did he want his money spent?" I still wasn't grasping what the goal was here.

"Quite simply," stated Borland, "Mr. Hazelton wanted to leave Glenville a better place for its citizens. He loved this town and felt that it was losing some of its character as it moved toward becoming just another bedroom community of Indianapolis. He wanted to retain its small-town identity and community spirit in ways that city government alone no longer can provide. He just wanted to do whatever possible to improve the lives of the residents here and to offer opportunities to those who might not otherwise be able to achieve their full potential."

Joe jumped in. "Did Uncle Shorty leave some specific directions for how to proceed? Are there particular groups or individuals who should receive some of the funds?" I could tell that Joe had reached his limit for patience. Now that the money was out of our grasp (not to mention the checkerboard), it was hard for him to sit through much more of Borland's lecture. I could see Joe's wheels turning. It was time to get on with the business at hand and then head back to our homes.

I think Borland could see that it was time to get to the point as well. "Mr. Hazelton thought very highly of you two. He saw you as outstanding examples of what was right with growing up in a small town that prepared you to lead successful lives. As he told me more than once as we prepared his will, you two seemed to (in his words) 'have your heads screwed on straight' and 'knew what was bullshit and what was not.' That was very important to him. So, in his will he has asked that you two administer his estate funds in a manner that you see fit to benefit as many deserving people as possible in town."

Joe and I exchanged dumb looks with each other. We still didn't understand exactly what this meant for us and why Uncle Shorty picked us to be involved. "Not that we don't have our 'heads screwed on straight,' but I have to agree with you that there are much more qualified people to handle this sort of thing. Isn't that true even if Uncle Shorty wanted to avoid a traditional philanthropy or foundation?"

"My observation, precisely," offered Borland with a slight rolling of the eyes. "However, it seems that Mr. Hazelton didn't get out much and you two remained etched in his memory as shining examples of what is good about Glenville." A hint of a smile appeared at the corners of his mouth.

Ouch. There's a condescending compliment if I ever heard one. "I thought you said you never joked about wills."

"I wasn't joking; merely stating what is painfully obvious. Others might handle this task more professionally than you two, but you are the chosen ones. It's his money and his choice how to spend it."

"What if we don't want to spend our time on this?" asked Joe.

Borland was quick to respond with a slightly suppressed smile, "Then I will be designated as the administrator of the estate and I will have full latitude to disperse the funds as I see fit."

With a split-second glance to me, Joe sent a clear message that I agreed with fully. Before the smile could leave Borland's face, I said, "We're in."

"But you don't yet know the terms of the commitment," stammered Borland. "You might change your minds."

I quickly responded. "We're in. We never joke about wills." There was no way that Joe and I would let an East Coast outsider handle something that would have such a profound impact on our hometown. Borland may be a bright and decent guy, but he's relatively new to Glenville. For whatever reason, Uncle Shorty wanted us to take care of his estate. Who are we to turn against his wishes? I also began to understand his wisdom in picking a couple of guys who no longer have many friends or contacts in the community. We will be less likely to play favorites than someone who currently resides in Glenville.

There was one very obvious question that needed to be asked yet again. Joe politely inquired, "How much money are we talking about? Have I asked that before? Because it feels like I've asked that before."

Good question. Let's face it, if we're dealing with a few thousand dollars, that's one issue. If it's hundreds of thousands or even several million, then that might take us some time. More than that would be a full-time job.

The little smile made an appearance once again on Borland's face. Why did I suddenly get the feeling that this task wasn't going to be as easy as I once thought?

Borland very calmly announced, "Well, gentlemen, Mr. Hazelton has asked you to distribute roughly fifty million dollars to the citizens of Glenville."

CHAPTER 5

THE BEGINNING OF A PLAN

Joe and I left Borland's office several hours later after hearing the lawyer read the entire last will and testament and signing lots and lots of documents. Since we were obviously skeptical about the huge amount in the estate, Borland produced an entire file of annual statements from Berkshire Hathaway that clearly spelled out how Uncle Shorty's money had grown each year. He explained that the fifty million (give or take a few thousand on any given day) represented the amount after all administrative expenses and transfer taxes related to the estate had been handled. Because the funds would go almost entirely to charitable causes and had originally been placed in a trust, the estate paid out a relatively small amount of tax up front.

Uncle Shorty had not gone into detail about how our work was to be conducted, but he offered insight about what he thought of various organizations in town. He left it to us to incorporate his thinking into our decisions, but did not restrict us from making our own choices. He realized that things might have changed over time and that we might discover something about a need in town that he had never recognized.

The one directive from Uncle Shorty that really surprised us was a time limit for distributing the funds. He didn't want this process to drag on because he understood it could become contentious as the word got out around town. He also understood that it would be an imposition for both of us to be away from home for too long or to have to continually return to Glenville.

Therefore, he set a very strict time limit on the process. We had exactly thirty days to handle our due diligence before committing the funds wherever we saw fit. Every little detail didn't need to be in place, but the determination of where the funds would go had to be completed. Uncle Shorty knew that completion in a month might be difficult, so he gave us an out. Borland could take over if other circumstances just wouldn't let us complete the task. That wasn't going to happen. We had made the commitment and we were going to see it through.

With our meeting finished, Joe and I would have normally realized that we had missed lunch and would be feeling severely out of sorts as a result. I'm not sure what "out of sorts" really means, but that's what you say when you're from Indiana. On this day, however, neither of us seemed to have an appetite. The session with Borland left both of us mentally exhausted and we just wanted an escape from our new reality.

"What do you want to do now?" I asked Joe.

"I need a break from talking about this," he responded. "I think I just want to drive around town for a while. How about you?"

"I want to take a nap." That's what you do when you're retired in your sixties and you've had a big morning. You take a little afternoon siesta and recharge the batteries so you can be productive for a couple of more hours and then fresh for the cocktail hour. At least that's what I do. I've actually mastered the technique. Plus, I could tell Joe was in a mood to just be by himself. That was fine with me. We'd pick up this conversation again when we were both ready. So, Joe dropped me off at the Residence Inn and slowly pulled away to wander around town. As I headed inside I wondered if he was going to hit the drive-through at White Castle for a couple of sliders to ease his journey. I wouldn't bet against it.

* * *

When Joe returned I had finished my "power nap" and had returned to watching the Golf Channel, which had put me to sleep in the first place. I know what you're thinking. This guy leads a pretty exciting life. It's true.

Joe plopped down on his bed and was quietly snoring within minutes. A half hour later he was stretching and moaning while I swung an imaginary golf club in the room, mimicking the actions shown by the expert on the Golf Channel Academy. For at least the third time that month I had experienced a moment of eureka as I discovered the true secret of making a perfect golf swing. That discovery would once again remain in my memory only until I got to a golf course.

"What's up?" Joe showed that he was alive by once again demonstrating his eloquence.

"Just perfecting my golf game and working up a thirst. The two go hand in hand."

"Where do you want to eat?" asked Joe. Several hours had passed since we talked about food, so we were long overdue. There were many options in Glenville and I'm sure we would try them all over the next few weeks if we went through with Uncle Shorty's plan. There were tons of pizza places, locally owned cafes, family-style restaurants, a couple of steakhouses, something called Smokin' Hog (that looked promising), a fine dining spot called Rockefeller's located in the old converted Public Library where our mother had worked, and lots of chain restaurants out by the interstate.

"It has to be a place with a bar," I declared. No surprise there. Joe knew that I enjoyed a beer in the evening after work. Since settling into the California lifestyle, I often switched to wine for my evening ritual. I don't like to lose control and overindulge, but sometimes I get caught up in the social aspect of drinking with friends. As I once told my doctor when he asked how much I drank, I openly admitted, "I'll have a beer or two or a glass of wine pretty religiously every night." Since all doctors know their patients lie about how much they drink, he asked "What about the weekends?" I paused and then stammered, "Well, on weekends I get a little more religion." That answer seemed to cover all the bases.

Joe, on the other hand, is not much of a drinker. He'll have something just to be sociable and he might even like the first sip or two. But I've seen him nurse one drink for hours. He's generally a good sport putting up with others who get louder and more boring with every drink. However, he sometimes gets antsy and likes to take advantage of their growing stupidity and practice his surgeon-like skills while he verbally dissects their latest inane comment. The drunken ones don't feel their organs being ripped out and those bordering on sobriety enjoy the show.

"Applebee's," Joe announces. Quick to the point, Joe has zeroed in on the perfect choice. Applebee's Neighborhood Grill is, indeed, in our neighborhood. We can walk there. It has the requisite bar and sufficient menu choices to keep us interested over a potential thirty-day period. Hell, we could even have a salad once in a while. Not likely, but we could. We both like the idea of a regular spot to meet and we're not too proud to eat at any chain restaurant. We'll sprinkle in some other restaurants along the way, but this would become home base.

Before we left the hotel, I had to resolve a question that kept nagging at me since Borland's revelation that Uncle Shorty had accumulated fifty million dollars. That's a lot of zeros—$50,000,000. Sure, he showed us quarterly reports from Berkshire Hathaway, but was it really possible for a guy with a very small investment to end up with that much money? I grabbed my laptop and looked up Berkshire Hathaway.

Right away I found a site that asked a question: what would an investment of ten thousand dollars in 1965 be worth today if it was left untouched, had all dividends reinvested, and received a rate of return comparable to that achieved at Berkshire Hathaway? The answer was nearly fifty million. Well, knowing that all information on the Internet is nearly infallible, I kept checking other respected financial sites and kept playing with the numbers. The theory played out and I was convinced that the estate was for real. I closed the laptop and looked forward to dinner.

* * *

Joe and I entered Applebee's and I could tell that the place would work just fine for us. It looked like any other Applebee's, complete with multiple TVs for watching sports; lots of booth, table, and bar seating; and a wall dedicated to local athletic heroes to make sure the patrons understood that this was "their" neighborhood grill. Glenville high school athletic achievements and pictures were displayed prominently. I might have had a small photo somewhere in the mix if Applebee's had been around when I was playing ball. It wouldn't have been large and I would only be part of a team photo, but it might have made the cut. Or maybe that's just wishful thinking.

I led the way and zeroed in on the bar. That's where I feel most comfortable when visiting a new establishment. You can sip on a drink, chat with the bartender, and unobtrusively check out the local clientele in the mirror. Since Joe and I had arrived pretty early for dinner, the clientele was slightly older than us (not that easy to accomplish) and likely was there to capitalize on an early bird entrée.

Our bartender worked her way around to our corner and flashed us a warm smile. "What can I get you fellas?"

How many times has that line been spoken in bars and taverns all across America since the time there were saloonkeepers and spittoons? I thought I'd test her knowledge. "Well, let me see. I'm feeling quite regal tonight."

"Crown Royal or Budweiser?" she responded without hesitation.

"You are good; very, very good," I complimented her. "I will have the King of Beers in a bottle, thank you."

"And how about you," looking at Joe. "Feeling 'regal' as well?"

"No, I believe I will begin my Jamaican vacation right here, right now." Joe delivered the line with a big smile. He wasn't really used to this sort of bar banter and he was a little disappointed when she immediately responded without hesitation.

"Rum and Coke it is." She turned quickly to fetch the drinks, dryly proclaiming, "Let the vacation begin."

"Don't take it personally," I offered to Joe. "I have the feeling she's heard them all. Yours really wasn't that tough to guess."

As soon as the drinks arrived, we got down to the business of figuring out our next moves. It was clear to both of us that we were committed to this project. How could we not be? Uncle Shorty picked us to do this for him and we couldn't let him down. And the reality was that we were both free to pursue this right now. Retirement was a beautiful thing. We could pick a more convenient time and come back. But why wait? We might have to buy a few more clothes to get by, but that's about it.

"Okay, let's start with the pros and cons of this little enterprise," I began. "What's the downside?"

Joe had clearly been thinking about this on his drive around town. "We're stuck in Glenville for thirty days, our wives will be understanding but not thrilled, people in town who get no money will be pissed at us, people who get money will want more, we'll probably have to deal with some asshole lawyers, we'll likely add ten pounds each eating our way through Glenville, and the two of us have absolutely no idea about what we are doing."

"Nice summary. Very uplifting."

"You asked for the downside," Joe quipped.

"I presume you have also given thought to the upside?"

Joe jumped right in. "It's a once in a lifetime chance to change a lot of lives for the better, we're playing with house money and can't lose a thing, maybe a few people will actually be grateful to us, our expenses are paid, and women might throw themselves at us for a share of the cash."

"Very funny. Anything else?"

"Sure. We have total control. When have we had total control of anything? We set the rules. Someone doesn't like our rules? That's just too bad. We also probably get to deal with some of the assholes we grew up with who will be looking for a slice of the pie. That could be fun. And, finally, we get to do this thing the way Uncle Shorty would want it done. He was right. We have our heads screwed on straight and we know bullshit when we see it. We don't exactly know what we're doing, but those two traits will probably carry us in the right direction. Overall, I'd say this project is going to be a pain in the ass and a lot of fun at the same time!"

I couldn't find any fault with Joe's logic, so we began the task of mapping out a strategy. We agreed that there were plenty of organized groups and organizations that we could meet with to start to get a feeling for the needs of the community. The mayor, school board superintendent, service club leaders, police chief, church leaders, and massage therapists all came to mind. The last one was quickly dismissed despite Joe's protest. We also both had a small network of old friends in town that would give us some honest input.

Our theory was that we could meet with lots of groups over the course of, say, the next two weeks. We would let them know that we had a small amount of money to distribute and were looking for ideas. Our intent was to never let anyone know the extent of our bank account and what the rules were for distribution (since we had none).

Assuming that we didn't cover all the bases with our start-up list, we would then put the word out through the local paper and hold a town hall meeting of some sort to give anyone and everyone a chance to state their case. We knew that could be a complete zoo, but didn't want to restrict our search just to the established organizations in town. One of Uncle Shorty's provisions was that we do our best to reach out into the community to find areas of need that might otherwise be overlooked. So, even though we were opening ourselves up to all the head cases in Glenville, we felt obligated to cover all the bases.

An hour later we had a plan. I'm the organized half of this duo (Joe being the creative half), so I compiled my notes on my laptop and set it aside to finally finish my dessert. During the evening I had consumed a few more adult beverages while Joe simply kept adding soda to his original Rum and Coke. His Jamaican vacation was too exciting for words. We dined on two of Applebee's finest steaks and agreed that we really needed to watch our meat intake over the next month. So, we'll watch it. We ate at the bar and got to know our bartender, Amanda Saunders, who morphed into Mandy pretty quickly as the night progressed. She was smart, funny, and not hard on the eyes. I could tell we had found a solid temporary home base for the next thirty days.

Tomorrow we start. I had already set up a breakfast meeting just to get reacquainted with an old high school friend. It just so happens that he was now the editor of the only local newspaper, *The Glenville Daily Reporter*. This guy would be a wealth of information. What could be better? We'd have another great breakfast with a side order of gossip. Let's get this show on the road.

CHAPTER 6
BREAKFAST WITH THE EDITOR

It was another beautiful spring day in Glenville and another opportunity to start with the most important meal of the day. Since my old high school friend was calling the shots that morning, we met at the Bob Evans restaurant. This was an excellent choice. The place looked and felt like the Cracker Barrel without all the extra crap they tried to sell in the adjacent store.

Joe and I perused the menus while waiting for my friend and quickly concluded that there were sufficient sources of cholesterol and nitrates to keep us happy. This morning we might throw in some wheat toast to balance the meal. We had both called our wives since yesterday and clued them in on our new adventure. As Joe had predicted, neither was thrilled but both understood that we had to see this through for Uncle Shorty.

Both couples talked about getting together at some point during the four-week stretch, but I suspected that everyone had doubts that it would happen. After thirty-plus years of marriage on both sides, you come to understand that breaks from each other are healthy. Sure, we mouthed the words about getting together but I'm not sure anyone really believed them. My wife, Beth, and Joe's wife, Carol, both had very full lives with plenty to keep them occupied. They are strong, independent women who had enjoyed productive careers and remained productive in early retirement. Neither had any need for a nostalgia visit to Glenville since it held absolutely no nostalgia for them. We met them long after our Glenville days.

Would we miss our wives and would they miss us? Absolutely. Would we see them this month? I wouldn't place any bets on it. I don't like the idea of being away from Beth for a month and I'd welcome her input about this new challenge if she could join me at some point. However, the reality is that this task and the town of Glenville hold a special appeal to Joe and me. It's not the same for our wives and I wouldn't blame them at all for letting us sort this one out by ourselves.

John Bourke cruised into the restaurant greeting several patrons along the way. He looked and acted every bit a small-town politician pressing the flesh with the local constituents. I imagine being editor wasn't much different than being a politician when it came to having your fair share of supporters and critics. The fact that he had lived his entire life in Glenville meant that he probably knew just about everyone and a little about everyone's business. He had done a stint on the city council a few years back, so I'm sure that John was well acquainted with any skeletons in the town's closet as well. He and I had kept in touch a few times over the years and I looked forward to spending a little time with him. Now I had even more reason to get his perspective on Glenville.

"Darren and Joe Kelly," John proclaimed to no one in particular. "It is good to see you boys back home where you belong! What's the matter? Did you miss our good cooking, fine weather, and sensible Midwestern values, or are you just divorced and destitute, looking for a fresh start?"

"You nailed it, Bourke," I quickly replied. "All of the above. You always were so perceptive. Actually, we were thinking about buying a newspaper and wondered if you would mind a few changes we'd like to make. We thought it would be good to bring an East Coast/West Coast flavor to the heartland."

That got his attention for a second. John hesitated briefly before declaring, "You're still full of shit!" As I said, he was perceptive. He shook our hands with great enthusiasm and settled his five-foot-nine, two hundred-pound frame into a chair at the corner table we had selected earlier. The waitress appeared instantly with menus and he quickly offered, "Hey, Suzie, how are you doing today? How's your mom? Is that big, dumb brother of yours keeping out of trouble?" The questions just flowed from John with no expectation of an answer. Suzie just laughed and sarcastically said, "Everyone is just fine and thank you so much for asking."

Suzie looked like she was about twenty years old and had worked in a restaurant for all twenty of them. She took our coffee orders and disappeared. John lowered his voice and confessed, "I used to date her mother for a while until I realized that she was hell bent on finding a husband to take care of her and the family. Suzie's a sweetheart, but not real bright. I'm pretty sure her career aspirations have peaked here at Bob Evans. She does volunteer work at the hospital as a candy striper. Wants to be a nurse some day. It's not gonna happen."

Bourke chuckled. "To give you an idea of her depth of intelligence, one day she tells me that she heard a good name for a baby at the hospital. She thought she might use it if she ever has a girl."

Bourke can barely contain his laughter. "She says the name is Chlamydia."

"As in the venereal disease? You're serious?" I asked.

"Hell, yes, I'm serious. You can't make this stuff up. She heard some of the nurses talking about a patient and they mentioned chlamydia. Suzie thought it had a pretty ring to it and locked it away in that uncomplicated mind of hers for future reference."

"And did you inform her that the name might not be appropriate for her future child?"

"Oh, no. I don't like to interfere in other people's lives." Bourke snickered at that false admission. "I wasn't lying about her brother either. He's a world-class dumbass. Hard to imagine what he might be thinking on any given day. But he's a pretty good kid who just seems to find trouble every now and again."

And so it went with John Bourke, editor of *The Glenville Daily Reporter*. We proceeded to engage in idle gossip. We asked about some of the characters we had known growing up in town. Every person we asked about, John had a story. "Whatever happened to Freddy the Painter?" Joe asked. "Did he ever get straightened out?" Freddy was a guy who was probably only in his early thirties when we were kids, but he looked about fifty. Freddy was not only an alcoholic, but he was partial to drinking Gillette After-Shave (for the miniscule alcohol content) when he had a few extra dollars to spare. I presume it kept his breath fresh as well.

Freddy called everyone Governor. "How you doin', Governor? What's going on, Governor?" I have a vivid memory of him hiding under a car in the A&P parking lot in a futile attempt to escape the wrath of his wife who spotted him coming out of the Hook's Drugstore with some after-shave. Freddy had a goofy smile on his face and motioned for me to keep quiet with his finger over his lips. His wife screamed at him while he just laughed and sipped on his after-shave under the car.

John laughed, "He was a helleva good painter, wasn't he? Best painter in town. Between the alcohol and the paint fumes, it's a wonder he could function at all." He added in a very matter of fact way, "Yeah, he's dead."

"Booze finally got him?" I presumed.

"Nope, his wife beat him over the head with a shovel when he drank away his pay check. I guess you could say the booze finally got him. She went away to prison for a while."

The reference to prison reminded me of someone. "I heard something about Ed Tolliver getting in trouble with the law. What was that all about?"

Bourke sat back and smiled. "Well, Ed was a fine, upstanding citizen for quite awhile after he got married. He quit engaging in some of his slightly illegal activities from his misspent youth."

"You mean like selling pot?" I asked.

"Precisely. He went to work at the Caterpillar plant. For five years his wife, Martha, would pack his lunch box for him every day and he'd go off to put in his eight hours. One day he forgot his lunchbox and the wife was worried that he wouldn't have anything to eat. So, she went on over to the plant and asked where she could leave Ed's lunch. They looked at her like she was nuts and explained that Ed lost his job there about a year before.

"Come to find out, Ed had resurrected his former occupation and was spending every day selling pot between here and Indianapolis. However, he always stopped to eat with great appreciation that fine lunch Martha had prepared for him each day. When she confronted him at home, he confessed to her and said he was making too much money to quit. She went out to his truck, saw a huge bag of pot tucked behind the seat, and drove right down to the police station and turned it in. They came and got him at the house and found a few more stashes. He got some jail time and now he and Martha are giving it another try. I reckon the moral of the story is 'don't forget your lunch box.'" Bourke had a good laugh over that one.

"You reckon that's the moral, huh?" Joe gave Bourke a look that suggested there was more than one dumbass in Glenville. Unfazed, Bourke just shrugged his shoulders.

"How about Bobby Paul?" I asked. In addition to being a former teammate, Paul was noteworthy for having two first names (though not as interesting or alliterative as Larry Lawrence, another classmate). His father was Bobby Paul, Sr. There was not a lot of creativity when it came to names in that family.

"He's sellin' used cars and living in the bottle."

"Hell, Bourke," I blurted out, "Is anyone doing okay in this town?"

"You're the one asking the questions. Plenty of people are doing fine; just not the ones you asked about. Might say more about the questions than the answers."

"How about Coach Mays?" He was my track coach.

"Dead."

"Mr. Hartley?" He was our high school principal.

"Yeah, he's dead, too."

I was getting depressed.

"What the hell did you expect, Kelly?" John asked. "You've been gone for damn near forty years. You think everyone is just frozen in time around here? Take a look in the mirror."

Now, that kind of comment is just hurtful and unnecessary.

Just then Suzie came around to take our breakfast orders. John had "the usual." I didn't ask. I had some eggs and corned beef hash. Suzie warned, "Now, that hash isn't homemade; it's just from a can." I told her that corned beef hash was just fine from the can when properly cooked to a crisp. She took a note.

Joe ordered eggs and bacon. When Suzie asked if he'd like fruit for a side order instead of potatoes, Joe just smile at her and said, "No, I'm trying to quit."

She didn't quite understand that. "You're trying to quit what—fruit?"

Joe just smiled and nodded for emphasis. "Yes, Suzie, I'm trying to quit fruit—at least while I'm on vacation." Suzie just shook her head and walked away. A lot of waitresses did that with Joe.

We eventually tackled our food with great enthusiasm and remained silent until we came up for air. Joe and I were thoroughly enjoying the experience. John, on the other hand, was eating oatmeal and fruit—apparently "the usual." He didn't look nearly as satisfied.

It was time to start the discussion. I gave John the highlights of our visit with Borland and the fact that Clarence Hazelton had left some money to be distributed to some members of the community who could use a little extra help. We described it as a modest sum, but one that was more than you might have expected from a guy like Uncle Shorty. I told John that we would appreciate his help in developing a plan to reach out to the right sorts of groups in town that might be good candidates for help.

"Why you two guys?" John didn't waste any time.

"We have no idea," I said, "other than the fact that he trusted us and probably didn't know who else to trust with his money. He didn't seem to stay connected with anyone after his wife died."

"Well, I guess he could do worse."

"Thanks for the endorsement," Joe quickly responded.

"I can help you; in fact, I'd be happy to help in this case," John said. "There are plenty of folks who could use a little good fortune and plenty of organizations in town that do good work with very little money. We could also use the newspaper to get the word out. I could do a feature on you two—'Brothers Return to Dole Out Cash!' That should bring the rats out of the woodwork."

"I don't think so." I could just imagine what such a headline would bring. "I think we'll leave the newspaper part until the end when we try to flush out anything we missed. We really don't want any publicity about the two of us. I'm sure that will slip out anyway, but we don't want to add fuel to the fire."

"Okay," John acknowledged. "Let me go to my office and I'll start making a list of organizations and folks you should contact. You mentioned some of them already, but I'll give you the right people who will give you straight information. Some of the jackasses running those operations have no clue what the real needs are in this town. Case in point, our young mayor is a horse's ass with big political aspirations. But there are good people on the city council that will give you solid information.

Likewise, the police chief was a punk who became a bully when he put on the badge. He tried to intimidate everyone on the force and most of the citizens around here. Folks say he's mellowed a bit and he has his wife to thank for it. I haven't personally seen evidence that he's changed, but our paths don't really cross. Hell, Kelly, you might remember the little asshole—Frank Hagman—Randy Hagman's little brother."

I did remember the Hagman boys. Randy was a couple of years older than me and seemed decent enough. But his little brother, Frank, was an obnoxious little shit that never shut up and thought he deserved to hang around with the older kids. He was at least four years younger than me, but big for his age. I remember one time he kept pestering a group of us when we were playing ball at the old Riley outdoor basketball courts.

The kid thought he should play and kept screaming about how much better he was than us. That didn't wear well on Tom Braswell, a high school senior and the biggest kid on the court at the time. Braswell picked up the miscreant and stuffed him head first into a trash dumpster near the court. That shut the kid up for the time being, but I did hear later that he might have also learned the wrong kind of lesson from it. It seems Frank started to turn his attention to kids his own age and younger and became known as a real bully. I soon moved away to college and never really heard much about him until now.

"I can't believe that little shit became a police officer—let alone the police chief," I said.

"Well," countered John, "he did and he's big, strong, ornery, and bright enough that you shouldn't underestimate him. Apparently, some people admire those traits in a police chief because he's held the post for quite awhile now. Be careful around him. If you looked at him sideways thirty years ago, I guarantee you he didn't forget it."

With that bit of cheerful advice, John started to ease his way out of his chair. "I assume you boys will be generous enough to pick up the check since I am going to be of invaluable help to you. By the way, I think you should start by just cruising around and getting a feel for this town again. You have some strong roots here, but it's been forty years and there really have been some changes—for better or worse. "Get out there and revisit your past, but get in touch with what's going on today. Visit some shops, drive around, check some real estate offices, and ask some questions of the locals like a couple of visitors would. Hell, maybe some old fart will even remember you." He laughed. "Then, when I get you a list of contacts in a day or so, you might have a better perspective on things." He paused before leaving. "Thanks for breakfast. Good to see you boys."

CHAPTER 7

WESTSIDE VILLAGE

Joe and I thought that John Bourke's advice to revisit Glenville with a new perspective was a solid idea. We began our journey back where it all started—on Garfield Drive where we grew up. We lived on the west side of town in a little subdivision called Westside Village. It was a great place—or so it seemed at the time. As we grew older, we came to understand that we didn't live on the rich side of town. We weren't poor; there were other sections of town that we could proudly look down upon. But by the time we approached middle school where kids from all over town converged, we knew there was a social class divide east and west of Broad Street.

Now it appeared that Westside Village had slipped down the social strata ladder just a few more rungs. Our little house had once shown a great pride of ownership just like the others in the neighborhood. It was a one-story, two-bedroom, one-bath stucco structure with an exterior wall of Indiana limestone slapped on the front section facing the street. Originally, it was probably about a thousand square feet of living space, but our parents greatly enhanced that by converting the single-car garage into a family room and adding a carport made of fiberglass panels to partially shelter our one car. This renovation not only enhanced our status in the neighborhood, but it suddenly allowed us to have a family room where we never left and a living room where we never lived.

The family room had a couple of comfortable old chairs, a couch, an antique rolltop desk, and a small TV that morphed from black and white to color over the years. The living room had uncomfortable blue furniture, family photos taken once a year at the local studio, and a beautiful dark mahogany baby grand piano. The piano set us apart from every other house I had ever been in within Westside Village. It's one thing to have an upright piano shoved up against a wall, but quite another thing to have the lid opened up on this gorgeous centerpiece in our living room. It completely dominated the room.

The piano was a symbol of many things in the Kelly household. First and foremost it was a symbol of our mother's determination to expose us to the cultural arts. Coming from the East Coast, she viewed the cornfields of central Indiana as a cultural wasteland. She would do everything possible to expose us to music, art, theater, and literature.

That piano was also a symbol of my mother's heritage. It had been in the family since 1929. In August of 1929, two months before the stock market crash, my grandmother took my mother over to Patterson, New Jersey, to purchase the piano. My grandparents financed it over forty-eight months. It was a Wheelock brand—not a Steinway, but still a quality instrument built in

New York City. It was a piece of the East Coast and all things cultural that she remembered about that area.

Growing up in New Jersey only a thirty-minute bus ride from New York City, our mother spent a fair amount of her youth visiting the great museums and attending Broadway matinees. Her world back then was a far cry from the reality of today's *Jersey Shore*. Joe and I would later imitate her treks to Broadway as we visited our grandparents in Little Falls, New Jersey, for summer vacations. From *Man of La Mancha* to *Roar of the Greasepaint, Smell of the Crowd*, our mother immersed us for two weeks a year in a world far away from Glenville, Indiana. At first I pretended to hate it, but the pretense couldn't mask my excitement as we entered the Shubert Theater or the great Radio City Music Hall. And what's not to like about the Radio City Rockettes when you're thirteen?

It was Joe who immediately took to the piano and fulfilled his mother's dreams. Joe loved singing and knew he was good at it from an early age. The piano was a natural fit and Joe's aptitude was reinforced with weekly lessons. Music would become a huge part of Joe's life. His interests ran the gamut of performing the lead in high school musicals, making a living as a rock 'n' roll disc jockey, singing on radio and TV musical commercials, owning his own professional recording studio, and eventually singing and playing guitar in the church every Sunday. He even cut his own CD of music in his early sixties that sounded great for a singer in his prime—let alone one whose best vocals should have been in his rearview mirror. That baby grand was the start of a life-long connection to music for Joe.

The good news for me was Joe's commitment to singing and playing took all the pressure off the second son. Mom had filled a void in her life and I was free to choose my own direction. That was easy—sports. My only obligation to the music world was her demand that I practice lines from each play that Joe was in during his high school career. In his senior year he was given the lead in Camelot. This was a big deal. All I can say is for weeks I played a very reluctant Guinevere to Joe's enthusiastic King Arthur. I still have clear memories of him singing throughout our house, "I Wonder What the King is Doing Tonight?" Joe, on the other hand, also had an unfortunate experience regarding the legacy of our piano. He likely met his first potential pedophile and continued to visit with him on a weekly basis for years while taking piano lessons.

* * *

Hugh Langston was allegedly the best piano teacher in town. When any kid was forced to take lessons, you could be certain that Hugh Langston's name would come up first. He had a studio with two baby grand pianos and seating for about fifty people to attend recitals for his young protégés. Langston was an older guy, very meek and gentle, and completely non-threatening. It was no wonder mothers loved him and trusted him completely to nurture their kids and give them a gift they could enjoy for the rest of their lives. It appears that he might have desired to give some of the boys another gift to remember their entire lives as well. My mother hired him to tutor Joe.

Long after we had left Glenville, Joe and I were talking about the Kelly baby grand piano that now sits in Joe's living room in Maryland. I had long heard the bits and pieces about Hugh Langston's reputation, but I never got the full scoop from Joe and had no idea how he felt about the situation.

"There's not really all that much to tell, but I'm sure I could embellish it for you to make it a better story," Joe offered. "You know what the old guys down at the barbershop used to say— never let the truth get in the way of a good story."

"Let's just stick with the facts this time."

"Okay, the facts are the guy was a really good piano teacher. He was also a little creepy, but not to the point that I immediately thought anything was wrong. I was only about nine years old when I started, so what did I know? I'm sure that few people in our world back then even knew the definition of a pedophile and I have no proof that Langston was one. I can tell you for sure that, as time went on, he began to creep me out more and more.

"Nothing dramatic. He just liked to put his hands on mine to show me proper position on the keyboard. I must have needed a lot of extra work in that area. And he really liked to touch my leg like someone might touch your arm to emphasize a point. He seemed to need to emphasize points for a long time. After awhile, long pants became my outfit of choice even on hot summer days."

"That doesn't seem too unusual. If the guy was your grandfather, you wouldn't think anything about it," I suggested.

"True, but when he broke out the red nail polish I began to wonder. I had a habit of resting one of my thumbs below the keys. His "punishment" for this laziness was to stop the session and very slowly paint my thumb red with nail polish. This ritual was repeated many, many times over the course of several years of lessons. He was always careful to remove the polish at the end of the session and then he'd warn me (with a smile) that he'd have to do it again if I persisted in adopting that sloppy habit. It took me quite awhile to catch on, but I finally realized that I was no longer exhibiting the 'egregious' behavior, yet I was still receiving the red nail polish reprimand."

"Why didn't you tell Mom and Dad?" I asked.

"I eventually did tell them, but I picked a particularly lousy time when I had been goofing off and not practicing much. They read my complaints as just a way to get out of piano lessons. I remember them glancing at each other in the kitchen after I laid out my case. Mom just said, 'Get back in there and practice!'

"So, that was basically the whole story. Nothing else happened. He actually backed off on most of the touching and I told him to cool it on the nail polish routine or I'd tell Mom. That stopped him in his tracks. I checked with a few other students and several confirmed that Langston did similar creepy stuff to them, but that behavior was overlooked since he also promised these guys that he would introduce them to his latest student,

Nancy Worthington. Nancy was a couple of years older than me and clearly had come into her own with the development of actual breasts—not just a stuffed bra. Practicing for a recital with Nancy was definitely worth a few extra rubs on the leg by Langston. After she quit taking lessons, it was time for me to call it quits as well. So, I convinced Mom and Dad that I had learned all I could learn from Langston and it was time to move on to someone else. They set me free."

* * *

That is the story of the Kelly baby grand piano. Perhaps the most compelling story line is the fact that my grandparents bought it right before the stock market crash and the subsequent Great Depression. My grandfather apparently had owned a very successful excavation and paving company with lots of employees and heavy equipment. When the economy tanked he lost nearly everything, but was able to scratch out a very modest living. While the creditors came knocking and the family business was downsized on a monthly basis, my grandparents never missed a payment on that baby grand piano. The piano then made its way to our Garfield Drive living room in Indiana and eventually settled in the Kelly home next to the Chesapeake Bay. It's hard to say where its next stop will be, but I firmly suspect that it will enrich the lives of those who take care of it.

CHAPTER 8

HOME AGAIN ON GARFIELD DRIVE

Joe and I sat in our car across from our old house and took in the view. It wasn't pretty. The place had seen better days. To begin with, Garfield Drive was full of cracks and small potholes that led to a driveway filled with weeds poking up through the broken concrete. In a weed patch formerly known to us as a beautiful front yard stood the remnants of what was once a majestic old maple tree. It now was a four-foot high stub that was left to slowly decay. The mailbox out front was leaning at a forty-five degree angle and had the look of a place where only bills accumulate.

The house needed a new roof, but otherwise seemed livable—just worn out. Interestingly, the curtains that one might normally find on the front picture window had been replaced with a large quilt that completely blacked out any view of the interior. You can draw your own conclusions. Joe offered, "Crack house." That description was the opposite of our idyllic childhood existence where the milk man made his deliveries to our side door each week and my father's laundry was carefully placed inside that same unlocked door on top of the washing machine every Friday.

Each week five identical folded white shirts with heavy starch would be delivered and five dirty ones removed. These were part of my father's carefully groomed attire at the Fort Benjamin Harrison Army Finance Center where he was one of the higher-ranking civilians in the finance department. He also bought three new suits every year at the annual one-day suit sale at the William H. Block department store in Indianapolis. Because of his frugal nature, those shirts would also serve as his after-work leisurewear until their next laundry cycle. An open collar and rolled up sleeves signaled the shirt could now be worn mowing the lawn or washing the car. That's about as casual as my father would ever be seen. I have only one memory of ever playing catch with my father in the side yard and he was resplendent in his slightly wrinkled white shirt.

We pulled up in order to see the back yard. There, still standing, was the basketball goal and concrete slab that my parents had built when I entered high school and searched for Hoosier stardom. It was now littered with toys and other discarded debris. The rim held no net, which was a sign of poor judgment and suspect character in a state that treated the sport like a religion. It was not at all unusual to have a basketball goal of some kind on your property in Indiana when I grew up there.

In fact, if you didn't have one, then neighbors knew one of three things about you. You had no children at all, you had no boys in the litter, or you were a foreigner and probably spent hours secretly kicking around a black and white ball in your back yard while occasionally bouncing it off your head. Remember, there was no such thing as organized girls basketball back then, and soccer was decades away from becoming the ubiquitous babysitter that now dominates youth sports.

However, the Kelly property was unique in that it actually had a flat slab of concrete to play on. It was small, but flat. Most goals just were planted in dirt or were secured over garages on driveways that sloped toward the street. Thus, your basic shooting height might range from ten feet at the basket to twelve feet as you worked your way toward the street. That will really screw you up when you get to a normal court.

The Kelly court was also unique because of how it was built. Joe, like many kids in our area, got a summer job in high school working for the State Highway Department of Transportation. He basically did flunky work hauling stuff around for the next layer of clock-watchers higher up in the bureaucracy who performed flunky work for someone else. Joe had the good fortune of working with a crew led by the Booker brothers.

The four Booker brothers did not live in Glenville. I knew that only because there were no black people residing within the city limits. At the time, I never gave that oddity of homogenous living a single thought, but later heard strong rumors that Klan activity had been a part of Glenville history and the lingering memory of it might still have influenced the make-up of our quaint little town.

So, the Booker brothers lived in a nearby town and taught Joe the ways of state employment. First, slow down. Second, take a coffee break. Third, get ready for lunch. However, in spite of working the system like everyone else, Joe respected the Booker brothers for their work habits once they decided it was time to work. They also treated Joe well and liked him. I remember the first time Joe came home from work and told me about the brothers.

"These guys have some strange names: A, B, C, and D Booker."

"So," I naturally asked, "What do the letters stand for?"

"Nothing. They stand for A, B, C, and D."

"You're telling me they had letters for names?"

"That's right," Joe replied in a matter-of-fact fashion. "I was told by 'A' that his parents were illiterate and just went with single letters so they wouldn't have to write their names. 'A' was the oldest, 'B' and 'C' were twins, and 'D' was just an accident."

I had no reason not to believe Joe, and when I met the Booker brothers I confirmed the story. Joe had mentioned to them about my parents considering an investment in a basketball court and they told him they could build it on a weekend for a good price. A "good price" was all that my father needed to hear. He didn't care what race they were or how many vowels they had in their names. They did a good job with the court and probably created a little stir on Garfield Drive when they all showed up that first morning jammed into their old pick-up truck.

* * *

Joe and I drove up Garfield Drive and made the turn on Jefferson Street (where Uncle Shorty and Aunt Meta had lived) and on to Madison, Polk, Monroe, and Winfield streets. You get the idea. Westside Village was into presidents. The area was much more fully developed now and stretched out to the Glenville Water Tower and beyond. That silver tower, as with small towns all over the Midwest, hovered above the community and served as an announcement that you had arrived in Glenville. As a kid, it seemed gigantic and mysterious. We could see it from our back yard and when my parents first moved to Indiana there were just open fields between the tower and our house. Westside Elementary, our local grade school, also looked up at the tower from the classroom windows. As young kids, the water tower dominated our very existence; we seemed to live our lives in its shadow.

Over the years the area between our house and the tower eventually filled with starter homes built mostly in the 1950s and 60s. They now sell in the $50,000 to $100,000 range, according to the real estate guide we picked up at breakfast. You might be able to pay for a bathroom for that amount in southern California.

We looped back to Garfield Drive and again drove past our home. This time we looked across the street and realized how ugly the view was from our house. Maybe that's why a quilt now covered the front window. When we were kids, living across from the loading dock of the local supermarket and adjacent drugstore simply meant we didn't have far to go to run a quick errand. It was also a source of income in the summer when Joe and I unloaded produce trucks at night and were rewarded with cash. While violating child labor laws, we really didn't care that our house looked out into the backside of a supermarket. It was convenient. Now it didn't look so great.

A few doors down, we stopped in front of the old Conrad house to reminisce about The Garfield Gang. Yes, that's right. Joe and I were part of a gang. Thugs. Enforcers. Well, actually we put on garage sales, had a lemonade stand, and held dog show competitions for the neighborhood (which were most certainly later ripped off to create "Letterman's Stupid Pet Tricks"). We even put on a world-class magic show when Joe received a magic kit for his birthday one year. He was, naturally, the Master of Ceremonies. We charged twenty-five cents per ticket for that one and made a killing. We made even more money from our concession stand where we featured bologna sandwiches on Wonder Bread with Miracle Whip. It's amazing how much profit you can pocket when you take everything from your parents' kitchen and have no cost of goods.

The Conrad brothers were the same age as the Kelly boys (around seven and ten); so it was a natural fit to create a gang. We envisioned something akin to Spanky and Our Gang, but likely without Buckwheat and Darla since there were no black kids around and no local girl could ever match up to Darla. We were very selective about who could join. Just because you lived on Garfield Drive didn't mean you could be in the gang. Phil Duncan lived just a couple of doors down from the Conrad brothers and he was a cool kid—a year older than Joe. Plus, he had a basketball goal with a dirt court and a huge field next door where we could play baseball and football. He was a lock for membership.

The Bender brothers down the street barely squeaked in just because we felt sorry for them and we needed someone to run errands for us. They were younger and did what they were told. Of course, our next-door neighbor, Luke Jackson, had a guaranteed spot in the gang. Not that he needed us, but we needed him for any sort of credibility that we might be able to generate outside of Garfield Drive. If for any reason at all we got into trouble with other kids outside the gang, all we had to do is mention Luke. That would end any and all harassment.

The Hunt brothers wanted to join the gang in the worst way even though they didn't technically live on Garfield Drive. They were over on Jefferson. They begged us. Again, these guys were exactly the same age as Joe and me. Parents in Indiana at that time must have had a mandatory waiting period of roughly three years before having sex again. That seemed to be the appropriate spacing between kids in our neighborhood. The older one could best be described as whiney and the younger one farted all the time and blew snot out his nose when he sneezed. He never covered his mouth and nose; just blew it out. We weren't going to have that in our gang. In spite of the parents' intervention on the boys' behalf, we held firm. The vote was 8–0 against. I felt a real rush of empowerment at the time.

We once considered girls in the gang very briefly since there were a lot of girls on Garfield Drive and on the surrounding streets. Joe was convinced that girls would be a disruptive force within the gang and that we were heading down a slippery slope by even considering it. I had no idea what an ideological slippery slope was at the time, but I could tell by Joe's insistence that it was no place I wanted to go. When Sally Markham approached the group for inclusion, Joe convinced everyone that her red hair and abundance of freckles signaled a rare disease that could prove contagious. The group wisely avoided that calamity and never raised the issue of girls in the Garfield Gang again. Naturally, that all changed when the older guys' hormones kicked in, but the gang had run its course by that time and was ready for disbandment.

The Garfield Gang was not only wonderfully community-minded in offering a generous slate of reasonably priced activities for the neighborhood, but we were ahead of our time as an outdoor adventure club. We could have been called the Sierra Club if we had known what a Sierra was at the time. We went on long-distance hikes through the cornfields all the way out to Bird Island, which was almost out of sight of the water tower. No one knew why the spot was called Bird Island. We never saw any birds there. It basically was a mud hole surrounded by a grove of trees. We saw lots of frogs, but no birds. But since Luke Jackson was the one who originally found it and deemed it to be Bird Island, we weren't going to argue about the name.

In the winter, we would track wild animals in the snow. We saw tracks made by rabbits, squirrels, birds, dogs, and either a leopard or a lion. There was great debate over the issue. We camped out under the stars in the summer—sometimes in a back yard, but more often in our carport where the gentle evening breeze blew through gaps between the fiberglass panels. I don't claim to be much of an outdoor enthusiast these days, but I still yearn for a good night's rest primarily out in the open and only partially protected by a carport.

The only real mischief we engaged in was creating a stuffed dummy that looked vaguely like a teenage boy, then placing it carefully in the middle of a street at night with ketchup poured all around the head and a bicycle tossed askew nearby. The gang would then hide in the nearby bushes waiting for a car to come screeching to halt. The driver would always jump out screaming, "Are you okay?" A moment of silence would pass as the adult took a closer look and realized the prank. The laughter would start to drift out of the bushes as the driver got back into his car yelling something to the effect of "You stupid kids. You could have caused me to wreck my car!" Like that was really going to happen.

Joe and I feel sorry to this day for taking that little prank one step further. Our mother was unfailing in her nightly visit to the one bathroom in our house. This generally occurred around midnight or so. Joe and I had the bright idea to make use of our crash-scene dummy by leaving him sitting on the toilet, grinning at our mother when she flipped on the light. The ensuing screams were not pretty—nor were the threats she made toward us soon thereafter. However, I'm pretty sure she was extra cautious in her nightly ritual ever since.

Joe and I pulled away from the curb and looped one more time back to our old house. This time we pulled forward and sat in front of the next-door neighbor's house where Luke Jackson grew up. No description of our neighborhood, the Kelly boys' childhood, and the Garfield Gang could be complete without examining Luke in greater detail.

CHAPTER 9

LUKE JACKSON

I imagine most kids had someone in their childhood who stood out among the rest because of a reputation as a tough guy. There is always a kid who is a little bigger and stronger than the rest. Far too often, that kid uses his size advantage to bully everyone else. Sometimes the tough kid isn't even the biggest kid; he's just mean and focused on inflicting harm upon anyone who crosses him. He simply believes that he is mentally and physically more capable of gaining the upper advantage and he imposes his will on others. By imposing his will, I mean he beats the crap out of you.

But Luke Jackson had a different kind of toughness. He wasn't mean. He wasn't the biggest kid. He didn't look for trouble. But trouble seemed to find him and he never seemed to be too bothered by that. Luke had a quiet confidence that simply sent a message to guys looking for trouble: "Don't mess with me."

The Jackson family lived next door to the Kelly's with only about twenty feet of grass separating the two houses. Luke was a year older than Joe and four years older than me. Luke's father, Leonard Jackson, was a nice guy who scratched out a living doing a variety of jobs. I remember him as The Omar man, driving a panel truck full of Omar bread products and delivering door-to-door. The commercials for the company sang out, "Hey, Mom, Here Comes The Omar Man." I'm pretty sure that commercial wouldn't seem quite as catchy in America, post-September 11.

Mr. Jackson also sold Filter Queen vacuum cleaners door-to-door. Eventually, he caught on at the U.S. Post Office in town. Of course, that job didn't come along until he had spent some time in the V.A. Hospital recovering from a nervous breakdown. He was watching Jack Paar late one night and went into a laughing fit. That behavior was not unusual since we could hear Mr. Jackson laughing loud and hard all the time next door.

However, this time he probably starting laughing about 11:45 p.m. and was found still laughing at sunrise the next day. He couldn't stop. Well, he eventually stopped, but that's where the V.A. stint came in, along with an appropriately balanced cocktail of pharmaceuticals. Nice guy. Always treated us kids right. His wife, Evelyn, apparently also had a breakdown of some sort, but she kept to herself so much that we couldn't really tell anything was wrong.

Given the questionable sanity of his parents, Luke seemed perfectly normal—just larger than life. Of course, that four-year age difference for me meant that Luke seemed to be a fully-grown image of young manhood with rippling muscles, a firm jaw, and steely blue eyes that could look right through me. Picture a young Clint Eastwood—as in Rowdy Yates from

Rawhide or the mysterious gunslinger in *The Good, The Bad and The Ugly*.

I'm sure Luke could have become Dirty Harry later in life. He was a man/boy of few words, fearless, quick to act, and capable of uttering one-liners that captured the essence of the moment. This was Clint Eastwood before he started talking to empty chairs. Luke didn't have to be big and strong. I suspect that in high school he was probably a little over six feet tall and about a hundred and eighty pounds. There were plenty of bigger guys, but none tougher. And not one of them was as calm, cool, and unperturbed under pressure or duress.

Legend has it that in high school two huge senior linemen from the football team got liquored up after the season ended and went out looking for trouble. They ran into Luke in the Burger Chef parking lot and made the mistake of calling Luke out. The parking lot was a horseshoe layout where everyone backed their cars into the stalls and faced forward into the horseshoe. It was the primary local high school hangout on weekend nights. A crowd gathered and circled the threesome to watch the show.

Luke just stood there quietly as the drunken duo taunted him and got the crowd revved up by telling them how they "would kick Jackson's ass." Luke was an outsider when it came to the group of kids who played sports. He certainly was athletic enough to play and could have easily excelled at any sport. He just wasn't someone who joined others in anything. Luke went his own way. As a result, the crowd backed the local football heroes in the standoff.

Luke allowed the taunting to go on for a few minutes and then quietly said, "Are you done now?"

Ramsey, the 240-pound mouthpiece for the duo, moved within a foot of Luke and yelled, "Hell no, we're not done; now we're going to kick your ass!"

Before the last word was fully completed, Luke's right fist whipped out and splattered Ramsey's nose all over his face. The blood instantly spurted out and covered his face and shirt. You could literally hear the sound of his nose cracking as it flattened against his face. A collective gasp came from the crowd. His enraged partner lunged at Luke to grab him in a bear hug, but Luke neatly sidestepped him, grabbed the guy's hair and slammed his face down into Luke's rising knee. Again, the sound of a shattered nose and accompanying scream of agony filled the air.

Luke was not even breathing hard. Both guys were sprawled out on the pavement. Always thoughtful and courteous in victory, Luke turned to the silent crowd that had been supporting the beasty boys and quietly said, "You should probably help those boys get to the hospital. They're going to be bleeding for quite awhile." With that, he turned away, got in his car, and very slowly drove out of the parking lot. Classic Clint Eastwood.

* * *

I knew Luke when he was much younger. My first memories were when I was around six years old and he was ten. Even then he was larger than life. One rainy spring day I had walked out into the field behind our house. It had been raining for days and I went out in my yellow rain slicker and boots to play in some puddles. That's what you did back then. You just went out. Your parents weren't worried about you as long as you had your rain gear on.

Apparently, I ventured out too far into the field and got completely submerged in the mud to the tops of my boots. I was like a cartoon character that could lean forward and backward almost touching my head to the ground, but my feet never moved. The novelty of that exercise wore off rather quickly. I started screaming for help, but the windows and doors were closed on our house because of the rain.

Suddenly I saw this human form approaching through the rain. Luke Jackson was striding forward in a T-shirt and a pair of jeans and he was quickly getting soaked. He didn't have any sneakers on since they would have just been sucked into the mud hole. He had a big grin on his face. I can't ever remember him grinning like that before. You usually just got a quick smirk and a grunt from him when he was happy. Why he was so happy to come out in the rain and into the mud to rescue a stupid six-year-old kid, I couldn't say.

"How you doin', little Kelly?" Luke calmly inquired. "Not so good, Luke. I got stuck."

"So I see. Heard you too—from my bedroom. Lucky for you I had the window cracked a bit. You might have been out here awhile."

Luke then lifted me out of my boots and carried me in his arms. The boots would stay until the rain stopped and the mud dried out. He walked to my back door carrying me all the way with that big grin still on his face. He knocked on the door and then said to me, "You'll probably have some explaining to do, but it shouldn't go too hard on you."

My mom opened the door and just stood there with her mouth open looking at Luke holding her baby boy. "Mrs. Kelly," said Luke, "I brought you a package that I found in the mud. He's all yours." With that dry announcement, Luke put me down, grinned at my mom, and simply walked away to his house. That's how Luke Jackson operated. He was cool even at ten years old.

That wasn't the only time Luke would rescue me. As I grew older and joined the legions of Hoosier kids who lived for basketball, I spent most of my waking hours down the street at the outdoor courts behind Westside Elementary School. Snow didn't stop the local kids from playing there on weekends since my mother was willing to sit in her car with the lights shining on the court on many a Friday night while I shoveled off the playing area in response to a favorable weather report for the next day.

I developed a decent game at a young age and played in pick-up games with kids who might have been three or four years older than me. We didn't have that many kids in the neighborhood and the older guys had to tolerate a few of us younger ones just to make up two teams. I was smaller than them, but could hold my own when it came to shooting. If I got a hot hand on a given day, I could get their attention. It was unusual for Luke to join in, but he must have been bored that day.

Thankfully, I was on Luke's team and we were playing some guys that I seldom saw on those courts. One of the older guys didn't like the fact that he had to play with younger kids. He especially didn't like it when I started raining shots in over him after Luke would set a pick giving me clearance over the taller players. I eventually put up a shot and was immediately greeted with a full frontal body slam as this guy just barreled into me without trying to stop. I collapsed on the asphalt surface like a rag doll.

"I've had enough of your shit, kid," the guy screamed.

The images that followed played in slow motion. I already knew the script and could see the ending of the scene. Luke was silently moving toward the offender. I knew the guy wouldn't like how the story would end. Luke grabbed his shoulder, spun the guy around, and delivered one shot to his gut that doubled him over and dropped him to the ground. Then a beautiful thing happened. The crazed idiot that slammed me to the ground started crying. He could barely catch his breath. He was absolutely blubbering. His friends stared at him in disbelief. The game was over.

Luke and I walked the one block home to our houses in silence. If there had been a sound track to this movie it would have been playing the whistling theme song from *The Andy Griffith Show*. My memories are now clouded with sounds and images that likely are out of sequence and have distorted the reality of the event, but I think Luke might have had his arm around my shoulder and offered me a Lifesaver.

* * *

The legend of Luke Jackson ran deep on Garfield Drive. From rescuing his friends from foul play to exceling at our local events, Luke was legendary in all things. Our summer baseball pick-up games were played across the street at the Duncan Field. Others would keep the ball in play, hitting line drives and scratching out singles. Luke would hit towering home runs over Monroe Street onto the rooftops of small shack-like houses. Tackle football games had to become two-hand touch games because Luke was simply hurting too may guys with bone-crunching tackles. He didn't mean to hurt anyone; he just ran at you full speed and didn't stop until you became part of the dirt underneath him. Even two-hand touch games were a foregone conclusion since Luke could outrun everyone or he could let a little guy like me run with the ball while he blocked everyone else out of the way leading to a touchdown.

However, it is safe to say that Luke's legend blossomed in his senior year in high school when he decided to paint the year of his graduating class on the Glenville Water Tower. I'm not sure when painting your class year on a water tower became a simple rite of passage. Eventually it became viewed as nothing more than graffiti. But in 1965 the Glenville Water Tower had never been touched by anyone other than the city employees of Glenville.

One early spring morning around 1:00 a.m., there was a tap on the bedroom window where Joe and I shared a room. Luke was standing in the flowerbed outside the window motioning to Joe.

"Are you ready?" asked Luke. I later learned that this was not a surprise visit for Joe. Luke had already planned this nighttime excursion into enemy territory and had enlisted Joe's support as his lookout sentry. Joe didn't tell me about the plan so I could maintain plausible deniability with our parents in case anything went wrong.

Joe pulled on his black T-shirt and jeans, then removed the screen from the window. He climbed out and grabbed the bucket of black paint that Luke handed him and then proceeded to follow Luke on the path that led out to the water tower. When they got to the perimeter fencing, Luke was prepared with a heavy piece of cardboard that could be thrown over the one strand of barbed wire on top of the fence. It was only about eight feet to clear the top and Luke cleared it with one big leap, grabbing a toehold on the fence and swinging up and over while bracing his hands on the thick cardboard on top. Joe then tossed the gallon can of paint over the fence and Luke caught it. He had a small flathead screwdriver with him to pop it open when he reached the perimeter railing above. The paintbrush was in the back pocket of his jeans.

At that point, Joe's job was simply to be the lookout in case a police car drove by on its nightly rounds. He was to alert Luke with a practiced call that sounded somewhat like a cow giving birth. It was a unique warning system created by the two boys specifically for this one job. Originally, Joe was supposed to climb the tower with Luke and keep watch from up there for a better vantage point. Joe would have nothing to do with that plan. He didn't want to climb the perimeter fence, let alone climb the fifty or so steps up the iron ladder.

Fortunately, the warning was not needed as Luke successfully climbed the ladder, opened the paint can, and proceeded to boldly go where no Glenville High School senior had gone before. "The Class of 1965" was emblazoned on the side of the tower facing town and was clearly visible the following morning when the sun came up. Luke had added to his legend and Joe was a proud and silent partner who hoped to never be discovered until long after leaving Glenville High School.

Actually, the hunt for the water tower painter became rather intense. Damn near everyone in town could see the thing and the city wasn't exactly swift in painting over it. Must have had to form a committee and study it for a while. It wasn't too hard to figure out that the culprit must have been from the senior class and likely a boy. So, all the boys were brought into the Vice Principal's office one at a time and given the opportunity to confess. Mr. Hathaway, the Vice Principal, first got on the P.A. system and announced that it would go easier on the perpetrator if he would confess. If no one stepped forward, then the entire class would be penalized and the real culprit would face criminal charges if they ever found him.

I suppose Luke didn't exactly step forward, but he also didn't let anyone else take the blame. He first let all the guys sweat it out one by one with their little visit to Hathaway. Some of these guys had never even been to the Vice Principal's office so a few of them were ready to cry. Luke enjoyed that immensely. It turned out that Luke was one of the last to be interviewed. When Hathaway asked him if he was the one that painted the water tower, he just shrugged his shoulders and said, "Sure, I confess."

Hathaway just stared at him, red in the face, and asked again, "You are the one who climbed up on that water tower and defaced it?"

Luke calmly responded, "I don't know anything about defacing it, but I did climb up there and proudly paint the year of our graduating class. I think it looks pretty great, don't you?"

Hathaway ignored the smartass question and asked, "Then why did you wait until now to confess? You could have saved me and all of these other kids from wasting our time with these interviews." Hathaway was now steaming and clearly wanted a piece of Luke.

Luke just shrugged his shoulders. "You said if the painter confessed, then it would go easy on him. I confessed. I didn't realize that I was supposed to step out of turn and cut to the front of the line." A very slight grin briefly appeared at the corner of Luke's mouth before a well-placed hand quickly concealed it from view.

When the dust settled after Hathaway swore and threatened to keep Luke from graduating, calmer heads prevailed. They chose to mete out a punishment that was far short of jail time or withholding a diploma. Luke spent the rest of the spring every day after school painting the bleachers at the football field. So, each afternoon he'd strip off his shirt and stretch his muscles for the girls who came by to give him moral support. After all, he had acted on behalf of the entire graduating class and gained immeasurable notoriety and respect in the process. He was the bad boy hometown hero unlike any of the jocks who wore the black and gold uniforms of Glenville High.

* * *

The final chapter in the Luke Jackson story is not a happy one. Sometime after high school graduation, there was a car accident out on one of the seldom-traveled county roads outside of town. Bordered by rows of cornfields and telephone poles, these roads were uniquely straight and notorious for providing the perfect setting for drag racing. On one particular summer evening, Luke ended up crashing his brand new turbocharged, convertible Corvair Spyder by rolling it several times through a cornfield. Two other guys weren't so fortunate. They crashed their '55 Chevy head on into a telephone pole. They died on impact. Luke walked away.

He never admitted to drag racing. No charges were filed. It was just a horrendous and avoidable loss of life. It hit Luke really hard and he left town soon thereafter. Some said he went to work over at the General Motors plant across the state. Others said he joined the military. As is often the case in small towns, a few ghost stories took root out in the cornfields where some say Luke can be seen walking down the road in the distance with two other figures. Even as he disappeared from Glenville, his legend survived.

CHAPTER 10

TOURING THE TOWN

We continued our nostalgia trip through the formerly vibrant downtown area. Unfortunately, it was no longer vibrant. Most of the retail stores had long since moved out by the interstate, leaving about three city blocks featuring an odd collection of little stores selling a variety of worthless crap that couldn't possibly generate enough in sales to make a living for the owner. A chocolate shop, small bookstore, discount tobacco shop, and a thrift store with second-hand clothes lined one side of the street. A local Pancake House occupied a corner spot and seemed to have a few customers hanging around. I suppose it could be argued that having a Pancake House might be perceived as one step above a Waffle House in terms of culinary sophistication.

Gone was the Glenville Theater, where sitting in the back row with your date usually meant you were going to get some action that night. In my case not much action—but action nonetheless, as long as holding hands qualifies. I saw *Goldfinger* there in 1964, with my parents (not in the back row). The introduction to Bond girl, Pussy Galore, was more than just a little awkward for all three of us.

The theater also had the distinction of being way ahead of the curve regarding special seating for those with disabilities. Sure, the place had a few spots for wheelchairs, but it also had the only fat chair I ever saw in a theater. A kindly old gentleman, Mr. Taylor, owned the place and knew just about everyone in town. He felt particularly sorry for a young man ironically named Jimmy Small. Jimmy, the son of a local farmer, was about twenty years old and not the sharpest tool in the shed due to a complication at birth. However, he was the nicest guy you'd ever want to meet. He also weighed about four hundred pounds. I am not exaggerating.

Jimmy loved the movies and never missed a new one when it came out. There was just one problem; Jimmy could not fit into a standard theater seat. Not even close. He would sit down on the floor in the back of the theater. So, as a special favor to Jimmy, the owner removed the bar that separated two seats in the front row and added some extra padding to cover the gap. Instant fat chair! A small plaque was placed on the backseat proclaiming "Reserved for Jimmy Small."

You might think that Jimmy could have been embarrassed by this gesture. Today a similar person would sue for discrimination. But in 1961, Jimmy Small had tears of joy in his eyes as Mr. Taylor ceremonially escorted him (with a large bucket of buttered popcorn and a Bladder Buster soda) to his personal seat. The Glenville Theater represented just about Jimmy's entire social life and now he had been given special status at his favorite place.

The only problem occurred one night when Jimmy didn't show up for a new show in town, *The Man Who Shot Liberty Valance* starring Jimmy Stewart. Once the lights went down in the theater, a scrawny little ten-year-old named Sammy Corwin decided that Jimmy was a no-show that night since he was always in his seat early. Sammy scooted on over to the fat chair and settled in for a special cinematic experience. It became real special about five minutes later when a dark shadow filled the screen in front of Sammy and four hundred pounds came crushing down on his world. No one ever sat in Jimmy Small's chair again.

Gone was Ricketts Hardware, the Five & Dime Store, the Glenville Banking Company, and a couple of family-owned furniture and clothing stores. Gone from the prime street corner spot was Johnson's Drugstore, a classic multi-purpose drug store enterprise built around a long soda fountain bar with swivel stools.

Chubby's Barbershop was just down the street. That is where most men and boys in town had their hair cut by Chubby and where all matters of social consequence were discussed. That included politics, the draft, religion, race relations (a short discussion since there were no blacks in town and a pretty uneducated and universal opinion about the subject), women, recent marriages, recent divorces, and basketball—Indiana high school basketball.

Without question, the main topic of discussion on Saturday morning was the game on Friday night and the one coming up Saturday night. Men would gather in the morning at Chubby's and just rotate through to get a hair cut while hanging around for hours. Any newcomer was welcomed in and put at the front of the line since the regulars weren't going anywhere. However, if you sat in the barber's chair, you better be ready to be grilled by the men about your thoughts on the latest Glenville team.

If you were a player on the team, as I was, it was an intense few minutes of answering questions about recent coaching decisions, playing time for certain players, and offensive and defensive strategies. All of the guys on the team felt like celebrities at Chubby's and we always received lots of support. The town loved its high school basketball team. But Chubby's is no longer there.

Later in the day back in the '60s, you could find some of the same men down the street at Ralph's Lunch. Yes, you could find the men, but you wouldn't spot any females. No women. Men only. It was a place where you could get a classic slider before anyone knew they were sliders or a wet tenderloin sandwich (the "wet" refers to gravy for the uninitiated). Later, the local Jim Dandy restaurant picked up on the wet tenderloin idea and created a cult following among the locals.

Perhaps of more importance, you could also get a drink at Ralph's. It was no soda fountain like Johnson's Drugstore. This was a dark, mysterious place where real men got real drinks and real greasy food. As a kid I would walk by and sneak a peak when the door opened. It was forbidding and exciting at the same time. If you lingered too long at the door, one of the regulars would yell at you to "get the hell out of here, kid!"

Across the street was the impressive County Courthouse, built in the late 1890s and featuring Indiana limestone in its intricate design. Joe and I took a couple of minutes to quickly walk through the marble main floor area and, naturally, thought it was much smaller than we had remembered. Yet, it was impressive in its solemn dignity and seemed to convey a sense of importance and history for the Glenville community. People were lined up at a window, presumably paying some sort of governmental levy, while others with sad faces whispered back and forth while sitting on benches. Joe and I figured they were soon headed upstairs to one of the courtrooms where the likelihood of good news was not real strong. We quickly moved on.

Joe and I left downtown and cruised past the old high school that had now been converted into some sort of retirement center. We went all the way to the other edge of town from our house to Glenville Park, where we spent many a summer's day at the swimming pool. We were shocked to see from our odometer that the entire trek was only about one and a half miles. Walking to the high school was only a half-mile and it was another mile to the park. Our infallible memories suggested that we had an exhausting walk to school and we covered at least five miles on those summer bike rides to the swimming pool. I guess not.

I can still remember trying to keep up with the older kids on those bike rides. Joe, Luke, and most of the kids from our neighborhood had full-size Schwinn bikes and I was still saddled one summer with something that was a step below their bikes and a step above a little bike with training wheels. What were my parents thinking? It was embarrassing. I'd pump my legs as fast as I could, but there was no way to keep up. Just as they were about to vanish from sight, Joe would usually loop back and ride with me the rest of the way to the park. I wasn't worried about riding alone, but I didn't mind Joe coming back either. Sometimes Luke Jackson would tell me to leave my little bike at home and he'd have me jump on his handlebars for the ride. It scared the crap out of me, but it was a great thrill. Of course, with Luke in charge I knew I would be okay.

As Joe and I slowly drove around Glenville Park, we were struck by how much it hadn't changed. It still was a large open area with picnic tables, tennis courts, and a little stream meandering through the sycamore and maple trees. The main difference was the old swimming pool had long since been torn down and replaced with a new community pool up on a hill overlooking the park. Whenever that change took place, it couldn't have been too soon. We all look back with nostalgia about the places where we used to play as children, but there was no mistaking that the Glenville Park Pool was already beyond its prime when we were kids.

The pool was an overcrowded aging structure—but it was a terrific place to spend a summer day. As a young kid it was a place to swim and play until you were exhausted. You could bounce off the springboard or, if you dare, climb the steps to the high platform and jump into the air screaming at full throttle, without a care about how you looked or sounded. Of course, as you got older, you were only there to be cool while checking out the talent and being looked over by other teenagers. For some, diving off the high platform became an artform demanding attention and admiration. It was clearly a conversation-starter and, after all, that's why you were there if you were eligible for dating.

The plaque left behind on the original site reminded us of the history. The pool was opened on July 4, 1930, and was touted as being a unique above-ground concrete structure. It cost a whopping $26,800 to build. Admission was twenty-five cents per swimmer for the day and ten cents per spectator. The whole spectator-at-the-pool concept seemed a little creepy, but if you were going to get your kicks that way you'd have to pay for it. The above-ground aspect of the place made it particularly weird since you would enter the locker rooms at ground level, change into your swimming suits, throw your clothes into old rusted metal lockers, and then cross through a wading pool area before climbing the steps up to the pool deck.

Presumably, this small water area was designed to wash off your feet, thus eliminating all the foul bacteria that you had accumulated from dog and bird droppings accrued from wandering around barefoot in the summer. At any rate, after about mid-morning this little wading pool had generally turned into a pleasant shade of brown. Somehow, I don't think it continued to serve a cleansing purpose prior to entry into the clean and pristine waters above. Perhaps that's why the swimming pool never looked particularly pristine. Or, perhaps, it had something to do with the fact that young clueless mothers were dipping their babies into the pool. Mommy was so pleased at the look of satisfaction on junior's face when his bottom was submerged in water. She just thought he liked to swim.

Joe and I cruised out of the park and immediately entered a complex of three baseball fields surrounding a relatively small structure bearing signage that announced the arrival to the Glenville Boy's and Girl's Club. Formerly called only the Boy's Club, for obvious reasons, this was my second home growing up. Joe was a regular as well, but I was a true sports junkie and he only had a passing interest as he moved onto other pursuits. On most summer days when I was old enough to play organized sports, my mother heard me shout out, "I'm headin' to The Club. Back by supper!" This was my "country club." The rest of those days were spent playing in little league games, followed by sodas and snacks from the machine, on to pick-up basketball games in the gym, and maybe ending with a game of dodge-ball that would both thrill and terrify me as a I found myself the target of older guys trying to knock me unconscious.

The expanded Boy's and Girl's Club still seemed modest in size and the ball fields were not in the best shape. Joe and I quickly speculated that this might be an area where an infusion of Uncle Shorty's money could go a long way. We know what a positive impact the place had on us and it still seemed to be serving the community. We wondered who ran it now and how it was governed. Back in our day, Jim Montgomery was the face and voice of The Club. He ruled with absolute authority and you did what he told you to do. He was there to help the kids who needed a little extra help and to discipline the ones who needed that as well. If there ever was an example of how one person could positively impact the lives of so many kids, "Big Jim" was that shining example. We'll be taking a hard look at today's version of The Club.

* * *

One last loop out to the edge of town and we found ourselves driving by the local bowling alley, the Glenville Lanes. Joe pulled into the parking lot and stopped the car so he could reminisce about his crowning achievement at the bowling alley. I didn't even know Joe ever bowled there as a kid. It just wouldn't have been something that Joe would have pursued.

"Oh, yes. I was quite the bowler. Only bowled one time in my life, as I can recall."

"And how did that go?" Clearly, there was a story here that Joe was anxious to tell.

"Well, a big group from our freshmen class showed up here one Sunday afternoon. Some guys who wanted to spend time drooling over Sally Duncan and her friends dragged me along. Sally was the real deal. She had begun to seriously blossom as a freshman."

"And you thought you could impress her with your non-existent bowling skills?"

"It was worth a try. So, we split up into teams and Sally asked what I normally scored in bowling. I didn't have a clue, so I asked her what score was needed for a perfect game. She told me that would be a three hundred. I quickly figured that I should be about half that good with no experience, so I told her and the others nearby that I generally scored in the one-fifty range."

"You didn't lack for optimism."

"Oh, that's never been a problem for me. I proceeded to take my position at the top of the lane when it was my turn. I had previously watched a few others and thought I had the hang of it. Well, remember I weighed about ninety-eight pounds at that time and the ball seemed like it weighed half as much as me. I swung back with a mighty effort and the ball flew out of my hand backwards and cleared a path of onlookers until it blasted into a rack of balls behind us."

"Very impressive. And were you appropriately humiliated?"

"Oh, God, no. I hammed it up and acted like I was just joking. They bought it. After all, they thought I was a one-fifty bowler. They figured I must have been goofing around. I grabbed the ball, ran back up the lane, and heaved it with two hands. Knocked down eight pins and came back grinning at the crowd with my arms raised. They loved it!

"How did it go after that?"

"I scored a thirty-five followed by another thirty-five. Though I was trying my hardest on every roll, the group thought

I was just messing around so they got a big laugh out of it. That was one of the first times that I realized how easy it was to entertain people."

We pulled out of the parking lot and headed back to the Residence Inn. I had the feeling if we made any more stops along the way, Joe would have a new story to tell me at each location. He had a lot of childhood memories locked away. I'd heard enough. It was time for another fine meal at my neighborhood grill.

CHAPTER 11

THE GLENVILLE ASSISTANT SUPERINTENDENT OF SCHOOLS

We continued our ongoing discussion with Mandy at dinner that night at Applebee's and then enjoyed breakfast the next morning at Cracker Barrel. Joe and I were properly fueled to have a 10:00 a.m. meeting with the assistant superintendent of schools. That wasn't too difficult to set up since I had gone to school with Sam Harkins and he cleared his calendar when he heard I was in town.

"Damn, Kelly, it is good to see you!" Sam was always enthusiastic and was a good friend in high school. "Good to see you, too, Sam!" He was from the east side of town, but came from common roots like us. He had fallen prey to the middle-age rounding effect as well and his thinning gray hair was hanging on for dear life. He still had an open and honest-looking face and just seemed to send a message that he was a good guy. Maybe that was just my inherent bias. His dad was a life-long teacher at the middle school and Sam followed in his footsteps, moving up to high school teaching. It wasn't hard to imagine him teaching kids, but it was more difficult seeing him as the second-highest-ranking administrator in the school system.

"Harkins, how in the world could you possibly be the assistant superintendent of schools? You barely made it through high school!" I decided to lay it on thick. "Did you even graduate from that phony little church college you went to in Kentucky? I heard you were suspended."

"Well, I was suspended for one semester," Sam admitted sheepishly. "Might have had something to do with drinking and smoking on campus—with the college president's daughter. He was just a little uptight about that sort of thing. She wasn't. But I liked the school in spite of its rules and, yes, you are fully aware that I did graduate." He looked over at Joe and rolled his eyes in mock exasperation.

"How did you land this job?"

"Well, that's an interesting story. I really wasn't exactly the greatest teacher in the world. I know you'll find that hard to believe. But I wasn't the worst either. I taught some history and civics and the occasional English course when we would lose a teacher unexpectedly. Once I got my lesson plans down pat, it was pretty easy to put things on cruise control and just sprinkle in a few guest speakers and educational films."

I interrupted. "I can't tell you how inspiring this is, Harkins. Makes me proud to know you're training the young minds of America."

"You're still a smartass, aren't you? Guess that's why I liked you. Anyway, I had a few little incidents over the years that almost got me fired. In the last week of one school year, we were basically done with any teaching for the senior class. We were just trying to keep the classroom from chaos as the kids geared up for graduation and summer break. This one little gal, Melissa Conway, had the bright idea to bring a *National Geographic* video to watch about glaciers or some mountain stuff up in Montana. I thought why the hell not? It would keep them occupied for an hour. This girl wasn't some sort of screw-up either; she was homecoming queen and heading off to Indiana University with some scholarship money. I figured she would know if it was a decent video."

Joe asked, "Why do I get the feeling this doesn't end well?"

"Probably because it doesn't. She brought it in the next day and we had the system set up. I went to the back of the room and started chatting with my teacher's aid—a bright young guy with a good future in education. We were looking at a *Sports Illustrated*, as I recall. Melissa put the video in and I wasn't paying any attention to it. The room was real quiet until I heard these moans and groans. I looked up and saw a naked woman and an equally naked man on the screen in a serious state of arousal demonstrating to our young children the professional quality of their chosen craft. I must admit that it was impressive. And the students were certainly enjoying it. I was a little hesitant to shut it off."

"Did the girl bring in porn on purpose?"

"Well, at first we thought she must have, but she was in tears over the whole deal. She was afraid we wouldn't let her graduate.

Come to find out later that Daddy had a pretty good collection of porn. Young Melissa thought she was grabbing the video about Montana glaciers, but little did she know that Daddy had accidentally left one of his "special" videos in the same area. It featured several well-endowed gentlemen with the title of *The Royal Mounties of Montana*. Never mind that Royal Mounties are from Canada. The alliteration worked for the porn industry." Sam paused, presumably to make sure I caught his ingenuous use of the word, alliteration. "It was an innocent mistake made by Melissa. On the other hand, I caught a ton of grief over the incident. The fact that it was the end of the year saved me."

Joe was trying real hard to follow this story. "So because you showed porn in the classroom, someone thought you were superintendent material?"

"Not exactly. The next year I had another incident. This kid, Travis Martin, was an absolute asshole. He disrupted class at every chance; he bullied smaller kids and had an unbelievable smart mouth on him. He had brought a few of our younger female teachers to tears with the crap that he would dish out. His dad was a pretty important guy in town—big athletic booster with lots of money from his contracting business. Other teachers were understandably hesitant to take any real action against the kid."

"Well, one day I had enough of his lip. He wouldn't shut up and I was actually trying to teach for a change. For some reason our classroom was moved that year and I was teaching in the science lab on the second floor. We had those big lab tables pushed against the wall next to the windows. I walked over to Travis's desk, pointed my finger at him and told him this was his last chance to shut up. He jumped out of his chair and squared off at me. That was a mistake on his part. He was standing with his back to one of those big, flat lab tables with a stainless steel top. I had intended to simply grab him by the front of his shirt and slam his ass down on the table to get his attention. He wasn't very big—just stupid with a big mouth."

"He got right in my face and yelled, 'Fuck you, Mr. Harkins!' I exploded and proceeded to toss him up on the table. I just tossed him a little harder than I had intended." Sam dropped his eyes and looked embarrassed by what he was telling us. "The kid slid across the tabletop and flipped over backwards right out the open window, screaming his ass off. The good news was it was only the second floor and there were bushes below to break his fall."

"Well, now I see why you were promoted to assistant superintendent," Joe nodded knowingly with a straight face.

"Exactly. Well, not exactly, but close. The good news was the kid's father heard that his boy dropped an F Bomb on a teacher and he told the principal that he would have done the same thing as me. That helped. However, the School Board started rumbling about my "temperament" and it took some fancy footwork by my principal to cover my tracks. He was a good friend with the superintendent who was a good friend with my father. They taught together at the middle school before my dad retired.

Joe suddenly took an interest in Harkins' reference to his father. "That would be the same Mr. Harkins that served as vice principal in charge of administering a large wooden paddle to students who were wrongfully accused of misconduct?"

Sam laughed. "He got you, too, huh?"

"Let's just say your father left an impression on me as I grabbed my ankles on one very memorable visit to his office. I see where you got your training."

"Well, I have to admit that his techniques might have been a little over the top, but you didn't screw up more than once, did you? Anyway, back to my story, there was an opening in the superintendent's office for an assistant who could handle budget issues and work with the union leaders on labor issues. They figured I could grow into the job and keep my pension intact. Who would have thought that I actually was pretty darn good at handling budget issues and I took great pleasure in battling with the union leaders. Never liked those guys even though I was in the teacher's union. Five years later I was given the title of assistant superintendent and that is precisely how I intend to retire in a couple of years."

"Joe," I said, "clearly, we have found the right guy to give us the inside scoop about the educational needs of Glenville."

That prompted Sam to ask, "Well, now that you mention it, Kelly, why are we having this meeting?" I hadn't really given Sam much information when I called for the meeting.

I proceeded to fill Assistant Superintendent Harkins in

about Uncle Shorty's money (without revealing the amount) and the thirty-day time limit we had to distribute it. He had lots of questions and we had very few answers, but it was easy to see that he was excited about the prospects of solving some budget problems. I finally pinned him down and asked him to name three top priorities for the school system where we might be able to help.

"I can't really do that," he said, "without knowing how much money we're talking about. If it were a few thousand dollars, I'd give you one list. A couple of hundred thousand would allow for an entirely different approach. And, are we talkin' about one-time funds or an annual annuity spun off from a foundation?"

I just stared at him. "God, you really have become a bureaucrat, haven't you? It's a one-time lump sum of money that could be spent all at once or it could be invested to grow so you could spin off part of the funds each year. And, for the sake of argument, let's just say it could be a sizeable chunk of money. So, think big." Sam didn't hesitate:

"Number 1: Building improvements. All of our schools need repairs that we just can't afford. Hell, we should tear some of them down and start over.

"Number 2: Program incentives. We have bright, young (and some veteran) teachers who have great ideas for new learning experiences. They might need computers, a variety of education software packages, scientific supplies, travel money for field trips, and stipends for classroom helpers to give a little individual attention ... all kinds of stuff. I get requests all the time. Great ideas. I just don't have any money to help.

"Number 3: Teacher incentives. I need a way to keep the best and brightest of our teachers. We are constantly losing our best to bigger school systems that pay more and we're stuck with the ones who are just putting in their time waiting for their pension. There are certainly other good teachers who just want to stay in Glenville, but it seems that group gets smaller every year."

Joe innocently asked, "Are they the ones showing porn in class and throwing kids out the windows?"

"Pretty much," Harkins deadpanned.

"Sam," I asked, "who would ultimately be in charge of this money if we sent some your way? Superintendent's Office, School Board, principals, Teacher's Union?"

"That's the problem. Once any money becomes part of the school system budget, the School Board who establishes priorities that trickle down through the system ultimately controls it. And when it comes to teacher's salaries, that issue becomes an item that has to be bargained for as part of the union contract. We can't just decide which teachers we want to reward without using a system that the union first agrees to. And, you know what that means. All teachers will be treated alike since the union doesn't go for evaluations and merit-based incentives."

"And what are the School Board members like?"

"It's a real mixed bag." Sam paused for a minute and looked thoughtful. "Some of them are real bright and dedicated to the kids and the school system. You remember Kathy Nelson from our class? She's on it and very good. Another woman moved into town a couple of years ago from one of the best school systems in Indianapolis. She's been great. But some of the members are just plain stupid, some are so smart they have no clue how the real world works, some have one-item agendas like sex education or teaching Creationism alongside Darwinian theory, and one guy only cares about creating the best sports teams in the state. A few are actually good folks who are just doing their best, but are usually overwhelmed and discouraged that the state keeps cutting the budget and there is no good news for the schools."

"That's so very encouraging," I acknowledged. "Once again, it gives me great hope for the children of Glenville."

"You asked. I answered."

"So, if we really wanted to help the Glenville school system in a manner in which I think Uncle Shorty would approve, then we probably wouldn't actually give the money to the school system. We'd find some way to work around the system to get the money where it could do some good."

Sam stared at me and simply said, "Exactly."

CHAPTER 12

TEACHERS, UNION REPS AND THE BOOSTER CLUB

As much as I like and respect Sam (despite his predilection for throwing kids out windows), I don't see him as the definitive word on the educational needs of the Glenville school system. Joe agreed.

It took us a couple of days, but we pulled together another meeting of people affiliated with the city schools. We just took a shotgun approach and sent out emails to a variety of folks provided on a list from our editor friend, John Bourke. We hoped that some would show up later that afternoon after school was over. Our note indicated that we represented someone wanting to donate a sizeable amount of money to the school system and we were looking for input. Apparently, the prospect of money got some attention since nearly every person contacted showed up in the small conference room at the public library at 4:00 p.m. Bourke had reserved it for us earlier.

What an interesting collection of folks. There were six teachers representing elementary, middle school, and high school levels. Two union representatives showed up even though we had only invited one. The secretary at the middle school was there specifically due to John Bourke's influence. He told us that Ms. Emily Rodgers would give us the most unbiased appraisal of the many needs in the system. She was his cousin and had worked in the schools for thirty years. The principal at our alma mater, Westside Elementary, was there along with the high school principal and the athletic director (also the assistant principal) for the high school.

Finally, two beefy guys introduced themselves as the Glenville Tigers Athletic Booster Club president and vice president. Once again, we had only invited one person from the Booster Club, but they must have figured that four hundred pounds of influence was better than two hundred pounds. When Joe saw them he raised an eyebrow at me that could only mean he had some history with one of them. One guy was too young for Joe to know, but the other guy was roughly our age and had a look that was only vaguely familiar to me.

I started with my usual general description about the fact that we were executors of an estate and that we were looking at all aspects of the Glenville community for possible funding. They wanted to know how much money was involved and I once again dodged the question but encouraged them to think big and we would work backwards from there.

The lead union rep jumped right in. His name was Martin. "Clearly, our teachers are the most important aspect of our school system. We must hire the best and do everything we can to retain them."

Joe dryly questioned, "Let me see if I have this right, Mr. Martin. If the teachers are the most important aspect of your schools, then where does that place the students? Second, third, fourth?"

Martin stammered, "Well, you know what I mean. Of course, students come first, but we must have the best teachers to help them achieve their goals."

"And what goals would those be, Mr. Martin?"

Martin confidently jumped in. "The goals established by the School Board, such as a mastery of certain skills and acceptable scores on standardized tests that would ultimately lead to acceptance to college. We need excellent teachers to get them there."

"I wouldn't argue that we don't need excellent teachers, Mr. Martin. Exactly how many Indiana students tend to graduate and go to college?" I could feel Joe boring in on this guy. I've seen it before.

"Well, I don't know exactly," said Martin.

"Would you be surprised to learn that only roughly sixty-five percent of high school graduates in this state go on to college? I guess that means we are failing the other thirty-five percent to reach their goals—excuse me, the School Board's goals."

"I wouldn't exactly call it failing!"

"Oh, really? So, sixty-five percent is a passing grade in your estimation? Very interesting. So, maybe the other thirty-five percent of our students have different needs or skill sets . . . or goals." Joe was now just yanking this guy's chain for the fun of it. No matter what Martin said at this point, Joe was going to shoot him down.

"Mr. Martin, if we were to somehow funnel a substantial amount of money toward teacher's salaries, they of course would pay a certain amount of their higher salaries to the union for the privilege of being represented by you. Of those dues, what percentage is spent by union leaders for political advertisements and lobbying on statewide issues without any input from the people who pay you the money?"

Martin's jaw dropped open and his face turned a few new shades of red.

It was time for me to insert myself and move this conversation along. "So, Mr. Howard (Westside Elementary principal), what could your school do with an infusion of money to help in any way you so choose?"

Howard was a younger man (somewhere around forty), tall, thin, wire-rim glasses, and had a very intense and intelligent look about him. My first take was he seemed like a pretty good guy, albeit maybe not the most approachable. There was a certain type of shyness about him that I suspect got in his way a bit. "Well, I've only been principal here for two years, but I can see that we have many needs."

"For instance?" I prompted.

"For instance, more interdisciplinary approaches to teaching that combine subjects like reading and science or math and art. We need to create incentives for students and teachers to have more fun in the learning process and to use technologies that are available to us but unaffordable right now. We need to reward creativity as well as success on standardized tests. We need to assume that kids learn in different ways and come at them with different approaches. That requires constant updating and training of teachers. We need to capitalize on resources that already exist in the community and encourage help from the community in teaching our kids. We need to get more parent involvement and that usually means more outreach counselors to work with at-risk kids. That's just the tip of the iceberg and they all require money to one extent or another."

"Wow," I offered with an obvious command of intelligent conversation. "You really get on a roll once you get started!"

Howard's head ducked down and his face reddened a bit. "I'm very passionate about kids and teaching. I think we're turning too many off to learning at a very young age."

Joe quipped, "Too bad you weren't here when Darren and I went to Westside. We could have used a little creativity. The old lady teachers who slapped rulers to my knuckles just didn't seem to bring out the best in me. I like you, Mr. Howard, and I can see you will do good things for Westside."

* * *

Joe and I were, indeed, products of Westside Elementary School in the late 1950s and early '60s. It might have changed a little since then. We had many of the same teachers. Mrs. Renfrew was in second grade, Gephardt in third, Wilson in fourth. I can still remember the smell of cigarettes and coffee on Mrs. Gephardt. She was one tough old broad. When we were adults, Joe once showed me his third-grade report card. It was clear why he kept it. His grades were mostly "Unsatisfactory" in all the major subjects. A few "Satisfactory" ratings kept him moving forward to the next class. However, in music and art, he achieved "Excellent" ratings across the board. "What does that tell you?" he asked me.

"Uh, you were a tortured creative soul trapped in a rigid system that didn't recognize or celebrate your brilliance?"

"Exactly!"

Joe continued to be an underachiever in high school even though I have no doubt he was brighter than most of the kids on all matters that count in life. At some point he confided in me that he flunked biology in high school, but changed the grade to a "B" on the report card that he had to bring home to our parents. He then made up the class in summer school without our parents even knowing what he was doing. With the expert tutoring he received from Sally Markham (yes, the same red-headed Sally who was rejected by the Garfield Gang), he was able to pass the class and wipe the "F" from his record. Classic Joe.

On the other hand, I was an outstanding suck-up in school that could crank out "Excellent" ratings by simply zeroing in on what I knew the teachers wanted to see and hear. I wasn't any smarter than Joe; I just enjoyed playing the game and he didn't. However, when it came to actually showing any genuine creativity or talent in music and art, there were more than a few "Unsatisfactory" ratings on my report card.

Joe always liked to say that my ability to tell people in authority what they wanted to hear was first clearly evidenced when I was eleven. I had entered a written contest to determine who would get interviewed to become next season's Bat Boy for the Indianapolis Triple-A League Indians. These guys were only one step away from the major leagues. Though I had absolutely no chance to serve in that capacity due to the distance from our house and the lack of transportation to the stadium, I was nonetheless determined to earn an invitation. Three finalists out of hundreds of entries would be chosen for an interview.

Joe joined me at the kitchen table as I put the finishing touches on my essay. He read the final draft and starting laughing. "Darren, you are so full of it! Do you really think they'll believe this stuff?" Joe still laughs about that memory of me composing my tribute to the Indianapolis Indians at our little kitchen table.

I admit that I laid it on pretty thick. However, if they wanted to hear about undying loyalty to the Indians, then that's exactly what I was going to give them. The fact that I'd only been to two Indians games didn't deter me from embellishing my attendance record by roughly a thousand percent. "Joe, I'm just giving them what they want to hear." At age eleven, my keen sense for ethical consideration was not yet fully developed.

The short version of the story is that I was, indeed, picked as one of three finalists. My mother, after considerable pleading from me, accompanied me for the interview to the organization offices of the Indians located right at the ballpark. Three suits asked me a few general questions before zeroing in on the obvious. "How do you intend to get to the ballpark for every home game?"

Well, I guess my answer of "we haven't quite figured that out" didn't go over so well. They thanked us for our time and told me what a great essay I had written. I got a bunch of Indians' memorabilia to take home. That was the end of that story. But I learned a great lesson. When you bullshit your way into an interview, be sure you have enough left in your bag of deceit to answer the follow-up questions.

My very favorite teacher was Mr. Hinton, fifth grade. He was a young (late twenties), athletic guy who seemed to take me under his wing for some reason. He kept telling my mother how I reminded him of himself as a boy. One day he asked if I wanted to go to his house for dinner and then head off to a Harlem Globetrotters game over in Indianapolis. This was huge. My folks didn't hesitate to let me go since they saw only a bright young teacher who obviously had the good sense to think highly of their son.

He picked me up at the house and we drove out into the country where he lived. All of a sudden I began to wonder if Mr. Hinton was married. I also wondered why he lived so far out into the country. I still was okay with the whole deal, but a nagging feeling started to eat away at me. What if this guy was some kind of creep who preyed on young boys? I mean, how many male elementary school teachers do you know?

We got to his little farmhouse surrounded by a good deal of acreage and went inside. No sign of a wife so far. Mr. Hinton disappeared into another room and came out with a pistol in his hand. My eyes must have been as big as basketballs. "What's the matter, Darren? Haven't you ever seen a gun before?" He grinned at me like he was having fun.

Just then I heard the back screen door slam and in walked a gorgeous young woman with a big smile on her face. "You must be Darren," she said as she offered her hand. "I'm Jenny—Mr. Hinton's wife." Then she turned to Mr. Hinton and exclaimed, "Now, Tom, what on earth are you doing with that gun?"

I was seriously confused. He has a wife . . . and she's gorgeous . . . so I'm thinking that he's probably okay. But then I wonder if the two of them are creepy and they plan to have some fun with me. Am I headed for the basement?

Mr. Hinton said, "I was just going to take Darren out back to our practice range and let him do a little target shooting. Have you ever shot a gun before Darren?"

"Uh, no sir, I haven't."

"Would you like me to show you how?"

"Sure!" That is, as long as you're not shooting at me.

Much to my relief, we headed out back to a homemade practice range and Mr. Hinton proceeded to teach me how to shoot a gun—with real bullets. It was awesome! We then ate a quick dinner fixed by his beautiful wife who visited me frequently in my dreams that night. Then it was off to see the Harlem Globetrotters. I was back home by 11:00 p.m. as promised by Mr. Hinton. What a night for a kid in fifth grade! If a teacher tried that stunt today he would be arrested before he finished offering the invitation.

* * *

But getting back to our meeting, I'd have to say that all of the teachers in the room were impressive. They were dedicated to kids and really wanted to find some ways to break through the budget problems that were holding them back from doing their best in the classroom. They echoed the Westside principal's sentiments about using new technologies that would excite the kids. There just wasn't any money for it.

The middle school teacher emphasized the need to bring back music and arts into school since both activities had been dropped due to lack of funding. The high school teacher realized the need to reach those students who would never go to college, but needed to learn some skills that would help them land a job after high school. I saw Joe perk up on that one. However, once they talked about rewarding teachers based on merit, the union rep jumped in with a cautionary warning. "Now, let's be careful about a system that might choose favorites or make rewards based on arbitrary factors decided by administrators."

John Bourke's cousin, the school secretary, quickly entered the discussion. "God, no. We wouldn't want to actually reward the good teachers and get rid of the dead weight around here!" It appeared that Ms. Emily Rogers came as advertised. She pulled no punches. "Why don't we just get rid of the union while we're at it and put those union dues into a fund to reward teachers who actually work hard at what they're doing, unlike the ones who just phone it in?" Mr. Martin chose not to respond to that one since I suspect he knew the secretary would chew him up and spit him out.

"Okay, moving along," I interrupted. "Let's hear about the high school athletic department needs. I can't imagine that you want new equipment, new facilities, or more assistant coaches. So why would you need additional funds?" Joe snorted. My sarcasm appeared to fly over the heads of the athletic consortium and they jumped right in with their list of priorities.

The athletic director, Mr. Pike, started to outline a list of needs that sounded very close to what I had just offered. He had his little speech prepared and wasn't going to alter it. We heard about the massive cut-backs in spending, declining enrollment, decaying facilities, and demand from Title Nine requirements that drove the need for duplicate practice areas in order to give equal opportunities to boys and girls. All of his needs sounded legitimate, but it was hard to say kids weren't enjoying a good sports program with what they had.

The Booster Club boys took a different approach. The older guy, Jim Penfield, grabbed the lead and attempted to personalize the discussion. "Now, Darren, you might not remember me, but I remember you. You played ball on that team that won the sectional basketball tournament in 1969." This guy was really digging deep now. Yes, we won the sectional for the first time in seventeen years at Glenville as part of the Indiana High School Basketball Tournament. The tournament was made famous with the movie, *Hoosiers*, and it dominated every small town in Indiana in March. Over six hundred schools entered the tournament that year and we made it to the final twenty-four teams.

I was a starter on the team and a decent scorer, but others played more dominant roles, including one remarkably talented young man who was obsessed with basketball. He averaged thirty-six points a game (before the three-point shot) and ended up as the fourth leading scorer in Indiana high school basketball history. I had no illusions about my contributions to that team in our senior year, but I sure enjoyed the ride. It was an extraordinary time in the lives of young boys who likely would never again experience that level of attention and at times even adulation. Penfield was clearly trying to appeal to my sense of nostalgia—and it might be working.

"You know what it feels like to be a winner in Indiana and you know what it takes to get there. Remember how the whole town was covered in black and gold on game days? Do you remember the electricity in the old gym? Two thousand people would line up outside on game nights to get one of those seats. Ten thousand fans were there at the sectional tournament! Remember winning that sectional and coming home with a police escort? And how about when all the players were lifted onto the shoulders of fans and marched around the bonfire at the park? Remember the pride you felt? Hell, the whole town felt that pride!"

Penfield was really on a roll. "Imagine what you boys might have done if you had better facilities, better training, and more specialized coaching to work with you individually. The bigger schools had that. That's why they usually came out on top."

Well, that and the fact that a small school of two hundred might have played a school of two thousand in the tournament. That was part of the tournament's allure. I suspect there was a slight difference in the depth of the talent pool among schools back then.

Penfield went on. "This is still a small town and we take great pride in our Tigers. We need help to be competitive, Darren; and your funding could help our kids be part of a top-notch program. Think about how proud you were to be a Glenville Tiger. Help these kids experience what you had."

I had to admit that Penfield had tapped into something in me that I had left behind long ago. There was something to be said for working hard in sports and getting rewarded for your work. It was a heady time for a group of young Hoosier teenagers. However, while Penfield spoke I was aware that he never addressed or even looked at Joe. I looked at my brother and he had a fixed stare on Penfield as he crossed his arms and leaned back in his chair.

"Joe," I asked, "What do you think about Mr. Penfield's notion of Tiger Pride? Are you feelin' it?" I knew something was
going on here and just wanted to give Joe a chance to jump in.

"Oh, I think Mr. Penfield knows all about pride. I suspect
he's still living off the pride he felt in his high school days. I
suspect that was the highlight of his life, perhaps with the exception of being the Booster Club president. But I'll try not to
let my low opinion of Mr. Penfield interfere with a desire to do
what's right with our funding choices."

The room was silent and Penfield just stared at Joe while
his face reddened. Joe's outward appearance remained impassive.
The big guy actually looked like he might come across the table
at Joe and that wouldn't have been pretty for Joe.

Penfield snarled, "Do you know what the difference is between you and me, Kelly?"

Joe was quick to respond. "I bathe regularly and use mouth-
wash?"

I ducked my head so Penfield couldn't see the look on my
face. I have to admit that was one of Joe's better lines. I was
about to lose it and when I glanced up I saw some suppressed
smiles on other faces in the room.

"Is that supposed to be funny?" Penfield was livid.

"Apparently not. I don't see you laughing."

Penfield ignored Joe's last remark and said, "The difference
is I made a name for myself in this town and you were nobody.
You were nobody in high school and you're nobody now. You

just happen to be in the right place at the right time with this money you're giving out."

I could tell that Joe was about to begin a demonstration of slicing and dicing an inflated ego, so I jumped in. "I think we're done here, folks. We appreciate your time and I want you to feel free to call me if you have follow-up ideas that we didn't cover today. We'll be making our decision by the end of the month and I feel pretty confident that some money (I can't say how much) will be flowing toward the schools." Might as well leave them hopeful and get the hell out of there.

CHAPTER 13

BACK TO APPLEBEE'S

Joe and I didn't talk much after the meeting and we just headed straight over to Applebee's. I needed a beer and I'm not real sure what Joe needed. Mandy greeted us with her usual smile and cheerful greeting, "How are the Kelly gentlemen doing tonight?"

Mandy was the kind of person who could brighten up a room. She just seemed to genuinely enjoy being around people and chose to see the best in them (though she wasn't above letting us in on a little town gossip now and then). She was about five foot seven with light brown hair, somewhere in her mid to late thirties I'd guess, a firm body that seemed as if it came from hard work rather than exercise classes, and an intriguing face that looked like it had some miles on it. By that, I mean she wasn't exactly beautiful by most superficial standards. But she was attractive in a way that might not get immediately noticed, and the extra smile lines and small wrinkles around her eyes suggested someone who laughed easily despite a life that was not particularly easy.

We had learned that she had been divorced for five years from a guy she met in school at Indiana University and married during their senior year. "He was nice enough, but completely unwilling to grow up after college. He was incapable of holding down a job for long or investing much effort in the kids." After marriage counseling and countless second tries at making things work, she finally asked him for a divorce. He apparently was more than happy to grant it and to move away to start a new life without a family. Young love can apparently take you only so far. Financial responsibilities and kids can sometimes present too great of a challenge.

Joe slowly sipped on a light beer while I finished off my first Budweiser and reached for the second that magically appeared in front of me. The meeting with school officials had apparently caused me to work up a thirst. Mandy moved off to tend to other customers.

I asked the obvious question. "What's up with you and Penfield?"

Joe just stared ahead. "Why do you ask?"

"Well, because you're usually a lot friendlier than you were in that room. You clearly knew Penfield from the past and you didn't like him. Not only didn't you like him, but you also demonstrated that disdain in front of other folks. You're usually much more discreet when you take shots at people you don't like."

"Yeah, I know. I was a jerk in there. Even to the union guy, though I don't regret that one. I shouldn't have let Penfield get to me."

"What's the deal?" I asked.

"The deal is I couldn't stand the guy when we grew up here and I guess I was just taken aback when he showed up at the meeting. It was like I was back in school. That guy started bullying me when we were in fifth grade and he never let up until we graduated from high school. Right before they took a picture of our fifth grade basketball team, he knee'd me in the groin. The picture that showed up in the newspaper caught me bent over holding my crotch and him laughing."

"And he kept doing that stuff all through high school?"

"Not exactly. He tried to shove me around for a while and just pull the usual dumbass guy stuff when you're bigger than everyone else. Nothing spectacular. But by high school, I discovered that I could pretty much talk my way out of anything and I could make him look bad in front of his friends if he started bugging me. We developed a tenuous truce in public, but he would always push me around when no one was looking."

I stared at him for a minute. "I guess you're not too interested in giving his Booster Club a lot of money, are you?"

"Hard to say. I think I can look at the needs of the school without thinking about him. It's just that I've had this recurring dream over the years about Penfield. Pretty funny that it would stick with me that long. I dream that we're at a high school reunion and I see him across the room. Everyone is there and having a good time just hanging around in small groups and laughing. He gives me that stupid grin of his that I perceive as incredibly insulting. I don't say a word and slowly walk across the room where he is standing with some of his old high school buddies. I smile at him and just bring my knee up as hard as is humanly possible right into his crotch. He doubles over and drops to the floor. I slowly turn and calmly walk out of the room as the Class of 1966 stares at my back. It was purely Luke Jackson-esque."

"Man, you really carry a grudge!"

"Apparently so. I've had that dream off and on for over forty years now. I once had a version where I just went up to him at the reunion and eviscerated him with some witty verbal attack on his manhood. But that version wasn't nearly as satisfying as a knee to the groin, so my subconscious always reverted to a more action-oriented hero."

I thought I had heard all of Joe's disclosures about growing up in Glenville. I guess not. "You are one very complex guy, Joe."

"Not really. I just want a little payback like most folks and never achieve it like most folks. It bothers me that I still think about it and, after seeing Penfield again, it will probably bother me more." Joe paused and just stared at his beer. "I wish I were a better person than that."

Some more silent time passed between us. Mandy eventually came over and took our dinner orders. We preferred just eating at the bar and chatting with Mandy when she wasn't too busy. Something was bothering Joe tonight. He usually enjoyed going over the day's events and commenting on some of the characters we had encountered. Not tonight. He didn't even show his usual enthusiasm when Mandy helpfully suggested with a smile that he might try a vegetable with his meal. Last time she tried a similar tactic, he asked if she had any kale or arugula. When she offered broccoli instead, he quickly responded, "No, only kale or arugula will do. If you don't have it, then I'll just have macaroni and cheese instead." Tonight, he just mumbled, "No thanks."

"What's up?" I ventured. "You seem a little off tonight."

Joe took a deep breath and let it out. "I got a call from home this afternoon before our meeting. Carol told me that the doctor's office had called and they want me to come in to go over some test results and they've scheduled some more tests for me."

"That's never a good sign."

"That's what I figured. I've been having this odd feeling in my leg now and then . . . maybe once a week. It's like a little tremor or spasm that can last for a few minutes and then it just goes away. It's been getting worse. I told my doctor about it and he ordered up some extra tests, including a complete body scan. I guess the results are in. Can't be good. It also doesn't help my state of mind that he scheduled an appointment with an oncologist for me."

That extra bit of news got my attention. I was scrambling for something positive to say. "You know how doctors never want to deliver test results over the phone. They're going to cover their asses quickly with additional tests just to make sure they don't miss something. He's naturally going to bring a specialist in to make certain they're interpreting the test results right."

"Agreed. I'm not jumping to worst-case scenarios at this point. It just got my attention and I can't stop thinking about it. I'll fly back this weekend, get a chance to spend time with Carol, and have the extra testing done on Monday. You can pick me up at the airport late Tuesday morning. I already got a pretty cheap flight, even on short notice."

"Joe, you need to take care of this stuff at home. I can handle things here and keep you posted as I move through the next set of meetings."

Joe shook his head. "No, this is important to me. Uncle Shorty wanted us to handle this and I think two heads are better than one in sorting through how to best impact Glenville with his money. It's not going to do me any good staying at home— no matter what news I hear or what pills I need to take. This task is one of the most important things we've ever done and I want to get it right."

"Okay." I had a lump in my throat and that's all I could say.

Joe nodded. "Okay."

CHAPTER 14

THE KELLY BROTHERS GO TO CITY HALL

Joe and I enjoyed another fine breakfast at the Bob Evans restaurant where our favorite morning waitress, Suzie, served us the most important meal of the day. She had learned not to ask Joe if he wanted to substitute fruit and instead asked if we would like a side of biscuits and gravy with our breakfast. That sounded like an outstanding idea to both of us.

We had a 10:00 a.m. meeting at City Hall to meet with a variety of people affiliated with city government. Even though John Bourke warned us that the mayor was "a horse's ass," we nonetheless thought we should start with him and let him decide whom to bring to the meeting. If we didn't think we got a fair sample, then we would seek out others later.

The group convened and Mayor James Riley introduced everyone on his side of the table. Unlike some small towns around the country where a mayor is more of a rotating figurehead among the elected council members, Glenville's mayor was directly elected to the post and served essentially as the city manager and chief spokesman for city government. In this case, it was well known that Mayor Riley's family came from political stock and he intended to follow the family tradition. His next stop was the state legislature, if all went according to plan. He was young and ambitious.

The group included the police chief, Frank Hagman. I saw no sign of recognition from him that he might have remembered me, but I didn't forget Bourke's warning about Hagman's powers of recollection. The city attorney was there along with the head of the Public Works Department. Representatives from Parks and Recreation, the Utilities Commission, the Arts Commission, the Planning Commission, and the Youth Foundation all showed up. Three of the seven city council members were also in attendance. If Rod Serling had been sitting in the corner of the room, it would have been clear to me that I had entered The Bureaucratic Zone.

After my usual introduction about Uncle Shorty's estate, the mayor started in with an overview of Glenville government and its many contributions to the citizenry of the area. He painted a very favorable picture of Glenville, but then blabbed on in excess just long enough for me to conclude that Editor Bourke was, indeed, correct. The guy was a politician to the core. That being said, it did appear that Glenville was still a city to be proud of and that these folks had a vested interest in preserving its finer qualities.

The city council members chimed in periodically clarifying what the mayor had attempted to articulate. Unfortunately, they somehow thought that telling us all about their financial problems down to the smallest detail would get our attention and warrant additional money from the Hazelton fund. When the city attorney blustered on in a convoluted way about a legal issue causing a financial hardship on the city, Joe made a rare error in judgment—he asked the guy to clarify.

"Well, I can try to simplify the concept, but it's a rather complicated issue."

Now he had Joe's attention. "Oh, gee, thanks. I love it when really bright people can break down complex subjects so I can understand them." Then Joe gave the attorney his most ingratiating smile. The guy was clueless.

Before the attorney could reply, I redirected the discussion to include others. After the Public Works guy and the Arts Commission lady had droned on about their areas, Joe and I were both glazed over and ready for a nap.

Joe turned to the Parks and Recreation director, Ms. Ralston, a pleasant-looking person who appeared to be about forty years old. In front of her was a huge three-ring binder. "Ms. Ralston, Darren and I read your last annual report and also the report commissioned two years ago by an outside review agency. Your department appears to be doing some very good work and we can see that more could be done."

Her eyes grew wide. Guess she hadn't expected that we would actually do any homework for this task and that we might have an interest in her area. Joe continued. "Darren and I happen to have a lot of good memories of the park, the community pool, and the recreation programs that were made available to us as kids. So, forget about everything else you had planned to show us and just tell me your top three priorities for funding if some money could magically appear."

To her credit, Ms. Ralston slowly closed the binder that she had instinctively opened when Joe started speaking. She smiled and then without hesitation offered three funding priorities.

"First, we need a major community center. We have great outdoor parks, but it's snowing and cold for at least five months a year and often raining when it's supposed to be nice. A space with room for a gymnasium, fitness classes, community meetings, and even an indoor lap pool would be outstanding. We spend most of our money on kids for good reason, but we have a huge baby boomer population in town and many of them don't have much in the way of resources or support groups.

"Second, we need more resources to expand our youth programs aimed at our youngest kids and also the teenagers who don't generally participate in school athletics as they get older. I need to hire young people who know what other young people want to do and who know what won't carry a stigma with it if kids participate. We have too many middle-aged people trying to do the same stuff over and over again with no better participation rates or better results. We need to hire some new thinking, but not career staff who require longterm pension funding. We can put our young, bright people to work. Pay them a good part-time salary that lets them know this is an important job.

That takes some money. Not that much, but more than we have now.

"Third, Glenville could be a model for all of Indiana in terms of its parks, bike and walking trails, and places where families can get together for free. With a small investment we could have great picnic facilities in all of our parks throughout the city. This might sound trivial, but good shelters with clean restrooms nearby can go a long way toward meeting the needs of families who can't afford to spend lots of money on restaurants and such. Of course, we need staff to keep the grounds looking nice and the restrooms clean, but we could be a model city in that regard if we do it right."

I looked at Joe. He gave me a subtle wink. We both liked this woman and her commonsense approach to the problems. Some money would be heading her way, but we had to make sure it could get to her programs without being diverted elsewhere. I also didn't want to play my hand in front of the others.

"Thank you, Ms. Ralston, that was just what we wanted in a presentation: short and to the point. We'll see what we can do to help if possible. We appreciate your time."

"Chief Hagman, I think you'll be our last presentation," I announced to the group. That got a reaction from the folks from Planning, Utilities, and the Youth Foundation who had not yet spoken. I knew that I'd already heard enough for the day and that meant Joe had heard more than enough. We had spent too much of our professional lives in meetings and we didn't need to sit through one more that dragged out because others had a need to hear themselves talk. "Don't worry, folks, you can just send me your list of priorities to my e-mail address. Remember, keep it short."

I really didn't want to hear from Hagman either, but I figured he had one of the biggest budgets in the city government and I might as well see what he had to say. I had no clue what crime was like in Glenville.

"Well, Joe and Darren, I appreciate the opportunity to share a little bit about our challenges here in Glenville," Hagman offered. Good start. It's always good to use first names and to kiss a little ass when starting to beg. You just have to be skillful about it so everyone doesn't feel dirty afterwards. I didn't need to shower yet.

Hagman continued. "Let's start with the facts. We have forty-two law enforcement employees and that translates to a little less than two officers per one thousand residents. Our reported crime is far less than in most cities. Last year, we had no murders, three rapes, one robbery, six assaults, sixty-eight burglaries, two hundred and ninety-three thefts, twenty stolen cars, and three acts of arson. Our statistics compare very favorably with other towns similar in size, but we are concerned about the spread of crime activity from Indianapolis."

Joe asked a fairly obscure question, "What's the most popular stolen car?"

Hagman didn't blink. "Ford F150 pickup."

Joe stroked his chin in a thoughtful fashion and declared, "Sounds about right." Then he shifted into his best radio voice and declared, "It is, after all, America's Best Combination of Torque, Capability and Fuel Economy."

With that important observation out of the way, I got to the issue at hand. "Chief, it sounds like you have a good handle on crime in this town. Why should we send any money your way when things seem to be going pretty well?"

Chief Hagman gave me a small, condescending smile. "Well, Darren, I'm sure you'd agree that even one rape or one assault is simply one too many."

Oh, God, he really didn't just play the "one-too-many" card, did he? I hate that crap. This is where more tolerant people simply nod their heads and appreciate that one bad thing in your life is one too many. I tried to keep an even tone in my voice. "Look, your crime stats are outstanding. Let's just accept the fact that a few bad things will happen regardless of how much money you throw at the problems. You're not getting to zero in your crime stats, but I'm sure that's your goal. I get it. Now, why do you need more money?" I wish I could be more tolerant, but I'm old and short on patience.

Hagman glared at me for a few seconds and then continued as if I hadn't said anything. Good move. The chief was showing more maturity than Bourke had characterized. "We are becoming a suburb of Indianapolis and, as such, big-city crime is starting to spread in our direction. We want this community to remain one of the safest in Indiana and to do that we must stay ahead of the problems—not just respond to them. I want to set up a task force to study potential gang infiltration into our city. Those stats I quoted didn't account for drug activity in town and we have plenty of that, just like any small town. We don't want that trend to grow."

Okay, good point. I thought Hagman might be right about the influence of Indianapolis on Glenville. When we grew up here, Indy was just a big city that seemed completely separated from us by miles and miles of cornfields. There was no interstate to get potential criminals in and out of town quickly. There simply wasn't a real connection to big-city crime. Maybe now there was.

Joe was staring at his laptop. "Chief, you say that big-city crime is starting to spread toward Glenville, but the data I'm looking at doesn't really support that notion." Uh, oh. Watch out chief!

"Crime in all the categories you mentioned has actually been only slightly up and down each year and, in most segments, you just completed one of your best years for crime statistics. Rapes, robberies, and assaults are all lower than most years in the past. Even thefts are down— apparently with the exception of Ford F-150s."

Hagman just stared at Joe. I decided it was time to jump in and offer an unlikely mature approach to ending this meeting on a high note. "Chief, it looks like you're doing a great job here and we understand that costs are always going up as you look to the future. Why don't you just send me a summary note with a budget proposal for what you think you need to address the rising drug issues and your concerns about gang activity?"

Chief Hagman finally turned away from Joe and simply said, "I'll do just that. I'll put a number on what it takes to keep this community safe. It won't be a budget for picnic tables and restrooms either. It'll be a budget to stop people from being assaulted and robbed and to keep kids off drugs. It will be a real budget for real problems facing this city."

Well, I guess he told us where he thought the priorities were for the city! An uncomfortable silence came over the room as people cleared out. I suspected it wasn't the first time that Hagman ended a meeting with letting the other city employees know where they stood in his pecking order.

I just looked at Joe after the last one filed out. "Did you have to antagonize the guy?"

Joe smiled and shrugged. "I got bored. Plus, as Uncle Shorty said, we know bullshit when we see it and I thought I'd seen enough."

CHAPTER 15

ALL ALONE IN GLENVILLE

It was Friday afternoon and I drove Joe over to the Indianapolis airport so he could catch his flight back to Baltimore. His wife would pick him up there and they'd make the one-hour drive over to their little town on the Chesapeake Bay. We were pretty quiet on the drive as I suspect we both were wondering what lay in store for Joe once he met with his doctor.

As we got closer to the airport exit, Joe spoke in a quiet voice. "A lot sure has happened in one short week. We get the chance of a lifetime to do some wonderful things in our home town and then I learn that maybe I've got something seriously wrong with me."

"Come on, Joe, that's a huge leap in logic to make at this point. You just might have some oddity that will be easily cleared up with the right meds. No need to assume the worst."

"Oh, I'm not assuming the worst at all. In fact, I'm quite neutral in my assumptions. However, you have to appreciate the irony of the two forces colliding at the same time. And I'm also acutely aware of how much I'm enjoying life right now at the ripe old age of sixty-three. There are so many good people in my life and I just want to enjoy them and contribute something to their lives if I can."

"Well, you'll still have plenty of time to do that."

"Any way I look at it, I'm humbled by Uncle Shorty's trust in us and I really want to do the right thing with his money. If I get some bad news back home, my desire to do right by the people in this town will likely be intensified. If I get good news (relatively speaking), then I'll feel that I dodged a bullet and can throw myself into the task with enthusiasm. In either case, we're going to get the job done and I'll be thankful that I had the chance to do it with you."

As he turned away from me to get out of the car, I quickly ran a shirtsleeve over my eye. If he noticed the redness in my eyes when he stuck his head back in, he didn't say anything. He just shook my hand and closed the door.

* * *

Back in Glenville it was time for my daily visit to Applebee's. Every day Joe and I intended to branch out in our Glenville culinary pursuits, but every evening we returned to Applebee's. We don't have a lot of imagination when it comes to food. Plus, the Budweiser is cold and Mandy is good company. I think she's about due for a couple of nights off starting tomorrow, so I might just have to see what else the town has to offer. However, I just hate eating alone in a restaurant. I'm starting to see an image of me watching sports in my hotel room surrounded by White Castle wrappers. Most people would think that's pitiful; I'm actually looking forward to it.

I sat at the bar chatting with Mandy as she went about her business. The more I got to know her, the more I liked her. As she walked away to help another customer, I felt a tap on my shoulder and heard a familiar voice say, "I'll bet you fifty dollars that I can beat you in a hundred-yard race outside on the parking lot right now!"

I didn't have to look around. "You never could beat me and you never will beat me because I'm far too mature now to engage in such foolishness. Plus, I think it would just destroy you if I left you in my dust one last time."

Jim Barton was a high school classmate who was an inferior athlete with a superiority complex. Not a great combination, but nonetheless entertaining for his friends. In high school he finally realized that he couldn't beat me in most sports, but he was convinced that he was faster than me. No matter how many times he challenged me to a race and how many times I beat him, he kept coming back for more. I'm not sure which was the bigger ego issue—his need to win just once or my need to once again prove my athletic superiority over him. Neither approach was healthy.

"Barton, how the hell are you?"

"Kelly, I heard you were hanging around in Glenville and had to come see for myself. I figured you wouldn't look me up, so I just decided to take the initiative."

"I'm glad you did, Barton. Sit down and join me. Can I buy you a beer or is that off limits?"

Barton had a history with alcohol and there was no point in dancing around it now. It was one of the reasons that many of his old high school friends didn't stay in touch any longer. He apparently got pretty deep into the bottle at one point, lost his driver's license for a while and had a hard time holding down a job. Since I had moved away long ago I just didn't stay in touch enough to really know the details.

Barton smiled and said, "Well, let's just say that I've decided that alcohol doesn't seem to work for me any longer. It was my best friend for a long time. I guess you heard that. But I quit five years ago and never looked back. I guess most alcoholics crave it when they quit; I don't miss it a bit. It no longer has any appeal to me. Guess that can happen when it damn near ruins your life."

"Good for you, Barton. I'm glad to hear it." And I meant it. Barton was a good guy who deserved a break. "By the way, how did you know I'd be here at Applebee's?"

"It's still a small town. Mandy mentioned to her sister about chatting all week with the Kelly brothers. I know her sister from work. Also heard from John Bourke that you were in town. Saw him at the barbershop. I figure by next week half the town will know that a couple of guys have some money to throw around and you'll find yourselves getting real popular."

Barton joined me for dinner and we swapped old stories. There were quite a few when it came to Barton. He was the scrawny kid that we tormented whenever possible because he just seemed to be a glutton for punishment. We tied him to a flagpole at the school once and left him there for hours. He would antagonize anyone just to get a rise out of the guy, knowing that he might even get his ass kicked as a result. Plus, he simply did stupid stuff that was hard to believe. One night we were innocently shooting off M80 firecrackers. For the uninitiated, those little bombs could blow your fingers right off if you caught a short fuse. Well, Barton somehow managed to light an M80 and, while turning fast to run away, ran face first into a four-by-four post. He managed to damn near break his nose and shoot his ass off at the same time!

Barton was also the inspiration for one of my most memorable accomplishments in high school athletics. In our sophomore year, Barton had signed up for the cross-country team. He only did it so he could get his picture in the yearbook. He planned to quit right after they shot the photo. I had been forced to join by the varsity basketball coach who doubled as the cross-country junior varsity coach. If a basketball player wasn't playing football in the fall, then he had to run cross-country to get in shape for the upcoming basketball season. As much as I pleaded to work out on my own and spend the after-school hours in the gym where I could improve my game, Coach didn't buy it. He assumed that I would just be goofing off with the other guys who didn't play football. He might have been right.

I hated everything about cross-country. Running anything longer than the length of a basketball court or a hundred-yard dash seemed like a gigantic waste of effort. Fortunately, Barton developed an outstanding training technique that he shared with me after a couple of mindless practices of running around the Glenville Park for an hour. We hung back from the group, climbed high into a beautiful maple tree with lots of foliage, and proceeded to relax while watching the other kids do laps around the big park. As they passed under us for the return back to the high school gym, we dropped down and slid into the rear of the pack, feeling appropriately invigorated.

Since this training technique was so successful, I thought I should try it out in real competition. Barton was supposed to join me in this effort, but he twisted his ankle jumping out of the tree at our previous practice. I had to go it alone. We were at an away competition where the course started at the high school football field and then immediately headed onto a three-mile path carved through a heavily wooded area. Barton was there at the meet limping around in support of the guys.

He did a little reconnaissance work beforehand to locate a perfect spot for my new approach to cross-country competition on this hot and humid early-fall day. The race started and I quickly dropped to the back of the pack, consistent with the expert training provided to me by Barton. I saw the huge tree with conveniently placed lower branches that he had marked for me with a red rag. I made the quick ascent before I could be spotted. The other runners headed off deeper into the woods for their silly trek toward total exhaustion.

I had a lovely rest in that fine maple tree and soon heard the sounds of the runners coming back through the woods. Jumping down at this point was a calculated risk since I couldn't be sure when a large gap in the pack might suddenly close and I could be discovered by those rushing up behind me. Of course, I could have dropped down when the final guy came through and I'd be safe from discovery. But then I would be last. I couldn't come in last. I may have hid in a tree, but I had some pride after all.

So, I found an opening about two-thirds of the way back in the field of runners and made my move. I dropped behind a guy from the other team who was gagging for air and looking like he could go down any minute. We came out of the woods and I could see the football field ahead along with the dozen or so spectators waiting at the finish line. Cross-country in 1960s Indiana almost didn't qualify as a spectator sport. My plan was to pass through one set of goal posts, appear to stagger down the length of the football field, and cross through the finish line under the other goal posts.

The lead pack had already crossed the finish line and I saw a group of about ten guys straining and gasping in front of me as they made the turn onto the field. All of a sudden I heard Barton yell out, "Come on, Kelly. Show us some speed!" Exhibiting no judgment whatsoever, I responded to Barton's taunt with a burst of speed normally reserved for my role as a moderately capable sprinter on the Glenville track team. I don't know what got into me, but I just had to pass that group of guys running down the hundred-yard field.

I sprinted like—well, like a guy who had been resting in a tree and who was now competing with stragglers that could barely put one foot in front of the other. Their necks were tightening up, each face was locked into a permanent strained grimace, and their skinny arms were just flailing around side to side. In comparison, I looked like a cheetah. I passed every one of them.

I crossed the finish line with a big grin while Barton yelled, "Nice finish, Kelly!" He was obviously pleased with his protégé. Coach was not quite so pleased. Perhaps it was the stupid grin on my face. Perhaps it was the fact that I had absolutely no sweat on my clothing while other runners looked as if they just ran through a shower. Perhaps it was the kids who I passed in the home stretch who were pointing at me to their coach and then pointing back at the woods.

All I know is that Coach walked up to me without the slightest appreciation for my splendid final hundred-yard dash and simply said, "You're off the team, Kelly. Report to the gym on Monday for conditioning drills." I was ecstatic, but of course I didn't show it. Barton was pissed. Now he had no one to join him in the trees during practice. Somehow I knew he would soon find another malcontent to replace me. I didn't care. My cross-country days were over.

* * *

Barton's finest hour came at a summer party the year after high school. Alcohol might have been involved. We had all been off to college for a year and the alleged smart one in the group, Rick Cole, who went to Harvard, told us about a great trick he learned at some Harvard drunken bash attended by other brilliant minds. It begins outside of the house where the party is held. You turn a sweatshirt inside-out, put it on a person who presumably has a death wish, and then pour a modest amount of lighter fluid on the raised nap of the sweatshirt's interior which is now facing outward. You then strike a match and light the fumes.

The theory is that the Darwin Award participant will appear to be on fire (and in truth he would be on fire!). Again, in theory and only according to Harvard legend, the sweatshirt nap would be giving off a flame but it would be harmless to the person actually wrapped in the piece of flammable clothing! It made perfect sense.

His "friends" would turn off the lights in the house, he would then burst into the room in flames and people would scatter, screaming and spilling beers as they panicked in fear. At just the right moment, the highly trained friends would then jump out with blankets and smother the flames before they had a chance to actually penetrate the entire sweatshirt and light the guy up completely. Clearly, all would have a good time. What can I say? We were nineteen and not even remotely sober. Cole was adamant that he had seen this stunt successfully performed. Presumably he was drinking at the time.

This brilliant plan almost worked. Barton, of course, volunteered. There was never any doubt. He followed the requisite steps in the proper sequence, but when we lit the sweatshirt the small flame just sputtered and died out. Not to be deterred from making a grand entrance to the party, Barton grabbed the lighter fluid. "Give me that. We need more lighter fluid to make this thing work!" He then liberally doused the sweatshirt front and back.

Seeing the liberal dose applied to the subject, none of us would accept the responsibility of actually lighting the match. Barton grabbed the matches from Rick's hand. "I'll do it. Just get the blankets ready and catch that light switch as you go in the back door." However, when the match touched the sweatshirt, the entire garment erupted into a flame that rose about two feet above Barton's head. Not only was the sweatshirt on fire, but Barton's hair was also on fire!

Acting with the instincts of a first-time human torch, Barton proceeded to take off running around the yard escaping our attempts to help him. No drop and roll. No hose. No pulling off the sweatshirt. Just panicked running with abandon. He finally stopped and ripped the sweatshirt over his head and screamed like—well, like a guy who had been on fire.

What was left of the hair on his head was literally still smoking. His eyebrows had little patches missing, his mustache was minus a big chunk on one side, and his once-hairy chest was now void of all hair and glowing red like someone who just spent ten hours on a beach with no sunscreen. It occurred to me that we might have discovered how the name Harvard Crimson was created.

* * *

That was Barton. He created many of his own problems, but clearly didn't deserve all the grief that he was given. There was an aspect to Barton that saw the world differently from me and I always appreciated how he could ground me when I became too full of myself. At the height of my modest Hoosier basketball stint I was enjoying the daily doses of small-town fame, which were based solely on my slightly above average ability to shoot a ball through a basket.

Barton and I were cruising the Glenville streets with two other friends in a '63 Chevy Impala. When we pulled up to a stop sign, a tall, gawky-looking kid named Ken Borkin saw me in the shotgun seat and gave a big, nerdy wave. I knew him from the freshmen basketball team. My elbow was on the windowsill of the door and my chin rested in my hand as I gazed out the open window with a practiced sense of casual indifference. With seemingly great effort, I managed to lift my little finger as a subtle acknowledgement that I saw the kid. That's all I gave him. A quick raised little finger that said, "I see you, I acknowledge that you exist, but you're a freshmen and I'm a senior." We pulled away from the corner.

Barton jumped all over me. "Kelly, you piece of crap! You acknowledged Borkin by lifting your little finger? You couldn't even make the effort to lift your chin off your hand and give him a decent wave? Do you know how you just made that kid feel? Like a piece of dirt, that's how. God knows why, but that kid looks up to all you guys on the team." Barton was on a roll and nearly foaming at the mouth. "That's right—you're a big deal to him. We all know that's a load of crap, but that's the way it works! Get over yourself and think about somebody else for a change."

I'm a sixty-year-old man and I still remember that tongue-lashing from Barton. He was absolutely right at the time and I knew it. That simple admonition changed me. I knew Barton wasn't just talking about Borkin; he was talking about himself as well. He knew what it was like to be ignored or even ridiculed and he wasn't going to sit by quietly while his friend demonstrated that same kind of boorish behavior he'd seen in so many others.

* * *

Over the course of our dinner at Applebee's, I learned that Barton worked for the Glenville Youth Foundation helping kids who were at-risk for one reason or another. Sometimes it was an abusive home, some were living at the poverty level, and others just had little supervision and were already on the police radar for petty crimes. Whatever the issue, Barton's job was to help them. "It doesn't pay much, but I cover my rent and don't have much other need for money—especially since I quit drinking."

Because of Barton's drinking history, not many employers in town would give him any work. The Youth Foundation saw a guy who had hit bottom and probably could help kids avoid some of his own missteps. Somebody really had to take a chance with that hire since I imagine Barton had some serious detractors. I have no doubt that a sober Barton would be very good at the job.

Our conversation reminded me that I had not let the Youth Foundation director give a report at our meeting. "Probably just as well," Barton observed. "She's about to retire and seems to feel a need to take thirty minutes for a two-minute presentation. You made a good choice. If her written report doesn't make sense, I can fill in the gaps for you."

We parted company and I took comfort in knowing that Barton had turned the corner and seemed to have his life back in order. I almost felt sorry for leaving him tied to that flagpole when we were kids. Almost.

CHAPTER 16

THE POUNDERS

Once I learned that Joe would be gone for the weekend, I thought I'd try to find a golf game to take my mind off of Uncle Shorty's task and Joe's health. I called an old classmate who I knew played golf. On one of the rare occasions that I ever opened up my Facebook account, I followed a few folks who had posted messages and eventually came across a picture of Bill Shipley swinging a golf club. He was a realtor in Glenville and, therefore, easy to find since his smiling mug shot was all over town. He also had already heard that I was in the area and was very open to having me join his regular Saturday golf group as a guest.

At 11:30 a.m. on Saturday I pulled into the entrance of what used to be called the Glenville Country Club. This place had been a mysterious symbol of wealth and privilege when I grew up in Glenville. Coming from the west side of town as young kids, we only knew one family that belonged to the country club and they seemed to have scraped together every penny they had to afford the membership. Later in middle school and high school I met plenty of kids who belonged to the country club, but it still held its allure and mystique for me. I don't remember ever being invited as a guest, and I didn't really expect to be invited.

Having played on some fine golf courses throughout America, I now had a very different perspective of the old country club. First, the new sign at the entrance welcomed me to Raven's Landing—not the Glenville Country Club. At first glance, it looked more like a place where crows hung out rather than the elitist image I had maintained in my memory bank for all these years. As I drove down the lane that separated sections of the golf course, I watched carefully for errant tee shots and quickly made my way to the safety of the parking lot. Oh, the place was nice enough and appeared to be well maintained. It just struck me that this once forbidden place was really nothing more than what would pass for a decent municipal facility in most small towns.

Like so many country clubs around the nation, it submitted to the economic realities of the times and changed from exclusive membership status to daily fees and optional annual dues. I assume that when I was growing up the local membership thought it was a grand place to escape the ordinary folks of Glenville. I'm surprised my mother hadn't pushed for a membership given her feelings about the cultural limitations of central Indiana. However, golf would never have been on her agenda and paying any kind of money for that privilege would not have been on my father's agenda.

I spotted Bill Shipley as soon as I parked and he came over to greet me with great enthusiasm. "It's good to see you, Kelly. I can't wait to take some of that California money from you out on the golf course!" There are a few fundamental truths in life. Most people in other parts of the country have a great disdain for Californians (based, I'm sure, on repressed envy). Also, all golfers have an inflated sense of their own abilities and unbridled optimism prior to hitting their first tee shot of the day when reality sets in. Golfers love to bet and take even the smallest wager from their competition in order to gain bragging rights until the next golf outing. Shipley was no exception.

After a few minutes of catching up, Bill led me to the driving range to meet some of his golf buddies. Bill had an extra set of clubs for me to use. There were about twenty guys hitting balls on the range and stroking some putts on the practice green nearby. According to Bill, they called themselves "The Pounders" presumably referencing the pounding they gave the golf ball and the pounding they gave each other in their competitive team format. I suspected that pounding a few beers down might also be part of the equation.

I made the rounds and shook some hands. I only knew a couple of the guys from high school. As each golfer greeted me, I got a brief character description from Bill. Along with a guy's occupation, he announced his nickname: Lawyer (Judge Judy) . . . doctor (Kevorkian) . . . car sales (Slick) . . . farmer (Rooster) . . . contractor (Hammer) . . . retired (Happy Hour) . . . stock broker (Blue Chip) . . . optometrist (Fore Eyes) . . . restaurant owner (Sal—short for Salmonella) . . . teacher (Mr. Rogers) . . . plumber (Wrench) . . . dentist (Painless) . . . accountant . . . (Debit) . . . and on and on. This was an eclectic group representing all walks of life. Golf seemed to be the common denominator, along with a sense of humor.

We had six groups of four and I played with Bill and two guys I didn't know. One worked for the post office (Stamp) and the other owned a couple of laundromats (Suds). My friend Bill, the realtor, was simply known as "House." He was a fairly big guy so the moniker fit for more than one reason. Because of my California connection, I quickly became "Tofu." It was a great day for golf and I didn't embarrass myself on the course.

The routine with this group was to return to the clubhouse for the nineteenth hole. Each guy previously put ten dollars in the pot to begin the day. Five dollars went to the pay-off for various achievements and the other five dollars went to buy a few pitchers of beer. Bill explained, "It's a small enough buy-in where no one feels like it's a burden. It only pays out a modest sum for the winners, so you don't feel like it's a big loss when you miss out and you still get bragging rights when you win. Finally, there is just enough beer so everyone gets a couple of glasses out of the deal and heads on home before they get in trouble— usually. Pretty simple. We play every Saturday at noon and not many guys miss a turn."

I listened to all the usual golf banter and could tell that this group really had a good camaraderie about it. The put-downs were plentiful but not mean-spirited. The praise for good shots and particularly good rounds were generous. However, the most boisterous guy in the group, Slick, just couldn't take it when the doctor droned on about his unusually good round shot-by-shot, as too many golfers tend to do. Slick screamed out, "Would you just land the plane, Kevorkian! No one cares enough to hear about every shot—especially from some damn eighteen-handicap hacker!" That drew a round of applause. It seemed that a car salesman taking a doctor to task was not necessarily an unusual occurrence in this group.

As the beer ran out and the payouts were made (to others), Bill turned to me privately and said, "I heard about this money you're trying to spread around. Seeing as how you are now an honorary Pounder, maybe you could set aside just a little bit for the Saturday group so we could do some road trips to other golf clubs or create some annual prizes." I didn't give him any reaction, so he continued.

"Look, I know you have better causes for the money, and I'm only asking because you're right here and I figure there's no harm in throwing it out. We wouldn't need much to make a small difference and you can see that this is a great group of guys. You know we'll put the money to good use!" That last statement was made with a big, wide smile and a wink. Bill was clearly on a fishing expedition, but not really expecting to land a big one.

I didn't waste any time giving him false hope. "Shipley, it is exactly because this is such a good group that I wouldn't give you a penny. I am not going to be the reason that a very good thing got ruined because someone thought it should be changed in some way. You guys have a perfect format, a great chemistry, and a common love of golf. Don't screw with it! Enjoy what you have!"

Bill just smiled. "Yeah, I can't argue with that. Go spread the wealth, Kelly. We'll be just fine."

I thanked him for the invitation and told him again what a great time I had. I had no idea what kinds of issues or troubles these guys might have had in their daily lives. But I knew for certain that for a few hours every Saturday, they had a really good thing going on and I wasn't going to be the guy who messed with it.

CHAPTER 17

THE GLENVILLE PUBLIC LIBRARY

That night I did, indeed, dine in my room on a bag of White Castle cheeseburgers and a couple of cold beers. I missed Joe, but I also enjoyed my private time. I called my wife and brought her up to speed on our latest meetings and my concerns about Joe's health. She was eating a salad and catching the national news at the time, so it felt as if I was right there with her enjoying our fairly routine yet somehow satisfying typical evening ritual. I decided she didn't need to know my entrée selection for this night.

Like me, she chose not to jump to conclusions about the news that Joe needed more medical tests. Ironically, Beth was the daughter of pharmacists and also a veteran of the pharmaceutical sales industry, like Joe. She tended to approach all medical issues from a scientific perspective based on her career background and academic training in biology. She had already started researching Joe's issues and asked me several questions that I could not answer. We finally both acknowledged the frustration of waiting, but knew that Joe and Carol must really be suffering from the fear of the unknown.

We had a great talk and I filled Beth in on all of latest Shorty Hazelton issues. When it felt as if we had covered everything, she did ask a very intuitive question that affirmed the closeness of our thirty-year relationship. "You're eating White Castles, aren't you? And watching SportsCenter?" I told her that I missed her and said goodbye. I could feel her smirk through the phone.

After my exciting Saturday evening in the hotel room, I just got out and enjoyed a leisurely Sunday in Glenville. I actually hoped that I didn't run into anybody that I knew since I just needed a break from thinking about the best way to distribute Uncle Shorty's money. You might think that giving away someone else's money would be a simple task, but I just didn't want to mess it up. I wouldn't have any trouble getting this job done, but I did fret over it more than I would have ever imagined.

I found myself driving around town and I eventually stopped in front of the old Glenville Public Library. My mother began working there part-time after she felt her two boys were old enough to handle the independence of not having their mother waiting for them every day after school. It was a stately old brick structure with lots of detail around the roofline. Two sets of exterior steps led up to the massive front doors that would always creak just enough to get everyone in the place to raise their heads in unison to see who entered. Unusually tall ceilings and hard tiled floors created an echo effect that amplified every whisper in the place.

This was a facility of great importance to the community. School kids didn't have the Internet to instantly look up historical references for their term papers. There were no computers to aid you with any of your research. You became adept at using the Dewey Decimal system and you made sure to keep on the right side of the library staff so they could help you find those obscure references you needed. Likewise, it was a community resource for older people in town who were avid readers and chose not to spend their money on new books. Downloading a book to your Kindle was not remotely on the horizon for that generation.

My mother ruled the library with an iron fist from behind the librarian's desk—or, more accurately, a vertical finger placed over her mouth as she loudly scolded "Shhhhhh!" at any offenders who dared to raise their voices above the softest of whispers. Young and old alike knew that a second warning would precipitate a personal visit from the assistant librarian. You just didn't want that to happen. You also never wanted to have any books overdue. An overdue book was a clear sign to my mother that you lacked integrity in all aspects of your life. You were destined for failure in whatever endeavor you might undertake. If you were a repeat offender, you became fodder for Kelly supper table discussions and were forevermore known as a "no-good rotter."

Yes, it might be perceived as a bit harsh, but Violet Kelly's standards were very high, to say the least. Heaven help Joe or me if we dared to date a girl who sometime in the past five years might have had an overdue book. If she had been a repeat offender, or worse yet, if her parents were also offenders, she was given the ultimate Violet Kelly putdown. She was a "but-nothing." It was her East Coast version of calling someone "trailer trash." You really didn't want to date a "but-nothing."

In addition to being a trifle over-reactive, my mother was a very clever woman. She knew that her boys' brains would turn to mush away from the rigors of schoolwork over the long Indiana summers. She had to get us interested in reading. She wasn't quite as worried about Joe since he was now diligently taking his music lessons and didn't seem to be as fixated on sports as his younger brother. There was no time left for reading in my summer days as I bounced from one sport to another down at the Boys' Club. By the time I made it home for supper, I was exhausted.

Then one day a book appeared on my bed at home. It was titled, *The Backfield Twins*. Twin brothers were featured in the story about high school football. I shoved it aside for days and then one night started reading it and couldn't put it down. The plot wasn't particularly complicated. The twins move to a new town. The regulars shun the new kids at school until they try out for the football team. They have skills. Suddenly they also have friends. And they have girl friends. Then girlfriends. Life is excellent. The end. I could almost identify with these guys. More accurately, I could fantasize about them . . . and their girlfriends.

My introduction to literature continued with books arriving home from the library via my scheming and conniving mother. *Sophomore Shortstop* was a classic. *The Catcher* and *The Perfect*

Pitch were baseball poetry. *One on One* and *Last-Second Shot* were basketball stories that inspired me to think about all the possibilities that Indiana basketball had to offer. I read dozens of sports books that first summer. I realized that great stories could lead you to dream about what might be possible.

Then one day a new book arrived on my pillow. It wasn't a sports book. I figured my mother made a mistake, because I was pretty sure that I was only capable of reading books about sports and I assumed she knew that as well. The book was *The Adventures of Tom Sawyer*. I first just glanced at it and skipped around to read a few paragraphs. I learned enough to know that some young boys got into trouble and there was a female interest as well (Becky Thatcher). That was enough for me. I read it as fast as my fingers could turn the pages. The *Adventures of Huckleberry Finn* followed. Then came *Treasure Island*, and on and on. Before I knew it *The Backfield Twins* was a forgotten chapter in my newfound life of literary exploration. She had won.

Staring at the old library (now a converted restaurant) brought back a wealth of memories about carefree summers, the power of books, and a mother who was so clever and so determined to "make something" of her boys. I just hope the new Glenville Public Library is opening new worlds for kids today like this old place did in the past for me and others. Joe and I will have to look into that as another source of possible funding. If my mother were alive, keeping the library viable would have made her very happy. And one last lesson learned—I've never had an overdue library book in my life. I don't want to be a no-good rotter.

CHAPTER 18

LONNIE MCDANIEL

When evening approached I had to make that all-important decision about where to eat. Mandy wouldn't be at Applebee's, so that meant I either opted for eating alone in a restaurant or repeating my in-room dining experience; If that were the case, I'd probably branch out to another fast-food place for variety. Steak 'n Shake would make a nice alternative.

I finally concluded that spending two straight evenings in my room would make me feel like a total moron, so I walked the short distance over to my home away from home, Applebee's. I chose a secluded booth this time and proceeded to break out my laptop to work on some notes for future meetings with other groups in town. There are few absolute truths in life, but one is that dining alone makes you look and feel like an absolute loser. The only way to mitigate that image is to appear to be busy with important work. Reading a book just for pleasure doesn't qualify. Loser.

However, busily sending text messages actually makes it appear to other diners that you have real friends somewhere. Even though you might only be hitting random letters with great enthusiasm, the process of fake texting is still an excellent cover technique. Reading a newspaper is also acceptable since that presumes you are intelligent enough to comprehend local and world events and that you have some degree of intellectual curiosity. Working on a laptop is the ultimate dining companion if a live human is unavailable or unwilling to join you. You look intelligent, important, and you presumably had enough money to buy the device.

I was actually having a relatively pleasant time sipping on a decent glass of Pinot Noir (overpriced, from California) and doing some research on church-related community services in town. Without any comment a man quietly slid into the booth seat across from me. He just stared at me with a very odd grin. It wasn't a grin that says, "It's good to see you." Rather, it was a creepy sort of half-smile that said, "Look what I found." I had no clue as to his identity.

The face continued to stare at me. He looked a little older than me, strong build with wide shoulders, long gray hair down to his shoulders, heavily lined face that had seen some hard times, a gray goatee, long sideburns, and the complexion of a guy who spends a lot of time in the sun during the day and a lot of time in the bottle at night.

"Okay," I said. "I give up. I'm sorry, but do I know you?"

His eyes grew wide in mock amazement when he exclaimed, "You don't remember me, Mr. Kelly? Why, I thought everyone in this town knew me, but you have been gone a long while, haven't you?" His stare continued, but the grin left his face.

Somehow I knew that being my usual smart-ass self might not be a good move with this guy. I simply stated, "You'll have to forgive me, but you have me at a disadvantage. I can't recall your name."

"Well, let me just paint a picture for you. Do you remember when you were around ten or twelve years old, you and that brother of yours came across something in the shed across the field from your house?" The guy paused as if looking in the air for the answer to his own question. "Oh, yeah, you opened that shed door and you found a big, furry, black dog hanging from the rafter with a chain wrapped around his neck! Why, I believe that beloved creature died at the end of that chain just kicking and squealing. You boys were a little late in finding him."

Now I was the one staring. "Lonnie McDaniel."

"Bingo!" McDaniel came out of his seat and slapped the table hard enough to make my laptop jump in the air and crash back to the tabletop. He quickly sat back and crossed his arms, looking very smug and satisfied with his little charade. I, on the other hand, was really shaken and trying like hell not to show it.

Lonnie McDaniel was not a guy to mess with and I really didn't like the fact that he had sought me out and was now sitting three feet across from me in an enclosed space. By every account I had ever heard and by what I had seen with my own eyes, Lonnie was a walking definition of a psychopath. He had engaged in antisocial behavior since he was a young boy, including violent and aggressive acts. Most notable, he never seemed to show any empathy for others or any remorse for his outrageous actions.

His story about the dog was true. Joe and I had adopted a big, loveable black dog that started hanging around our house. Our parents checked the usual sources for lost dogs and we were just about to take him to the vet for shots and tags when he suddenly disappeared. Joe and I canvassed the neighborhood and eventually peeked into the old, abandoned shed that Lonnie mentioned. There was Blackie hanging from that chain. Joe and I were devastated. The whole scene was just sick. We knew it was McDaniel that must have done it when one day he cruised by on his bike and called out over his shoulder, "How's that black dog of yours doin', boys?" He just laughed and laughed as he sped away.

McDaniel was a year older than Joe and just plain mean. He would fight anyone if something set him off. He didn't always win since he would often pick fights with bigger, older guys. But no matter how bloodied he was, he always left the scene with a big grin on his face. By the time he was in sixth grade he had already been busted for robbing a cigarette truck over in Indianapolis. He jumped inside when the driver was making a delivery into a store and came out with as many cartons as he could stuff into a gym bag. The only problem was a police car pulled up just as he jumped out of the truck. That got him some time in juvenile hall.

Other animals turned up mutilated and the rumors always included Lonnie, though he was seldom held accountable. He was twice accused of burning down vacant structures, but the charges didn't stick when the kids who called the fires in suddenly developed a case of amnesia. His most notorious action as a kid was when he stole one of his father's rifles and planted himself on a hill just below the water tower.

He was in high school at the time, but apparently took the day off for some target practice. During the middle of the day, he fired a shot into the sixth-grade classroom at Westside Elementary School. The bullet pierced the window and embedded in the chalkboard at the front of the room. The room was empty since everyone was on lunch break. It was presumed the shooter knew that no one would be there and simply wanted to send a warning of some kind.

Lonnie was never charged, but he had been absent from school, people saw him that day with something that looked like a rifle case, and he was heard bragging later about "sending a message" to one of the teachers at Westside. Mysteriously, the gun was never found and the father simply filed a stolen gun report with the police.

When McDaniel finished high school, he joined the service and went off to find "legitimate" ways to hurt people. Last I heard he was headed to Vietnam. I also heard rumors that he spent time in prison. Now here he was over forty years later with the same crazy look in his eyes, staring at me.

"What do you want from me, Lonnie?"

"What do I want from you? Well, now, is that any way to treat an old friend? Maybe I just want to reminisce a little bit. Maybe have a glass of that fine red wine you're drinkin'. Maybe I just want to reconnect."

"We were never friends, Lonnie."

"Well, I guess that might be so, but I always thought I could have been friendly with the Kelly boys if you two didn't have your noses up in the air so much. Is that the way it still is, Kelly? Still got your nose up in the air looking down at fellas like me?"

"Lonnie, I don't even know you. I haven't seen you in decades. Let's cut the bullshit. Why did you sit down here?"

McDaniel gave me a look that gave me chills. I forced myself to keep staring at him with little expression, but I was shaken. I had taken a tone with him that was risky and I could tell that he didn't like it. His jaw was clenched and he started to rub his temples as if a migraine had just kicked in. He finally looked at me and simply said, "I hear you have been burdened with a sizeable amount of money and I intend to relieve you of some of that burden. I'm here on a goodwill mission. I intend to convince you that my need for that money is equal to if not greater than the other needs of this community. Oh, they can have their share. I just want my fair share as well."

"So, you're telling me that you're in charge of some sort of charitable organization? Is that what you want me to believe?"

"Mr. Kelly, if that's what will make you comfortable, then by all means I want you to believe that I am indeed in charge of a charitable organization. I intend to use the money you give me in a very charitable fashion and I will personally see to it that every dollar is well spent."

"Well, Lonnie, unless Joe and I see some evidence that you really do have some sort of organization that does charitable work then I'm afraid we'll just have to keep Mr. Hazelton's estate proceeds focused on the legitimate needs of this community. Somehow I don't think I'll hold my breath waiting for that evidence."

Lonnie just smiled. "Oh, Mr. Kelly, I wouldn't want you to hold your breath. In fact, I encourage you to continue breathing. I encourage you to take the sort of bold leadership that will allow you to continue breathing at your leisure. You see, I only want the best for you. And the best for you is to see things my way. If not, you just never know what sort of accidents could befall a guy like you. I mean you are getting on in age. Things do happen, don't they?" His wide grin revealed tobacco-stained teeth that were chipped and crooked.

"I can't believe you just threatened me."

"Why, Mr. Kelly, did you perceive my statement as a threat? Well, I only meant it as a statement of fact. Good things sometimes happen to people who share good things with others. Bad things sometimes happen to people who withhold good things from others. You just never know, but things do happen. There are consequences to our actions, don't you think?"

"I've heard enough. Why don't you just leave, Lonnie?"

"Well, now, Darren . . . can I call you Darren? It seems as if we should be on a first-name basis since we're getting to know each other again. Darren, I'll be heading out now, but I want to leave you with this thought. You may think that people don't know how much money you've got to throw around, but you'd be surprised how information slips out. I happen to know that you are dealing with at least several million dollars—not just thousands, as most folks think. And as much as you might want to give me the majority of that money (and I truly appreciate that sentiment), I realize that just wouldn't look right. So, I'm proposing that you donate a mere $100,000 to my charitable organization and it will just get lost among all those other donations. Don't you worry; I'll give it a good cover so it won't raise suspicion."

"And if we don't give you the money?"

"Well, then ... Darren ... I'll just have to have another little meeting with you, and it won't be in a public place. Let me ask you a question. Does it require both you and your brother to administer this money? In other words, should one of you become "incapacitated" could the other brother go ahead and finalize the deal? You don't have to answer that now. Just give it some thought. I'll be in touch."

McDaniel started to get up and paused. "Oh, and please do give my regards to your wife, Beth, out there in Ojai. Nice name—Beth. What is that—short for Elizabeth? Rather old-fashioned, isn't it? I understand she's also an animal lover. Likes to walk her dog every morning. That's good." He paused and just grinned at me. "It will make it easy for one of my associates at our charity to find her in case there is any important news we might need to pass along from Glenville. You take care now, Darren. Good to see you again."

CHAPTER 19

JOE RETURNS TO GLENVILLE

I picked up Joe at the airport in Indianapolis on Tuesday morning and couldn't wait to hear the latest news about his health. "What's the word from the doctors?"

He didn't say anything at first. He just stared ahead and then heaved a heavy sigh. "Still a lot of questions that need answers, but there are some possibilities out there that don't seem very attractive to me."

"What's that mean? What about the tremors in your leg?" I didn't have any hesitation about pumping Joe for information. We had always been like that—sharing everything in our lives without any effort to keep anything private. Over the years I had heard more than I ever needed to know about kidney stones, catheters, and hernias. Likewise, he patiently listened to my multiple accounts of knee surgeries and minor setbacks. Nothing was off the table as far as I was concerned. But, I now wondered if Joe would be hesitant to share information if it was truly life-threatening. We had never reached that point before as brothers. Up to this point we were still invincible.

After a long pause, he quietly said, "It might be cancer."

I didn't say anything, but kept stealing glances at him as I tried to stay focused on my driving. He just stared straight ahead.

"What's that mean—it 'might' be cancer?"

"It means that I have a small lesion in my brain that is creating pressure, which in turn is causing some neurological issues for me, like the tremors in my leg. It's like I'm having a mini-seizure of sorts. And that's not all. The hits just keep on coming. I apparently have some other 'hot spots' that look suspicious in my lungs and my groin area. Might be cancer; might not be. Doctors don't seem to like to use the 'cancer' word unless they are absolutely certain. I can tell you that they called all this stuff everything but cancer and it still sounded to me like they were talking about cancer."

I just tried to stay focused on the process without thinking too much about what all this meant. "What's next? How do they determine if it's cancer? How do they treat it?"

"All very good questions, my brother. I wish I had more answers—for you and for me. Right now I'm taking medicine to reduce the swelling in the brain. That could take care of the leg tremors if it works. They took a different kind of body scan and those results might give us more information about the 'hot spots.' If they can't figure out what's going on, then it looks like they'll have to do a biopsy on the tumor or maybe even take it completely out of there. One way or another, I may eventually be headed for a craniotomy. Never even said that word before this happened. Never really knew what it meant exactly. I do now. And I'm not real thrilled about it."

I was really having a hard time staying focused on driving, but at the same time it was good that I had to keep looking straight ahead. If I looked at Joe I think I would have lost it. As it was, I was blinking back tears in my eyes and hoping they wouldn't start running down my cheeks so he could see. He didn't need to be worried about his brother along with everything else. "So, what the hell are you doing here instead of being home where you can get the right medical attention?"

"Another very good question. I am here, little brother, to assist you in completing this task for Uncle Shorty. We may have to step up the pace a bit. Remember when thirty days seemed like an unreasonably short period of time to get this done? Seems a little long to me right now. Look, the doctors said the swelling was minor at this point and they were optimistic the medicine would work and the tremors would stop. If it doesn't work, then I will be heading back to Maryland and you're on your own. We won't know the results of the other tests for a few days and even then I might just be taking more medicine, which I can do just as well here."

"What about Carol? Doesn't she want you home?" I couldn't imagine Joe's wife not wanting him to be with her and to be closer to his own doctors in case something happened.

Joe quietly laughed. "Yeah, that was an interesting discussion. Carol is a very pragmatic woman. She knows how important this business with Uncle Shorty is to me and she knows I will be going crazy sitting at home while you're out here working on this alone. She decided she didn't want a crazy man at home and that I would be better off staying busy rather than dwelling on something that we had no control over. I promised her that if my symptoms changed at all, I'd be on the first plane home. And I'll promise you the same thing. The doctors were okay with that plan for now."

I finally broke the silence. "How are you doing?"

Joe looked over at me. I'm not sure if he could see the streaks down my face. "I'm okay for now. You know I've always been a glass-half-full kind of guy, so I'm going to assume the best for now." He paused for a minute. "We have a long way to go with lots and lots of treatments available at whatever stages I may have to go through. I've got all the insurance in the world and I'll just take it one day at a time. For now, we don't know that much so I'm not going to dwell on it. In the unlikely event that I suddenly find out I have an advanced stage of cancer, then I expect that I'll have a very different attitude. One day at a time. Check with me later. For now, let's go put Uncle Shorty's money into the right places."

I swallowed hard and just kept looking forward at the road, blinking rapidly to keep the tears in check. I had this sickening feeling that I might lose my brother and I knew I could be overwhelmed with emotion if I focused too much on his situation. I studied every sign along the road and focused on the cars ahead.

Let's just get through today and then we'll see about tomorrow. One day at a time.

* * *

To quickly change the mood in the car I decided to fill Joe in on my visit from Lonnie McDaniel. I told Joe about Lonnie's physical description, how he admitted to killing Blackie, his demand for money, and his threats against Beth and me.

Joe was quiet for a few minutes and then started in. "Well, let's first dismiss that stuff about Beth. That was just an idle threat since he knew it would get to you. The guy is not going out to California to threaten your wife. He has both of us right here. What more does he need? Besides, he probably just got that information off of Facebook. I've seen the picture of Beth and the dog on there and I wouldn't doubt that she mentioned something about daily walks. What, did you think he's got someone camped outside your house right now? Don't give this guy too much credit."

Good point. And it's true that all I could picture was some creep up on the street from our house waiting for Beth to head out for her morning walk. I knew those thoughts were illogical, but I just couldn't shake them. "Hell, Joe, I've never been threatened like this before. The guy really got to me. Even though he presented a very civil exterior, I could see a temper just seething beneath the surface and a stare that looked right through me. I'm not saying that I believe he would kill someone, but I sure believe that some physical abuse is definitely on his agenda if he doesn't get his way. I suspect he'd really enjoy it even if it didn't get the results he wanted."

"Well," Joe commented with mock sincerity. "Let's just be thankful that he picked you instead of me. You're a younger man and can probably handle a severe beating better than me. Besides, he's probably afraid of my bad-ass reputation."

I laughed. "Thanks for your concern. Wait until you see this guy's face. He has that 1,000-yard stare that soldiers in war talk about. It's like the life has been sucked out of him. Somehow I don't think he's afraid of you . . . or anyone else on this earth. He might be afraid of the demons in his head, but that's about it."

Joe then stated the obvious. "We need to go to the police. We can't handle McDaniel on our own and we can't let him distract us from what we came here to do. Maybe he has some outstanding warrants. At the very least, he did make a threat against you. I'm not sure if that would hold up by police standards, but it's a start."

Taking our concerns to the police was certainly the next logical step. That is, except for the fact that we were talking about the Glenville Police Department. First, I'm pretty sure that Joe and I had both just insulted the police chief last week and we know the guy carries a grudge. Second, my history with the Glenville Police goes back to a time over forty years ago and it doesn't exactly inspire confidence. Granted, that was another lifetime and I need to move on, but some images are hard to shake.

* * *

In the summer of 1969 I had just graduated from high school and needed a summer job for some spending money before heading off to college in the fall. Instead of actually finding a real job, I joined some other slackers and formed our own pseudo-corporation called Operation Manpower. The brain trust consisted of my core group of friends at the time—Barton (eventually Youth Foundation mentor), Harkins (future assistant superintendent), and Rick Cole. Cole was a smart guy, class president, one of the state's best distance runners, and the recipient of a scholarship to Harvard. Not exactly your typical small-town Hoosier kid. Despite his numerous achievements, deep down he was just as lazy and immature as the rest of us. We turned down jobs if they interfered with planned social activities—like lying around and watching an old movie in the middle of the day.

We put out flyers all over town announcing that we would do any and all odd jobs—painting, mowing, car washing, house cleaning, baby-sitting, house-sitting, and anything else a prospective employer could imagine. We eventually did all of the above at one time or another including a two-week stint digging out a crawl space under the house of a rich guy who clearly had more money than common sense. We never were sure why he wanted the space, but we didn't care since he paid good money. We celebrated the end of that job with a case of beer consumed in the crowded confines of our archeological dig.

Harkins had an uncle on the police force, so he approached the guy with a proposal for keeping the police cars nice and clean all summer. The plan was for Operation Manpower to come down to the station once a week to thoroughly wash the exterior and clean out the interior of the six squad cars. We would do this at the shift change so we could clean some of the cars going out and others just coming in off a shift. It was a sweet deal and it got the officers out of cleaning their own cars. At the risk of abusing a stereotype, I do know the officers thought the task of cleaning was beneath them and I'm sure that getting all those donut sprinkles out of the seat cushions was difficult. Stereotypes exist for a reason.

One week the water had been shut off to the police station due to a water-line repair up on the street. We arrived for our car washing duties and were informed that we couldn't accomplish the job. Cole, being the smart one in the group with high credibility due to his Harvard acceptance, suggested to the dispatcher, Sargent Thomas, that we just run the cars to a self-service car wash on the other side of town. The sargent hesitated a minute and just looked at us. You could tell he was gauging whether he could trust us. He did. He shouldn't have. He tossed us the keys to two cars and told us to have them back in less than an hour. "No longer than an hour. Straight there and straight back here," he warned. What was he thinking?

Sometimes the definition of "straight" can get lost in translation. For some it might mean to take the shortest route to and from your destination. Others might feel that an alternate route is more suitable as long as it still takes approximately the same amount of time. The employees of Operation Manpower defined "straight" as the quickest route out of town where we could open up those powerful V8 engines on a straight, empty country road to see how fast they would go! I can attest that hitting a hundred and twenty miles per hour was absolutely no problem at all. Barton and Harkins did the driving; Cole and I handled the sirens, lights, and screaming. It was exhilarating! What a rush!

We eventually turned around in some farmer's gravel drive-way and proceeded to race back again to the outskirts of town. We killed the siren and lights and brought our speed down to normal as we then turned into the driveway of one of the first houses off of Maxwell Road. Barton was driving the lead car so Harkins just followed. The house belonged to Jake Hogan, the next big deal in Glenville athletics. He was the quarterback and point guard who thought he could make everyone forget about our graduating class of truly superior athletes. Hogan believed he was special and treated everyone around him as inferior. He was the epitome of what Barton hated in high school jocks.

So, we did what seemed perfectly normal to us in our temporary duties as officers of the peace. We blasted the siren, flashed the lights, and got on the bullhorn.

"Jake Hogan, this is the Glenville Police Department. Come out with your hands up!" No movement from within the house.

Maybe no one was home. A couple of additional blasts from the siren did the trick.

"Come out with your hands up or this will not go well for you!" Out comes Hogan with his hands in the air and an absolute look of terror on his face. He must have seen his entire high school athletic career going down the drain. We were howling inside the cars, but kept the windows up so Hogan couldn't hear us.

But suddenly we knew our little escapade had gone too far. Mr. and Mrs. Hogan slowly walked out the front door with their hands in the air and a look of astonishment on their faces. Their appearance quickly turned to anger as they moved forward and got close enough to see through the front windshield of Barton's car.

While Harkins hit reverse on his car, Barton made one last effort to minimize the damage.

He grabbed the bullhorn and stammered, "Uhhh, our mistake. Wrong address. Everybody—as you were!" He hit reverse and we raced away, hoping that at least the Hogan family couldn't actually make out the identities of the misdirected officers.

We then immediately went to the car wash, carried out our cleaning duties with eight hands moving at synchronized high speed, and carefully drove back to the police station. On the way, an elderly woman spotted the police cars and came out on the curb to wave us down—presumably for some sort of an emergency. I just waved to her from my shotgun seat and smiled, hoping that she wouldn't think me too callous. She looked at me. I looked at her. She seemed quite distraught, but we were under orders to go straight to the police station.

We parked at the headquarters and casually went up to the dispatcher's desk and dropped off the two sets of keys. "Everything okay?" asked Sargent Thomas.

"Just fine. No problems."

"You need some reimbursement from the pay machines at the car wash?"

Cole looked relieved and pleased. "Well, yes, that would be real good. Thank you."

The Sargent rose from his chair, red in the face. "You can thank me because I'm not going to report this little incident to anyone else around here. You can thank me because I convinced Mr. Hogan that nothing like this will ever happen again. And you can thank me because I'm not telling your parents about your little prank. Now get out of here and keep your mouths shut about this unless you want to come back and spend a little time in our facility to learn your lesson. Do you understand?"

"Yes, sir. We understand perfectly. Thank you, sir. Thank you!" In an incredible gesture of hope and optimism, Cole paused at the door, "Does this mean you won't be needing us next week?"

Sargent Thomas just stared at him. "I'll take that as a 'no' then," Cole conceded. We were out of the building and into our car before the door to the police station closed after us. Not a word was spoken as we drove for about a mile. Then Barton simply said, "And thank you, Sargent Thomas, for not having a clue about our drag racing and passing up little old ladies in distress. Thank you. Thank you." The car rocked with laughter.

* * *

And now you know why it's hard for me to think very seriously about the capabilities of the Glenville Police Department. Any department that would trust their police cars to four eighteen-year-old kids is in serious need of a new operations manual. But, again, that was over forty years ago and, as they say, there's a new police chief in town. And he's a bully. And he carries a grudge. Other than that, I think our meeting should go quite well and the Police Department will be a tremendous help to us.

CHAPTER 20

THE POLICE DEPARTMENT

At 2:00 p.m. Joe and I pulled into the parking lot of the government center where the police headquarters were located. I had to admit that it was a lot nicer than the little shack they occupied in the 1960s where I washed police cars out back. I had called ahead and made sure that Chief Hagman would be available to hear the concerns of one of Glenville's former residents who had been threatened by a local citizen. We entered the lobby and were immediately confronted by a bulletproof window with a speaker built into it and a guy in uniform sitting behind the glass. I'm pretty sure the cops back in the old facility didn't have bulletproof glass separating them from the public. I'm not sure it was even invented back then.

"We're here to see Chief Hagman. Darren and Joe Kelly. He's expecting us."

He looked us over and waived toward a row of empty chairs on the other side of the lobby. "Have a seat over there and I'll let the chief know you're here." Of course we'd have to wait. This was Hagman's turf and he would make sure that we knew we were just visitors here. He'd probably even remind us that he held the keys to the jail cells in case we wanted to question his wisdom in any way again. I wasn't here to question him. I wanted his help. I just wasn't sure he could really offer any help.

We spent the fifteen-minute wait guessing where the hidden camera was located that allowed Hagman to watch us while gloating about the enormous amount of power he held over mere citizens. Joe was pretty certain he saw the eye move in a photograph of one of the former police chiefs. The picture of the Indiana governor also stared at us, and I cast my vote for his cuff link that was placed just a little too carefully across his desk facing in my direction.

A buzzer sounded and the heavy door opened to the inner sanctum. The chief paused inside the door and waved us in. We went down the hall and entered a comfortable office that had all the signs that this was the place Chief Hagman claimed as his personal territory when he was at work. It actually was a pretty nice space with a minimum of the obligatory smile and handshake photos. Instead, the walls were covered with family photos and oil paintings depicting a variety of Indiana landscapes ranging from fall foliage to summer cornfields to meandering streams in heavily wooded areas.

Joe was drawn to the artwork. "These are really good. Is it a local artist?"

Hagman just shrugged. "I guess you could say that. The artist is my wife. I agree—she's very good."

Okay. I didn't see that one coming. Hagman didn't exactly strike me as the art appreciation type and the marriage of an artist and a cop seemed just a little unusual. My open mouth must have given away my thoughts.

"What's the matter, Kelly? You didn't think I was the artsy type?"

"In a word—no. That one caught me by surprise. I figured you might have vintage handguns lying around and maybe some photos of dead criminals, but I wasn't expecting beautiful artwork."

Hagman laughed. "Yeah, I know. That one surprises everybody. My wife started painting when she was in high school. She took lessons and immersed herself in it and just got better and better at it. She can't paint fast enough now. People are lined up all over Indiana to buy her paintings before they're done. Hell, I could probably retire on her income alone, but I'm having too much fun playing police chief." He offered that last line with an impish grin and a wink. This was a side of Hagman that I had not expected.

The chief could still see that I was puzzled by his attitude. "Kelly, you're just dealing in too many stereotypes. Now, I bet you have this image of me based on the opinions of some small-minded people in town that I'm a real hard-ass and that I hold a grudge."

"Don't forget 'bully' as well," I offered.

"Yeah, I heard that one, too. And it is true that as a younger man I was all of those things. I'm a grandfather now. That will give you a different perspective in a hurry. Hell, I've mellowed so much I almost make myself sick. I give people the benefit of the doubt all the time and every now and then I even let people off with warnings. That's why I'm being so nice to you boys right now. You both shot me down a little in that meeting, but I get it. You figure the Police Department is doing okay and others might need that money more than me." He paused and shrugged his shoulders. "You're probably right. My department could use the money and it would help the community in the long run. However, we'll get along without it if that's the way it works out."

Joe jumped in. "Then why did you make that scene at the end of the meeting, barking about how your budget would solve real problems? That looked like a guy who was used to bullying his colleagues."

Hagman laughed. "Yeah, I thought that was a pretty good line—'fighting crime instead of building restrooms.' It had a nice ring to it. Hell, I used to push those people around so much that now I just let go with one of those lines for the fun of it. I'm just trying to stay in practice to make sure no one thinks I've gone soft. That gal, Ralston, from the Parks Department is real good at what she does. Of course, I'd never tell her that. She's right about how she could make Glenville a model community for open spaces where families could gather. We also need the recreation facilities she talked about. She's pretty sharp. She'd make good use of your money and she's probably not going to get any of that stuff done without it."

I saw Hagman in a completely different light and I wasn't quite sure what to make of it. On one hand I respected John Bourke's assessment of people in town and he certainly didn't seem to think Hagman had changed appreciably. However, maybe Bourke's role as editor had put him at odds with Hagman over the years and he couldn't shake his past perceptions of the man. On the other hand, maybe Hagman was just a smart guy who was putting on a show for us. It was hard to say.

"Why are you guys here?" Hagman asked. "I planned to get that budget over to you in the next day or two."

I jumped right in. "Do you know Lonnie McDaniel?"

The chief laughed. "Do I know Lonnie? Do you mean Glenville's most notorious career criminal? Of course I know Lonnie McDaniel!"

"Well, Lonnie paid me a visit last night at Applebee's and threatened me with bodily harm if we didn't make a sizeable donation to his personal charity with Mr. Hazelton's estate money."

The chief quit smiling at that point. "He actually threatened you? He used words like 'I'll cut off your fingers' or 'I'll take a baseball bat to your knees?' I only use those examples because that's the kind of thing Lonnie likes to do to people . . . and animals."

"Gee, that's comforting. No, he didn't come right out and say anything like that. He just said we'd have to meet again in a private place if I ignored him and then he asked if Joe could administer the estate if I were to become 'incapacitated' in some way. He even mentioned my wife in a threatening way, but without saying anything specific about what he might do to her."

Hagman smiled just a little. "Yeah, that's Lonnie. He's no dummy. The boy can choose his words carefully when he's not caught up in some sort of rage. We've underestimated him too many times over the years and come out on the short end of the deal. For the most part, he knows how to stay just one step away from a jail cell."

I was incredulous. "You mean this psychopath has never done any serious jail time? This guy was terrorizing the town back when we were kids!"

The chief responded, "I'm not saying he hasn't done some jail time, but he's been out more than he's been in. Hell, he apparently spent time in military confinement when they caught him abusing some local villagers in Vietnam during his second tour over there. I guess he messed up some old men and women pretty bad and spent a couple of years in a military lock-up before they dishonorably discharged him.

Then he ended up in Indianapolis and was in and out of jail for fairly small stuff like burglaries and an occasional robbery where he would beat the crap out of someone in the process. He finally hurt someone bad enough to get five years up in Michigan City. When he was close to getting out, he went after another prisoner with a homemade weapon and damn near killed the guy. That got him another seven years."

"How long has he been back in Glenville?" I asked.

"Oh, probably about five years I'd guess. As far as I know, he went back to Indianapolis after prison, but eventually made his way back here. He moved into an old farmhouse way out west of town and generally only shows up in town to buy supplies or to get drunk at JJ's Tavern out there off of South County Road. It's just an old dive bar where only serious derelicts would ever go. Lonnie fits right in."

"So, you're telling me that he's kept his nose clean for the last five years here in Glenville? That's hard to believe with a guy like him."

"Oh, I didn't say that," Hagman responded quickly. "It's just that he hasn't done enough to get caught so I could throw him in jail for a while. We picked him up on a couple of drunk and disorderly charges, but that's about it. He allegedly cut up a guy with his knife out at JJ's one night. We responded to an anonymous call, but by the time we got there the victim was gone and no one was talking any longer. There was plenty of blood around, though. Must have really sliced the guy up judging by the amount of blood.

"We had always heard that Lonnie was partial to carving on people and animals with his knife. He's a sick bastard. We also had a couple of arson calls where people accused McDaniel of threatening them a couple of days before the fires happened. There were never any other witnesses and no evidence of Lonnie ever being in the area. I don't doubt that he set the fires, but I couldn't prove a thing."

Joe said what we were all three thinking, "Sounds like we should be taking Lonnie's threat seriously."

That observation hung in the air for a minute before the chief admitted, "There isn't a whole lot I can do to protect you, unfortunately." I suddenly had a flashback to four teenage boys racing down a country road in two police cars.

Hagman continued, "I can make sure that we try to keep an eye on Lonnie and I can follow your movements when you alert me to where you'll be. However, we don't have enough manpower to keep Lonnie in sight all the time and we might not be able to follow you if something comes up that requires all units to respond elsewhere. The only good news is that you'll be done with this estate business in a couple of weeks and gone from Glenville. We don't have to stay on high alert for long so we can put some extra manpower on for the short term."

"Chief, I appreciate your help, though I have to admit that I'm more than a little worried about this psycho coming after me. I saw the look in his eyes and it was beyond scary."

Joe quickly offered, "Don't you worry little brother. I'll protect you."

I stared at Joe until he busted out laughing. "Yeah, I guess that doesn't give you much comfort, does it? Hell, if you have to depend on me to protect you, then you better be making your funeral arrangements." I'm sure Joe had never been in a fight his entire adult life and only flirted with the notion as a kid.

Once Phil Wheatley, another twelve-year-old that weighed roughly a hundred pounds more than Joe, attacked him right in front of our house. My brother managed to grab the guy in a headlock and hold on for dear life. This was a technique he had perfected on me over the years. Fatso flailed around and tried to punch Joe but he couldn't get in a clean shot. My mother came out of the house and just yelled at Joe, "Don't you give up, Joseph!"

Joe just held on since he knew he'd be dead the minute he let go. After fifteen minutes, Fatso had enough and promised he wouldn't retaliate if Joe would let him go. Joe dropped the headlock and backed away cautiously— ready to run if necessary. Fatso was tired and just shook his head and lumbered away.

"Joe, somehow I don't think your legendary headlock technique will work on McDaniel."

"Yeah, maybe not. Chief, how about you deputize me and issue me a sidearm so I can be of assistance to my little brother?"

Hagman rolled his eyes. "First, this isn't the Wild West in the 1800s. We don't deputize people, organize lynch mobs, or refer to our weapons as sidearms. Second, the likelihood of you shooting yourself is far greater than the likelihood of you intentionally shooting McDaniel. Thank you for your interest in law enforcement, but I think I'll deny your request."

"Mighty short-sighted of you, Chief. I could have made the Glenville Police force proud when I came to the rescue and planted some hot lead in McDaniel just as he was about to cut off Darren's hand with a chainsaw."

"I'm sure I will forever regret passing on the opportunity to witness your fantasy in its full glory." Hagman didn't crack a smile. "Is it hard being wrong about most things in your life?" This time he smiled.

Joe nonchalantly replied, "I try not to be too hard on myself."

"Okay, gents. How about we focus on the realities at hand? Chief, I'll keep you posted on my plans and I'll assume you'll do your best to watch out for Lonnie. I can't let this guy get in the way of what we're doing and he might just be bluffing for kicks anyway, right?"

Hagman nodded, "Lonnie has been known to make idle threats. Then again, he's been known to follow up on some of them."

That admission didn't help my state of mind. Joe and I got up and we each shook Hagman's hand. The gesture seemed to acknowledge that we were now all in this deal together. I had come to think more highly of the chief during our visit and I suspected he really would do all that he could to protect me. The problem was that there was little that he realistically could do. There was no way to keep Lonnie under surveillance full time and I would likely be at risk if he truly wanted to send me another message.

CHAPTER 21

GET ME TO THE CHURCH ON TIME

The next morning Joe and I had a meeting set up with many of the church leaders in town to talk about their various community outreach programs. Again, John Bourke had helped us with tracking down the right contacts and paving the way for a meeting. We really didn't know how to handle this category of service provider. It seemed that they would all have their own agendas and their own source of funding through their church structures and parishioners. The list of churches in Glenville seemed huge compared to the number of citizens. There were lots of options to punch your ticket to heaven. The trick was picking the right one.

We found thirty-eight separate churches listed that included the usual suspects of Catholics, Methodists, Presbyterians, Lutherans, Baptists, Quakers, and Seventh Day Adventists. Other church names not quite so familiar to me included Church of the Nazarene, Pentecostal, Wesleyan, Church of God, Apostolic, and your basic Bible Church. An additional small list sounded more like they belonged in Roswell, New Mexico. I didn't see a place for Buddhists or Jews. Must not be a big demand in Glenville.

We decided to approach this issue with an attitude of "we don't care exactly what you believe in as long as you are doing some worthy outreach to help those in need." My brother and I do not come from a strong religious upbringing, though Joe became attached to the Methodist Church later in life. In fact, I was surprised to learn how important the church and his relationship to other church members had become to him over the years. He was very active in community service events and in fundraising for church programs and improvements. He seldom talked about it with me since he knew that I had never reached out in that direction myself. When he once briefly mentioned the enjoyment he and Carol experienced in their church, he quickly acknowledged, "Don't worry, I'm not going to start working on you to do the same as me."

Our father was an Irish Catholic. Our mother was raised in the Lutheran Church. We somehow attended the Presbyterian Church as a default compromise. Maybe it was the closest to our house. Actually, to say that we attended the church was a bit of a stretch. Our parents didn't attend church except for the token Easter or Christmas service. They had a serious break from their religious practices shortly before moving to Indiana after they lost my sister to cancer (retinoblastoma) at the tragically young age of seven years old. She had lost vision in both eyes at age two and lived another five years undergoing treatments that ultimately failed to stop the cancer. Joe remembers her, but I was too young.

The loss devastated my parents. At a time where their faith might have provided comfort, it apparently drove a wedge between them. It's hard for me to understand, but they both somehow felt that the absence of a unified faith between them contributed to the final outcome of the tragedy. Each blamed the other's lack of faith—or more accurately the lack of the "right" faith. Instead of seeking comfort in church, my mother pragmatically threw herself into volunteer work with the Glenville Cancer Society and ultimately became its chairman, providing a vital service to the community. I only fully understood their struggles with organized religion later in life after my father died and my mother, in failing health, attempted to clarify some of her religious beliefs in the hope that I might give faith "a second look."

Joe and I did attend church with our parents on those infrequent Easter and Christmas services when they felt sufficiently motivated by guilt. As hypocritical as it was to attend only on those few occasions, we simply followed our parents' lead. Somehow I guess it filled a void for them, but apparently it wasn't fulfilling enough to repeat the experience throughout the year. We even went to youth bible study classes that were held prior to the regular worship service on Sundays. Actually, when I say we "went to" the classes, I mean we "arrived" at the sessions and only attended when all other options failed.

Our typical Sunday experience was to be dropped off by one parent or the other in front of the church for the hour-long bible study class. Following the class, the drill was for the Kelly brothers to walk around the corner away from the church parking lot to be retrieved in a stealth fashion by our parents so as to avoid the accusatory gaze of incoming churchgoers who might wonder why the family wasn't attending the service. This all seemed perfectly normal to Joe and me.

The reality is that the Kelly brothers seldom made it to the bible study class anyway. Joe had other plans. Once we were dropped off at the front door to the church, we waited and waved goodbye to our mother or father as the car pulled away. When the car turned the corner out of sight, Joe and I made a straight line to the Glenville Ice Cream Company store where the elderly owner, Mr. Townsend, was busy getting his store ready for business later that day. In fact, one of his first customers was the Presbyterian Church, since they offered ice cream in the Fellowship Hall every Sunday after service. He didn't open to the public until 11:00 a.m., but Joe and I showed up regularly just after 9:00 a.m. and stared through the window until he let us in. The first time he wasn't sure what to make of these two boys wearing their Sunday best standing outside his store. Instead of making up a story, we uncharacteristically opted for the truth.

"We ditched the bible study class and thought we might see if you'd let us try some of your ice cream," Joe said.

Mr. Townsend just laughed and laughed. "You just waved goodbye to your parents and thought you could sit here and eat ice cream instead of learning about Jesus?"

The guy was laughing, but we weren't sure which way this deal was going to go for us. He might have been a religious man who couldn't let these boys get away with such sacrilegious behavior. Joe didn't hide from the truth. "Yes, sir, that's pretty much what we thought."

Mr. Townsend laughed some more. Apparently, he wasn't much of a church-going fellow himself and he thought our choice of ice cream over the teachings of the bible was hilarious. He waved us in and offered us anything we wanted. After that first Sunday, it was a very rare occasion when our faces weren't plastered to the Glenville Ice Cream Company store window by approximately 9:02 a.m. We never paid for any ice cream and we had some really good talks with Mr. Townsend over the course of about three months. You might say it was somewhat of a spiritual experience. Other people seem to apply that term liberally to everyday occurrences, so why not us? We eventually got busted, as all kids do when they brag about their exploits, but our parents gave up on making us go to church or bible study. Mission accomplished.

* * *

So, here we were again at the Presbyterian Church in Glenville, Indiana. We chose the location for the meeting just for nostalgia purposes and we thought it would be funny since the Presbyterian minister would likely think he had an inside track on our funding once he learned we attended church there. He would be sorely disappointed if he knew the real story. The group drifted in one by one around 10:00 a.m. They gazed around the place taking in the sights and smells as if for the first time. I got the impression that there wasn't much cross-pollination in Glenville's religious beehive.

We greeted each one and I experienced the most professional series of handshakes I had ever encountered. These people had perfected the art of the handshake through their Sunday morning rituals. They all looked me in the eye and smiled their warmest smile, gave me the hearty one pump of the clasped hands, touched my arm gently with the other hand, and then just held it there for one last second to once again convey their sincerity. It was an impressive byproduct of their trade.

Joe and I once again rolled out our road show with the usual description. This time I added my caveat about not being interested in favoring one church over another for any reason other than their community outreach. The Baptist minister quickly raised his hand. Joe seized the opportunity to call on him by saying, "Yes, sir, what would you like to confess?" I dropped my head. The minister looked confused. Joe just stared at him with an open expression of anticipation.

"I don't have anything to confess. I just have a question."

"Very good," said Joe. "Let's hear your question." I was starting to get the feeling that Joe was going to run this meeting like a show from Dr. Phil.

"I was just wondering what your religious backgrounds were and do you now regularly attend a church? That might help us understand your perspective a little better."

Joe didn't hesitate. "I regularly attend Saint Mattress of the Springs on Sunday mornings. It's non-denominational."

I quickly added, " I'm partial to the Church of the Holy Comforter."

The Methodist representative didn't miss a beat. "And I'm sure you both enjoy listening to Reverend Sheets with the able assistance of Deacon Pillow."

Joe slammed his open hand down on the table and proclaimed, "I like this man! He gets it! Darren, let's give him all the money!" Joe liked to celebrate an appreciation of sophomoric humor.

Everyone laughed, but it was clear that some of them had no idea about what had just transpired. Joe once again clarified. "You folks don't need to know how we practice our religion or if we practice one at all. And we don't care how you go about giving comfort to your congregations. We just want to figure out if there is a way to help you fund your outreach efforts that touch the lives of poor or needy people in this community. Maybe that won't work and you should just all continue doing whatever you do in your own way. We don't know. We just came here to see if there are any possibilities."

And that was the truth. Joe and I really didn't know how to handle this group and whether there was any way to coordinate their community efforts. We decided to approach it like any other business or committee meeting that we'd ever been in professionally. We just got the participants to focus on the greater goal and to leave their personal agendas behind as much as possible. We started to identify what they had in common and tossed aside their differences. After about two hours of slogging through some great ideas, we had settled on some common ground that seemed to warrant further examination.

There were families in Glenville who needed help and the churches had volunteers who could assist. These church organizations were already providing various forms of counseling, job training, help for the elderly, emergency services, and transitional housing. I was impressed at least with their attempts to help, not knowing if their efforts ultimately made a difference.

Joe and I decided that was as far as we would likely get that day and thanked everyone for participating. It seemed apparent to us that our funding could be helpful to this group, but the mechanics of how that could be done were still pretty fuzzy. Clearly, church outreach programs are intended to help the needy, but each has its own agenda to steer new members to their own particular church. That type of inherent bias could make a cooperative effort challenging. In talking afterwards, we both noticed a few of the church leaders who appeared to have the necessary skills to work together in forming a consensus.

The Methodist minister, Reverend Maxwell, a bright guy with a sense of humor, was on our radar. The Lutheran reverend took a very diplomatic but no-nonsense approach to the nutcase from Our Lady of the Green Valley who wanted to stage a love-in down at Glenville Park at midnight. She would have fit in nicely in California. Apparently, the Lutherans favor work over dancing in the park. We approved in this particular case. The Catholic priest seemed to have the right stuff. He completely ignored a snide remark about his church's work with children and was effusive in his praise for others' efforts. He was a fairly young guy with a lot of enthusiasm for the community.

As we left the church and headed to our car, I asked Joe what he was thinking. He looked back at the Presbyterian Church and then looked across the street where the Glenville Ice Cream Company once stood. "I'm thinking that I need some chocolate-chip ice cream. Let's go find some."

CHAPTER 22

STATE HIGHWAY INSPECTORS AND THE JEWEL TEA MAN

We lined up two more meetings for the next day—one with an outfit that helped senior citizens in town and another with the Glenville Boys and Girls Club. We eventually made our way back to Applebee's to enjoy the cocktail hour and dinner, visit with Mandy, and review the day's events while looking ahead to what still needed our attention.

Mandy seemed to be particularly perky following her brief time off from work. "Well, if it isn't my two favorite out-of-town customers!"

"That's really special, Mandy," Joe said with dripping sarcasm. "How many other visitors from out of town come back day after day to Applebee's?"

"Well, I'll have to think about that, but whatever that huge number might be, you two gentlemen are my favorites in that category."

We settled in at the bar in our usual spots and chatted with Mandy while she poured a beer for me and gave Joe a Coke. He had decided that his infrequent attempts at drinking alcohol were really just a waste of time. He didn't care for the taste and admitted to me that mixing alcohol with his medicine just didn't seem like a good idea. It was hard to argue with that logic. Mandy was excited that one of her teenage nephews had landed a decent job for the upcoming summer. Apparently part-time jobs were scarce for teenagers and full-time work was nearly non-existent for high school graduates who wanted to stay in town.

As a result of that discussion, Joe and I were prompted to reminisce about some of our summer jobs in Glenville. Much had changed in the job market. Kids of our age never seemed to have too much trouble finding jobs. Joe and I didn't always stay with them for long, but there always seemed to be another waiting around the corner. Mandy seemed to get a kick out of our stories since she kept working her way back to our side of the bar, prompting us for more. I'm pretty sure she thought we were lying most of the time.

Of course, Joe and I had both worked for the State Highway at some point. That's where he met the Booker Brothers and first heard the line that stuck with him for life, "Son, you need to slow down." Joe's most notable job with the State Highway came after his first year of college. Because he was a "college boy," he was entrusted with one of the ancient yellow pick-ups and assigned the duty of "small projects concrete inspector." That meant that Joe Kelly, probably only nineteen years old at the time, was the guy who would ensure that the concrete used in small state-funded jobs passed the state requirements. That included small bridges scattered around central Indiana built in the late 1960s. Older employees handled the large projects. Joe performed what's called a slump test on the mix. Scary thought, huh?

Mandy thought so. "You mean when I drive over a bridge in this county, I can be comforted knowing that some pimple-faced teenager was in charge of seeing that it will hold up when my car passes over it?"

Joe tried very hard to appear offended. "To the best of my knowledge, none of my little bridges had any catastrophic failures." Mandy was just a bit shrill in replying, "You've been gone for forty years! How would you know?"

"Good point, but I still stand by my assertion. However, you know when you drive over a small bridge out in the country and you get that little bump under your tires where the bridge meets the pavement?" Mandy nodded, "And some bumps are bigger than others?"

"Yeah, well, some of those bridges might have been mine. It took me a little while to get the testing just right and I might have read the results wrong a few times before I hit my stride. Some bridges may have settled a little more than anticipated."

Mandy looked at me, "Is that story true?"

"It is absolutely true and I have another one for you." I couldn't resist telling my State Highway story to Mandy since I felt I had learned a valuable lesson in ethics as a result of my efforts. My job came in the summer before my senior year in high school when I was assigned to the Brandywine Quarry operation. Truckloads of sand, gravel, and stones came out of this work site on the way to various state highway jobs.

Each load had to pass over a scale and be weighed so the state could be charged the proper amount by the quarry owner. My sole job was to sit in the shack adjacent to the scale, read the number registered as the total load weight, and then hand the driver half of the two-part official state inspection slip attesting to the declared weight. For eight hours a day, that's all I had to do.

No big surprise, I got bored real quick. Mrs. Evans, the wife of the quarry owner, checked in on me several times a day to see if I wanted something to drink or eat. She was a real nice lady. After about a week, I was nodding off in the booth between truck weigh-ins. She caught me in the act one day and asked me if I'd like to get some exercise working with her little ten-year-old boy to improve his basketball game. Their house was adjacent to the quarry and they had a nice blacktop basketball court out back. She said she'd cover my duties in the booth and issue the weigh slips for me.

Mandy jumped in. "So, let me get this straight. You're being paid by the state to be a watchdog over the quarry operations, but you opt to play basketball and let the quarry owner's wife be the watchdog instead?"

"Well, when you put it like that it doesn't sound quite as innocent as it really was. In fact, she was so nice that she had me meet her two daughters who were instructed to make sure that I had plenty to eat and drink while I was helping her son, Randall." Mandy rolled her eyes.

"These two young gals were only about twelve or thirteen. Rhonda and JoJo were their names. They were real sweet and obviously wanted to make an impression on this high school boy who suddenly showed up in their yard. Their specialty was baking pies—and I discovered during that summer that my specialty was eating pies. They'd just sit on the porch for hours watching me play basketball with their little brother. When I took a break, they had pie and iced tea waiting for me and they'd just giggle while I ate."

Mandy asked, "How long did this basketball-playing and pie-eating love fest last?"

I looked at her like she'd asked a stupid question. "Why, all summer, of course!" I never worked another day in the booth. I only got nervous once when I noticed Mrs. Evans in the house one day and wondered who was running the booth. It turned out that she just left the pad there for the drivers to complete and stamp. To this day I'd like to think that everybody acted honestly in that operation and no harm was done. I know I sure enjoyed myself; Randall became a better basketball player and the sisters went on to win several County Fair ribbons for their pies—no small thanks to my excellent feedback.

Joe and Mandy just stared at me. Joe asked, "So that's your ethics lesson that you took away from the experience? No harm, no foul?"

"No, of course not. As an older and wiser man, I realize that it was wrong for me to take the state's paycheck and neglect my duties. In fact, the state may have even incurred some excessive charges if Mrs. Evans was actually dishonest. However, my personal take on this is that sometimes you just have to trust in people, Joe, and I am full of good will and trust. My real ethical concern was whether I should have been charging her for those basketball lessons. I put in a lot of hours with that kid. That was probably a missed opportunity."

Joe just looked at me and shook his head. "You are so full of it."

"Yeah, I know, but that is a true story nonetheless."

* * *

Mandy drifted away to attend to other customers and probably because she could see the brothers needed a little personal space while they challenged each other's credibility. But when she came back she was ready for more. "Got any more stories about your incredible work ethic, boys?"

We had plenty. I started in. There was the time that I worked for the state highway as an "inspector" on an asphalt road crew. My job did not involve actually knowing anything about laying down asphalt; I was just assigned to walk along and account for how many hours the crew worked, how much material they used, and how many miles they covered in a day. I put it all in an official log and collected my paycheck.

Well, the contractor was supposed to have a flagman on the job to make sure traffic slowed down, but the guy quit the first day on the job. Since the contractor couldn't proceed without a flagman and I was just standing around all day, he convinced me to grab a flag and perform the duty. Thus, I collected one paycheck from the state and another from the contractor every week.

Mandy asked the obvious question. "And you thought that was okay for you to collect two paychecks?"

I looked at her thoughtfully. "Well, it did briefly occur to me that there might be a conflict of interest in there somewhere, but as a twenty-year-old kid I hadn't yet developed the well-tuned sense of ethics that I have now. So, no, I didn't really have a problem with it at the time. Of course, later in life I saw it as a great learning opportunity for which I am forever thankful."

Joe was smiling at Mandy as she just shook her head. "True story, Mandy. I saw both pay checks one time before he cashed them. I have to admit that I was proud of my little brother. Darren, tell her about your job as The Jewel Tea Man."

Mandy asked, "What's a Jewel Tea Man?"

Joe and I just shook our heads in mock disdain and pity. "God, you have led a deprived life, child," Joe solemnly observed. "If a man drove a big brown panel truck filled with household goods distributed by the Jewel Tea Company, then he naturally became a Jewel Tea Man. It was like a mini Walmart on wheels that would pull right up to your door."

Shifting into his very best radio voice, Joe educated Mandy. "The Jewel Tea Company started with just tea, spices, and coffee, but eventually branched out into other fine foods and necessary household items demanded by the enterprising and forward-thinking modern housewife." Joe smiled and continued in his normal voice. "If the driver didn't have what you wanted, he would take your order and then deliver it two weeks later when he worked his route back through your neighborhood. Think of it as the precursor to the Home Shopping Network."

I continued with the explanation. "Since I was a college boy home for the summer, I presumably had the necessary intelligence to handle the job. I was taught to show up at 6:00 a.m. to stock the truck for the day. Then I was given a map with all the locations where I should stop. The expectation was that I shouldn't stop selling until 5:00 p.m. when the husbands would start returning from work and it was time to get supper on the table."

Mandy sarcastically observed, "That sounds like a long work day for a young man with such a strong work ethic as yourself."

I ignored the implied criticism. "You're damn right it was a long day . . .and the third day I had a flat tire. But I always figured that this job could be a young man's dream. I had serious fantasies about showing up at a house where a young, beautiful, lonely housewife waited for her visit from the Jewel Tea Man every two weeks. She'd be wearing nothing but an apron and we'd sit down on her couch and I'd show her my collection of cosmetics and perfume while she showed me what it meant to be starved for affection."

Mandy laughed with an insensitivity that was not very attractive on her. "So, did you ever meet your fantasy housewife?"

"No, what I typically met was a haggard woman opening the front door with an old terry cloth robe hanging half-way open exposing a body that demonstrated the unyielding and devastating effects of gravity. There were always kids running around yelling and screaming. If I was real lucky, the woman would be sucking on a cigarette. That was the reality of The Jewel Tea Man."

"How long did you last?"

"Exactly one week. My parents were not pleased. However, I landed another job building swimming pools the next week where I learned the value of promising people a dream and then delivering a dose of reality. As you might expect, the Indiana swimming pool business had a short season. I learned from my boss that you got a signed contract, dug a hole in the ground, and then disappeared to dig another hole elsewhere as soon as possible. The goal was to get as many signed contracts as possible in the spring while intimating a beautiful summer of swimming ahead.

"People with a hole in their back yard typically didn't back out of a contract. We would then do our best to build out all those swimming pools—always responding to the owner that squawked the loudest and threatened to sue. Some got to swim that summer; others saw their pools finished just before the leaves started to drop."

I looked at Mandy and then admitted, "Plus, during this time I started having fantasies again about lonely young house-wives who would lie outside in their bikinis begging us to hurry up and finish the pool so we could all jump in together. That never happened either."

"You had a lot of fantasies as a young man, didn't you?"

"You have no idea how difficult it was to be a young guy with raging hormones and a complete inability to relate to the female species."

Mandy showed her very best sincere expression. "Oh, you poor thing. And I can see that you still struggle in relating to women." With that, she turned and went back to serving other customers.

"What did she mean by that?" I asked Joe.

* * *

Joe just shrugged and shifted gears. "Remember when I sold Collier's Encyclopedias?

Actually, I didn't remember that chapter in Joe's work career. Must not have lasted very long. "Let's hear it." I knew if Joe wanted to tell a story, then it probably had merit of some sort.

"It was the summer before my sophomore year in college and I saw a flyer about how to make big money selling ency-clopedias door to door. I showed up at the designated meeting place where other young guys like me were split up into groups of four and assigned a manager. My manager was a guy named Bruce Simmons. I later learned on our drive to my territory that he was a former meat cutter at Emgee Market. He was tall and skinny with greasy hair slicked back on the sides. The tobacco stains on his fingernails further enhanced his image.

"It appeared that the only skills necessary to become a bon-afide manager in the Collier's Encyclopedia organization was to sell twelve sets of encyclopedias and to own a fast car. Bruce drove a very respectable 1966 Buick Riviera. The car was necessary to get your four 'salesmen' to their designated selling areas scattered around a four-county territory in central Indiana. They would be dropped off in the morning and picked up late that afternoon."

At this point in Joe's story, Mandy came back over to our side of the bar. She had only been a short distance away and had apparently caught the part about selling encyclopedias. "So you were one of those guys knocking on doors and pestering house-wives, too? What kind of fantasies did you carry around?" She looked over at me with a smirk.

"Mandy," Joe quickly replied, "my only fantasy was to ed-ucate the young minds of America and make them better equipped intellectually to go out and further enhance the stature of this great nation. That's all. I preferred my housewives to be fully clothed with a checkbook in hand."

I couldn't believe I hadn't heard this story before. "How'd you do, Joe? With your line of bullshit, I'd think you'd be perfect for the job."

"Yes, little brother, I was indeed perfect for the job due to my inherent desire to help others and my innate ability to convince them of what was necessary to get ahead in life. All mothers want the very best for their children. My job was to convince them that their precious darlings would be left behind in a cesspool of the uneducated if they didn't have the advantage of the information contained in the Collier's Encyclopedia."

Joe was shifting into high gear now as he remembered his days on the cutting edge of providing an educational advantage to those who could afford it. "Bruce was very instructive. For three whole days of training we walked through wealthy neighborhoods as he pointed out the best homes for potential sales.

"Bruce would say, 'You first look for signs of yard apes, Kelly. Look for toys, swing sets, bikes—yard ape stuff. Make sure it's all in good shape and well cared for. That's a sign of parents who are motivated to give their kids the best. Those parents want their kids to have every advantage, including the advantage of the Collier's Encyclopedia collection.'"

Joe continued, "We would select a house and go up to give our pitch. Bruce would, of course, take the lead and sweet-talk the housewife for a bit. He'd then turn to me and introduce his assistant as a young man who was brought up in a 'Collier's Encyclopedia household. He is now a college student!' I'd give the lady my very best and most intelligent smile. Bruce would always ask, 'Wouldn't you like your children to grow up and go to college someday? Of course you would!' He'd then assure the worried mothers that the rich material inside the Collier's Encyclopedia would give their children every advantage to get ahead of the rest of the kids trying so desperately to get into a university."

Joe was smiling and seemed to be feeling quite nostalgic about the selling skills of the former Emgee Market butcher. "Bruce was good. He was very, very good. He'd close a deal and then push for more. 'But, wait, there's even more with this offer for just a slight upcharge.' In my three days of training, I saw him close five deals. The sales commissions were substantial since those books were grossly overpriced. As Bruce wisely told me, 'Kelly, we're not just selling books. We're selling dreams.' With my college-boy routine, I figured I'd be rolling in commissions before the summer was over."

"Why do I get the feeling your summer didn't work out that way?" I asked.

Joe ignored me. "By the third day I was ready to go out on my own and collect the commission. But when Bruce called into the home office late in the day he was told that he had to pick up another manager's salesman (as in a twenty-year-old kid) who was left stranded way over in Huntington, a full hour away. The kid needed to be taken home. The manager had dropped the kid off to work the territory and then got drunk in a bar and arrested for fighting. He was just another example of the quality management program at Collier's.

"Bruce was upset because he had a hot date that evening and didn't want to be late. We proceeded to turn a two-hour round trip into a one -hour version by pushing speed limits of a hundred twenty miles an hour. Bruce knew every speed trap on those county roads. He'd slow down just in time and then punch it so hard my head would snap back. I've never been so scared in my life. He was cussing a blue streak, chain-smoking, and blasting the radio.

"When he reached under his seat for a bottle of whiskey, I knew my days as a salesman for the Collier's Encyclopedia Company were numbered—one way or another! It was at that point that I made my peace with the Lord. I said, 'Lord, if you get me through this mess, I'm not coming back to this job and I won't be deceiving those nice housewives.' Well, the Lord must have been listening that day. We found the kid and made it home safely, fueled by Bruce's hormones and whiskey."

I didn't need to ask, but I did for Mandy's sake. "Did you go back to the job? That money must have been pretty enticing."

"No, I did not return the next day. They called the house and I just hung up. I had already made my deal with the Lord out there on that county road going a hundred twenty miles per hour with a crazy man. And that was not a deal that I was going to turn my back on."

Mandy looked at both of us. "I don't know which one of you is more full of it. Again, she turned away to attend to customers who I'm sure weren't nearly as interesting as the Kelly brothers.

Joe thoughtfully observed, "You know what her problem is, Darren?"

"She doesn't appreciate a good story?"

"No, she doesn't appreciate the fact that kids our age really did have lots of jobs back then."

"Of course, but we didn't know what the hell we were doing!"

"True. That's very true. And we were probably given more responsibility than we ever should have had. But we sure gained a lot of experience along the way, didn't we? You heard what Mandy said—jobs are pretty scarce for young people. Maybe there's something we could do about that."

I was intrigued, but confused. "I'm not sure I follow you. Do you want to hand out jobs with Uncle Shorty's money?"

"I'm not sure, but there might be a way to subsidize jobs for small employers or even create a kind of job corps program to train high school graduates in skills they could use while earning a paycheck at the same time. I really don't know. It just seems that there is a gap here that maybe we can fill."

"You're starting to sound like a socialist, Joe." My brother had been known to rant now and then about government programs that just hand money to people with no expectations in return.

"Well, it might sound that way," Joe admitted. "Then again, I might just be a capitalist trying to stimulate the local economy. Let's just leave the labels to others and see if we've stumbled onto something here. The concept needs some more thought and research, but we don't have a lot of time." He then looked at me in a way that suggested he fully understood the double meaning of his words. I looked away.

CHAPTER 23

I AM NOT A SENIOR!

Since Joe and I had two meetings scheduled for the day, we naturally needed to enthusiastically engage in our most important daily ritual at the local Bob Evans restaurant. Suzie wasn't there on that morning, so a rough-looking woman who appeared to be around fifty served us. She had thinning hair, sunken cheeks, a sallow complexion, leathery arms that resembled a belt I once had, and a raspy voice that likely reflected a lifetime of smoking. The folks at Bob Evans really knew how to whet your appetite.

Joe and I tried not to make eye contact as we gave "Bunny" (so noted on her nametag) our request. We went easy that day and just ordered pancakes. We then waited for Bunny to clear the area so we could talk. She didn't move. "You the guys with the money?" she asked. How were we supposed to answer that? I glanced at Joe for help.

"Well, Bunny, whatever do you mean by that statement? We're just two guys in here having a little breakfast before we move on down the road."

Bunny snorted. "From what I hear you boys aren't going anywhere until you pass out a bunch of money given to the townsfolk by some rich guy with no family. Word is that you're dealing with several million dollars."

Then Bunny did a very scary thing. She tried to act sexy. It's hard to describe, but she leaned over the table and sort of whet her lips slowly shaking her bony hips from side to side. The fact that her leaning forward exposed a long vertical scar peeking out from her partially unbuttoned blouse did not really enhance the desired effect.

"How about you two handsome men send a little of that money my way?"

We just stared at her with our mouths wide open. Undeterred, she simply went for the direct approach.

"We don't need to make a big fuss out of it. Just make sure to leave me a very, very generous tip when you leave. You know, like those celebrities do sometimes when they want to help someone—someone like me who is poor and deserving of a break." She said this last line while at the same time revealing a big, gap-toothed smile heretofore camouflaged by her other alluring physical attributes.

Joe leaned over toward Bunny in a conspiratorial manner. "Bunny, do you mind taking a check?"

Bunny smiled and said, "Just as long as that check has several zeros on it." She just turned and walked off with an exaggerated swaying of her bony hips.

Joe turned to me. "Enjoy your breakfast, little brother. I fear it will be the last we'll be dining at Bob Evans."

We did, indeed, enjoy our breakfast in spite of multiple appearances by Bunny to refresh our coffee and flash us her winning smile. We left sufficient money for our breakfast, but Joe took out another twenty-dollar bill. He then grabbed a napkin, took out his pen and made a large checkmark on it. Over the checkmark, he drew five zeros. He then placed the twenty dollars on top of the napkin.

I looked at him and asked, "One of the oldest gags in the books, huh? Is that supposed to make her happy?"

Joe just smiled and said, "I gave her a check with several zeros, as requested. I also gave her a generous tip, as requested. What more can a guy do? I fulfilled her request. Now, let's get the hell out of here before she comes back."

* * *

Our first meeting of the day was with a group called Seniors Helping Seniors. According to their website, this group offered a variety of services to the community's elderly population. They offered rides to the grocery store along with shopping assistance. Rides to the doctor's office were common as were stops at the pharmacy. An assistant would even go with a person to take notes as the doctor or pharmacist explained test results, drug interactions, or future actions that needed to be taken. Trips to physical therapists were part of the general package of services as well. Lots of other services were mentioned, such as home food deliveries, counseling, day care, health care advocacy, and clothing assistance. This all looked on the colorful website as if the organization was fairly robust. The reality that Joe and I witnessed was a little different.

We arrived at the Seniors Helping Seniors Center and parked in a five-car parking lot outside of a small building on North Street. The building itself appeared to be a converted residential cottage. It was in need of at least a fresh paint job and I suspected the termites were holding up a couple of the columns on the front porch. A sign next to the front door proclaimed "Welcome Young and Not-So-Young." Joe looked at me and asked, "Which are we?"

When we arranged the meeting with these folks we were told that we would have their entire staff available. A grand total of five people greeted us in the living room of the old house. They appeared to range in age from a seasoned eighty-something to an outright youthful woman of no more than sixty. In other words, she was about my age.

We learned that three men and two women made up the entire permanent staff of this organization. And when I say "staff," I don't mean that they get paid. These people just show up to work each day and attempt to organize other volunteers who give them an hour or two of their time to be of service to others in the Glenville community. During the course of a week, they might have forty to fifty other seniors volunteering their time and energy.

I was really impressed with the number of services they provided with an all-volunteer staff. "First, I must say that your website is impressive and the list of services you provide with just a volunteer organization is amazing. Who did your website?"

A guy that looked to be in his early seventies raised his hand. "That would be me. I'm Bill."

"Bill, this is really good stuff. How'd you learn to put a website together?"

"Well, the fact that I used to be in computer programming for the last twenty years of my career didn't make a website much of a challenge." Bill had a small smirk on his face that basically suggested, "You dumb shit; did you think I suddenly became an old man out of nowhere? I had a job. I had a career. I didn't suddenly forget how to use my skills."

I got the message loud and clear. It's easy to look at an older person and completely ignore what skills and talents they might have developed over the years. We tend to see the declining physical abilities and assume the brain is working in tandem with the exterior. Clearly that wasn't the case for Bill nor for the rest of this group, I suspected.

Joe jumped in. "I have a problem with your website."

"Oh, what's that?" asked Bill.

"Have you ever considered changing the name? I mean, 'Seniors Helping Seniors'—how boring is that?" Joe has always objected to the "senior" description, or at least ever since he became one.

Joe offered, "You can be over sixty and not see yourself as a senior. That sounds like you have one foot in the grave already. If you want to build some traffic to this place, then I would suggest that you consider getting rid of the senior label."

Another woman in her late sixties, Clare Simmons, smiled at Joe just as our mother used to do when he was transparent in his protests. "Mr. Kelly, I can see that you have a sincere concern about the label." She paused and smiled again. "I can also see that you have much bigger issues than just our name. We really don't need to build traffic, as you suggest, since we have more needs than we can fill. Our goal is to increase our volunteer base and maybe even hire some permanent paid staff to keep this place running when the five of us aren't able to do so in the future."

Joe smiled and said, "Just think about it, okay? The name is very limiting."

"We'll take that under consideration," Clare deadpanned.

That little exchange seemed to break the ice and we jumped into a good conversation about all that this group was trying to do and all the areas where they needed assistance. Their two vehicles for transporting seniors were in bad shape. One had a lift for wheel chairs and it often liked to stop halfway into the van and then reverse back to the ground. This could go on for five minutes before it finally lurched upward, successfully placing the wheelchair and its occupant into the van. Apparently Mr. Crowder, a ninety-year-old man with increasing dementia thought he was on a carnival ride. He'd scream with delight and throw his hands up into the air.

It turns out that our five "staff" members were all former professionals in a variety of fields and they saw a huge problem in the community that needed attention. Clare was a former practicing psychologist who now offered her services for free, but was overwhelmed with the demands of a senior community that included problems associated with simple loneliness to severe dementia and even psychoses.

"This town has done a good job of providing opportunities and services for youngsters and even young families in need," she said. "However, anyone over sixty-five with limited resources and no family are simply ignored. We are the only organization in town making any attempt to help this group. The city talks about building a senior center, but they don't have enough money and the project is pretty far down the priority list."

It was clear that these were good folks who could use some financial help. In addition to all they did for others, they also had to engage in fundraising and grant writing to keep their operation afloat. Joe and I gave them our usual line about having a modest amount of money to share among many groups, but promised them we would do everything we could to provide some sort of help. In reality, we knew before we walked out the door that the staff of Seniors Helping Seniors would be pleasantly surprised with how much help we could give them.

Just as we were stepping outside, Clare stood at the opened door and very casually mentioned, "I suppose you might like to know that your friend, Mr. Hazelton, actually took advantage of our services a few years ago. After his wife passed away, he needed help getting to his doctor appointments and running some errands. He was a very sweet man. Some of our clients can be quite demanding, but I remember Mr. Hazelton as very appreciative and kind. I just thought you'd like to know."

Not only did we appreciate the information about Uncle Shorty, we also took note of Clare Simmons' understated way of sharing her personal impression of our friend. Other people might have led the entire conversation with that bit of information to score points with us. For her, it just seemed to be a genuine side note to their ongoing mission of helping others.

Joe was quiet when we first got in the car, but then offered, "Makes you want to go home and volunteer to help your community, doesn't it? These people are doing some good work and they're right about old people being left behind." He paused, "They need to change that name, though. I hate that 'senior' description."

"Do you know what you are?"

"Many things, but I'm sure you are about to zero in on just one."

"You're in denial. You can't accept how old you are! Plus, you're full of shit."

"Well, first, whenever you want to make a derogatory statement about me, you often resort to a very limited number of descriptions such as the phrase, 'full of shit.' For a man with as many advanced degrees as you have, your choice of words to demonstrate your displeasure is rather pedestrian, don't you think? If you insist on using that line of inferior symbolism, then I find that the word 'crap' has a slightly more sophisticated ring to it. Don't you agree?"

I didn't answer since I knew he was stalling to gather momentum. It was a classic Joe Kelly debate strategy.

"Secondly, I am not just a 'senior.' I'm simply a mature individual in my early sixties. I am an educated professional with a wealth of life experiences. I have character etched into my face. I have maintained a good sense of humor about most things, I'm still intellectually engaged in my world, and I have proven that I can still be of service to others. I can experience great enjoyment playing guitar and singing and apparently provide a little enjoyment to others as well."

I couldn't keep quiet any longer. "Do you claim a senior's discount at the movies? Are you a member of AARP? Do you ask six out of ten people to repeat what they just said? Do you get up to go to the bathroom more than once during the night? Does taking a nap rank among your favorite activities? Are you eligible for Social Security? Do you go to bed earlier as each year passes? Is your TV set loud enough to be heard by your neighbors? If you answered 'yes' to at least three of these questions, then you are indeed a senior. It's not a bad thing. Get over it."

Joe's face remained contorted as he processed my excellent and thorough analysis. "I don't accept your theory and they still need to change their dumb name. End of discussion."

CHAPTER 24

THE GLENVILLE BOYS AND GIRLS CLUB

If there was one organization in town that fostered great childhood memories for me, it was the former Glenville Boys Club. It was my home away from home until I entered high school when organized school sports and lusting after girls became higher priorities. Sure, there was the swimming pool in the summer and some days were just spent hanging out and getting into small mischief that we perceived as major crime sprees. But most days were spent at "The Club." It was our version of a country club, and it had everything a kid could possible need.

There were three baseball fields—two for Little League and the larger field for American Legion ball. The Little League fields had actual dugouts with concrete block walls and an outfield fence that was short enough to allow for homeruns that would have been routine fly balls elsewhere. The Boys Club was apparently all about building self-esteem. Inside the building was an open room with a pool table and Ping-Pong table. There was a soda machine with the coldest Nehi orange soda known to scientists at the time. I seem to remember a small room with tables and chairs designed to encourage after-school studying. I never saw anyone ever enter that room.

The primary center of activity at The Club was the huge (in my ten-year-old mind) gymnasium with a full court and several side baskets. It had a stage at one end, and a small door, always open, at the other end to presumably let the prevailing stagnant, humid, Indiana summer breeze cool off the hot, sweaty bodies inside. There seemed to be a design flaw that hampered the desired effect. The open door did, however, effectively serve to stop all action on the court as basketballs and dodge balls occasionally flew out to the nearby street, hitting a passerby or causing a car to screech to a halt.

I loved playing basketball in that gym even though the floor was made of vinyl tiles (presumably made with just the right amount of asbestos). Conversely, I hated playing dodge ball. There is nothing fun about a sport where a ten-year-old, five-foot tall, ninety-pound scrawny kid gets blasted by a gargantuan thirteen-year-old who has already started to shave. When Big Jim blew that whistle and announced it was dodge ball time, you didn't have a choice. All ages were thrown into one bloody battle where only the strong survived. I'm sure there were several deaths in those games. The staff just dragged the kids off quickly so no one could see their eyes rolled back in their heads. "What happened to Johnny?" "Don't know . . . last time I saw him was two weeks ago when he got smashed in the face by one of Kracker's heat-seeking missiles."

Little League baseball was not quite the organized conglomerate that it is now. Who would have ever thought that eleven and twelve-year-old American kids would be playing on television in Williamsport for an international championship against some kids from Taiwan? That thought certainly didn't cross my mind in 1960s Glenville, Indiana. The coolest part about baseball each summer was getting your team shirt. These weren't slick uniforms with embroidered names. We got a T-shirt. It was a T-shirt with your team color and your team name screened on the front.

We weren't the Yankees or the Dodgers. We were simply Thompson's Paint & Stain, Rickett's Hardware, Bill's Bakery, Glenville Banking Company, and the 84 Lumber Company. If you were lucky, you might get Prescott's Mortuary as your sponsor. That lucky team always got the black T-shirts as the perfect complement to the business. And team cheers were so easy with that sponsor: "We'll stab you and slab you"... "We'll put you on ice"... "Get the embalming fluid; these guys are dead!" There apparently was no such thing as political correctness back then. The parents in the stands always laughed at our cheers.

However, if you were very unlucky, you'd get Betty's Big Hair Salon as your sponsor. No one wanted Betty's Big Hair Salon. Couple that name with a pale blue or yellow shirt and you were in for one rough season.

So, Joe and I naturally approached our meeting with the Boys and Girls Club Board of Directors with a bias based on all the positive memories we had at The Club. These folks would really have to screw up this presentation to avoid getting at least a little financial help from Uncle Shorty's fund. The cast of characters included the chairman, Dennis Harmon, a guy about my age who seemed to be a pretty decent sort. Five others joined him and they seemed to represent different aspects of The Club's program offerings. One guy, Reggie Phillips, the high school baseball coach, oversaw all the baseball operations, and it took all of ten seconds to dislike him. Never trust a guy who greets you sitting on a chair with arms and legs crossed and a scowl on his face. Instead of getting out of his chair to shake hands, he just nodded an acknowledgement that we existed. Joe and I exchanged a quick look.

One pleasant surprise in the room was an old high school classmate, Eddie Shields. Eddie was quite a character in our school. He was a starting lineman on the football team. One night he was particularly worried when he had to face off against an all-state lineman and decided to fortify himself with a shot of whiskey from his uncle's flask offered to him behind the stands. When Eddie headed out to the field and saw his opponent in person for the first time, he allegedly ran back to his uncle and barked, "You better give me another shot!" Apparently, he more than held his own with the all-star opponent—though it's hard to determine if it was the whiskey or just the adrenaline rush.

The self-proclaimed "twelfth man on our ten-man basketball roster," Eddie's only job in practice was to harass, intimidate, and physically abuse our star player in order to toughen up the kid for games. Eddie took the coach's challenge very seriously and caused the star to later comment, "The toughest I was ever guarded was in practice each day that year." The fact that Eddie also stole the high school basketball uniforms so the Boys Club kids could use them one time made him a legend at The Club. It was good to see him still involved with kids as a member of this board—though no doubt some might not think his legacy was exactly the right role model.

The only other person who stood out introduced herself as Mrs. Roberts. She was enthusiastic in her hand shaking and gushed about how wonderful it was to meet both of us. She clearly had heard about the money because we weren't that wonderful. She was a fourth-grade teacher at Westside Elementary and volunteered to be involved with the after-school program at The Club.

The actual work of running all these programs fell on a wiry, hyper-looking guy sitting at the end of the table. Ray Pendleton was the director of The Club, and we learned that he had a paid staff of ten people. He seemed to be a friendly sort who was not used to sitting in a meeting. His knee was bouncing up and down and his fingers seemed to be quietly playing the drum solo from The Surfaris' "Wipe Out." I think he was more comfortable with a whistle around his neck, monitoring the corridors and fields of the Boys and Girls Club. I later learned that his talent for finger drumming was exceeded only by his love for his work and the extraordinary number of hours he spent at The Club. For this effort, he was handsomely paid the equivalent of an auto mechanic's salary.

I gave my usual introduction about Uncle Shorty's estate and let the folks know how Joe and I valued our time spent at the old Boys Club. I then asked the chairman, Dennis Harmon, to give us an overview of The Club's success stories and to also help us understand their financial challenges. Before he could speak, Phillips (baseball guy) butted in, "Did you two play baseball when you were here?"

Joe answered. "Well, sure we did. Every summer."

"Did you play Legion ball, too?" His question was laced with an attitude that suggested you were only committed to baseball if as an older teenager you went on to play (after Little League). This was beginning to remind me of the church leaders who wanted to know what religion we practiced.

Again, Joe took the lead. "Darren continued to play, but I moved on to other things."

At this admission, Phillips jumped on Joe. "What could be more important than playing baseball in summer?" He looked at Joe as if he was some sort of alien creature.

At this point, I knew we were in trouble. Joe wouldn't let this moron off the hook, but he also wasn't likely to admit that he preferred playing the piano. That would send us down an ugly path. So, he said what could only seem normal in Joe's mind, "I sold beer and pot to other kids. Had an uncle who bought the beer for me and he also grew a big marijuana patch on his farm. I was the distributor and got a cut of the action. It paid better than baseball." Then Joe just sat back and smiled.

Phillips just stared, trying to determine if Joe was yanking his chain. He shook his head and said what was really on his mind. "I'm not convinced you two even have any money to give out. There are more than a few folks in town who think the same way and wonder if you boys are just out having some fun and wasting our time. Some say you're planning to get everyone riled up and then write a book about it that trashes the town—that you have some sort of vendetta against Glenville."

"You, sir, have a vivid imagination!" Joe exclaimed. "I like that. I figured you for a guy who never had a creative thought in his life, but here you are living in a fantasyland inhabited by vengeful former residents who are determined to wreak havoc and cast a pall of death and despair over the beautiful hamlet of Glenville! Is anyone named Carrie involved in your nightmare?"

"You can make fun all you want, but we have no proof that any of this is real and I'm not about to grovel at your feet asking for money." With that proclamation, Reggie Phillips headed out the door and returned to his world of balls and strikes and kids who listened to him and didn't give him any crap. The door slammed behind him.

For a few seconds no one said anything. Mrs. Roberts' jaw just hung open as she tried to process what she just heard. I'm sure she was convinced Joe was a former drug dealer. Harmon, the board chairman, and Eddie Shields just started laughing. Harmon managed to say "Man, that was priceless! Phillips really had his shorts all knotted up, didn't he? That was good—very, very good." He couldn't stop chuckling.

Joe always appreciated a good audience for his humor, so Harmon had just moved over to the positive side of our ledger. Just for fun, Joe asked him, "How do you know he wasn't right? Maybe there isn't any money."

"Because I checked you out before coming to this meeting. I meet Tom Borland every couple of weeks for breakfast down at Earl's Café. I asked him about you gents and he first just clammed up with his usual confidentiality line, but then I simply asked if the estate was for real and if you two have authority over it? He said yes. Then I asked if the amount of money was worth my time to have a meeting. He said yes again and nodded his headed quite vigorously—in a noncommittal, client-privilege sort of way. That's why we're here."

"Good," I said. "Then let's get on with it. We've wasted enough time. Tell us what you're doing well and tell us where additional funds would help the most. And cut to the chase so we're not sitting here forever. Joe has to make a drug run across town in an hour." I winked at Mrs. Roberts and she leaned back as if I'd smacked her in the face with a marijuana plant.

We heard pretty much what we expected to hear. Funds were tight. Enrollment in all programs was up. The usual summer-time stuff that Joe and I experienced as kids still rolled along pretty well since use of the gym didn't cost much and baseball teams still were sponsored by local businesses. The old gym where we played was built in 1954 and a new one was added in 1993 (so even more kids could be bludgeoned at dodge ball). Some financial debt was still associated with that remodel and it added to the board's burden.

Parents still volunteered to coach. Most were great; a few were jackasses. There was nothing new about that. Umpires and field maintenance was a drain on their small budget, but that was clearly a necessary expense. However, now The Club was expected to fill a niche during the school year with after-school programs. With so many households where both parents worked, there was a heavy demand for a low-cost and safe place where kids could go after school.

For parents with some money, the low-priced transportation from the schools at the end of the day and the supervision at The Club were a great bargain. However, when you're living at the poverty line and working two minimum-wage jobs, any cost can seem insurmountable. A subsidy program had been created for very low-income families, but it was completely dependent on fundraising efforts, and there were many other organizations in town clamoring for the same donations.

Mrs. Roberts, now recovered from the shock of Joe's pot distribution story, added some clarity to the discussion. "I watch these kids leave my class every day after school. Some are picked up by their stay-at-home moms, some get on a couple of the church vans that operate after-school programs for their members, and many get on the Boys and Girls Club bus to come here until one of their parents gets off work. But then I watch others just wander off the school property. These are first through sixth graders. Some are in groups; some just go off alone. I don't know where they're going. Some might be walking home, but I see others wandering around town when I leave school an hour or so later."

Joe offered, "Well, walking home alone isn't necessarily a bad thing. Darren and I did it every day from Westside and we turned out okay."

Mrs. Roberts looked at Joe as she most likely did with her most dim-witted fourth-grade students. "How far from school did you live?"

"Uh . . . about a block."

"That must have been very hard on you. Was your mother waiting for you at home?"

"Uh . . . yes, until she took a part-time job at the library." Joe then hesitated. "Now that I think about it, I guess she mostly worked while we were at school. She was generally home."

Mrs. Roberts summed up their discussion. "So, you only had to walk one block to a home where your loving mother waited to provide care and structure to your lives so you could get your homework done and relax a little before your father came home for the perfect family dinner."

"Don't forget the milk and cookies after school," Joe added.

"And with all that support, you still became a drug dealer!"

"Hey, hey, hey . . . I was kidding about the pot and alcohol! It never happened. I was just having a little fun with Phillips. Lighten up, will you?" Joe was now laughing. "You made your point. And, by the way, Darren and I turned out fine—by most standards."

Harmon was laughing again. Mrs. Roberts seemed to finally get it. And Joe had no trouble understanding the real message. Life had changed in forty years. Mothers weren't always home after school. Kids had more ways to get into trouble now with time on their hands. And worst of all, there seemed to be more predators out there who looked at kids as targets.

We talked a little more about The Club and heard some details from the Club director. I glanced at Joe and could see that he was ready to wrap it up, so we finished with our usual promise to do what we could to help. I was struck by the fact that we seemed to end meeting after meeting with fairly positive feelings about the work being done and the need for additional funds. Our choices were not going to be easy.

CHAPTER 25

HERE'S . . . JOHNNY!

Joe and I were talked out by the end of the day. We decided that even chatting with Mandy at Applebee's was too much effort, so we just grabbed some burgers and fries from Steak 'n Shake and headed back to The Residence Inn. There would likely be an NBA game on TV and that's about all the stimulation we needed for the night. A couple of Indiana boys could always waste a few hours watching basketball and not feel a hint of remorse for being unproductive.

After the food was polished off and we were both semi-comatose, lying on our beds watching a game between the Pacers and Atlanta, there was a knock at the door. Joe and I exchanged the universal look that asked "Who the hell could that be?" Neither of us having an answer to the unspoken question, I got up and opened the blinds so I could see outside.

A distorted face was pressed against the glass and I could hear a muffled "Here's . . . Johnny!" I quickly realized that smashed nose and mouth belonged to none other than Lonnie McDaniel doing his very best impression of a psychotic Jack Nicholson in *The Shining*. He picked the perfect character to emulate. Lonnie pulled back from the glass and shouted, "Let me in!"

My first thought was there was no way that I was going to open the door for that psychopath. Why in the world would I do that? It would be like every horror movie you ever saw when you whispered to yourself, "Don't do it; don't do it. Don't go down that dark hallway to the closed door at the end!" But then, of course, the dispensable actress would creep down the hall and get sucked through the door by a vacuum force so powerful it pulled her beating heart out of her chest and bounced it across the room. That's pretty much what would happen if I opened the door for Lonnie McDaniel.

I looked at Joe for help. He casually propped up on his elbow and said, "Might as well let him in."

"Are you nuts?" Due to my extensive training in counseling, I often revert to technical jargon when expressing my opinion about someone's grasp on reality. "You do realize that he's crazy and that he threatened me?"

Lonnie was now slowly and quietly knocking on the door in a rhythmic fashion so as to not warrant the attention of anyone in the area.

"Yeah, I get that part. But what are we going to do—ignore him out there? Or are you going to call the police and tell them—what? Someone knocked on your door? Let's get this crap out in the open. If he threatens you again, now you have a witness."

"Oh, great. And if he hacks off my arm with a chainsaw, I'll have a witness, too. You're pretty smug when you're not the one on his radar."

Joe called out loud enough to be heard outside, "Hey, Lonnie, you don't have a chainsaw with you, do you?"

A surprised voice replied, "Hell, no, I don't have a chainsaw. What is wrong with you guys? I just want to come in and talk a bit."

Joe looked at me. "See, he doesn't even have a chainsaw. Let him in. Let's deal with this head on."

I opened the door and stepped back into the room wondering if I would be greeted with a gun pointed at my face. Lonnie stepped in slowly and carefully closed the door behind him. He looked up with that creepy grin of his and said, "Hello, boys! Looks like you're having a big night here in wonderful Glenville. Are you tuckered out from talking with all the do-gooders in town?"

Lonnie's long, gray hair was disheveled and his T-shirt and jeans had oil stains as if he'd just come here after working on a car. He looked much worse than when I saw him previously in Applebee's. His hands were filthy and he reeked of cigarettes. The smell of whisky was prevalent and the source was confirmed as he reached into his back pocket for a flask and took a big swig in front of us.

He held out the flask toward us and asked, "You boys want to join me?"

We both just looked at him and said nothing as we waited for his next move.

"No, I didn't think you Kelly boys would want to drink with ole Lonnie." He cackled and then started a short coughing fit that confirmed his apparent life-long love of nicotine. The guy was a mess. But he was a scary mess that was currently dominating the small room.

Joe broke the silence. "What do you want, Lonnie?"

"Why, Joe Kelly, it's good to see you, too. How've you been doing all these years? I'm fine. Thanks for asking." McDaniel's smile suddenly disappeared.

Lonnie's intensity changed noticeably when he spoke. "You boys are running out of time on your good will mission and I just wanted to check in with you to see how it was going. I hope you hand out lots of money to the good folks of Glenville, but I didn't want you to forget the hundred grand that will be sent in my direction—for my charitable foundation."

Joe took the lead. "So you have a charitable foundation now, Lonnie?"

"Yes, sir. I guarantee you that all the money will go to a good cause."

"What kind of cause might that be?" Joe asked.

Lonnie grinned at Joe and just said, "Well, that would be confidential information not made available to the public at this particular time."

Joe smiled at Lonnie's description and then tried to get at the real issue hanging over the room like a dark thundercloud. "And what if we choose not to fund your fine organization since there are so many other worthy groups in town who need that money?" If McDaniel was going to make a threat, now was the time to get it on the record so we'd have something for Chief Hagman to work with.

Lonnie smiled at Joe and said, "Then I'd probably have to follow up on my previous conversation with your little brother until you and he saw the error of your ways and made sure my charity was funded."

"Is that a threat, Lonnie?" Joe was trying to seal the deal.

McDaniel stared at Joe with a look that quickly became a mixture of hatred and rage. Joe's comment had set him off.

"You think I'm playing games here, Kelly? You think I'm worried about making a little threat that you'll run to the police with? While you've been out there enjoying your perfect little lives, do you know where I've been? Do you have any idea the shit I've done to people who crossed me?"

McDaniel was right. Joe and I were out of our comfort zone. We really didn't know what we were doing and this guy was now scaring the crap out of me. We were trying to talk sense with an enraged ex-convict who had nearly killed a man in prison.

Just then Lonnie suddenly grabbed the table lamp, yanked the cord from the wall socket, and smashed the lamp on the tile floor right in front of Joe. Pieces of the ceramic base flew everywhere as Joe and I ducked and covered our faces. It obviously didn't take much to cause Lonnie to lose control.

Lonnie screamed at Joe. "Do you feel threatened now, Kelly? Is that what you want from me? So you can go running to your little police chief and tell him that big, bad Lonnie threatened you?"

Joe and I remained quiet and didn't move. There wasn't a sound in the room except for Lonnie's heavy breathing. But just then the entire mood in the room changed. Instead of continuing his rant, Lonnie calmly grabbed for the chair by the desk and quietly sat down. He reached for his flask and took a long drink. Then he carefully set the flask on the table and stared at us. This sudden calm was just as alarming as his brief outburst. In a strange way, it was even more unsettling.

Lonnie then reached into his front pocket and took out a small pocketknife. He unfolded it and attempted to clean the dark grease out from underneath his long fingernails. He just quietly sat there for several minutes and diligently worked on his nails.

He broke the silence by observing, "It looks like this little knife is no match for the amount of crap that I've got under these nails." He looked up at Joe and me and just smiled as if we were his best buddies engaging in idle conversation.

"That's the way it is with knives. You have to match the right knife with the right job. I know a lot about knives, boys. Did your police chief tell you about that? I'm real partial to them. Yeah, some knives are good for gutting deer and some are good for cleaning fish. Some are good for skinning all sorts of critters and some are good for cutting the throats of mean dogs. And some knives—just some knives—are particularly good at cutting people." Lonnie turned and stared at each one of us individually.

"You see, I don't need to kill people. Hell, I'm not that bad. I just like to cut them. I like to see them bleed and I like to make sure they'll have scars to remember me by." He spread his hands wide and grinned. "It's just what I like to do. It's sort of like a hobby to me."

Then he stared at Joe. "So, Joe, this is not a threat. It's just an explanation. If I don't get what I want, then I will proceed to do what I enjoy the most. I'll engage in my hobby. I will quickly find your brother alone somewhere and I will teach him a lesson. And when you see his face after I get done, I will have taught you a lesson as well. You could have easily stopped that unfortunate event by simply writing a check—and you wouldn't even have to use your own damn money!"

Joe and I remained silent, not moving an inch. As eerie as Lonnie's calm demeanor was, we both clearly preferred it to the more violent alternative. We weren't going to interrupt.

McDaniel slowly rose from the chair and closed the pocket-knife. Placing the knife back in his front pocket, he then pulled out a piece of paper and placed it on the table.

"Here's the account number and the name of my wonderful 'charity.' Don't bother trying to trace it. A little buddy of mine in prison taught me how to set up an untraceable account that is perfect for a quick deposit. The money then moves on immediately to another account that I can access. It will just get lost among all those other accounts held by the good organizations of Glenville. No one has to know anything about it and I'll be long gone from this hick town. You won't have to worry about me again."

Lonnie took two steps toward the door and paused. "Go ahead and run to your police chief, boys. He won't be able to find me. It's time for Lonnie to lie low until he gets paid." Lonnie opened the door and looked back directly at me.

"But if you cross me, Darren—well, you just don't want to do that. You see, I just don't really have much to lose and I'd take great pleasure in carving you up." He smiled again at both of us. "Thanks for inviting me in, boys. It's been a real treat."

The door closed and Joe and I just stared at each other. I think I was in some sort of shock because I couldn't even speak at first. This little dose of reality with McDaniel illustrated that we were way out of our league. Lonnie had completely dominated and controlled us. I had absolutely no thoughts about being able to overpower him if things had turned ugly. He just toyed with us and we knew he was in control. Joe looked down at the smashed lamp. A silent moment passed before I finally said, "Good idea to let him in, Joe."

Joe nodded. "Yeah, but it was a smart move to make sure he didn't have a chainsaw."

CHAPTER 26
HOW TO WIN FRIENDS AND INFLUENCE PEOPLE

"You just opened the door and let him in?" Chief Hagman needed to work on his empathy skills. He didn't seem to understand that Joe and I had been traumatized. We had arrived on his doorstep at the police station the next morning looking for help.

"Joe told me to let him in."

"And you always do what your brother tells you to do?" I'm pretty sure Hagman was channeling my mother at this point. If he reached over and tried to brush the hair out of my eyes, I was really going to get spooked.

"No, I generally don't do what Joe suggests, but in this case it seemed like a good idea to confront the issue and be done with it. I just didn't think confronting the issue included a threat to carve up my face."

Joe offered, "On a positive note I think the record should show that I verified he did not have a chainsaw in his possession before entering the room."

Hagman turned a quizzical eye on Joe. "And how, exactly, did you verify that point?"

"I asked him and he responded that he did not have one. A man's word is his bond." Joe smiled at Hagman as if he had just uttered one of the great truths in the history of mankind.

"And a psychopath's word is also his bond? You do realize they lie a lot?"

Joe hesitated only a second. "It is true that a psychopath's word is slightly less bondable than a normal man's word. One should proceed with caution. I just had a good feeling about the whole chainsaw thing. It would have been so cliché and melodramatic. I didn't see the scene in our hotel room playing out that way. Of course, I didn't see a knife in Darren's future either."

Hagman looked at Joe without blinking. "Remind me not to ask your advice again about anything having to do with Lonnie McDaniel."

At this point Chief Hagman turned back to me and we went over and over the exact words that McDaniel had used in making his demands and threatening to cut me. When he was satisfied that he had the whole story, he just leaned back in his chair and let out a sigh. I didn't find that action to be particularly comforting.

"The reality is that Lonnie has been pretty smart about this whole deal. First, he didn't demand a large percentage of the funds that he thinks you have because he doesn't want to draw attention to it. Second, he knows you have complete control over the money. You're the administrator of the estate. Sure, it's still blackmail and extortion, but there is nothing stopping you from meeting his demand. Third, he's right about transferring the money in a manner that we can't trace. And, fourth, he won't have any trouble staying away for the next week or two while you wrap this up. He gets his money and splits for a new start. It's not a fortune, but it will last quite a while for a guy like Lonnie."

I then asked the most important question on my mind. "Do you think he'd come after me if we don't make the payment to him?"

"Absolutely. Based on what he's done to other people, I think he would come after you with a vengeance. I have no doubt that he would want you to suffer."

"Hell, Chief, don't sugarcoat it," Joe dryly commented. "Darren will be sliced up like a Halloween pumpkin and small children in the street will run and scream at the sight of him."

As much as I generally appreciate Joe's sense of humor, I have to admit that his commentary wasn't particularly helpful. In fact, drawing attention to your brother's impending disfiguration just seemed a tad bit insensitive. But I would have likely done the same to him.

The chief chimed in. "The question is whether he'd have the energy or the attention span to pursue you once you leave town. I doubt it. I mean the guy is a complete loser who hasn't exactly proven to be a mastermind criminal. My guess is he'll quickly move on to his next great idea. I think you should wrap up your business and get out of Glenville.

I asked the chief, "What do we do now? What are my options?"

He once again instilled great confidence with a casual shrug of his shoulders. "I wish I could tell you something positive, but I really can't. Oh sure, we'll go looking for Lonnie, but I suspect he has enough holes to crawl into around here. I'll even call the FBI office over in Indianapolis, but I can just about guarantee you that Lonnie's threat won't raise to the level that warrants sending any agents over here to check it out.

"I'd say you're safe until you announce your decision about the funding. It's your business if you go along with his demand and no one except you and your lawyer will know either way. If you don't give him the money, then you need to let me know so I can do my best to protect you while you're still here in Glenville. Maybe Lonnie will get stupid and try something before you leave town. Otherwise, you're off to California and you have to hope that I'm right about his lack of ambition."

* * *

Joe and I left the police station and went out in search of comfort food at a place where the waitress wouldn't attack Joe with a meat cleaver. We found Earl's Café, a breakfast eatery in the old downtown area where the locals apparently hang out and get caught up on the town gossip. And sure enough, the first person we saw sitting alone at a corner booth was none other than Lawyer Borland. He waved and motioned for us to join him. Joe and I looked at each other with a "why not?" expression and walked over.

"Gentlemen, I haven't ordered yet, so why don't you join me? We have a few details to follow up on and I'd love to hear how it's going for you."

Joe said, "From what we hear, you are already familiar with some of our discussions around town."

Borland smiled and nodded. "Yes, it's still a small town and folks do like to talk. You two have become one of the main discussion items around the local hangouts. Most people are just trying to figure out if you're for real and if there is any substantial money involved. Though I weighed the ethical considerations with due earnestness, I decided I wanted you to be taken seriously so I did confirm with several organizations that you were legitimate executors of an estate. However, I never disclosed anything about the amount of money you have to distribute or the terms outlined by Mr. Hazelton."

"Well, as long as you weighed the ethics with due earnestness, then we're okay with it." It seemed that Joe was in a generous mood that morning while only taking a mild jab at Borland's somewhat questionable approach to the issue.

The waitress approached and asked if we'd had time to look at a menu. She was not as young and perky as Suzie at Bob Evans restaurant, but thankfully not as lizard-like as our good friend, Bunny, at the same establishment. In fact, she was perfectly normal and pleasant. Joe glanced at her nametag and said, "Alice, just give me a breakfast that contains eggs and bacon. Surprise me." It should be noted here that Joe could often be seen walking around his house in a T-shirt featuring a picture of several sizzling strips of bacon accompanied by the explanation "Bacon Makes It Better."

"Yes, sir, one Bacon Delight Omelet coming right up." Turning to me, "And for you, sir?"

"Ditto—with coffee, please."

As Alice turned to leave, I asked Borland if he was going to order. He just smiled and said, "It's Tuesday, so she knows what I want."

Joe stared at Borland for a few seconds. "You people live very regular lives around here, don't you? Waitresses don't even need to take your orders, everyone gets dialed in about the local gossip, and life moves from Point A to Point B with very few detours along the way." I was waiting for a further insolent observation from Joe, but it never came. He just stared at Borland and seemed to be lost in thought.

Regardless of Joe's intended meaning, Borland viewed his observation as a deserved compliment. "That's why I love it here, Joe. It's a simple life and it suits me just fine. Now, how are the discussions going and is there anything I can do to help you finish up?"

I gave Borland the general overview of our many talks with individuals and groups around town. I decided he didn't need to know about Lonnie McDaniel. If we decided that getting rid of Lonnie by paying his demand would allow us to accomplish Uncle Shorty's goals, then Borland didn't need to be dragged into that reality until it was necessary. Plus, the fewer people that knew about McDaniel, the better it would be for us in general.

Borland was enthusiastic about the progress that we made. "I think you hit most of the groups that I would have recommended, but you might want to check in with the hospital. Just the fact that we have a private hospital in a small town is a pretty big deal and I know they are constantly fundraising to stay afloat. The other thing that's missing are the individuals who have fallen on hard times who wouldn't show up on the radar of these organized groups. I don't know exactly how you reach out to them. Then again, you can't help everyone and maybe you just have to approach this from a group standpoint and let those agencies do more outreach to find those in need."

The rest of our breakfast discussion was pretty casual. Borland told us more about how he migrated from the life of a rich Virginia/Washington, D.C., civil litigation specialist to a small-town lawyer who now takes on anything and everything associated with the law. He told us that the move saved his marriage and he was now happily raising a family of three boys. His wife's family lived in Glenville and she basically gave Borland an ultimatum about moving back to be close to her aging folks. He made tons of money back east, but he was a workaholic and had nearly lost the family that he loved.

It seems that Glenville has helped him tremendously and now he is determined to give back to the town in any way possible. It was starting to make sense how Uncle Shorty might have picked this guy and why Borland was so insistent that he could become the executor if we were unable to handle it. What Joe and I first read as greed may have simply been his desire to carry out this task in the manner that Uncle Shorty would have wanted.

"Okay," said Joe, "I now get your motivation and I'm glad we're on board together. But why in hell do you talk the way you do? Everything was 'splendid' and you couldn't stop calling us 'gentlemen.' Now your latest is 'due earnestness.' You do realize, I hope, that you are not exactly fitting in as the stereotypical Hoosier lawyer."

Borland just laughed. "I know, I know. I still sometimes sound pretentious, but I use to be far more ostentatious in everything that I did."

The fact that he just confidently used the word "ostentatious" in a sentence still makes him a little suspicious in my mind.

"Believe me, I have changed dramatically since I arrived in Glenville, but it still creeps back into my speech patterns when I'm meeting new people. That's just nervousness. It's the product of a mother who taught high school English in Virginia and raised me on BBC dramas." Joe and I looked at each other with a congratulatory nod. We had nailed the Agatha Christie connection when we first met Borland. "And, yes, I did go to private schools. Of course, at Yale I was surrounded by similar preppies trying to impress each other.

"Then I discovered that juries generally liked my style of elocution and mistakenly equated it with an elevated level of intelligence. So, I laid it on thick in court and that style seemed to carry over into my private life. Let's just say that a pompous know-it-all approach really doesn't work well in normal marriage communication. I'm still trying to break old habits. I have been asked the same question by others in town who at first distrusted me."

We talked a little more about what still needed to be accomplished. Borland would be drafting a number of contracts related to various groups that we intended to fund at some yet undetermined amount. Our goal was just to allocate the funds and, literally, get out of town. That would leave Borland with lots of administrative work to complete the task, and Joe and I would plan to check in with him and respond to his questions long-distance.

As we wrapped up, Borland paused and seemed to hesitate in saying something to us. Finally, he asked, "Do you guys know someone named Luke Jackson?"

Joe and I looked at each other with raised eyebrows. I answered for both us, "Sure, we knew Luke. He was our next-door neighbor growing up."

"That's what he told me."

Now it was Joe's turn. "That's what he told you—as in a real person talking to you—or a ghost that came to you in a dream?" Joe obviously still wasn't sure about Borland.

Borland looked confused and answered, "He was in my office yesterday. He wanted to prepare a will and claimed that he picked my name out of the phone book. He indicated that he wanted to deal with someone who didn't know him since rumors might get around that he was back in the area. He wanted to be left alone."

Always capable of stating the obvious I asked, "And the fact that you're telling us this somehow doesn't qualify as starting that sort of rumor?"

Borland laughed. "Yes, I can see that it might appear that I've violated his trust already. But, no, he actually gave me permission to tell you. I'm afraid that I made a mistake by leaving a file on my desk. It was closed, but the label clearly showed Joe and Darren Kelly. Mr. Jackson glanced at the file when I was clearing it off my desk and commented that he knew those names. I informed him that you were clients of mine and that you were in town for a short period of time. That's all I said." Once again Tom Borland wanted us to know that he was careful as he flirted with violating our confidentiality.

"After we concluded our business, Mr. Jackson left me a cell number and indicated that you could call him if you were so inclined. He truly seemed to lighten up and smile when he discovered you were in town. Otherwise, he was a very serious individual."

Borland gave us the phone number and we then went our separate ways. As Joe and I walked to the car, there was no question about our next move. Time to reunite with our boyhood legend—Luke Jackson.

CHAPTER 27

LUKE JACKSON RETURNS

Joe made the call to Luke as we were walking back to our car. It was a brief conversation and I could tell that Joe was getting directions to Luke's place. He had offered to meet Luke in town, but apparently that wasn't the plan.

"Well, that was interesting," said Joe. "Luke didn't want to meet in town, but invited us out to his farm for lunch. He lives way the hell out on West County Road 100—halfway to nowhere. Guess he really does want to be left alone."

We spent the rest of the morning following up with some people from the library and then paid a visit to the hospital, as lawyer Borland had suggested. We went in unannounced and just wandered around in the public areas a bit to get the feel of the place and made an appointment with the administrator in charge for the next day. Joe was very quiet and had an odd look on his face as he looked down the corridors where patients were housed.

Just to make things a little more awkward, a guy in a hospital gown came out of a room pushing a rolling rack with an I.V. bag hanging from it. He looked to be about our age, and a woman, presumably his wife, was holding onto him to provide a little balance. He glanced at us as he slowly moved by and said, "Hope you gents are just visiting and not checking in." He grinned at us with a defeated look in his eyes and slowly moved on. I didn't dare look at Joe.

We quickly left the hospital and headed out of town in the direction of Luke Jackson's farm. It felt very odd to think we were going to see Luke again after over forty years. This could either be a comfortable renewal of boyhood recollections or a very awkward meeting that demonstrates how you just can't go home. Joe shared some of the same concerns. He, of course, was closer to Luke in age and really had more of a bond with him. I was just the little brother who idolized Luke as a larger-than-life action figure.

We found the address without too much trouble and drove down a long gravel road to an older farmhouse with a barn and several additional buildings nearby. Even though this was clearly a working farm, the place looked immaculate. All the buildings had a fresh coat of paint, farm equipment was lined up in a row ready for inspection, and even the two German shepherds on the porch sat up ready and alert without barking or making a move toward our car. I thought to myself that the rumors about Luke going off to the military just might be true. This place had discipline and structure written all over it.

The front door opened and out stepped the guy I expected to see. There was no way that the years would have transformed Luke into some pudgy, balding old guy. I wasn't disappointed.

The person who stepped out was wearing a T-shirt, jeans, and work boots. He was deeply tanned, lean and tall, and strolling toward us with a confident and casual stride. His hair was mostly still dark with gray speckled throughout. His shoulders were still broad and his waist disgustingly small and flat. Of course, no surprise, his arms looked like twisted steel cables capable of enormous strength, but not bulging like some steroid-laced body builder. Luke had the face of a guy in his sixties, but the body of a much younger man.

He greeted us with a big smile and an enthusiastic and firm handshake. Clearly, he also was a disciple of the Kelly "no man-hug" policy. We exchanged all the predictable opening lines of people who haven't seen each other in a long time while knowing that soon we'd sit down and have some more substantive conversation about life's passages. The door to the farmhouse opened and a petite woman with long dark hair stepped out and waved to us. She appeared to be Asian, but I wasn't sophisticated enough to ascertain exactly where she might be from.

Wearing a sundress and sandals, she flashed a very warm smile and her eyes were mesmerizing. She was younger than Luke, but it was hard to pinpoint by just how much. Her fair skin was mostly smooth and flawless, but the laugh wrinkles around her eyes showed signs of a graceful aging. As she stepped off the porch, I noticed her give a very subtle hand signal and the two shepherds immediately dropped to the porch in a submissive position with their heads on their front paws. Impressive.

"Joe and Darren, meet my wife, Ling."

I started to put my hand out, but Ling quickly gave me a big hug and then followed with the same for Joe. This move also fit nicely into the Kelly hug policy. Always discourage hugs from men but enthusiastically accept hugs from beautiful Asian women. "I'm honored to have you visit our home. When Luke heard you were in town he couldn't stop telling me old stories about life on Garfield Drive. I've never heard so much about his childhood."

Ling spoke with a slight accent, but it was obvious that she had been speaking English for a very long time. We later learned that she was from China and that she and Luke had returned to the States several years ago. Joe and I didn't want to pry since we had no idea where Luke had been all these years. All they would offer was that they had met in China and Luke was able to assist Ling in leaving that country. They apparently then lived together in several other countries for many years, but the description of where and when remained very vague.

As we talked over lunch the conversation started with Luke's prodigious childhood exploits. Though he claimed that we blew his actions way out of proportion, he nonetheless laughed hard and long at Joe's descriptions of the tower painting, the fight in the Burger Chef parking lot, defending me on the basketball court, and pulling me out of the mud in our back yard. He even acknowledged the story about his father laughing non-stop through the night. "What people didn't realize is that my mother was crazier than Dad. She was barely in touch with reality. He was the stable one of the two—he just got a little goofy that night. After that stint in the VA hospital, he seemed to be just fine."

And so it went as we got caught up. Joe and I offered plenty of details about our last forty years, but Luke was more interested in hearing about us than sharing much about his own life. When we finally reached an awkward silence due to Luke's reticence to talk, Joe just came out with it. "What have you been doing all these years, Luke? You must have been in the military, right?"

Luke slowly smiled in an almost wistful manner as he stole a glance at Ling, who smiled back at him. "Look guys, I'll only give you the condensed version of my past forty years. I simply don't want to talk about it very much. It's the past and it wasn't always very pleasant—until I met Ling. Even then, it was often pretty challenging."

Again, Luke paused and just stared out the window for a few seconds. "You're right, Joe. I joined the army and headed right off to Vietnam. I survived two tours there and managed to escape that horror with my limbs intact. But it took its toll on me. I became numb to the killing and I was fearless in taking on the toughest assignments. That might be because I really didn't give a damn whether I lived or died. I had no real future waiting for me back home. My CO (commanding officer) approached me when my second tour was up. He pulled me into a meeting with some other officers and offered me a special assignment to stay in the military. The money they offered was substantial compared to normal military pay, but they made it clear that I would be involved in secretive and dangerous missions all over the world."

Joe asked, "So it was like Delta Force and the Navy Seals?" Joe had just demonstrated his entire knowledge of special military operations based on movies starring the likes of Chuck Norris, Sylvester Stallone, and Charlie Sheen.

"This was even before those units were created to conduct counter-terrorism strikes. What I got involved with later evolved into those units, but we were on the ground floor and actually kept a lower profile than either of those outfits. The brass wasn't sure how we would be used at first, but they knew they wanted an elite fighting force that could go places where the regular military couldn't go. We trained for two years before we even saw any action. It was the hardest two years of my life, but we formed a unit that was damn near invincible. We became killing machines. No task was too hard. We rescued hostages, killed drug lords, captured terrorist leaders, and infiltrated huge weapons operations and dismantled them. We were assigned a task, trained for weeks and months to accomplish it, then moved in and got it done."

"And I presume no one back home in America even knew you existed?" Joe asked.

"Not in the early years. We couldn't communicate with anyone at home and the army didn't want anyone to know of our existence. Later, the politicians needed to let the public know that the U.S. was effectively fighting terrorists, so they started to glamorize the notion that we had these special fighting forces. Believe me, there was nothing glamorous about it. There was satisfaction in pulling off a mission to further the best interests of the U.S. and there is nothing to match the camaraderie of a fighting unit like ours. But we lost good men along the way and we killed people at point-blank range. You don't forget the feeling of cutting a man's throat with a knife. It's not pretty."

Joe and I exchanged glances. Our old friend had been living a life that was part of a world we couldn't even begin to comprehend. Joe pushed a little further. "But that's a young man's profession, Luke. You couldn't have been doing that stuff into your fifties."

"Well, I was in pretty good shape and good at my job, but I stopped going on missions in my early forties and became a trainer for all the new recruits in our unit. It was during that time that I met Ling and we managed to create a life for ourselves living on remote training bases around the world. That's all I can tell you. We finally got out, collected all the pay that I had saved up over the years, and eventually , moved back to Indiana to run this farm. We love it. It's peaceful and quiet—and no one is shooting at me."

Joe and I just sat back and said nothing for a minute. I had never once imagined that Luke would have taken that path, but it also wasn't surprising at all to hear his story. It was pure Luke

Jackson. He always went his own way and he was tougher than any kid I ever knew. I guess he naturally became that same sort of man.

Luke quickly shifted the subject back to us. He knew we had been to see Lawyer Borland and wondered what brought us back to Glenville. So I gave him the quick overview about Uncle Shorty's money. Since he knew Shorty Hazelton as well, he was just as surprised as we were about the enormous wealth Shorty had created. I told him about all our meetings and even briefed him on the Lonnie McDaniel problem. "We could have used you in our motel room that night, Luke, when Joe so graciously invited Lonnie in to threaten us."

Luke gave Joe a confused look, but asked me, "So the police are basically just going to wait and see what happens. Is that it? Are you going to give him the money?"

I suddenly felt very timid and spineless as I answered to a guy who had put his life on the line all over the world. "I don't want to cave in, Luke, but I also don't like the idea of being sliced and diced by a psychopath. I'm not sure the money is worth the risk."

Luke didn't comment right away, but I could see his wheels turning. "It's just not right," Luke quietly declared. "I remember Lonnie. We were in Vietnam at the same time. Our paths crossed one time back at a base camp. He was stoned and trying to act like he was my buddy since we grew up here together. I blew him off, but I could tell he wasn't right. The guy doesn't deserve to take that money away from people who really need it."

It was no surprise that Luke would see the issue in black and white as he did. After all, he had the necessary skill set to deal with a guy like Lonnie. I had the necessary skill set to capitulate and get out of town with my skin intact.

Luke sat silent for a minute and then glanced over at Ling who gently smiled at him. He turned to Joe and me and let out a heavy sigh. "This is why I'm so screwed up. I came back to this farm to find peace and quiet. Another man could easily ignore your issue and just wish you well. But I can't ignore it. It's not right for Lonnie to threaten you and it's not right for him to get his hands on Shorty's money. My problem is I have to do something about it."

Joe jumped in. "Luke, we didn't mean to burden you with this. We just came out here to see you again. We had no intention of dumping on you. It's our problem and we'll deal with it."

"Oh, I know you didn't mean it. It's just how I'm wired and now I won't rest until I can get this straight somehow." He looked over at Ling and just shook his head slowly and smiled.

Ling said to us, "You have to let Luke help you. Otherwise, he'll be miserable, and then I'll be miserable with him. If he does this, then we can go back to our simple life."

Joe asked the obvious question. "What do you plan to do?"

Luke gave Joe a quizzical look, as if he was contemplating that question himself. "I'm not going to kill him, if that's what you're asking. I'm not a murderer. I just intend to convince him that bothering you again would be a very, very bad idea. Since the guy's a little unstable, I'm not exactly sure what approach will work best. Even psychopaths have something deep inside that can be manipulated if you can find it. Let's just say I can be very persuasive when necessary." Luke then gave us a piercing look that told us the discussion was over. For a second, there was something very challenging in his eyes. Then it was gone and he smiled.

We finished up inside, said goodbye to Ling, and walked with Luke out to our car. Luke asked us when we planned to make the final announcement about the disbursement of funds. I gave him a date that was seven days away. The game plan was to have a public meeting where Borland would handle the reading of the will and we would then list the people and agencies that would be receiving funds. Joe and I wanted to clarify our approach and reasoning in that one meeting so we wouldn't have to go over and over the issues. We'd give my friend, editor John Bourke, an exclusive just prior to the meeting so he'd have all the facts. We intended to get out of town soon thereafter—especially if we were worried about Lonnie.

"Okay, I'll take care of Lonnie by that date. You don't need to worry about him. Go ahead with your plans and do the right thing. Don't ever mention my name to anyone and we'll all go on living our lives as if nothing happened. You need to trust me on this."

Joe said, "Luke, but you don't even know how to find Lonnie. Will you at least let us know what happened before the meeting so we can decide whether we need to pay him? It's our decision, after all. If you can't convince McDaniel, then Darren will be in danger if we don't give in to his demand. As much as giving him the money might be wrong, it still might be the right move for us."

Luke opened the car door and gestured for us to leave. "I'm asking you to trust me. I'll take care of it and you won't have to worry about Lonnie. It's what I do. You just take care of your business. You're doing a wonderful thing for Glenville. It was great seeing you guys."

With that, Luke turned quickly and walked back toward his house. Ling was standing on the front porch and slipped her arm around his waist as he turned to give us a short wave. Then they opened the door and disappeared inside.

CHAPTER 28
BRAIN DRAIN

We slowly drove away from Luke's property. Not a word was spoken for several minutes. Joe finally broke the silence. "Wow, I didn't see that coming."

"Me either. I wasn't surprised that Luke didn't think we should pay Lonnie, but I didn't think he would suddenly take over and hand us a solution to our problem. I felt like he just pulled me out of that mud hole again."

Joe was deliberate in his speech when he spoke again. "Well, maybe he will solve the problem and maybe he won't. Let's face it; the guy is one serious badass with special military training and a forty-year history of licensed killing. But that was all done with the resources of the U.S. military complex behind him. He's alone now and operating on Lonnie's turf. He has no idea where to find him. And if he does find him, he has no idea just how crazy this guy might really be. I'm not ready to accept the fact that Luke can pull this off in time. I think we need to be ready with Plan B just in case."

I couldn't argue with Joe's logic and I wanted to be prepared one way or another when we announced our plan for the distribution of funds. I only hoped that Luke was successful and would let us know prior to the meeting.

* * *

We had no other meetings for the rest of the day, so we decided just to head back to the hotel for a couple of hours and try to collect our thoughts. I sat at the desk in the room and made a list of people we still had to see. It was now a very short list. Unfortunately, it included the town hall meeting where we intended to let anyone or any group we missed have a chance to make their case. Joe and I feared that it would be an absolute zoo inhabited by a particular species of Glenville village idiots. However, we also thought there might be a few legitimate areas that we had overlooked. At least we could claim that we did our due diligence in reaching out to the community. John Bourke had already run the ad in the paper for several days and the meeting was scheduled for the next evening at 7:00 p.m. in the Westside Elementary cafeteria.

As I jotted down notes on my laptop, Joe was sitting on the edge of his bed quietly playing a tune on his guitar. On road trips, he always carried a nifty little Yamaha "silent guitar" with him. It was collapsible and traveled well. The beauty of this instrument was it produced only a barely audible sound of fingers picking on nylon strings while Joe could hear the music perfectly amplified through a set of earphones attached to the guitar. Throughout our stay in Glenville, I'd look over at Joe and he'd be quietly rocking out to some song only he could hear. I usually paid no attention to him while I read or watched SportsCenter, but this time he was quietly singing some lyrics I had never heard before.

I'm gonna have myself a craniotomy
I'm just as happy, just as happy as can be
There's some stuff in my head
And the doctors they all said
We got to see now just what it could be
Shave my head; make it nice and smooth
Put me to sleep and I'll take a little snooze . . .

"Joe, what in hell is that song about? Did you just make that up?"

Joe pulled out his earphones and asked, "What did you say?"

"I asked you why you were singing a song about a craniotomy!"

"Well, my brother, that is because I'm letting my creative juices flow as I ready myself for an unpleasant chapter in my life. I've actually been working on this little tune for a few days now. I call it "Brain Drain." Kind of catchy, don't you think?"

"Why are you suddenly thinking this way? Has something changed?"

Joe put down his guitar and heaved a heavy sigh. "Yeah, things have changed. I didn't want to bother you with it until I knew more, but the drugs I've been taking for the past few days haven't worked. I'm still having the tremors in my leg, which means there must still be pressure on my brain. The seizures are getting stronger. I've just been lucky that they didn't occur when you or anyone else could see it happening. It scares the crap out of me.

"I called Carol and she called the specialist at Johns Hopkins who reviewed my original brain scan. He wants me to come home and get another scan. Since the drugs don't seem to be working, the only option is to remove the lesion so they can get the swelling down. That will also let them biopsy the mass to see if it's cancerous or just something benign that is causing this side effect."

I was stunned. I had just assumed that Joe was doing better since he hadn't talked about any further tremors. We had been so busy that I guess I put his problems on a back burner. If I was honest with myself, I had to admit that I just didn't want to let myself go there. Now I looked at my brother and I couldn't hold back the tears in my eyes. I couldn't say anything. I just lowered my head and silently wiped my eyes with my shirtsleeve, as if that would somehow cover up what I was feeling.

"Hey, Darren, I'm sorry to drop this on you. I've had a day or two to get used to the idea and that's why I started knocking out this goofy song." When I glanced up at Joe I could see that his eyes were red but he was keeping a better handle on his emotions than me. "If I had time I was going to cut a quick CD in my studio at home and give it to my neurosurgeon just for kicks. I told you this guy looks like he's about twenty years old. He's the top guy at Johns Hopkins for this kind of stuff, apparently. Maybe he could play it while he's cutting my skull open!"

Typical of Joe, he was ready just to move ahead and deal with it. That's what I'd have to do as well.

"When are you leaving?"

"Well, the doc says I probably shouldn't fly just to be safe, so Carol is flying in to Indy the day after tomorrow and we'll drive back. We'll be heading straight to the hospital instead of going home. That way I can be here for our town hall meeting tomorrow night and you'll have to wrap up any loose ends without me after that. I'm sure we can keep doing some FaceTime right up to the final meeting and you can keep me up to speed with any developments on Luke and McDaniel. I'm real sorry, Darren, that I can't see this all the way through with you. I really wanted to be there when we announced our plan."

"You don't have to worry about any of this. I'll keep you posted every day except, of course, when you're having your head cut open. I might not want your opinion that day." Might as well start joking about this now. It's the only way that I'll be able to cope with it.

"Okay, then we'll just keep moving forward. As I said from the beginning, we'll take this a day at a time and we'll respond to whatever news the wonderful world of medicine has to offer. I still have a lot of living to do."

With that proclamation, Joe grabbed his guitar and put his earphones back in. "I'm thinking about this for an ending to the song. I'm still working on it."

I got a surgeon; he's a rock star, that's for sure
He's been doing this since he was only four
Says he'll be done in an hour and a half

Sure hope he's right, 'cause the drugs may not last
Why am I not worried?
Friends are asking me
This ain't rocket science
It's just brain surgery!

CHAPTER 29

WANDA AND DOREEN

Following a couple of hours devoted to note-taking, guitar-playing, and napping, Joe and I were ready to slide over to our neighborhood grill to see Mandy and the rest of the early regulars. After Joe's last admission, I needed a beer to at least temporarily provide a little comfort. I was also counting on Mandy to partially lift the dark cloud that was suddenly following the two brothers around.

Mandy didn't fail us as she greeted the Kelly brothers with a big smile like an old friend from the past. We settled in and started chatting about her day and the continual challenge of raising two young boys. She always amazed us with her insight about people and the positives and negatives of life in a small town. She seemed to volunteer for every possible opportunity in support of the school system. Regardless of the issue, she always maintained a supportive and non-judgmental way of viewing others. She really had talent and an aptitude for helping others that reached far beyond her job as a bartender. However, those traits were also the likely reason why she was so good at her current job and so well-compensated. Her tip jar overflowed and a large number of customers seemed to always choose camping out at the bar instead of elsewhere in the restaurant.

Even though this evening would likely be Joe's last dinner at Applebee's, we decided not to let Mandy in on Joe's need to return home. Joe just wanted to escape that reality for a while and enjoy the evening. A few of the regulars stopped by to say hello to us. We had become nearly permanent fixtures and by now the word had spread about our mission in town. Some folks just were being friendly and some were embarrassingly obvious in their lame attempts to ingratiate themselves with us. What did they think—we were going to whip out a checkbook and drop a couple of grand on them?

When we were about halfway through our dinners, two women quietly slid into the bar stools on either side of us. Joe and I both did a very unsubtle double-take since these women were quite attractive—and attractive women did not generally waste their time chatting us up. Both appeared to be in their early forties, one blonde and one brunette, and both in exceptionally good shape. A little too much make-up probably covered up some road miles, but I wasn't one to nitpick at this point. To a couple of twenty-something guys, these two gals would be aging cougars. To men our age, they were in the prime of their lives.

Joe never liked being interrupted while he was eating. It was a sacred time for him. The blonde version sat on the stool next to him and made a big mistake by asking, "What are you up to stranger?"

Joe didn't look up as he slowly moved a forkful of mashed potatoes toward his mouth. "I'm knitting a sweater." He sometimes became downright irritable when he was interrupted.

Mandy walked up and smiled at the two lovely bookends, "Hi, Wanda . . . hey, Doreen—I see you've made the acquaintance of the world-famous Kelly brothers." The brunette next to me spoke first. "Well, actually, Mandy, we have yet to be formally introduced to these gentlemen. We just sat down and hoped to share some ideas with them, if they didn't mind. In the meantime, you can just bring us two glasses of Chardonnay, please." Mandy flashed me what I perceived to be a warning look with her raised eyebrows as she turned to retrieve the drinks.

Wanda turned to me with what I'm sure was her very best practiced smile and put out her hand, "I'm Wanda, and you must be Darren Kelly." I shook her hand and she quickly managed to place her other hand on top of mine. "I'm so glad that we finally get a chance to meet, Darren." What's that supposed to mean? She's been longing to meet me? Who is this woman?

With one introduction out of the way, Joe initiated a preemptive strike and said to the blonde on his right, "That would make me Joe, and you would be Doreen, correct?" Joe didn't take the fork out of his hand in a doomed attempt to signal a greater interest in eating rather than talking. Doreen laughed a little too much at Joe's opening line and just reached out and squeezed his shoulder, "Oh, Joe, I knew you had a sense of humor. I saw your Facebook page and it has humor all over it."

I turned to Joe. "Since when did you have a Facebook page?" I seldom checked my Facebook activity and was stunned to learn that Joe had even ventured into that world.

Joe shrugged his shoulders. "When I made my CD, I decided I needed to get the word out and Facebook was an easy way to do that. In the process, I actually connected with a bunch of old friends and it's been pretty cool. In fact, I now have about five hundred 'friends' who just can't seem to get enough of me. I've never heard of most of them, but when someone asks to be your friend, it's hard to say no."

Doreen offered, "That's what I did. I just asked to be your friend and you said 'yes' right away. And now here we are. We're friends sitting at a bar." Okay—Doreen just might be a stalker. But with her looks, it just might be okay.

"Which begs the question," Joe said. "Why would you be looking me up on Facebook and why are you two very attractive ladies wanting to spend time with us?"

Just then Mandy returned with the wine and quietly commented as she turned away, "Now there's the million dollar question, isn't it?"

Wanda took the lead in explaining their sudden attraction to the Kelly brothers. "Well, we heard that you gentlemen were in town and the rumor mill has been pretty strong about this estate that you are overseeing. Of course, the announcement for the informational meeting came out in the paper this week and that just confirmed the rumors. We thought it would be in our best interests—and yours, of course—if we had a chance to speak to you before that meeting. We have a business venture that could use some additional funding."

So that was it. Our irresistible charm was not the reason (or at least not the only reason) that two attractive, younger women suddenly took a great interest in us. Money. It always comes down to money when a guy in his sixties suddenly looks attractive to a woman twenty years younger. He can think whatever he wants. I look younger than my age, I have a great sense of humor, and I'm in excellent shape . . . blah, blah, blah. Money. It's all about the money. I suddenly felt very deflated.

Joe and I had a long history of failure when it came to the girls of Glenville. The highlight of my entire youthful experience with girls was walking hand in hand to first grade with my neighbor, Joyce Seagram. She was a tall blonde beauty who already looked like a model in my mind. Plus, her father built one of the first bomb shelters in town in case of a tornado or the imminent Soviet Union nuclear attack. I already had fantasies about her pulling me into the shelter just before the blast went off, where we would live together for the next ten years. But she grew another four inches in first grade and towered over me. It started to look like she was dragging her little brother off to school and that just didn't work for her. She set her sights on third graders. It was a sad but amicable breakup.

That rejection stayed with me until middle school when I saved up a huge amount of money (at least twenty dollars) to buy a charm bracelet for Becky Windham. She barely knew I existed, but I thought (like most guys) that the bracelet would get her attention and then I could win her over with my wit and a promise of more jewelry. I stood across the street from her house for thirty minutes, hiding behind a tree while I rehearsed the lines I'd use when she answered the door. The more I rehearsed, the more I was certain that she'd laugh in my face. I eventually just sneaked away—convinced that rejection was a certainty. She never knew just how close she came to the start of a beautiful relationship that could have lasted a lifetime. And, with that action, I had embarked on a life-long pattern of avoiding embarrassment and rejection by never making the first move with a girl.

Joe was the same. He only seemed to attract exceptionally weird girls who never seemed to fit in with the other kids. The Van Winkle girls (age ten and seven) down the street from us on Garfield Drive both took an interest in us. The older one, Gretchen, really tried to impress us by cooking lunch one day— boiled weenies on Wonder Bread. It was the first time Joe and I had witnessed the marvel of red dye floating to the surface of boiling water.

Following lunch, Gretchen took Joe into the bathroom (her mother was at the other end of the house) and tried to convince him that they should both drop their pants and show each other their private parts. "We're moving to Cincinnati in a month and I just want to see what a boy looks like down there (she points) before I go." This was apparently a ten-year-old girl's version of "I'm shipping out for the war in the morning and this might be our last chance together." Joe didn't buy it. He had seen what she did to those weenies and it scared him. He grabbed me and we ran home.

Eventually in high school, Joe and I were able to settle into fairly traditional boyfriend-girlfriend relationships. This was due to the kindness of girls who took the time to find out that these two shy guys could actually make them laugh sometimes and they both had perfectly acceptable hygiene habits. What more could you ask for in a guy? Our relationships were simple and wholesome. Other guys bragged about their sexual conquests—generally related to what "base" they had reached in the back seats of their cars at the National Drive-In Theater. I never fully understood the whole baseball/sex analogy.

First base really was ambiguous as a starting point but always seemed to include exploratory expeditions with tongues. Second base appeared to involve the partial removal of one piece of clothing or at least the uncoupling of snaps or hooks. Getting to third base was also loosely defined but always required exhaustive effort and a promise to love and cherish forever while never telling another soul what went on in that back seat.

Actually arriving at home plate was subject to wildly differing interpretations but generally involved avoiding the catcher's block and actually touching home plate in some fashion, even if through multiple layers of clothing. Of course, hitting a Grand

Slam was reported to be the ultimate triumph in the baseball/ sex analogy and allegedly resulted in the car rocking to the point that it tipped over in the back row of the drive-in. To my knowledge, no one ever witnessed this phenomena first-hand but it was reported by several guys who never stopped smiling in high school.

I, on the other hand, was simply happy to have arrived at the baseball stadium holding the hand of an actual girlfriend. I wasn't about to risk rejection by attempting to jump on the field and round the bases. And that brings us back to Wanda and Doreen, who have taken an uncommon interest in two guys who don't normally attract an uncommon interest from women. They were after a piece of Uncle Shorty's money and I was sure that Joe and I were looking better by the minute.

Wanda took the lead. "We want to start a community-minded program called The Glenville Holistic Spiritual Center. It will be a place where all ages can come and enjoy a variety of healing arts that will help the citizens of Glenville become more 'centered' in their lives and open to change in their spiritual awakening." At this point Wanda placed her hand on my arm to really get my attention. "Darren, have you ever experienced an authentic Swedish massage?"

"No, but I once ate a plate of authentic Swedish meatballs and they were delicious."

Wanda ignored my attempt at humor and kept rolling along. "Well, I'm a licensed massage therapist and I guarantee you I can make you feel absolutely wonderful after an hour in my experienced hands." She gave me a conspiratorial wink and I began to sense a better understanding of the perks that come with money and power.

Doreen jumped into the conversation while Wanda's hand lingered on my arm. "And I'm a trained lymphatic therapist in addition to being licensed in hydrotherapy. We also have another gal who is an expert with crystals and can help people relieve their energy blocks with the right vibrational match. With enough funding from you two gentlemen, we could add Sufi healing sessions, herb and acupuncture therapy, and maybe even a psychic medium who could help people reach out to their loved ones in the after-life."

Joe couldn't resist. "And what exactly does a lymphatic therapist do?"

"Well," Doreen explained, "the trained therapist performs a procedure called lymphatic drainage, which cleanses the patient of all sorts of toxins."

"I see. And you've actually performed this 'drainage' procedure?"

"No, not exactly," Doreen admitted. "But I took a two-week online course to get my certification and I did perform the procedure on a doll that was included in our training kit. I think I'm ready."

"Oh, so do I, Doreen," Joe offered with enthusiasm. "A two-week course seems more than sufficient to drain the lymphatic region of its toxins. Good for you. If you couple that with a good hydrotherapy job, I'd think that the patient would be cleaned out for months."

Doreen was beaming. She had found a soul mate in Joe. "Joe, let me guess. You must be a Capricorn, right? What's your sign?"

"It's a Stop Sign." That's all Joe said.

"Oh, silly. I know we must be compatible. What kind of women do you like?"

Joe didn't blink. "I like my women completely anonymous and delivered to me via the Internet from websites that include the words 'hot' and/or 'desperate' in the title. I'm also partial to detached voices on the phone that charge me ninety-nine cents a minute."

Doreen and Wanda just looked at each other not knowing what to say next.

I tried to change the subject. "You two are from California, aren't you? You cannot possibly be from Indiana!"

Wanda smiled and massaged my arm some more. I could tell she had talent. "Darren, you are a very perceptive man. Doreen and I grew up in Glenville, but left for Hollywood to make our fortunes right after high school."

"How'd that work out for you?" Joe asked without a noticeable hint of sarcasm.

"Well, it was a lot harder to become actresses than we thought. We had a few background roles in commercials and then eventually landed some film roles in smaller, alternative productions. That only lasted a few years since there was a high demand for younger girls." With this admission, Wanda and Doreen exchanged sheepish grins. "We bounced around between odd jobs, but eventually made our way back home and started offering our different therapies that we learned in California."

Joe and I glanced at each other with only one question in mind: porn stars? They didn't actually come out and declare themselves in that category, but all the evidence seemed to point in that direction. We were sitting here with two beautiful women who needed our money—technically, Uncle Shorty's. They were clearly willing to do anything for it, and had demonstrated that they were skilled in a variety of "healing arts." The Kelly brothers had never been in this situation before. It was difficult to even fantasize this big.

Of course, the fact that we were happily married men and these two lovely ladies lived on another planet prohibited this wonderful fantasy from overcoming our sense of reality. Also, the fact that Mandy was standing off to the side behind the bar listening in and smirking didn't help matters. Doreen's goofy smile and Wanda's increasingly uncomfortable pressure on my arm made it clear that this fantasy would have to just take its place next to the Jewel Tea Man's desperately gorgeous housewife and the pool contractor's bikini-clad homeowner—oh, and being trapped in the bomb shelter with Joyce for ten years.

Joe saved us with a bold move. "Girls, we'll take care of your drinks, but I think you should run along now. You see, I have cancer—and it's the contagious kind."

Doreen quickly removed her hand from Joe's shoulder and I could feel Wanda leaning back away from me on her stool. Being the sharper knife in the drawer, Wanda commented, "I didn't think cancer could be contagious. I never heard of such a thing."

"Well, you'll be hearing all about it soon. It's a new variety and I'm one of the lucky ones to get it first. Darren probably has it by now, but he just doesn't know it yet."

With that little announcement, our fantasy evening started moving quickly toward the door. Wanda called out over her shoulder. "You keep us in mind when you dole out that money. We could help a lot of people in this town."

Joe shouted back. "You bet we will. I might even stop by for a massage or some hydrotherapy! You girls take care, now." With that last exchange, Wanda and Doreen moved quickly toward their car.

Mandy joined us and we all started laughing so hard we had tears in our eyes. Joe, in particular, had a hard time stopping. I realized it was the first time I had truly laughed out loud since Joe shared the news about his health problems. "I can't believe you played the cancer card!"

"Well, I figured drastic times called for drastic measures. Plus, I thought I'd see how it felt to say it out loud. It was pretty strange. Guess that's why I added the contagious part."

Mandy gave Joe a quizzical look. "What do you mean you wanted to see how it felt to say it out loud?"

Joe wasn't going to go there and he was quick on his feet. "Oh, we have a very close friend who just found out he likely has cancer and we're still coming to grips with the idea. It's been hard to verbalize."

Mandy immediately bought it and, characteristically, showed concern for a person she didn't even know. "I'm sorry about your friend, Joe, and I really hope he gets better."

"Thanks Mandy. I hope so, too. I really do."

CHAPTER 30

WRAPPING UP LOOSE ENDS

The next morning Joe and I had our final Glenville breakfast before he would head back to Maryland early the next day. Bunny, our disgruntled leathery waitress, might be waiting at Bob Evans to personally cash Joe's check with a frying pan to the side of the head, so we opted for another trek to Cracker Barrel. We arranged to meet John Bourke there since he wanted more background information on the story he would ultimately write for the *Glenville Daily Reporter*. While waiting for John to arrive, we spent the time getting ready for the meeting that night and discussing strategies for ultimately dispersing Uncle Shorty's money.

The reality was we didn't expect much to come out of the meeting. Like most bureaucrats charged with a task that involved public input, we had already privately sought out the opinions of people who seemed to have credibility. At least the institutions they represented had credibility, so the representatives were a necessary component to be consulted. When the public is "invited to comment," the invitation is generally designed to create the illusion that all input will be considered equally in the process. Politicians are masterful at this ploy.

Joe and I had to be honest in admitting to ourselves that we were just as guilty to some extent. We had done our due diligence and worried that we might only hear about funding for "Naked Acres: A Clothing Optional Community" or a proposed "Glenville Pot Festival." But, we still felt that there could be some worthwhile input that might shift some funding in a particular direction.

While we waited for the editor to arrive, Joe and I laughed some more about Doreen and Wanda. We had both called home the night before to share the story with our wives. They laughed at the tale, but somehow didn't seem too surprised. Joe and I were both struck by the fact that we often found ourselves over the years in awkward situations with bizarre women. The reality was that we had both enjoyed long professional careers with a variety of strong, intelligent, and gifted women. We had married similar women. Our mother was a strong and determined woman. That was our norm. Yet, throughout the years, when we were together, we seemed to attract the likes of Doreen, Wanda, and Bunny, the waitress.

Why didn't a nice female doctor sit down to talk with us at Applebee's about the needs of the hospital? How about one of my classmates who went on to be vice president at the bank? Why didn't Mandy introduce us to some of the more upstanding, professional women in town who might have good ideas about how to distribute Uncle Shorty's estate? No, we end up being accosted by the Holistic Spiritual Center girls and the creepy waitress. Maybe we come off as simple-minded guys, so we attract women from a pool of similar personalities and intellect. Whatever the cause, we're stuck with it. Thank God we found the right women to marry. We'd be in trouble otherwise.

John Bourke arrived and dropped down in his chair with a heavy sigh. "I'm going to miss you boys after this is all over. I haven't seen the rumor mill so active in town since Russell Wheeler, our local judge, got accused of having affairs with the assistant district attorney and his court reporter at the same time."

I wasn't about to go for the bait and encourage another one of Bourke's stories. I knew my silence would just kill him. I said nothing.

"Don't you want to know what happened to the judge?"

"Nope, we have work to do here and I don't need to hear another fabricated John Bourke story."

Bourke looked a little hurt. "Kelly, I never have to fabricate stories; I just embellish them a bit." Then he laughed. "Are you boys getting a little impatient to get out of Glenville? Well, my point is that you two have generated a fair amount of rumors around here yourselves. It'll be interesting to see what comes out in the meeting tonight."

In John Bourke's announcement and story in the paper, we had asked him to avoid the term "town hall meeting" since it might suggest that we really wanted the whole town to show up. If five people showed up, we'd be happy. He came up with an appropriately innocuous title, "Investing in Glenville's Future—

An Informational Meeting on Community Needs." In his cover story, he generally described the fact that an estate had been left to assist with community needs in Glenville.

Of course, no dollar amount was given and Joe and I were only briefly mentioned as the executors of the estate. Those agencies already interviewed by the estate executors were encouraged not to attend since their needs were already documented. Bourke even added a time frame of two hours for the meeting in the hope that people would get a clue that they couldn't ramble on forever. That was probably optimistic thinking on our part.

We gave Bourke some background on our various discussions around town. We had promised him the full story when we first met and we wanted him to understand our thought process. Of course, two important encounters were left out of the discussion. One was with Lonnie McDaniel and the other with Luke Jackson. With breakfast finished, our friend seemed satisfied that he had the makings of a good story. It would be an even better one when he learned the magnitude of the estate and just how much it could help. He'd attend the meeting that night and the last meeting when we announced the plan. In the meantime, I promised him a final interview before I left town. Little did he know that he'd be meeting only with me; Joe would be long gone to Maryland by then.

* * *

We had one final meeting scheduled that day at the hospital. In terms of established organizations that are designed to help people in town, the hospital was the last one on our list and no doubt the one with the largest budget of them all. As we approached the hospital, Joe surprised me. "Why don't you take this one by yourself? I think I'll just drop you off and go for one last drive around town."

"What's the matter? You don't want to see guys your age shuffling around with their asses hanging out the back of their gowns?" Might as well state the obvious.

"Yeah, and I don't need to hear that guy warn me about checking in. I think I'm going to get my fill of hospitals when I return home. I'd much rather enjoy a pleasant drive."

He dropped me off and gave me a little smile and a nod of his head as he pulled away from the curb. I felt a wave of loneliness wash over me just then. This would be the first meeting where Joe wasn't by my side exchanging glances of understanding with me, probing the participants with questions, and generally offering unique observations that emanated from his wonderfully skewed perspective on life. I realized how much this journey over the past few weeks was about time we spent together as brothers just as much as it was about the task at hand. I really wasn't looking forward to this next meeting.

I checked in at the hospital administration office and was soon greeted by a very professional-looking woman who appeared to be in her early fifties. Mrs. Humphrey gave me a firm handshake and a pleasant smile as she welcomed me back to her private office. She was quite tall, at least five foot ten, and appeared to be very fit judging from her perfectly tailored business suit. It was clear that she was a busy person who wanted to get right to business.

"Do you know who I am, Mrs. Humphrey?" Though the opening line could be misinterpreted, I figured we might as well cut right to the bottom line.

"Yes, as of this morning when I checked my calendar. I asked my assistant to fill me in and she had lots of stories about two brothers returning to Glenville to administer an estate that some say is quite sizeable. I presume you're here to discuss the needs of the hospital and I'm happy to share information with you and to be as helpful as I can."

This was good news. First, this lady was quick and to the point. Second, the fact that she hadn't read about Joe and me in the paper gave me hope that most other people hadn't clued into our meeting tonight. Maybe we could avoid the zoo that I feared.

"Mrs. Humphrey, I'm going to be real straight with you. We have some funds to administer and many, many worthy organizations that could benefit from that funding. Some really have very little to work with right now. Others, like the school system for instance, seem to have endless opportunities to improve with some additional money. There is no doubt that a hospital like this one is a huge benefit to a small community, but your operation really seems pretty robust compared to some others in town. Why should we funnel money to an organization that seems to be already doing well on its own?"

She started in on a list of services provided to the community and noted from memory statistics for every category in the past fiscal year. I heard about the number of patient days, emergency room visits, surgical procedures, radiologic procedures, physical therapy treatments and an extraordinary number of lab tests performed. Mrs. Humphrey knew her stuff and she was very proud of the service the hospital provided to the residents of Glenville. They were improving lives in many cases and literally saving lives in many more. I let her go on for quite some time since she was so knowledgeable and I really was curious about the role of a hospital in a relatively small town. Joe would have brought this discussion to a conclusion much sooner, but Mrs. Humphrey would have impressed even him.

"If some money were to be made available to you, how would you use it?"

"Mr. Kelly, we are a private, non-profit hospital. We get by, but there are always needs. Medical equipment is extraordinarily expensive and is in constant need of upgrading. Our facilities are old and require repair and renovation. Our staff is underpaid compared to larger hospitals. Medicare payments are shrinking and we rely more than ever on fundraising provided by our Hospital Foundation. I can only tell you that every dollar spent here would go toward the greater good of this community. You could not choose a better recipient of funds to know that your donation was well spent."

Mrs. Humphrey was making me a believer, and responding to the health needs of the community was certainly an easy choice. Yet, I couldn't help but think that Joe would not let such a glowing report slide by so easily. I can just hear him ask, "So would you mind providing us with a list of supplies you use in the hospital and show us their cost versus what you charge patients? Would we find any twenty-five-cent pills that are charged out at twenty-five dollars? How about fifty-dollar socks to keep the feet warm? Got any two hundred-dollar bedpans? And while we're at it, could we get a list of all your procedures conducted for the past year and compare your patient charges to the state-wide average in Indiana? We just want to be certain that the citizens of Glenville are not paying an extraordinary premium compared to what they could get by taking a twenty-five-minute drive to Indianapolis."

That's what Joe would do. He would try to shake things up a little with some good old-fashion confrontation. Sometimes I think Joe was channeling Mike Wallace from *60 Minutes*. He'd hold the hospital accountable and make them prove that they were worthy of Uncle Shorty's money over other deserving groups in town.

But I had lost my energy and enthusiasm for such sparring matches. It just wasn't as interesting without Joe. The hospital might be a model of efficiency or it might be gouging the local patients. It likely fell somewhere in between the two. I'd gather what information I could and we'd just have to make our best decision on what we had.

So, I asked Mrs. Humphrey to send me whatever comparative data she had available and to get it to me right away. I told her what I was looking for without being at all accusatory. She still looked at me as if I had somehow questioned her integrity and her hesitant reply of "I'll see what I can pull together" didn't inspire confidence that I would get much of substance. So be it. Our work was nearly done and I was anxious to finish. I took out my cell phone and called Joe to pick me up.

CHAPTER 31

THE TOWN HALL MEETING

People started to arrive at the Westside Elementary cafeteria about fifteen minutes before the announced 7:00 p.m. starting time. We had chosen the site primarily for nostalgic reasons, since Joe and I had gone to school there and our house on Garfield Drive was just a block away. It just seemed fitting that he and I would have this last night together in Glenville in our old neighborhood before he headed back to Maryland to his other reality.

I looked out the cafeteria windows and saw the familiar Glenville Water Tower standing tall with its red beacon flashing a warning to any planes that might be flying by in the approaching night sky. The basketball courts behind the school were empty, but I could see a mother and father pushing two young kids on the swing set. I wondered if they had walked down from their home on Garfield Drive after supper.

Our friend, Superintendent Harkins, had used his pull to reserve the school site for the meeting. It was a nice casual setting that I hoped would set a productive tone for what I feared might be a challenging group to manage. What would you expect when you announce that you have some money to give away and you're looking for people who have problems that need to be solved? We might have issued an invitation to every nut job in town.

I just hoped that wasn't the case and we'd hear about some worthwhile issues that we had missed in our other interviews. Joe and I watched from a side room as the first rows started to fill. We had hoped for a crowd of less than fifty. By 7:00 p.m. there were about a hundred and fifty people in the room.

I scanned the room and saw editor John Bourke smiling in the back. He gave me a wink. Chief Hagman was in the other corner putting on his best tough-guy look for the crowd. He had a couple of other officers around the perimeter just to help us send a message that we expected an orderly meeting. I could also see clusters of folks representing the many groups that Joe and I had interviewed. Mrs. Humphrey from the hospital was even there with a few guys in suits. Guess they wanted a look at the competition. I saw most of the church leaders, Dennis Harmon from the Girls and Boys Club, the loquacious mayor along with an entourage of bureaucrats, and the staff from the seniors center with a fairly large contingent of older folks.

I was surprised to see Mandy sitting in the back of the room and even more surprised to see Doreen and Wanda just a few rows ahead of her. Perhaps our porn queens had done a little research and realized that cancer didn't tend to be contagious. I nudged Joe and pointed out the girls. He rolled his eyes and quietly said, "We need to make a quick exit when this thing is over."

I had one more surprise for him. "You don't know the half of it. Your waitress friend, Bunny, is sitting in the third row on the left and she's looking right at you!" Joe couldn't help himself. He took a quick peek and there was Bunny pointing a bony finger at him. The good news was she was smiling. Maybe she had a sense of humor about Joe's big check. The bad news was her blouse was unbuttoned again.

Time to get started. Joe and I walked to the front of the room where a table had been arranged with two chairs and a microphone at each setting. I was sure the senior members of the audience would appreciate the amplified sound, as would the Kelly brothers. Two microphones had been placed on stands in the audience where people could line up and make comments, or ask questions, or just babble.

I took the lead on behalf of the Kelly brothers and thanked the group for coming to the meeting. I gave my usual brief explanation about the Hazelton estate and its intention to help the citizens of Glenville. This time I made an extra effort to describe Uncle Shorty a bit more and to give those attending a better understanding of why he chose to leave his money to create a long-term benefit to the community. It was very gratifying to share more about Shorty and Meta Hazelton since most people in town didn't know them. It gave me a chance to humanize this couple instead of allowing them to remain just another anonymous source of funds for the community.

Then I described some ground rules for the meeting in hopes of creating some order to what potentially could become disruptive if the wrong people commandeered the microphones. I explained how each speaker would have a ten-minute time limit and that we would turn off the microphone at the end of that period. I explained that no decisions would be made that night. We were just interested in hearing from everyone and trying to put all of their concerns in perspective.

I also tried my best to let folks know that Joe and I were instructed to use our own judgment about awarding the money and that our intent was to focus on community-wide programs rather than respond to individual problems that might need a financial solution. I hoped that might cut off some of the bad-luck stories about people needing individual bailouts. My strategy clearly was a bust when the first person approached the microphone.

"I'm Randall T. Tubbs and I live out on County Road 300. I'm a farmer." Joe leaned over and whispered, "Gee, I never would have guessed that." Randall Tubbs was wearing overalls with a long-sleeve T-shirt underneath and a well-used John Deere hat on his head. His right sleeve was pinned back onto his shoulder, presumably because there was no arm in the sleeve.

"You might notice that I'm missing my right arm. Had an accident last year working on my combine. Took it clean off. I'm not here to complain about that. That'd just be spittin' in the wind. But I can say for a fact that being a one-armed farmer isn't as glamorous as it might sound." That line got a few laughs from the crowd. "I can't keep up with what it takes to grow a crop and that means I can't make any money to pay my expenses and I can't provide my share of food to this here community of Glenville. Seems to me that everyone loses."

I tried to get to the bottom line. "And what would you have us do about your dilemma, Mr. Tubbs?"

"Give me some damn money so I can get help to work my farm! That's what I'd have you do! I don't care how you go about it, but I think some hard-working folks like me who have fallen on tough times should maybe have some kind of fund set up to help us get back on our feet. That's all I got to say. I'm not here to beg." With that, Randall T. Tubbs went back to his chair and sat down.

That singular appeal for help opened the floodgates for individual problems. We heard about a single mother, Louise Ratcliff, who had a sick child with a disease I'd never heard of and no insurance to cover the costs of curing it. Charles Green lost his job at the Caterpillar plant six months ago and couldn't make his mortgage payments. His wife didn't work and they had four kids. A little old lady, Marge Wilson, told us in a halting voice how an "investment counselor" had stolen her entire life savings after she trusted him with everything she had. He was later arrested, but the money was gone. She had nothing and was being evicted. She broke down in tears and several people jumped up to help her back to her seat. It was heartbreaking.

There must have been a dozen legitimate stories about family hardships. Bad things had happened to good people. More stories were told about being out of work. Several women were primary care givers to parents and had to make monthly choices about whether to spend money on food or on drugs to help the parent. A disheveled-looking man stepped up to the microphone and described in a very clear and coherent manner that he just needed a roof over his head during the winter. He had no place to go and no money. Another man who appeared to be homeless attempted to speak, but just wandered off into a monologue of gibberish before shaking his head and sitting down in the corner. I wanted to fix their problems on the spot, but knew that I couldn't just blindly take that approach.

However, there were other appeals that weren't so compelling. Mr. Cooper needed money to invest in a new car technology powered by soybeans. Linda Butterfield had the desirable goal of weaning people off of sugary sweets with her prune cupcakes that "tasted just like the real thing without all the sugar." Right. And Bud Light tastes just like Budweiser. Joe Scanlon simply wanted to expand his auto repair shop. He figured he was providing a community service and we could help him do a better job of it by funding his expansion.

Two young boys approached the microphone stand. A helpful man lowered the mic for them. The boys said they were homeless and living in an abandoned truck in a salvage yard outside of town. A collective gasp came from the crowd. The young fellas were very composed as they told of their long cold nights with no food. For kids who were homeless, these two boys looked remarkably fit and clean. Their tale of woe may have momentarily worked on the crowd, but it was clearly flawed.

Joe quietly asked the boys, "Guys, how much money would you like us to give you? You just say the word and it's yours."

The older boy jumped right in. "Well, we figured that maybe we could get a thousand dollars from you and then we could get some real good food and maybe fix up the truck a bit. You know, maybe get a mattress and some blankets. We'd really appreciate it, mister."

"Are you sure your names aren't Huck Finn and Tom Sawyer?"

"No, sir, we're Tommy and Jake Hall from over there in Pendleton—shit!" Young Tommy had just realized his mistake. It was hard to live in nearby Pendleton while also living in a truck outside Glenville.

Joe just laughed. "Boys, I appreciate your initiative and I'm very glad to learn that you don't have to live in that truck any longer. It was a good effort. Keep it up and you'll probably be politicians one day. Don't you worry about this, but I'm afraid Chief Hagman over there will need to reunite you with your rightful parents or guardians." Hagman looked at the boys and smiled while motioning for them to join him. The boys started to trudge off when a quiet applause rippled through the audience. The boys lit up and waved to the crowd like they were hometown heroes. It was a surreal scene. I leaned over and asked

Joe, "What the hell are they clapping for—nice attempt at swindling money? Good job of lying?"

"I guess they just appreciated the effort. You know, every kid is a winner—no child left behind."

Following that scene, the mayor of Glenville must have felt the need to restore the good name of politicians as he jumped up to the open microphone. "I would just like to remind you gentlemen of your opening remark about attempting to serve the needs of the greater community of Glenville. We have well-established government programs here in town to assist people who have fallen on hard times and I think your money would be best utilized and most effectively monitored in the hands of the elected leaders of this community. We will be looking out for all our citizens—young and old alike. I just don't see why you have to look at this issue so hard when you have a system in place ready to put that money to good use. As the mayor of Glenville, I am ready to lead the effort to distribute the funds appropriately throughout our various agencies."

A voice from the crowd bellowed, "Oh, shut the hell up, you little prick! You'd probably take that money and build a statue of yourself outside the courthouse!"

"Who said that? I demand to know who said that!"

Mr. Randall T. Tubbs rose to his feet. He might have been shaking his right fist, but I couldn't be certain. "You can demand all you want, you little piss-ant, but the city don't need the money. The people do."

I jumped in to quiet the laughter from the crowd. "Okay, Mr. Mayor, we have heard your perspective and, likewise, we believe that we fully understand and appreciate the perspective of Mr. Tubbs. Let's move on. Are there any other suggestions for Mr. Hazelton's funding?"

A small, somewhat frail looking woman moved to the microphone. She wore thick glasses and had her hair pulled back and tied off in a fashion that could be described kindly as haphazard. She had mastered the look of the "earthy" librarian or distracted scientist with a bland print dress that fell to her ankles, a light wool sweater that seemed a size too large, and tan socks inserted into sandals that had a distinct Birkenstock quality without the brand name.

A surprisingly strong and clear voice came out of the small person at the microphone. "I'm Ms. Templeton and I teach Environmental Studies at the high school. It's an elective in the science department. I have a degree in biology and a masters degree in environmental studies. Last year I applied for and received a large private educational grant to study some of the more unusual elements of the wetlands restoration that is located just east of the high school. I did this all on my own without involving the school administration.

"When they found out I was using the funds at my own discretion without school oversight, they attempted to take away my grant money. I threatened to sue the School Board and they backed off with the provision that future educational grants must come through them. It's none of their business how I handle my own grant money as long as my expenditures meet the grant guidelines. So, I'm coming to you for funding to bypass this overbearing and oppressive board in order to bring a unique and quality form of education to my students."

Well, that was certainly a cohesive and impressive statement that caught the attention of the crowd. Never a fan of large bureaucracies, I felt some empathy for this disheveled-looking science teacher. However, I took a glance at Assistant Superintendent Harkins in the back of the room and he was rotating his pointed finger at his temple and giving me the universal sign indicating, "this person is loony."

Joe was curious. "Ms. Templeton, exactly what were you studying out there in the wetlands?"

"Well, we were studying the weezuns and the way they lived."

Joe looked confused. "Excuse me, you said you were studying the 'reasons' out there?"

"No, silly, we were studying the weezuns—you know, the little fairy creatures that inhabit wetlands." As Ms. Templeton stared at Joe as if he were an idiot, he leaned toward me and whispered, "I just thought she had a lisp. This should be good."

"They create little colonies and communicate with humans via leaves and rocks and other forms of life. We studied them during winter (as they hibernated under the ice), through the thaw, and then into spring. I took my students out each period to witness this phenomena firsthand and to learn how to communicate with the weezuns. They loved it. At the spring showcase for parents, our class was able to show how they made masks out of mud and leaves and twigs and other gifts from the weezuns. The parents seemed to be truly surprised at this novel approach to learning."

"I'm sure they were, Ms. Templeton. I'm sure they were. And just how large was this grant?"

"It was $100,000 for one year and I would like to ask for the same amount from your fund to be administered outside of the School Board's jurisdiction." A low murmur worked its way through the crowd.

Joe's mouth dropped open. "You got $100,000 for making some masks out of mud and leaves?" He caught himself before saying anything more, paused and just smiled. I'm not sure if he was more shocked at the audacity of this person in front of him or the idiocy of a grant program that would fund her project. "And exactly how did you manage to spend that amount of money?"

"Well, The Center for the Study of Wetland Weezuns in New Orleans produces a number of educational materials that I bought for the students and for the spring showcase. Then there were boots and tools for working in the wetlands and advisors from the Center who flew out to help us. They were quite expensive—but worth every penny given their expertise. Then, of course, I had to fly out to New Orleans several times for refresher courses. They have wonderful wetlands there."

"Well, that sounds perfectly reasonable, Ms. Templeton. Darren and I will take your request under advisement along with all the others we have heard tonight. Thank you." This, remarkably, was said with a straight face.

As Harkins rather indelicately slashed his open hand across his throat in the back of the room, I asked one other question. "Oh, Ms. Templeton, before you go I have one last question. Do you have a contract to teach at the high school next year?" Harkins was vigorously shaking his head back and forth.

"Well, not exactly. That is to say that I was only on a contract for this one Environmental Studies course last year and I have not heard yet whether I will be asked back. I assume I will, particularly if I have a large grant that can benefit the school."

"Okay. Well, good luck to you, Ms. Templeton."

The wetlands presentation seemed to let the air out of the room. No one wanted to follow it. The groups that Joe and I had already met with wisely remained seated. They didn't want to be associated with some of the strange requests we had throughout the evening. Eventually a few more people spoke mostly on things such as fixing roads, supporting the arts community in town, setting money aside for downtown improvements, and building either a youth center or a senior center depending on the age of the speaker.

We had heard enough. I wrapped up the meeting with one last encouragement to send any further ideas to editor John Bourke at the paper. He would collect them and see that we got them in time for our self-imposed deadline, which was only now five days away. Five days and I could finally get back to my California life—where incorporating twigs and leaves to talk with an imaginary wetland creature was just another normal day in paradise.

CHAPTER 32

JOE GOES HOME TO MARYLAND

Joe and I spent our final evening together dining on some fine burgers from Steak 'n Shake and discussing what we took away from the meeting. We laughed at length about some of the characters—the one-arm farmer being our favorite. But we also struggled with some of the legitimate hardships brought forth. It had to be incredibly difficult for those folks (including farmer Tubbs) to stand up in front of the community and ask for help. We wanted to help, but just weren't sure if we should get down to that level of detail in trying to solve every problem in Glenville.

Joe asked, "Do you ever get the feeling that we're slipping into some sort of Orwellian existence here with trying to control everything in town with this money? I sometimes think we're playing Big Brother. I know it's not that extreme, but the whole thing makes me uncomfortable at some level."

"I had the same nagging feeling, but I didn't think about *1984*. I had a dream the other night and we were walking around with B.F. Skinner." Joe has heard me talk before about the behavioral psychologist who was known for motivating with reinforcement practices.

"Isn't he the guy that got in trouble for raising his kid in a large cage and treating her like one of his experiments?"

I didn't want to get into a debate with Joe about Skinner's theories since they were fairly radical but still germane to our discussion. Skinner believed that the notion of free will was just an illusion and that human behavior was almost entirely dictated by either being positively or negatively reinforced. I have to admit to seeing some degree of relevance in that sort of thinking. Joe would love to argue the theory.

"Anyway, can I get back to my dream? The guy was a little strange, but brilliant in his own way. In fact, his work inspired me as an undergraduate to train a rat, Leroy, to shoot little basketballs through a tiny basketball goal."

"You trained a rat to shoot hoops—and you named him Leroy?" Joe shook his head. "Only in Indiana."

"Absolutely. I got high praise for the project in an experimental psychology class. Anyway, Skinner wrote this book about a Utopian society where positive reinforcement was used to control all the citizens' behavior. In my dream, you and I were strolling around with Skinner talking about how we could create positive behavior by slowly dishing out the money in small increments to provide continuous reinforcement. We could essentially create our own Utopia here in Glenville."

"And were the citizens appropriately trained to bow down at our feet?"

"Very funny. My point, smartass, is that I've obviously been troubled by the weight of this decision as evidenced by my dream. And I, too, am concerned that it's unrealistic for us to solve every problem that we hear about. I think we need to paint with a broad brush or we'll never complete the project."

* * *

After several hours of sifting through our notes and discussing various tactics, Joe and I called it a night. We had substantially talked through everything and I would next meet with Borland to sort through some of the logistics of how to proceed. Once Joe got home and learned more about his health, he and I would get back on FaceTime to finalize a plan. He was feeling optimistic that night since he hadn't experienced a leg problem in hours and wondered if there had been a change of some sort.

Joe and I were both quiet the next morning as he packed his bags and got ready for the trip home. We were heading out early and didn't even leave time for our customary breakfast at one of the fine local eateries. A quick cup of coffee in the room gave Joe a chance to look around one last time. "I'm going to miss this place. Our talks . . . your snoring . . . endless hours of SportsCenter . . . stinking up the room with White Castles."

"Inviting a psychopath into our room?"

"Yeah, that too." Joe laughed, but then got very serious and I could see his eyes getting red. "Mostly I'll just miss our talks. It's been a hell of an experience, brother. I wouldn't have missed it for anything. I'm glad Uncle Shorty brought us back together again. You and I have something pretty special."

I already had tears in my eyes. "I feel the same way, Joe."

"So," he paused. "Is this getting a little weird now?"

"For us? Absolutely."

"Okay. That means it must be time to go!" Joe headed for the door with his bag and guitar case. I quickly followed.

We slowly pulled away from the hotel and turned toward Interstate 70, which would take us back toward Indianapolis and the airport, where Carol would be waiting for us. It was too early for much to be open, but a Shell station was lit up and we needed to get gas for Joe's car. We pulled in and stopped alongside a gas pump right in front of the small snack shop where an attendant sat with his face buried in the morning paper, not paying attention to us. There were no other customers.

Joe got out and started to fill the tank when a black pick-up truck pulled on the other side of the snack shop where there was another bay of gas pumps, including one for diesel. I didn't pay any attention to the truck or its driver as I checked my cell phone for messages. After a couple of minutes, Joe got back in and said, "Did you see who just pulled in?"

I hadn't noticed earlier, but just then I saw Jim Penfield, Joe's old nemesis and current Booster Club president. He was walking out of the snack shop with a cup of coffee in his hand, heading for his truck. I looked at Joe and said, "What a pleasant way for you to leave town—seeing your old friend in your rearview mirror."

Joe had a funny look on his face. "Yeah, that's just what I was thinking." He pulled our car forward and positioned it out of the way of any new customers and pointed it toward the exit onto the street. He then smiled at me and said, "I'll be right back. I just want to say goodbye to Penfield and let him know that there are no hard feelings. It's time one of us was mature about this and I need to finally get over that revenge dream about him."

I looked over at Penfield and saw him pumping gas into his truck with his left hand and sipping coffee with the other. He was facing toward Joe and suddenly realized who was walking toward him. Joe waved to Penfield and I could tell that he said something to him, but I couldn't make it out. A big smirk broke out across Penfield's face and he said something that I also couldn't hear.

You know how people start to slow down as they approach someone else? Whether they are going to shake hands, hug, or just stop short and shoot the breeze—they generally start to slow down a few steps away from the other person. Joe didn't. In fact, it appeared that he began to pick up speed in his last few strides. I suddenly realized that things were about to go very wrong. I watched, as if in slow motion, Joe took one last quick stride and lifted his knee into Penfield's crotch as hard as he possibly could. Joe is not an athletic guy, but if the judges were scoring without international bias, his knee-to-the-crotch effort was clearly a ten. It was perfection—that is, if extreme humiliation along with extraordinary pain and suffering were your objectives.

Penfield's mouth dropped open at the moment of impact. His eyes bulged at Joe. His coffee cup flew from his hand and, fortunately, the pump handle remained in the car as he released his hand from it. He fell to the pavement like dead weight and then curled up into a ball with his hands attempting to offer comfort to his crotch. I was certain that comfort would not arrive in that region for hours. I quickly glanced at the snack shop to see if the attendant was watching. He was clueless, still buried in his newspaper. No other customers had arrived at the station either.

I watched as Joe slowly turned toward our car. He didn't hurry. He didn't say anything to Penfield. He just strolled back to the car and gave me a sheepish smile. I was stunned. This was so out of character for Joe. I am certain that he never struck another person in his life. The great headlock battle with Phil Wheatley was the closest he had ever come to inflicting harm and I'm pretty sure that the fat kid only saw that as an annoyance.

He got in and pulled out of the station. We then slowly drove to the interstate and continued in silence for about ten miles. I couldn't take it any longer. "What in the world possessed you to do such a thing?"

Joe glanced at me and smiled. "Well your choice of the word, 'possessed,' might be rather accurate. When I left the car I really thought I would be the better person and just put Penfield behind me. As I approached him I just said, 'Penfield, we need to talk.' He responded by saying, 'Kiss my ass.' Well, I wasn't inclined to do that, so instead I simply gave in to an immediate visceral reaction to him. I had never felt such a sense of rage in my life and, before I could even think about it, I landed that knee in a manner that he will never, ever forget."

"It was, indeed, a well-placed knee delivered with considerable force."

"Thank you, brother. I'm glad you could be a witness. And though my dream always contained numerous witnesses to Penfield's humiliation, I'm glad there weren't any bystanders this time to back up a complaint he might want to file." Then a look of panic swept over Joe. "There weren't any witnesses were there?"

"Nope. No other customers and the attendant paid no attention. Penfield is even hidden by his truck from the snack shop and the other pumps if someone drives in. He can lie there quite awhile in the fetal position and I suspect that is exactly what he'll be doing. I doubt he'll suffer any permanent damage, but I can nearly guarantee you that he won't file a police report and be subjected to further humiliation. Can you imagine how Chief Hagman would react?"

Then it got quiet for several miles. The adrenalin rush had worn off and the reality of what had just happened settled in. Joe shook his head and let out a heavy sigh. "You know, I held onto that dream for a long time. The guy really got to me. I hated him from fifth grade until I left this town. Then the feelings just rushed back in when I saw him on this trip. I am way too old for this crap and to be acting this way." Again, another heavy sigh escaped from Joe. "I wish I were a better person, Darren. I really do. Actually, I thought I was better than that and I'm ashamed that I let my emotions get the best of me."

I knew that Joe really meant what he said. He was a good person—a very good person. I knew that he felt diminished in some ways by his action. I also knew he was human. "So, how'd it really feel when you were fully committed and you could see the shock on his face?"

Joe smiled widely. "It was one of the most satisfying feelings I have ever experienced in my entire life! I may pay for it in many ways down the line, but I can't escape the sheer sense of triumph I felt at that moment. It was great!"

We never spoke another word on the trip to the airport, but we exchanged grins several times along the way.

CHAPTER 33

A Visit with Ronnie Ratcliff

We got to the airport just in time to pick up Carol as her plane arrived. Joe and I parked in short-term parking and went to greet her as she cleared the security area. She and Joe exchanged a long, meaningful hug as I hung back to give them some time. Carol came over with tears in her eyes and gave me a quick hug before we all quickly headed for the exit. She only had a carry-on bag to be used for their possible stay near Johns Hopkins when they got back to Baltimore that evening.

We wasted no time. Joe and I had said everything we needed to say to each other over the past several weeks. The feelings we shared didn't require any further words to become more meaningful. A quick hug for Carol and a handshake for Joe, then I was off to the car rental counter to pick up the rental that I had reserved for the next few days. As I starting walking away, I was once again gripped by a strong feeling of loneliness just as when Joe decided not to do the hospital interview with me. I slowed and looked over my shoulder to give them one final wave, but they had already turned toward the parking area with Carol's arm wrapped tightly around Joe's waist and his arm draped around her shoulders.

* * *

I got back to Glenville by mid-morning and felt an urgency to get started on a variety of loose ends. I knew that Borland and I would need many hours together over the next few days to at least initially put some broad parameters in place. Joe and I had concluded how some of the money should flow, but we were stuck on exactly how it should be administered, who should be held accountable, how parts of it might be further invested, and just how we could leverage the money to get the most out of it.

Even though fifty million dollars seemed like an enormous amount of money when we first heard about it, that sum could quickly dwindle if one were to heavily invest in buildings, equipment, and major renovations. Joe and I did a fair amount of research to determine building costs for recreation centers, schools, gymnasiums, and general office construction. Very basic school classroom construction of about 50,000 square feet could cost ten million dollars in Indiana. A recreation center designed to accommodate all ages with indoor pool, fitness room, and meeting space could easily reach twenty to twenty-five million. A basic 25,000-square-foot gymnasium with no seating or locker rooms would set you back about five million dollars. If funds were set aside for the hospital, the cost for renovation and equipment far exceeds all other types of construction. Ten million dollars might pay for a small wing or several rooms full of specialized equipment. Poof! Uncle Shorty's fifty million is gone!

My first stop of the day was to see a Glenville High graduate, Linda Wilde. Her last name in no way reflected her personality. Linda was apparently the top C.P.A. in Glenville, but she had built her career and reputation with a large firm in Indianapolis where she quickly rose to partner status. After fifteen years climbing the corporate ladder and beginning to raise a family, she and her accountant husband had returned to Glenville to establish their own practice.

According to Borland, Bourke, and several others we spoke to in town, Linda was considered the top person for dealing with small businesses, non-profits, and charitable foundations. She was reported to be smart and reasonable, charged a fair price, and was known to be excruciatingly serious and boring about the business of saving money for her clients. That's just what I wanted in an accountant.

After an hour of hearing about tax implications and conservative investment strategies, I just held up my hands and said, "I don't know what the hell you just said, but you're hired." That brought the first smile to her face. Wilde and Borland would be a perfect professional pair to help get this money to where Joe and I wanted it to go. It was clear to me that we needed professional help since my knowledge of the law was limited to episodes of *Law and Order* and my understanding of tax strategies consisted of annually signing my name to a tax form.

After the accountant, I spent the rest of that day and the next seeking out several others in town just to nail down a few things before I had my final meetings with Borland. I checked back briefly with Clare Simmons at the seniors center to clarify a couple of issues they had raised on our visit. I liked the gang at the Center. Maybe it was our similarity in age. Maybe it was because they had helped Uncle Shorty. I also chatted with my friend, Sam Harkins, about some of the issues he had mentioned about school building renovations and repairs. I additionally wanted his thoughts about some of the athletic facilities issues, since I figured following up with Penfield could prove detrimental to my health.

Joe had asked me to follow up on the status of music programs in the schools since that was important to him and we really didn't learn much about it in our previous meeting. I tracked down some key people and verified what Joe and I had expected. The formal programs had dwindled to almost nothing except for a small band effort at the high school. Everything was done on a "pay for play" status outside of the school budget. The instructor clearly was engaged in a labor of love since the stipend he earned was negligible.

A few more quick stops just to track down some items that came out of our town hall meeting and I was finally down to one last potential visit. I really had mixed feelings about this meeting and wondered why I had let myself get sucked into it. I came very close to backing out, but ultimately found myself sitting in the driveway of Ms. Louise Ratcliff, the young single mother who spoke at the town hall meeting about her sick son. Every rational thought in my mind told me not to get any closer to this issue or any other similar issues. But Joe and I had talked about it and agreed that it wouldn't hurt just to understand what was going on and to see if help was even possible.

I had called ahead and was greeted at the door by Ms. Ratcliff and a small boy, Ronnie, who was clutching her hand and staring at me. He looked as if he might be eight to ten years old, but it was hard to say since he was so frail and gaunt looking. I greeted him in the awkward way that adults typically greet children who are ill—trying to hide my heartbreak, attempting to appear upbeat, and glancing away quickly, seeking help from his mother. We moved into the living room while the mother and I talked and the boy just stared at me. After about ten minutes, he quietly interrupted us, "My mom says that you might be able to get me well again. Is that true? Can you do that?"

"Ronnie, I really don't know. I just came here to meet you and to learn more about your situation from your mom. I really don't know if I can help—but maybe I can. That's all I can promise. I'm sorry I can't promise you more."

"That's okay. I'm glad you're here." With a last look at me, Ronnie turned and asked his mom if he could go watch TV and then slowly walked away when she nodded to him. I watched him go and then looked at a woman who was having a hard time holding it together. The tears streamed down her face as she watched Ronnie go into the other room.

When she had composed herself, she explained more about Ronnie's disease and the potential treatments for it. It was a blood disease that slowly broke down the patient's immune system and caused certain organs to work overtime. Kidney failure appeared to be growing more likely by the month as his test results were becoming more alarming.

There were treatments to stop the progression and even evidence that the disease could be completely eliminated in some cases. The treatments cost a fortune and Louise had already spent everything she had and all that her parents could give her. Fundraising efforts in town produced a generous donation, but it was barely enough for a month's worth of medicine. According to Louise, the boy would surely die in the not-too-distant future.

I felt an overwhelming sense of sadness as I left the Ratcliff home. I really didn't know if any amount of money could help Ronnie, but I promised Louise that I was still willing to look into it further. I got the name of the specialist who was treating Ronnie and planned to follow up with her. I had to know if I had just heard a mother's optimistic view of likely treatment results or whether the medical staff might paint a picture that was bleak in contrast.

God, I was starting to feel as if I was sitting on some sort of panel making a decision about who gets health care. I hated the feeling. It's a lot easier to paint with that broad brush and never really worry about the details. Real people with real problems have an inconvenient tendency to get in the way of expedient decision-making.

CHAPTER 34

THE NEIGHBORHOOD GRILL

I strolled into Applebee's for my evening meal and conversation with Mandy. I could practically hear Barry Manilow singing her name in the background as I waived to my favorite bartender and was greeted with her usual warm smile. Tonight was different, however. "Where's Joe?" she asked.

I really didn't want to go there, but Mandy deserved an explanation. The three of us had spent a good deal of time together over the past few weeks. "Remember that friend of ours who might have cancer?" I could see my comment register on her face. "Well, that wasn't exactly a friend. That was Joe."

"What do you mean that was Joe? I don't get it." I waited for the realization to set in and then saw the look of recognition on Mandy's face. Her hand came up to her mouth as she whispered, "Oh, no."

I then proceeded to fill her in on the whole story—the tests and scans, leg seizures, the pressure on his brain, and the impending brain surgery to remove the lesion. It had not been definitely declared cancer, but the odds were leaning in that direction. At some point in my description, Mandy reached over the bar and put her hand over mine. She had tears in her eyes.

"So, I'll be here for three more days to wrap things up," I quickly said. "We'll announce the plan for Uncle Shorty's money on the third day and I'll then head back to California."

Mandy tried to collect herself by wiping down the bar that was already perfectly clean. "When will you know more about Joe?"

"I don't know. He gave me a call and said that he arrived at Johns Hopkins yesterday evening and checked in for the night. All he said was that he was meeting the neurosurgeon first thing in the morning and that he'd let me know the next steps. I haven't heard from him today."

"Promise me that you'll let me know if he's okay," Mandy demanded. "Even if you don't know anything until after you go home, will you promise me that you'll let me know how he's doing?"

"Sure, Mandy, I promise. You're part of the Kelly brothers' lives now, so you can be certain that I'll keep you posted. I promise."

We quickly changed the subject and moved on to important issues like alcohol and food. By now I had tried nearly every entrée on the Applebee's menu, so I decided to cycle back to the first night we ate there and have another steak in Joe's honor. The accompanying glass of wine was purely for me.

Since it was a slow night, Mandy eventually had some free time and hung around at my end of the bar. I filled her in on some of my meetings around town and let her know in a very general way about where Joe and I were headed with some of Uncle Shorty's money. Not surprisingly, she was very insightful in asking questions about various people and organizations. She had a good sense for the politics in town and an even better sense for some of the personal challenges that faced her friends, neighbors, and the customers she saw every day.

I finally had to ask. "Mandy, why in the world are you still holding onto this job? You are way too talented to just be a bartender."

"Well, first of all, thank you for the compliment and also for the condescending insult. Did it ever occur to you that I choose to work here because I enjoy the interaction with customers, I can make decent money, and I can have a flexible schedule to spend time with my boys? Being a good bartender at the right restaurant can be a great job. It's not like I'm working at Sam's Wet & Wild Lounge."

I looked at her and almost believed her. "And, so, this is it? This is how you see your next ten years in Glenville?"

She looked at me and laughed, "God, I hope not!"

"I didn't think so. Nice speech, though, on behalf of misunderstood bartenders everywhere."

"Look, Darren, this place really is great. My customers are mostly very good people and my boss is a gem. But, no, I can't say that the work is particularly fulfilling and I'm not exactly challenged intellectually. It's a job. And there aren't many like it in town with decent pay and flexibility."

"What if I could help you change that?"

"You mean find me a better job here in town? I don't think it exists."

"Well, you never know what might come your way if you just make yourself open and available to it. Uncle Shorty's money will make a lot of changes in Glenville and you just never know what opportunities might be created. Just stay open to the possibility, okay?"

Before Mandy could ask another question, my cell phone rang.

* * *

"Hello."

"Hey . . . what are you having for dinner?"

"Joe! How's it going? I thought I might hear from you earlier. What's the game plan?"

"Well, the game has already started, my brother." Joe sounded strange. His words were coming out slowly and his voice had a raspy quality to it. There was a good reason for it. "I just got out of surgery a few hours ago. I am now the proud graduate of the school of craniotomy! My "Brain Drain" song was quite prophetic after all."

"How in the hell could you have brain surgery so fast?"

"Well, I might have left out one little piece of information when we last talked. I pretty much knew that I was heading for surgery even before I left Indiana. They had already scheduled me for prep in the morning and surgery in the afternoon. The doc just wanted one more scan completed before he made the final decision. I thought I'd just surprise you with the news.

"You should see me. I've got this turban thing wrapped all around my head. I'll send you a picture as soon as we finish here. Guess I have some kind of staples holding my skull together. I just have a little headache and the whole thing took less than a couple of hours. Of course, I'm pretty juiced up on morphine, so I guess I wouldn't know how much my head really hurts."

"Yeah, you sound a little sloppy. So, what's the word? What did they find?"

"I guess they found a lot of swelling, but he was able to remove the lesion. The wiz-kid doc told Carol afterward that he got it all. Now it's just a matter of finding out if the lesion was cancerous and whether the swelling will go down. All things considered, I guess the operation was a success and we don't have any other bad news at this point."

I had a million questions, but I could tell Joe was tired. I'd just ask one more. "How long before you know the results of the biopsy?"

"The doctor was pretty vague about it. He said it would be several days. My guess is before they tell someone he has cancer they might want to run the tests a couple of times to be sure. Whatever. I can't control that. I'm heading home in a couple of days if all my signs look good. I hope to be set up with my computer so we can hook up on FaceTime to watch your meeting when you announce the plan for the money."

Joe was already moving forward. That didn't take long. "Okay, Joe, you get some rest now. I'm meeting with Borland over the next two days and I'll give you a call to iron out any last-minute details. If you're too tired when I call, just let me know and I'll run with it. I know I won't do anything that you wouldn't approve of anyway."

Joe wished me luck and said goodbye. Pretty ironic—he's wishing me good luck. The guy just had brain surgery. Good thing it wasn't rocket science. Mandy looked at me the entire time I was on the phone and had pretty much figured out what was going on with Joe. "I can't believe he had surgery today! When will they know the results?"

"He says it will be a few days. He'll likely go home in a couple of days."

Mandy and I talked about Joe some more as I finished my dinner and then she got busy with other customers. As I sat there alone, I thought about how the entire process seemed so incredibly surreal. Within a matter of weeks Joe and I had been thrown into this estate issue, we were stuck in Glenville for the duration away from our wives, I was threatened by a crazed psychopath from our past, and Joe just happened to develop serious health issues that led to brain surgery and a possible cancer diagnosis. As I mentioned before, spring was generally an amazing time in the Midwest. It's just not usually quite this eventful.

CHAPTER 35

WATCH WHERE YOU'RE GOING

I left Applebee's with a full stomach, pleasant warmth from the wine, and the satisfaction that Joe had cleared a major hurdle on his road to recovery. At this point, I would simply remain optimistic about future test results. A large parking lot separated Applebee's from our Residence Inn and I began to work my way through the parked cars. My phone buzzed and there was a message from Joe with an attached picture. I opened the photo and was greeted by Joe's smiling face with his head wrapped in white gauze. He looked pretty tired, but the smile was unmistakably pure Joe enjoying the irony of the moment in his post-surgical state.

My head was still down as a passenger door suddenly flew open in front of me causing me to run right into it. I backed away apologizing profusely for my dumb mistake when a voice from inside the car said, "Darren, you need to keep your eyes open around here. You never know what you might run into."

"Lonnie." That's all I could say. I was frozen in place as he got out of the car and stood right in front of me. His face was so close that I could smell the whiskey and cigarettes on his breath. He had that same smirk on his face that I'd seen before.

"Darren, I just thought I'd pay you one more visit to reinforce for you just how serious I am about getting my money. Where's that brother of yours? Don't you boys do everything together?"

"He's a little under the weather. He decided to stay in the room tonight." As soon as I said it, I hoped that Lonnie didn't plan for us to walk over to the hotel. I didn't want to get caught in a lie and then find myself alone with him in the room.

"Well, that's a shame. But I really don't need to see him anyway. You're the one I'm going to carve on if that money doesn't end up in my account. You know that's true, don't you?" Lonnie was starting to get worked up and leaned into me a little more.

"I know that's your intention, Lonnie. I heard you loud and clear."

"It's not just my intention, Kelly. It's what I will do. That's a fact!"

"You'll get your money, Lonnie. It's not worth it to me to go against you. As you said, it's not my money anyway." I figured I still had time for that decision, but right now getting out of this situation was the priority.

McDaniel smiled and relaxed a bit. "That's a good boy, Kelly. You just make sure that happens and you'll never hear from me again. But if you don't make it happen, I guarantee you that you'll be looking over your shoulder until the day that I come to collect." With that, he got back in his car, closed the door, and slowly pulled out of the parking lot.

As he pulled away, I looked at his license plate and punched the numbers and letters into my phone. Even though I had just been threatened, I was feeling incredibly proud of the fact that I was calm and actually able to operate my phone at a nominal level. Admittedly, I still have trouble retrieving phone messages. My daughter had shown me how to quickly jot down numbers after watching a very instructive episode of *Law & Order* where the perpetrator (or perp, as we like to say) was caught through the efforts of an eyewitness.

I wasted no time in calling Luke Jackson. I had entered his cell phone number into my contacts list the morning that Borland gave it to us. He answered on the first ring.

"Luke, you won't believe what just happened."

"You were just threatened by Lonnie McDaniel in the parking lot at Applebee's?"

Silence. "How did you know that?"

"Maybe because I was about ten rows over from you at the time."

I was stunned. "You were right here and you didn't make a move on him? He could have killed me!"

"Now, Darren, why would Lonnie want to hurt you at this point when you control the money. He just wanted to scare you. You were never in any danger. If I don't convince him to go away, that might be a different story in the future." Silence—a great technique for raising my blood pressure. "But that's not going to happen."

"But you could have grabbed him and hauled him off somewhere for interrogation."

"Wrong time. Wrong place. I'll pick the spot and the best time to do it."

"Okay, I get that. Do you want his license plate number?"

"Did you happen to notice what state that license plate was from? Illinois. It's a fake—probably taken off a scrapped car. Besides, a license registration would be tied to his home address and he isn't about to hang out at home."

I needed to increase the breadth of my cop shows on TV. *Law & Order* just wasn't giving me the necessary sophistication to match the criminal mind. I was clearly out of my element.

"Luke, how did you know Lonnie would be here tonight?"

"I didn't. But I've been following you the entire day and figured that Lonnie would eventually make another move on you before your Thursday deadline. He did."

"What are you going to do now?"

"I'm going to continue following that Illinois license plate up ahead of me and see where it takes me. Now that I have Lonnie in my sights, I won't leave him until we can have a little chat. Go back to your hotel, Darren. The show is over. I'll take it from here." He hung up.

CHAPTER 36

TIME TO LAWYER UP

With only two days to go on my Glenville odyssey, I walked down Main Street to Sam Borland's office. This is where it all started nearly a month ago. It's when Joe and I first learned about Uncle Shorty's estate, when we took on the challenge of trying to accomplish what Shorty intended, and when we started our quest of eating our way through Glenville.

Reaching for Borland's door reminded me of the first time we met the lawyer. His stuffy, East Coast image had surely changed for the better and I had grown to like and respect him—as much as you really can respect any lawyer. Actually, that's not fair. I'm not among those who routinely and glibly use the word "lawyer" as a pejorative term. Certainly, some have clearly earned the negative stereotype, but Borland is okay. He's better than okay. He is very bright and capable and I can now see why Uncle Shorty selected him and stuck with him.

My plan for the next two days was to work through the general plan with Borland and the accountant, Linda Wilde. Though Uncle Shorty's stated intent was to minimize the amount of administrative overhead associated with his estate, there was just no way to distribute and monitor fifty million dollars without some professional oversight. That was especially true when our plan called for multiple accounts and agencies to receive money, each with its own unique parameters and guidelines attached. It would have been easier to just throw all the money into one big foundation and assign a group of people to act as a board of directors in dispersing the funds as they saw fit. Joe and I weren't that lazy. Plus, we had some very specific notions of where the money should flow and how much certain groups should get.

So, Borland and Wilde agreed to charge reduced hourly fees in exchange for a long-term commitment to monitor the legal and accounting issues related to the estate. To their credit, they both saw the immeasurable value of how the Hazelton estate could impact the Glenville community and they were anxious to be a part of that effort. Joe and I intentionally created a plan that would need revisiting from time to time and we intended to adopt a strategy that would not spend all of the money at once. We figured the vagueness of Uncle Shorty's directive allowed us to purposefully set aside some of the money to be used as new initiatives and issues presented themselves in the future.

As our planning progressed through the two days, we identified finite amounts of funds for some groups and created more fluid approaches for others who would request funding from a larger fund with community-member oversight. In some cases, Joe and I had very particular ideas about who should serve on boards and committees. In other cases, existing folks were in place and we didn't need to get in their way with more bureaucracy.

The bottom line was people in Glenville would ultimately have to make some tough decisions about funding choices. Joe and I couldn't realistically make all of those choices in such a short timeframe. However, we felt confident that we could set up a system to make it palatable for community members to do so in the future. At some point, you just have to trust people to do the best job that they can do. We knew enough people in town that we trusted and we had come to know even more in our recent time spent in Glenville.

As our second day reached mid-afternoon, Borland surprised me with a question. "Would you ever consider reaching out to another potential donor in order to further maximize the impact of Mr. Hazelton's estate?"

"There you go again, Borland. Would I want to 'further maximize' Uncle Shorty's money? What the hell is that supposed to mean? Spit it out."

Borland laughed. "Fair enough. If I had a client who was interested in a large philanthropic gesture toward the city, would you consider joining forces in order to perhaps double the impact each of you could otherwise have individually? For instance, if you didn't want to fund an entire building or renovation, would you be willing to fund half of it if the other donor came through with the remaining half?"

"You could make that happen?"

"I don't know, but I can tell you that I have previously had confidential discussions with this person and she is very interested in the idea. Until you and Joe came along, we saw no other legitimate funding source on the horizon. However, I'm meeting with her late today and I could broach the subject if you would approve. I didn't want to ask you until I saw how you were approaching the distribution and I think this plan would still fit with your overall goals."

"Let's do it. See what she says and how much she's willing to give."

Borland paused. "There is only one catch."

"Of course, there had to be a catch."

"It's really not that bad," Borland said. "This donor is what we like to refer to as a 'last donor' on a project. In other words, she wants to see how much other money will be put up and then she will finish off the project and will have the structure named after her family. It's very important to her to leave a family legacy here in Glenville."

I thought about that little twist for a minute. For nearly a month, Joe and I had enjoyed the complete freedom of operating on our own with no ties or restrictions created by others. This new plan didn't feel quite right from that perspective. On the other hand, the distribution of Uncle Shorty's money was not about the Kelly brothers' comfort level. It was about creating the greatest positive impact for the community using Uncle Shorty's estate.

"Tom, it seems clear to me that Uncle Shorty was never concerned with his legacy or getting his name on a building. He kept his wealth a secret until his death and then left no instructions about memorializing his gifts in any way. If we could double a portion of his money in order to leave a lasting structure to benefit Glenville, then I'm sure he would be in favor of that tactic. You know what Joe and I were interested in building, so go get your client to make it a reality. Without her, I doubt that we have enough money to make it happen. In the meantime, I'm going to have a little talk with our politically ambitious mayor to see how the city might also contribute to this idea."

Things were moving in a hurry during these last hours, but I was comforted by the fact that we didn't need to have everything figured out down to the last dollar. We just needed commitments from a variety of people and a structure in place to make things happen after Joe and I were no longer in Glenville.

CHAPTER 37

OPERATION MANPOWER DINNER

I wasn't going to spend my last night alone eating White Castles in my room and I still had a little business to wrap up. I invited to dinner my three old friends from our 1970s summer business venture, Operation Manpower. Jim Barton, Sam Harkins, and Rick Cole were happy to have one final reunion before I left town. Operation Manpower—what an ironic name we picked for ourselves that lazy summer after high school. We were just a bunch of silly kids looking to work just enough to cover our summer expenses, but not so much that the work hampered our social lives. There wasn't a "man" among us and we clearly had no "power." But it was some operation.

Much to the others' surprise, I suggested a restaurant out of town on the way to Indianapolis. I didn't want the interruptions that we'd likely get at Applebee's, or any other restaurant in town for that matter. Harkins was well known as a life-long teacher and school administrator. Cole and his family were well known in Glenville. He now lived in Indianapolis, but he visited his elderly mother in town often. If people saw him, they would want to stop by and say hello and be remembered to his mother. Glenville people were friendly that way.

It was hard to say who might want to talk with Barton. From what I gathered, he knew a rougher crowd from his drinking days, but now dealt with an appreciative and thankful group of folks familiar with his current work. I imagined that some mother might come up and give him a hug, but maybe an old drunk that he owed money might slug him and knock him out. That would make for an awkward dinner. Therefore, we headed out of town.

Once the food was ordered, I got down to my last bit of business with the boys. "Guys, I need to know if I can count on you to help me out with seeing that this estate money gets to the right people. Joe and I are going to keep our hands in this adventure for a while, but we really can't attend to the details from California and Maryland. I need people here in town who know what is really going on and who I can trust to give us the straight scoop if something isn't working out the way we planned."

I then explained that I'd likely be taking the lead for the Kelly brothers for at least the near future due to Joe's health issues. I briefly filled them in on Joe and asked them to keep that information quiet for now. They were understandably shaken by the news about Joe.

Cole spoke for the group, "Whatever you need, Darren, we're here for you. This is a good thing for Glenville and we'd like to help in any way we can." He looked at the other two and quickly received affirming nods from both. "What do you need us to do?"

"Well, at the very least, I need you all to serve on a foundation board that will have some oversight responsibility for some of the money. A portion of the funds will go directly to existing groups in town, but other money will need to be invested and parceled out over the years. I just want to make sure I have a group that is completely trustworthy to make those decisions in an honest and thoughtful way. I don't care about trying to select representatives from different parts of the community or filling slots with elected officials. I don't care about gender, race, religious views, wealth, or poverty. I care about trust.

"Joe and I get to make the rules and we agreed that our number one rule was to only deal with people that we trust. Our second rule was to follow our instincts and not be swayed by conventional thinking about how this money should be spent. We'll direct it to be spent in a manner in which we think Uncle Shorty would approve. We may not get it all perfect. I'm sure there are professionals who deal with this sort of philanthropy all the time and they would likely handle the estate differently. Well, Uncle Shorty didn't call on them. He called on the Kelly brothers and this is what you get."

Cole weighed in with the question I was anticipating. "Darren, the way you're approaching this makes me think that you're dealing with a sizeable amount of money. How much?"

I laughed. "What's the rumor mill around town?"

Barton: "A low of two million."

Harkins: "A high of twenty million."

Cole: "Now that I see how earnest you are about it, I'm betting it's on the high side of the rumor mill. Don't leave us hanging here, Kelly. What's the number?"

I didn't hesitate. "Do you think we can make an impact on Glenville with fifty million?"

"Holy shit!" Harkins' mouth was hanging open.

"You know, Harkins, for an educated man and a leader of our youth, you really need to clean up your language. I find that 'holy crap' is a more nuanced and sophisticated exclamation." Joe always could influence me.

"Holy crap!" Barton was always a quick study.

"That's a sizeable estate," Cole quietly observed. Spoken like a true Harvard man who has a passing familiarity with sizeable estates. "No wonder you've been low key about the amount of money. People I've talked with in town think you'll be passing out a few thousand here and a few thousand there. They have no idea."

Over the course of dinner, they pumped me for more information. I gave them an overall feeling for the plan, but didn't get into the specifics. They had agreed to do whatever I asked, so I didn't feel a need to fill in all the blanks. I did, however, want their opinion on others in town that could be trusted to serve on various boards or committees to monitor the flow of funds.

They weren't always unanimous in their thinking, but the gang generally agreed (whether positive or negative) on most of the people I mentioned. I had pulled together a list of people

I had met in the past month along with a few classmates who had stayed in town. The responses to each name were clear and succinct as I bounced around on my list.

Barton: "Jerk."

Harkins: "Asshole."

Cole: "Idiot."

Harkins: "Stay away from him."

Cole: "Great guy."

Harkins: "Trustworthy."

Barton: "Smarter than Cole."

Cole: "Hey—don't get carried away."

Barton: "Boring, but bright."

Cole: "Super person."

Harkins: "Married a proctologist."

Cole: "Why does that matter?"

Harkins: "Questionable judgment."

Barton: "She's a saint."

Harkins: "Never heard a negative thing about her."

Cole: "He's a misogynist."

Barton: "What's a misogynist?"

Cole: "Hates women."

Barton: "I love women."

Harkins: "We know."

Cole: "Big heart."

Harkins: "Big ideas."

Barton: "Big ass."

Cole: "Are we still talking about the same gal?"

Barton: "She's the complete package. Brains and beauty."

Cole: "You are truly enlightened."

And on and on . . .

As I suspected, it was still hard to keep the members of Operation Manpower focused, but I managed to get decent confirmations for the handful of people that I needed once the guys settled down and got serious.

As we wrapped up the dinner and I paid the bill, Barton looked at me directly and asked, "Are you sure you want us involved in this in such a public way? I mean, we all have some skeletons in our closets. Actually, mine all pretty much came out and walked around Glenville for about twenty years. But, you get the point. You could probably choose some more outstanding citizens to be your watchdogs. I guess Cole qualifies and maybe Harkins is marginal if you don't count the kids he throws out windows. What about me? You'll catch some grief about me."

"Barton, what part about trust did you not understand when I was speaking earlier? Sure, you guys can still be absolutely inane . . ."

"If I knew what that meant I might be insulted."

"You can be foolhardy—like me—but you all are my friends and I trust you completely to do the right thing to the best of your ability. Now, there was a time when I wouldn't have trusted you to do the right thing because I know I didn't trust myself to do the right thing. I do now. And, Barton, you've never given yourself enough credit and that's what got you in trouble. Get over it and take the leadership role that's being handed to you."

I paused for effect and looked at each one of them. "Besides, I really don't know anyone else in town that well, so you three were the logical choice by default."

"Geez, Kelly," said Barton. "I was just starting to get all teary-eyed and you have to go and be an asshole again."

"Joe and I have been given a gift. We have a unique chance to change lives for the better. The fact that we can share that gift with old friends makes it even more special. And before you thank me, just remember that I'm leaving town and you boys will be the ones catching shit from the people that got left out of this little lottery."

Barton was quick to correct me, "Actually, we will be catching crap from those people and I'll be happy to do so."

CHAPTER 38

THE LAST BREAKFAST

My last full day in Glenville had finally arrived. Tomorrow I would catch a morning flight back to California where I could live in relative obscurity with my wife. No one would be asking me for money, no one would feign interest or enthusiasm for my witticisms, and no one would threaten my life with a knife—unless I decided to go down to L.A. for a Dodgers game.

I started the day at a final breakfast meeting with John Bourke to go over details of his newspaper article about the Hazelton estate and its impact on Glenville. I wanted to make sure he had plenty of background on our decisions in the hope that the information would soften the blow to those who didn't receive money or not as much as they had expected.

We met at his favorite spot, the Bob Evans restaurant, and thankfully had Suzie as our waitress. After exchanging his normal pleasantries with Suzie, he ordered his "usual" helping of oatmeal and fruit. I decided that it was time to wind down my "vacation" eating and simply settled for a small stack of pancakes. Plus, gorging myself on breakfast didn't have the same appeal without Joe there to share the experience.

The silent figure sitting across from me did not look particularly excited about his order. I had to ask. "What's with the oats and fruit diet, Bourke? Are you trying to impress the Californian with your healthy choices?"

"Hardly," he moaned. "I had a physical a few months ago—first one in about five years. The doc says I tested positive for trans-fats, he could see lumps of butter in my veins, and that I was about a gallon high on the grease meter. Or he said something to that effect. I have to change my ways and you are seeing the first efforts at doing so."

Before we got down to business, I shared with John the news about Joe. As with others who learned about it, Joe's situation visibly affected Bourke. He grew quiet and just lowered his head for a minute.

"You know, I really like that guy. Always did. Even though he was a few years ahead of us, he was just always genuinely nice to all of your friends. He was really proud of you. I talked with him several times when he came back from college to watch your games in high school." He paused again and just stared at me. "I hope this turns out okay for him. Keep me posted on it, will you?"

"I will. I promise. We're both optimistic at this point. They got rid of the lesion, so maybe more good news will soon follow."

I quickly shifted the discussion to the meeting that night and filled Bourke in on the plan. I shared with him our thinking about various choices. He didn't agree with all of them and thought we might have slighted one or two of his favorite areas, but was nonetheless enthusiastic about all of the positive impacts the estate funds would bring to Glenville. He would be sending me copies of his article and any follow-up editorials and articles just so I could get a feeling for the reaction.

We wrapped up our breakfast meeting and I left an extra generous tip for Suzie. She deserved it for putting up with Bourke on a regular basis. He graciously offered to her on the way out the door, "Suzie, say hello to your mom and that dumbshit brother of yours for me!" She just shook her head and smiled at him like he was her favorite uncle.

* * *

My only other meeting before our 7:00 p.m. announcement was with the mayor. I had contacted Riley the day before when Borland had mentioned the possibility of another donor who was willing to commit substantial funds toward a major community center. Rather than appealing to the mayor's civic pride, I suggested that this project could go a long way toward cementing his legacy and giving him a springboard toward a higher office in Indiana state politics. He seemed to resonate to that line of thinking—if you consider drooling part of resonating.

My meeting today was to seal the deal and to make sure he had the authority and funds to contribute to the project. I told him that I only needed fifteen minutes of his time since I really didn't want to spend one minute more than necessary in his presence.

"Mr. Mayor, it is a pleasure to see you again." And when I say "pleasure," I mean it is extremely painful for me to kiss your ass like this to accomplish my task. "I think we have a chance here to do something very special for the citizens of Glenville."

"Mr. Kelly, I have checked out all of the potential stumbling blocks that might get in the way of our completing this terrific project and I'm now completely satisfied that we can move forward. As I mentioned on the phone, we have been building a contingency fund for a community center for years, but we are still far short of the necessary amount to commit to the project. With Mr. Hazelton's money and that of your mysterious donor, the city can be the third piece of the puzzle to create a truly state-of-the-art facility that will serve as a prototype for small cities all across Indiana. The city attorney has assured me that I have the authority to commit the funds due to the emergency nature of the timing and because the money was previously identified for this purpose."

"Great. That's all I need to hear. I'll direct Mr. Borland to draft the paperwork and he'll work out the details with your city attorney." I started to head for the door.

"Mr. Kelly, there is one more item that we need to confirm. You mentioned on the phone that I, as mayor, would play a central role in the announcement of this partnership. Would you have any problem if we described this financial package as something that was initiated by the Mayor's Office in collaboration with you and the other donor? I think it would be beneficial to the citizens of Glenville if they knew their city government was working on their behalf."

I gave Riley my very best stare. I held it just long enough for him to finally look away. I knew this moment was coming since I had hinted on the phone at allowing the mayor to take credit without actually spelling it out for him. I just wanted to see him grovel for it.

"Let me get this straight." I wondered how long I could drag this out. It was just so much fun. "You want me to allow you to take credit for orchestrating this financial alliance? You want it to be presented as your idea? That would be the very same proposal that I actually brought to you out of the blue and handed to you gift-wrapped and ready to be opened? I just want to make sure I have it right. Is that what you would like me to do?"

The mayor attempted to stare back at me, though his eyes shifted slightly to the right just before he spoke. "Yes, I think that would be in the best interests of everyone. The donor wants anonymity at this stage, you are merely representing Mr. Hazelton and need no further recognition, but the city's leaders could benefit from the good will generated from this sort of initiative." And when he said "leaders," he clearly meant only himself. Spoken like a true politician. This guy could go places.

I laughed out loud. "Mayor, I will announce with enthusiasm that this was all your idea." With that proclamation, I turned and quickly left the room. I smiled as I walked out of City Hall. The younger version of Darren Kelly would surely have agonized over the thought of letting this guy get credit for something dropped in his lap. I might have responded with an emotional vitriol that could have jeopardized the entire plan. The more mature Mr. Kelly actually enjoyed the charade and really didn't care at all who got the credit for the ultimate accomplishment. The donor could have her family name on it and the mayor could demonstrate exemplary leadership. In any case, Uncle Shorty would have accomplished his goal of helping the community.

CHAPTER 39

SHOW ME THE MONEY

It was finally time to end the Shorty Hazelton estate saga. The meeting was scheduled for 7:00 p.m. at the high school auditorium and a general announcement had been placed prominently on the front page of the *Glenville Daily Reporter*. John Bourke had suggested the location since it provided an easy exit strategy from the back of the stage in case some of the Hoosier natives became restless upon learning that they would receive little or no money.

Even for those receiving funds, there would likely be endless questions and I really wanted to defer those to Borland at a later date. After nearly a month of immersing myself in the task and dealing with the threats from Lonnie McDaniel, my immediate goal was just to get back to Ojai as quickly as possible to be with Beth and to enjoy my very quiet and peaceful life.

Bourke didn't realize that his exit strategy theory also was potentially applicable to Lonnie's threats. I had not heard from Luke Jackson and was entering the meeting without any clear direction on that front. Having a clear path to my car waiting outside the auditorium might prove to be the smartest move I made all month. Just in case, I asked Chief Harkins to post an officer at the stage door where he could make sure that Lonnie didn't greet me from the back seat of my car.

I showed up early to set up my laptop and to connect with Joe on FaceTime. Very quickly I saw his smiling face on the screen. His turban had been replaced with a large gauze bandage on the back of his head, but he looked remarkably normal from the front. He and I had talked several times on the phone as I kept him updated on my progress. I could tell that he tired easily from our conversations, but he was as sharp as ever.

"So, Darren, are you going to excite the crowd like they're at a game show or just bore them to death with charts and graphs? I really think yelling 'Come on Down' would be a nice touch to get the crowd cranked up. You could hand folks a big fake check and take a picture with each winner! Hell, you could hold the laptop up and I'd be in the picture, too!"

"Thanks for that input. Just remember that you can disappear as soon as I close the laptop, so don't cause me any grief or you will no longer be a part of this party. I'm making this short and sweet. I'll announce where the bulk of the money goes, refer folks to Borland for follow-up, and get on the next plane to California."

"What about Lonnie? Any word from Luke?"

"Nope—and that has me worried. Is it even possible that Lonnie could somehow get the jump on a guy like Luke Jackson? Or maybe he gave Luke the slip?"

"Relax. A guy like Lonnie is not going to get the best of Luke Jackson. It would be typical of Luke just to take care of business and not even tell you. He just assumes that you took his word for it." Joe paused for a minute. "But, just in case, did you hold back some of the money if you needed to pay off Lonnie at the last minute?"

I looked squarely at the screen so Joe would know I was serious. "I'm not paying Lonnie a penny, Joe. Either Luke takes care of this or I accept Chief Hagman's assessment that Lonnie isn't ambitious enough to follow me out to California. If he threatens me again, then I'll figure out what to do next."

Joe looked at me and smiled. "Well, it's your face he's going to carve up, brother. Good luck with that. I've got my own problems."

I laughed hard at that one. Of course, Joe didn't mean it. And that was the point. He respected my decision and wasn't going to wallow in the potential fallout from that choice. Time to move on.

The crowd started to file in and moved toward the front since we had roped off the back of the auditorium. I wanted to keep the atmosphere as intimate as possible. There would be no microphones in the crowd since I really didn't want to engage in conversation about our decisions. I placed a table microphone in front of me just so the elderly folks in the crowd could hear me clearly, but I decided to sit at a table with my laptop next to me rather than take a more formal position behind the podium.

I also asked Tom Borland to sit on stage with me since I would be introducing him as my local contact for all administrative matters pertaining to the distribution of funds from the estate.

My laptop sat facing me on my left and Borland was on my right. I suddenly became aware of Joe quietly whistling a tune that our grandfather had taught us, "Pistol Packin' Mama." I glanced over at him with a look that indicated my displeasure.

He smiled with mock concern. "What—do you want it louder? Stick that microphone over here next to the laptop. I'll entertain the folks while they get settled." Joe was a self-proclaimed world-class whistler, but I didn't think this was quite the right venue for a breakout performance.

"Just try to shut up and let me get through this. It's weird enough having you staring at me over there."

"Just think of me as your conscience. I'll whisper to you when I think you're blowing it. Hey, by the way, are my girl-friends there tonight?"

"Yep. All three of them."

"Three? I just meant Doreen and Wanda."

"Yeah, they're in the back—and still looking good. And right down front is your favorite waitress, Bunny. She looks particularly fetching tonight. I think she got her hair done in anticipation of seeing you. Plus, she's doing a lousy job of hiding a flask in her lap and looks a little glassy eyed. Do you want me to turn the laptop around so you can wave to her?"

"Uh, that's okay. Carry on."

* * *

The crowd was larger than at the town hall meeting when we had just been gathering information. After a month of speculation and rumors, I guess it was just too tempting for many in town to miss this event. Most of the folks were back from that first meeting, though I was sorry to see that our one-arm farmer was absent. Must have had something more glamorous to attend.

The loony wetlands teacher was present, looking particularly hopeful. Huck Finn and Tom Sawyer must have been safely tucked in at their cozy home since the abandoned truck no longer needed improvements. I didn't see any Pounders, either. Probably still at the nineteenth hole. My buddies—Barton, Harkins, and Cole—were there and I'm sure they were curious to see how everything would play out.

All the principal players were there, but they came in very, very large numbers presumably to demonstrate their earnestness. Representatives were present from Seniors Helping Seniors, the school system, the hospital, the Boys and Girls Club, all of the agencies of the city government, the mayor (of course), Chief Hagman, and students. There were lots of students in the back of the crowd. There were students wearing athletic jerseys over their regular clothing, students carrying musical instruments, elementary-age students, and high-school students. Two enterprising guys carried a small portable chalkboard with the chalked message: "This is an example of our school's state-of-the art technology."

There were probably about five hundred people in attendance. Obviously, some still had a misguided sense that they
could influence the decision by lobbying at the last minute.
Joe and I didn't spend nearly a month in Glenville just to wait
until the final night to see who showed up. What were these
people thinking? Maybe they thought they could change our
minds with persuasive arguments or emotional pleading after
the meeting. Thus, the backstage exit.

One face caught my attention. Joe's good buddy, Penfield,
was sitting off to the side with his younger Booster Club col-
league. I covered my mic and leaned toward the laptop. "Hey,
Joe, Penfield is here. Maybe he thought he could have a chat
with you after the meeting?"

"Is he still covering his crotch?" Joe asked innocently. "You
know, Darren, one thing about having brain surgery and worrying about the results—I am soooo over the entire Penfield thing.
I have gained a new perspective on life. Give him my regards if
you see him."

With that bit of sarcastic insight duly noted, it was time
to start the meeting. I welcomed the group and noted that Joe
was joining us via FaceTime connection from Maryland. No
further explanation of Joe's status was necessary. I introduced
Tom Borland and indicated how he would be handling much of
the administrative follow-up once I left town. I then started by
reminding everyone why we were there and to whom we were
indebted for this opportunity. The bulk of the Hazelton story

had been thoroughly covered by John Bourke in the newspaper, but I wanted to emphasize a few points.

"Shorty Hazelton was simply a good friend to the Kelly family as Joe and I grew up here in Glenville. Perhaps he wasn't special as judged by normal standards, but he was a very special person, indeed. The man we knew was kind, caring, funny, interested in our well being, and also interested in the well being of Glenville. Looking back on those years I can remember Uncle Shorty reading the *Glenville Daily Reporter* with great interest and commenting on all sorts of local issues. As a teenager, I frankly only cared about what showed up in the sports section. But now I get it. Shorty Hazelton really cared about Glenville, and he demonstrated that caring in the most amazing way upon his death.

"It might be one thing if Shorty and Meta Hazelton had been from wealthy families or had developed wealth and lived a luxurious lifestyle throughout their years. You might expect people like that to leave some portion of their estate to a worthy cause or two in town.

"But the Hazelton's lived a very modest lifestyle in a modest little home over in Westside Village. They lived within their means and had no family. They just demonstrated an extraordinary amount of financial discipline and maybe a good deal of luck in picking a guy like Warren Buffet to monitor their small initial investment over fifty years ago. As a result of their financial choices and a desire to improve the lives of Glenville, the citizens of this town will become the recipients of one of the largest gifts ever bestowed upon the community from one of its very own."

There was a low, quiet rumble in the audience as people leaned toward each other presumably wondering just "how large was large." With the timing of a seasoned politician presenting his well-rehearsed stump speech, I waited to regain their full attention.

"Folks, tonight Joe and I have the privilege of acting on behalf of Shorty and Meta Hazelton. We would like to announce our plans to distribute a substantial amount of money among various citizens, community groups, and governmental agencies. The total of those gifts from the Hazelton's estate amounts to roughly fifty million dollars!"

The previous quiet rumble immediately grew to a much louder background noise of excited chatter, laughter, and more than one "Holy shit!" Big smiles appeared on the faces of many people with whom I had spoken. A few optimists prematurely celebrated with high-fives. Students in the back with musical instruments quickly started blowing aimlessly through their mouthpieces. Clearly, some funding for musical training would be greatly appreciated.

As the audience noise continued, I heard a voice to my left quietly say, "Very nice timing, Darren. You have a real flair for the dramatic. Are Doreen and Wanda excited?"

I covered the mic and looked at Joe's smiling face on the screen. "Yeah, they're blowing me kisses. I'm not sure what Bunny is doing."

I turned back to the excited crowd and realized that people were already counting their money. I guess fifty million dollars sounds substantial enough for everyone to get a piece of the pie. There would be a lot of pieces to go around, but some would be much smaller than others. And some groups would go home hungry. I started with the largest commitment.

"Folks, let's start with the single largest gift that can be shared with the entire community. Mayor Riley approached us with the idea that the Hazelton fund could be stretched even further if we would consider a matching fund scenario to double or even triple the amount available to build a state-of-the-art community center. The mayor committed five million from the city reserves that had been earmarked for a future community center construction project. Through the joint efforts of the mayor and Mr. Borland, a third donor (who will be identified later) was discovered who could match the Hazelton commitment of ten million plus the five million from the city to create a thirty million dollar total building fund. With this amount of funding, Glenville will have an incredible community center with a variety of indoor recreational spaces, meeting areas, classroom spaces for adult learners, and other resources for both the younger and older members of this town."

The crowd broke out into an enthusiastic round of applause as the mayor beamed from his seat and accepted the congratulations of those around him. The voice next to me said, "Gee, I didn't realize how astute and enterprising our young mayor had become in my absence. What wonderful leadership! Darren, you have either sold your soul to the devil or you have become a wise and generous person in your old age. Well done."

When the applause died down and Joe stifled his commentary, I continued with our list of donations. One of the largest commitments went to the Senior Citizens Center (five million). What can I say? When you turn sixty, you gain a very different perspective on the needs of the elderly. This group was already doing so much with almost nothing. They could now buy new vehicles and hire some professional staff to better coordinate the work of their volunteers and to head up additional fundraising efforts. After the applause quieted from that announcement, Joe clearly offered his opinion. "They still need a new name!"

A similar amount went to our favorite childhood hangout, the Boys and Girls Club. We earmarked some of the money for the after-school program to allow low-income families to get a subsidy to make the care affordable. The rest we left to the folks in charge and presumed they would spend it wisely. Joe and I had no fear that staff salaries would suddenly triple. We felt confident that money would go where it was needed most to improve the experience for the kids.

Next in line was the Glenville school system. Or, more accurately, the kids who attend the schools were next in line. Taking the advice of the assistant superintendent in charge of throwing kids out the window, we earmarked most of the money for a fledgling group called the Glenville Educational Foundation.

This collection of concerned citizens had been formed only a few years back. They conducted small fundraisers and donated money to the schools in the form of supplies and one-time checks to outstanding teachers. Their donations thus far amounted to little more than twenty thousand dollars each academic year, but they seemed to be gathering momentum and had added an impressive list of community leaders to the group in the past year.

Joe and I had met with them and learned that they were completely independent of the School Board and the local parent-teacher associations. They had representation that went well beyond parents who currently had children in the system. It was an impressive group of citizens (including some teachers), but all had full-time jobs or families and very little extra time for extensive fundraising.

That group suddenly found itself with five million dollars and a mandate to spend the money for improving technology in the classrooms and rewarding innovative teaching practices with one-time stipends. Some additional restrictions would be imposed to limit how much could be distributed in any given year, but I didn't need to go into that detail in the meeting. Joe and I wanted to guard against the chance that the group would rush out and equip every classroom, K–12, with state-of-the-art technology that quickly became obsolete in a few years. Our goal was to provide the latest in teaching aids for many years to come.

The Kelly brothers had discussed at great length ways to help out the various athletic programs in the schools and in the community at large. Despite Joe's feelings about Penfield, he was an advocate for alleviating the pressure felt by kids who never had enough indoor practice space for basketball, volleyball, conditioning, etc. We had talked to many parents who described picking up their kids at 10:00 p.m. after basketball practice since the boys and girls teams all had to share court time in one gym. When you consider that there are freshmen, junior varsity, and varsity units for every basketball squad in high school, that's a lot of kids to accommodate on cold winter days when playing outdoors is not an option. And, after all, we are Hoosiers. Basketball is a way of life.

We had done enough basic research to believe that five million dollars could build a sizeable practice facility with no frills. This money would have to go through the School Board since the facility would be on school land and would be owned by the district. If the cost projections came in higher than our allotted amount, the school district would have to commit to the additional funds or the donation would be withdrawn (minus the initial development costs to get a reliable cost estimate). Harkins had told us that some state matching funds would likely be available for a project that already had such a large portion funded, so we felt confident that things would work out.

Joe made sure that smaller amounts went to the school music and drama department to fund instruments and production costs for plays. Other funds went to the city recreation department, specifically to finance the bike trails, picnic areas, and restmoms throughout the Glenville Park that Ms. Ralston had envisioned in her presentation to us. We funneled some money to a centralized church effort to coordinate food drives and temporary shelters for the homeless. The churches were already doing a good job, but acknowledged in our meeting that some centralized efforts could really improve the impact they could have on the community.

Chief Hagman got his funding for the development of a task force to deal with drug and gang influences, though the allotted money wouldn't be enough to sustain it for many years unless other funding came along to augment it. Knowing the chief, we figured he could demonstrate the usefulness of the task force and successfully lobby for additional money when it became necessary. Plus, Joe and I thought Uncle Shorty would appreciate the gesture. He was a law and order kind of guy.

Returning to one of our priorities of trying to help those who simply can't get by on their own, we funneled some money to the existing Glenville Mental Health Clinic. This group was mostly tax funded, but also relied on donations. We had learned about them from Mandy and realized that they served a surprisingly large number of people with chronic mental illness. Some were treated on an outpatient basis and others lived in a shelter. A little extra money could go a long way in augmenting their state and county budgets.

We thought the work that Barton was doing with at-risk kids could be expanded. Joe worked with a wonderful mentor group in his Maryland town that successfully paired volunteers in the community with at-risk kids for commitments of a minimum of one year, spending at least one to two hours a week together. Joe had personally worked with two teenagers for several years helping with homework, encouraging them to reach for college, going on trips to expose them to another world outside of their neighborhoods, and just being there as a friend and role model.

One boy lived with his elderly grandmother at nearly a poverty level and Joe may have been the best thing that ever came into his young life. He wasn't alone. This was a very successful program that reaped huge benefits in the community. The blueprint for a Glenville Mentor Program was already available and we had a plan for its inception. Somehow the program could be merged with the Youth Foundation. I saw a future there for Barton, if he was willing to step up, and if my new best friend, Mayor Riley, was willing to engage in some fairly innocent quid pro quo politics.

And finally, in this collection of somewhat smaller donations (if you call one to three million small), we added a very vaguely defined concept we named the Glenville Youth Job Corps. The concept still needed work, but the general idea went back to one of our Applebee's discussions about summer jobs and all the great experiences we had growing up. If a program could be established to fund local employers for half the salaries of part-time student workers during the summer, several good results might occur.

First, employers could get some fairly inexpensive help when they needed it most. At full price, they might hesitate to hire extra help, but half-price might be worth the risk. Second, young people could gain valuable work experience and have a ready-made placement service, helping them get their first job. And, finally, those employers might find that hiring the extra labor actually helped to generate more income.

If you started with a one million dollar fund and invested the balance wisely, such a program could last quite a few years and perhaps establish a solid trend of local hiring. It would be good for the kids and good for the community. If employers decided they didn't like the plan, then the money could go back into a central fund for future distribution.

So, with this last collection of odds and ends, we had committed roughly thirty-eight million of the total estate. We needed to retain a small portion of the remainder for ongoing administrative overhead for legal fees, investment costs, and accounting expenses. But a sizeable chunk still remained available and our decision for that money would likely draw some heavy criticism for a variety of reasons.

CHAPTER 40

WHAT ABOUT ME?

As I looked out at the audience, I saw many smiling faces and still others that stared at me with quizzical looks that suggested they wondered why their favorite causes had not yet been mentioned.

"How's the crazy wetlands lady doing?" Joe's voice startled me.

"She's staring a hole through the back of your head right now."

"Too late. I already have a hole back there."

"Good point. She doesn't look happy. The hospital gang looks like they just had a group colonoscopy. The teacher union rep seems confused, Wanda just blew me another kiss, and Bunny has fallen asleep with the flask in her lap."

The reality was that we had covered a lot of ground with the Hazelton funding so far. We had created the opportunity for an amazing community center, helped older people in need, attended to the community's youth in a variety of ways, did our part for law enforcement, dramatically improved the technological capabilities of the schools, offered incentives for innovative teaching, helped community efforts in dealing with mental illness, funded a much-need athletic facility, and helped the churches in their work for the hungry and homeless.

However, we had not yet given any money to the hospital, which certainly served an important role in Glenville. We just felt that the health-care issues were too complex to wade into and hospital equipment costs would have taken too much away from the estate. Plus, we knew the hospital's fundraising efforts were pretty robust.

Though we offered some one-time teaching incentives, we really didn't feel that we could address issues of salary inequities as my friend, Harkins, had hoped. The school district needed more classroom space and major repairs, but we felt that was the role of the School Board to sort out and a choice the tax-payers could make if they felt the need was paramount. There had also been numerous proposals for repairs and replacements to community assets around town, but we viewed those as city responsibilities.

We gave nothing to the arts community even though the city-employed arts commissioner had worked the Kelly broth-ers pretty hard when she caught us at Applebee's one night and pushed the idea of a series of sculptures around the city. While she was talking about the influences of Rodin, the French sculptor, we were both thinking about Rodan, the menacing, winged Japanese-film creature that waged epic battles with Godzilla. Somehow there was a serious disconnect in the dis-cussion.

We could have donated money to the historic preservation of the downtown area, but we didn't since there did not seem to be enough left to preserve. We could have given money to a proposed skateboard park. Maybe that would be necessary in California—but Indiana? Come on. Go find a basketball . . . or learn to jog . . . and pull your pants up and turn your hat around.

We turned down several church proposals, a theater concept, a major land purchase for a proposed shopping mall, and an addition to the library. That one we almost funded, but it seemed to us that the library was doing great compared to what we had as kids. And, of course, there also would be no hydrotherapy or lymphatic drainage sessions paid for by the estate.

It really came down to the fact that Joe and I wanted to first focus our attention on those groups of people in need (the poor, elderly, homeless, and young people who need opportunities to succeed and often a gentle push in the right direction). The Community Center really represented something for everyone in terms of a place of refuge, healthy activity, and learning. We knew there were some gaps in our logic when it came to what we funded, but we did our best. We then decided that the remainder of the money would not be reserved for community groups, but rather we would establish a fund to help individuals and families who had fallen on hard times through no real fault of their own.

Just as I was about to announce the final portion of our funding, I stopped and stared at the back door to the auditorium. A lone figure had just appeared in the doorway. I took a deep breath and then spoke into the microphone, "Folks, give me just a minute to consult with my brother on something." There was a small rumble in the audience, but it must have seemed fairly normal that I needed to talk with Joe.

I put my hand over the microphone and whispered to the face on the laptop. "Guess who just showed up in the back of the room?"

"Lonnie?"

"Nope."

"The Ghost of Christmas Past?"

"Nope."

"Luke Jackson." It was a statement—not a question.

"Yep. He's just standing there with his arms crossed leaning against the door jamb."

"How's he look? Any cuts or bruises?"

"None that I can see. What do you think I should do?"

"Well, Darren, it seems to me that you finish your meeting and get the hell out of there and enjoy your trip back home to California. If Luke is standing there, then that means Lonnie is not. If Lonnie is not there, then that means your troubles are over. Luke is just letting you know."

Just then Luke fixed his gaze on me and gave me a small, almost imperceptible salute with his right hand. He then smiled and just turned and vanished. That was it. Weeks of worrying about Lonnie McDaniel and wondering what to do about him were over with a quick acknowledgement from Luke Jackson.

I don't know what happened and I don't want to know. I guess Luke had that "talk" with Lonnie and he saw the wisdom in what Luke had to say. That's the end of the story as far as I'm concerned, but what a story it was. The legend of Luke Jackson clearly lives on for the Kelly brothers.

"He's gone, Joe. He just gave me a little salute and left."

"Very military of him. Good. It's over. I never doubted him. Now, wrap this thing up, will you? I'm getting tired and won't be able to maintain my sunny disposition for much longer." It was easy for Joe to dismiss Lonnie. He wasn't the one who had been threatened. I also never could shake the image of a young Lonnie McDaniel laughing at Joe and me after he bragged that he had hung Blackie from the rafters of that old shed. The guy was a sick bastard and I had feared him. But I no longer feared him. That look on Luke's face told me all I needed to know. It was over—one way or another.

I shifted back to the microphone and explained to the crowd that no further money would be earmarked for any particular existing group or service. A groan went up from those who had been hanging on for better news. The hospital suits looked like they could use a good blood transfusion. Wanda and Doreen were no longer blowing kisses.

"Folks, we never intended to try and fix every financial problem in this community. We thought we'd funnel money out to the agencies that were already equipped to help others. And, to a great extent, that's what we did. However, at our first town hall meeting, Joe and I met some people who had fallen on hard times. Families had lost jobs and were close to losing their homes. A farmer was injured and just need help to bring in his crops. And a little boy had become seriously ill and needed medicine that the mother couldn't afford. I met that little boy and he changed my mind about everything. Many other families contacted us since that meeting. Joe and I decided that we couldn't turn our backs on these folks."

I paused and looked out at Louise Ratcliff in the audience. She had come to the meeting without Ronnie. I'm sure she didn't want to build up his hopes, but obviously she was still hoping for a miracle of some sort. I'm not a big believer in miracles, but I do think an inexplicable series of events can occur to change a life for the better. Somehow Uncle Shorty made a decision about Glenville, and Joe and I did our best to carry out his wishes. Now, perhaps, a little boy can live as a result and a mother can watch her son grow up to be a man. Louise just looked at me and cried. The doctors had told me that their prescribed treatment would likely cure Ronnie if the family could find a way to afford it. That's all I needed to hear. The Ratcliff family would get immediate funding while we sorted out what to do about others.

"So, even though we know this plan is imperfect and that eventually the fund will run out of money, we intend to set up a volunteer oversight board of community members to review requests for emergency funds and loans to help people get through hard times. We'll refer to this last pot of money as the

Hazelton Fund—a selfish move on my part just to keep Uncle Shorty and Aunt Meta's name remembered here in Glenville. These funds won't be intended as a permanent solution; we're not providing a lifetime of income to anyone. We just want to help get people back on their feet so they can go about the business of being contributing members of the community again.

"For instance, in some cases we will work to match up people with a need for help along with those who have a need for work and income. At our previous meeting, Mr. Tubbs expressed a desire for help on his farm following his accident; meanwhile, Mr. Green had just lost his job and needed work. He has the necessary skills to help Mr. Tubbs, so the Hazelton Fund can finance his salary at the Tubbs farm until other work comes along. That's just one example of how we intend to proceed."

I let that notion sink in and I could see there were questions in the audience that I didn't intend to answer that night. "Mr. Borland will be helping to establish this board and its guidelines with guidance from my brother and me. I've asked Mr. Rick Cole to serve as the chairman for the group of volunteers who will initially serve. This will not be easy and we realize that these people will be placed in a difficult position as they sort out the guidelines for funding and then actually have to deny some requests from fellow Glenville citizens. But for every denial, we hope there are many more positive outcomes for families and individuals in need. We just have to believe that if Shorty Hazelton saw some of these immediate needs, he wouldn't hesitate to reach out to those people."

I glanced at Joe and he gave me a thumbs up—a sign of his approval for what I said and probably a gesture of relief that it was over. I again thanked the crowd and let them know that John Bourke would provide follow-up articles in the newspaper with more information. I might as well boost his circulation while I was feeling generous. With that, I pushed the microphone aside and stood up to gather my belongings.

Then a funny thing happened. The room erupted in applause. Serious applause. Not the tepid, perfunctory clapping of hands you might hear following a retirement speech for a guy no one really liked. No, this was the real deal—complete with an awful racket from the instruments in the back of the room. I saw several people wiping tears from their faces. Some I recognized; others were strangers to me. I had not seen that reaction coming. I guess I had become so focused on what we couldn't do that I forgot about all the positive feelings generated from the Hazelton gifts. It was a wonderful sight. I never felt better about the town of Glenville.

I looked at Joe and he had a big grin on his face. I turned the laptop around so Joe could see what I was seeing. The crowd was on its feet. Even the hospital people were smiling and applauding. Despite the disappointment some may have felt about our choices for funding, it appeared that the folks of Glenville thought that something very good had happened that night. So did I. . . . I just wish Uncle Shorty could have seen it, too.

EPILOGUE

Almost a year has passed since that night when the Glenville community received word about how Shorty Hazelton's estate would be distributed. Great progress has been made. Tom Borland proved to be an excellent choice for putting the wheels in motion and seeing that guidelines were created for the various funds. He also was charged with investing the remaining funds appropriately so the estate could continue to grow to some extent even as the community drew down on it. When I met with Borland on a quick visit to Glenville, he seemed to really be enjoying himself and I had no doubt that the Hazelton Fund was not being fully charged for his services. He had found a home in Glenville.

Rick Cole had organized the board members for the Hazelton Fund and had led them through the creation of a set of guidelines. He had the help of Sam Harkins and Jim Barton on the board along with John Bourke, the editor. I had also asked Don Howard, the Westside Elementary School principal to serve in addition to Reverend Maxwell, the Methodist minister who demonstrated a sound intellect and a sense of humor when Joe and I met with the church group early in our process. Dennis Harmon, chairman of the Boys and Girls Club Board also answered the call.

Several others were added on the recommendation of my three trusted Operation Manpower cohorts. Yes, these were the same guys who raced police cars and created a human fireball to liven up a party. Now I trust them to make incredibly important decisions about the lives of others. It's a good thing I left town. But one interesting addition came directly from Joe and me. It probably raised a few eyebrows.

Ms. Amanda Saunders, formerly known as Mandy, the Applebee's bartender, was asked to serve on the Hazelton Board. She reluctantly accepted after trying to convince us that she was not worthy of such a position. On the contrary, we convinced her that she was the perfect choice. She loved the community, had children in the schools, probably heard every hard-luck story that had ever been shared in Applebee's, and she had a kind, caring, and gentle soul. She understood the challenges facing many in town, but she would be intelligent and demanding in her assessment of whether people really needed money to solve their problems.

Mandy not only served as a volunteer on the board, but she was no longer at Applebee's since she had joined the law firm of Thomas Borland, Esquire. Borland quickly discovered that his continued work on behalf of the Hazelton estate along with his past clients from his previous work in the Washington, D.C., area was already a full-time job. It left little time for taking on the many Glenville clients who had responded to his newly acquired name recognition.

The fact that Borland had moved to Glenville to spend more time with his family led him to accept my suggestion that Mandy just might be the perfect assistant in his office to help with the load. She already had a pre-law degree from Indiana University and she could pursue a paralegal certification part-time in Indianapolis or with online coursework. When Borland offered a starting salary that was already well above what she was making, Mandy jumped at the chance for a new career.

True to his sense of "politics as usual," Mayor Riley had no problem with seeing the wisdom of a promotion for Jim Barton. The previous manager of the Youth Foundation had retired, an infusion of funds had arrived to create the Glenville Mentors program as part of the existing city department, and Barton was a perfect example of someone who had suffered hard times and risen above it. It was a good story for a mayor to tell his constituents. Of course, this only occurred after an appropriate posting of the job and the mandatory interviews of two other candidates who never had a prayer of getting the job. You have to follow procedure after all.

Chief Hagman's task force was just starting to get underway and he seemed to be getting softer on others all the time. Being a grandfather had seriously mellowed him. Lonnie was never heard from again. The strongest rumor of his disappearance came from his drinking buddies out at J.J.'s Tavern. They said he came in one night with heavy gauze bandages wrapped around one hand and blood still seeping through the white cloth. His face was battered and swollen. He pounded down several shots of whiskey and told the boys he was heading for Texas. It was just a tale told by a bunch of drunks, but I think I'll go with it just to put my mind at rest.

* * *

There is one last story that needs to be told as I try to gain perspective on all that has happened since my brother and I got that important call from Lawyer Borland. It's not an easy story to tell. In fact, it's excruciatingly painful.

Joe didn't make it. He died of cancer roughly four months from the day he had his brain surgery. The pain is still so fresh that it's hard for me to talk about him without bringing back the raw emotions of his final days. I'm trying to become more measured and stoic when reflecting on memories about Joe to others, but my voice catches and I know my reddened eyes are a complete giveaway. My dominant feeling is one of loss, but I'm trying to focus more and more on our memories and on the great life that Joe had a chance to live. I've learned that grief is a very private and consuming emotion. And at least in my case, it's not easily shared with others.

It all happened so amazingly fast. After I returned to California, Joe and I resumed our phone calls and FaceTime sessions every few days. He first learned that the cause of his brain tumor was melanoma. As he said, "Not really a big surprise there." The doctors had first warned him that his brain tumor was not the kind to have just started in the brain. It most likely had migrated from somewhere else and melanoma would be the likely culprit.

Like most people, I thought melanoma started as some visible malady on the skin. Joe learned that sometimes the initial disease is completely hidden until it has started to metastasize to other parts of the body. By the time the seizures had started and the swelling in his brain was identified as the culprit, the disease was already well on its way to claiming his body. Our phone calls became a roller-coaster ride of surging optimism to plummeting doses of reality either from the doctors' updates or from obvious signs of Joe's failing health. The most notable effect was the slow loss of control over his legs.

Early on he laughed at himself for missing his bed and "folding up on the floor like an accordion." Carol once had to call the nearby Fire Department to get help lifting him back onto the bed. Joe noted, "These two guys were really strong and clearly hadn't missed any fire-house meals."

At one point a doctor apparently mentioned that there were alternative therapies available as well. Joe asked him, "What—you mean like eating ground-up apricots or something?" That was a short discussion. On another day he and Carol went out to a restaurant and he reflected on the experience. "One day I was healthy just like you. The next day I'm the guy on the walker being helped to his seat while everyone stares and thinks, 'poor bastard.'"

In a particularly sober moment, Joe shared with me that, "Last week I thought I could handle this. It's a pain in the ass, but I can tolerate it. Now I'm not so sure. I'm not the guy who is going to try every possible treatment hoping to prolong my life. I'm not chasing the miracle cure. I may just have to let this disease run its course and quit fighting it. I'm not there yet, but I can see it in my future."

I'm glad Joe couldn't see my face as he told me this. I was quietly falling apart on the other end of the line. The silence was so long that he finally prompted, "Hey, Darren, are you still there?"

His descriptions shifted from "I get weird, almost evil thoughts sometimes at night" to "God, there are some really good and kind people out there." He talked about "jerk" doctors and the "really wonderful compassionate" ones. As always, he made fun of those who didn't measure up and praised the ones who deserved it. Sometimes he made me laugh; sometimes he made me cry. At one point he summed up our phone calls: "I can't express how much these phone calls mean to me. I can say stuff to you that I just can't say to other people."

On one phone call, Joe was particularly philosophical and reflective. "You know, Darren, someone once said, 'life is about the accumulation of memories—not things or possessions—just memories.' I've done pretty well in that department. My head and my heart are filled with good memories and good people."

"That's a good line, Joe. I'll have to quote you someday on it. Who said it originally?"

"I'm not sure. Might have been Aristotle. Might have been a Hallmark card. Might have been Doc Holiday on his deathbed in the movie, *Tombstone*." Joe still had his sense of humor.

Without warning, the physical gains Joe had briefly made suddenly evaporated and he was once again exhausted and losing more mobility each day. The professional care given to Joe was outstanding. The support from Carol and friends was extraordinary. His treatment ran the gamut from surgery to expensive medications to radiation therapy. Nothing could stop the insidious nature of the disease. When they learned that the cancer had spread throughout the spinal cord area and Joe's use of his arms and legs was essentially nonexistent, it became clear that the end was near and that further treatment was no longer warranted or wanted by Joe.

I had wanted to visit him long before the illness progressed to its final stages. However, Joe kept putting me off thinking that he would get better and that we could then have some fun going on day trips. When it became clear that the situation was getting worse and that Carol could use help with the heavy lifting, Joe agreed to have me come out and stay at the house. I spent the next two weeks watching him slowly die. From the day that I committed to making the trip until a few days later when I arrived, Joe's condition had dramatically deteriorated. The decision had already been made to stop the radiation treatment and hospice was called in to help.

A hospital bed had been delivered to Joe's master bedroom. For the first few days, I sat at the foot of the bed and traded off with Carol in just being there for Joe at all times. We laughed about old stories from Glenville and we talked about the work we had done on behalf of Uncle Shorty. Joe was in remarkably good spirits in spite of his clear knowledge that the end was near. No one would say if it would be weeks or months, but all of the medical staff thought it would be sooner rather than later given Joe's deteriorating physical condition.

Then, with little warning, his ability to communicate in a lucid manner began to fail him. He searched for words that were no longer there. At first those frustrating experiences made him angry, but then he simply resigned himself to it and smiled a little when the word just wouldn't come. Sometimes a nonsensical word came out of his mouth and he would just look at Carol or me and smile. "That wasn't a word, was it?" One of us would answer, "No, I believe you made that one up." He'd laugh and say, "Oh well—stupid brain."

And finally, just as the hospice pamphlets predicted, he became much more fatigued and also starting having some hallucinations. I marveled at the fact that his hallucinations didn't scare him at all. He was just intrigued by them.

"Hey, Darren, how are you doing?"

"I'm doing fine, Joe."

Silence. Joe just stared at me.

"How's that guy behind you doing?"

"You see a guy behind me?"

Joe's eyes grew wide. "Oh, yeah!"

Then he'd blink a few times and just give me a little smile as if to say, "Okay—I get it."

Once I walked into his room and he was swiveling his head back and forth with eyes wide open staring at the ceiling. "Look at that! Just look at that! Do you see this, Darren? It's an absolute freak show!"

"Joe, I'm sorry, I can't see what you're seeing."

"No kidding? Aw, man, this is some show. It's very interesting—some of it quite profound. Too bad you can't see it."

He was hallucinating on his deathbed and he felt sorry for me that I couldn't experience what he was seeing. Yes, quite profound after all.

While Joe was still lucid he began planning his own memorial service, or a Celebration of Life for Joe Kelly, as it became known. Joe's love of music would dominate the event and he even approved the songs to be played. He really wanted everyone to have a great time and to "blow the people away with the music." As his mind deteriorated over the last few days, he never stopped planning the event even though his thought process wasn't quite clear.

"Darren, I'm pretty sure we're good on water. We have about twenty gallons. And I think we have plenty of buffalo meat." I didn't think buffalo meat was an East Coast delicacy, but I wasn't about to interrupt.

"And make sure you make enough sandwiches for Bodie Miller. Bodie likes his sandwiches." Presumably, Joe was referring to the Olympic downhill skier. I wasn't aware that they were close personal friends.

"And, Darren, can you wash a pair of pants for yourself so they'll look nice? They have to be creased. Can you do that?" Clearly, I had failed Joe along the way in making myself look presentable. He'd have none of that sloppiness at his service.

And finally, looking quite content with the planning process, Joe looked out his bedroom window at a beautiful Maryland day. "You know, I believe this will be an unusually soft-stool summer." It's hard to argue with that sort of prediction. I just nodded.

* * *

Joe was incredibly peaceful and reflective in those final weeks. His faith remained strong and he truly had accepted whatever lay ahead for him. He wasn't just mouthing the words that others wanted to hear. There was an ingrained belief about his future that brought him a sense of relief and calm. I was so happy to see that for him and more than once stifled a feeling of envy for a concept so foreign to me.

My memory of him during those last weeks is not focused on the final days when his mind wandered and his body succumbed to exhaustion. I prefer to think about that first night that I sat up with him in his room when his mind was still perfectly sharp.

He was propped up in the hospital bed. After laughing about an old story, Joe grew quiet and serious.

"Darren, I'm a very lucky man. I've had a terrific life, a wonderful marriage, and a marginally acceptable brother."

"Your praise overwhelms me."

"Good, I didn't want you to get a big head. I really have been blessed. I don't feel cheated at all. Sure, I wish I had some more years left, but I can only feel an overwhelming sense of gratitude and thankfulness for all that I've had. And, isn't it amazing that the Kelly brothers were fortunate enough to be picked by Uncle Shorty to carry out his wishes? How cool was that? I know you'll do a terrific job following up in Glenville and the people we put in place will do a great job."

Then he just smiled and let out a heavy sigh that seemed to be a mixture of fatigue and contentment. He turned toward the window to signal that he was done talking for a while.

I looked at Joe and knew he was right. I knew our parents would be pleased with our efforts and I felt certain that Uncle Shorty and Aunt Meta would also approve of the results so far. I stared at Joe that day and realized the Kelly brothers had come a long way from their lives as young boys on Garfield Drive. Joe had been dealt a terrible blow and I didn't realize that day that everything was going to slip away very quickly over the next few days. Yet, as we sat there together we both experienced a feeling of satisfaction. Here we were in our sixties dealing with his rapidly declining health, but we still found even more meaning and joy in lives that had already seemed remarkably full.

It almost made me feel as if we'd finally grown up. Almost.

ACKNOWLEDGMENTS

Though an acknowledgment page generally allows an author to show his appreciation for those who helped in some way with editing and producing a final product, I need to begin with a slightly different approach. This book is dedicated to my brother, Michael Joseph Kirby. Nearly two years ago Mike and I created the idea for this book while we were eating breakfast at a small café in Fort Myers, Florida. That fact might help explain why Joe and Darren spend so much time in the story at various breakfast spots around Glenville.

As we talked and laughed that morning, I grabbed a *USA Today* newspaper and started jotting down ideas in the margins. Childhood characters and events poured out of us and I filled the margins of that newspaper with notes. When I returned home I quickly built on those sketchy ideas to create the outline for *In The Shadow of The Water Tower*. Over many phone calls, Mike and I agreed on the basic outline and I began working on the first draft. I had only completed five rough chapters before Mike first exhibited physical problems that would later be explained as the early signs of cancer. That's all Mike was able to review with me, though I shared thoughts with him about the book's progress over the next few months.

As Mike's disease progressed, we talked about weaving his illness into the story about the two brothers. After all, much of the book dealt with the relationship between them and it seemed disingenuous to exclude such a significant event. Mike was all for it. "Write it the way it plays out," he told me. Of course, at the time we were both optimistic that Mike would beat the odds and recover from whatever was attacking his system. Unfortunately, that didn't happen.

I want to make it clear that "Joe" is not exactly Mike, but they are very close in so many ways. Joe said and did some things that Mike likely would not have done. Joe acted on his impulses and blurted out sarcastic comments that Mike would have generally kept to himself or only shared with a select few. However, the bond between the fictional brothers is clearly based on the relationship between Mike and me. Nearly all of the childhood stories are based on actual events. Mike's illness progressed much like that of the fictional character and he faced the end with all of the humor, thoughtfulness, and dignity exhibited by Joe in the story. And, by the way, the song lyrics to "Brain Drain" really were created by Mike to share with his neurosurgeon. Mike supported me and encouraged me to complete this novel and I primarily have him to thank for helping me achieve this goal. I only wish he could be here to share the experience with me.

Though Mike's role in helping me with this novel was unique, others also assisted when it was finally time to get some honest feedback about the completed first draft. The following friends and family members offered their constructive suggestions to improve the book and I am indebted to them for taking the time to assist me: Mary Kirby, Kaitlyn Kirby, Christina Morrison, Nicki Robinson, Tom Keys, Rob Robinson, Bob Boyd, Mary Redman, Tom New, and especially Mike DeRousse who spent extra time going over the draft manuscript with me. Jennifer Gehlhar, from Hillcrest Media, provided professional editing that greatly improved the manuscript. I thank you all for your contributions and encouragement.

CPSIA information can be obtained at www.ICGtesting.com
Printed in the USA
LVOW06s1838140914

404024LV00001B/11/P